The Orphan
Sisters

SHIRLEY DICKSON

The Orphan Sisters

bookouture

Published by Bookouture in 2019

An imprint of StoryFire Ltd.

Carmelite House
50 Victoria Embankment
London EC4Y 0DZ

www.bookouture.com

ISBN: 978-1-78681-715-0
eBook ISBN: 978-1-78681-714-3

To Wal, who has always believed.

PROLOGUE
May 1945

Etty eyed the folded newspaper on the kitchen table. The head-line blared, in big bold letters, '*VE DAY- IT'S HERE!*'. Hearing excited voices as neighbours celebrated outside in the street, her heart soared.

News had spread over the past couple of days that the war in Europe was over and excitement ran high in Whale Street. Mrs Moffatt, who ran the corner shop over the road, had suggested victory celebrations, and a street party and bonfire in the cobbled back lane were planned. Not one to miss an opportunity, the shopkeeper sold rosettes, posters and Union Jack flags, charging, respectively, one to two shillings. The possibility of bad weather had been a source of great agitation for the revellers but apart from a spot of rain and the odd roll of thunder, the day proved warm with peeks of sunshine.

Wood from bunk beds thrown out of air raid shelters was piled high in readiness for tonight's bonfire, while an effigy of Hitler waited its fate on top.

Earlier that day, Etty had put the kiddies in the pram on the doorstep to watch, while she helped decorate the street. Red, white, and blue bunting crisscrossed overhead while posters and rosettes decorated walls and Union Jacks hung proudly out of windows. Trestle tables covered with white tablecloths lined the street, set with cups, saucers and tea plates, and party hats made out of newspapers.

Later indoors, Etty had made a plate of spam sandwiches and a carrot cake, using dried eggs as the fresh kind were on ration. The two kiddies were having an afternoon nap in the back bedroom and Etty planned to take the food outside later and join in with the celebrations.

Now the war was over, she marvelled, she might be able to buy anything she fancied and there'd be no need to take her ration book to the shops.

At three o'clock sharp, she switched on the radio and listened to Prime Minister Winston Churchill's dramatic voice as he announced to the nation from the cabinet room at Number Ten Downing Street, that the war with Germany was over. A huge roar went up from the crowd outside and then united they sang 'For He's a Jolly Good Fellow.' A surge of relief engulfed Etty – the longed-for day had arrived and the war was over.

But it was King George VI's earlier broadcast, transmitted by loudspeaker to thousands of folk assembled in London's Trafalgar Square and Parliament Square that really moved her. For in it, the king paid tribute to those men and women who had laid down their lives for victory. With a pang of sadness, Etty thought of those she'd loved and lost and all that might have been. She quickly wiped away a tear.

Etty checked the time on the mahogany clock, standing on the mantelpiece above the range. Half past three. Her husband should be home soon.

She surveyed the kitchen-come-dining room. Eyeing the wooden stacking bricks the two kiddies had been playing with earlier in the playpen, Etty's eyes misted. *Blast the war changing our lives forever.*

*

She was startled by a knock at the front door. Wiping her hands on her pinafore, she padded along the dim passageway, wondering who the caller was. Opening the door, she gaped at the ghost from the past who stood before her.

The woman, elderly and emaciated, with a lined, careworn face, wore a baggy ankle-length coat and man's trilby hat.

'Dearest child,' she cried in a feeble voice. 'I've found you at last.'

As Etty stared incredulously at the woman, the present ebbed away, images playing in her mind's eye. She was transported back to that long ago, fateful day.

'Be quick girls,' Mam called as she hurried along the street. 'Today we're off for a ride in a tramcar.'

CHAPTER ONE
November 1929

It struck Esther as odd that Mam carried a suitcase that weighed her down on one side. She didn't think much of it, though, because today, Mam told them, they were going somewhere special and Esther was excited about it. Even a ride in a tramcar was a thrilling experience for Esther who, at four, hadn't yet acquired her older sister Dorothy's ability to deal with the unexpected.

It was a cloudy grey sort of day, not the sort of weather they'd usually go out for a trip. Mam never took them out this time of morning and she certainly never wore her best swagger coat, cloche hat and a touch of vivid red lipstick unless it was a Sunday.

Hurrying to catch up with Mam, Esther passed the butcher's shop window where Aunt Olga – the butcher's wife, a tray of sausages in her hand – stared out at her.

'I'm off someplace special,' Esther mouthed.

A look of confusion crossed Aunt Olga's face and she called to someone over her shoulder.

'Be quick I say,' Mam commanded from further along the street.

Esther, giving Aunty Olga a little wave, ran to catch up.

They passed rows of redbrick houses that shouldered the streets, their tall chimney pots belching clouds of grimy smoke into the grey sky. The cobbled back lanes they walked along were lined by high yard walls with coloured glass cemented in the top.

'Why is—'

'To prevent kids from climbing over,' Mam cut in, anticipating Esther's question.

Hardly had Mam put the suitcase down on the pavement by the tramcar stop when a man approached them and tipped his cap.

'You've a bit of a handful, pet,' he said. 'Will I give you a hand with that suitcase?'

'Please,' Mam replied, and managed a smile that didn't seem quite real. 'That's very kind.'

'You must be going a fair distance by the size o' the luggage.'

'A fair distance,' Mam repeated, noncommittally, and Dorothy, who was hanging on to her hand at the other side, let out a funny sound as if she was crying but didn't want to be heard.

'What's wrong wi' the bairn?' the man asked.

Mam snapped at him, 'It's none of your business.'

Then the tramcar came rattling around the corner of Frederick Street, and the young man hoisted up the suitcase and dumped it on the platform. With a last glance at them and a shake of the head, he vanished swiftly inside.

Esther was lifted up and set down on the platform, but Dorothy, who was nearly eight, managed to climb up on her own.

Clinging on to Mam's hand, Esther stared at the people sitting on the tram's long wooden benches. An old man who wore a silk muffler around his neck rose stiffly from his seat.

'Here, missus, take me seat for you and the bairn.'

Mam thanked him kindly and hardly had she sat down, and lifted Esther onto her knee, then a bell tinged and the tram lurched forward. Dorothy stood in the aisle next to them and Mam put an arm around her waist to steady her. Dorothy, pale faced, stared dully into the space ahead and Esther couldn't fathom what was wrong with her. But after a moment, with so much happening, she forgot all about her sister and, as excitement mingled with trepidation whirled in her stomach, Esther looked up at the kindly gentleman, who hung on to a leather strap that dropped from the ceiling.

'We're off someplace special,' she blurted out.

'Hush, child, behave.' Mam's body tensed and her lips pressed into a thin line.

At that moment the conductor came alongside in his smart uniform, holding a ticket machine.

'Where to, Missus?' he asked.

'One and a half to Westoe, please.' Mam rifled through her purse and handed him some pennies.

The tramcar trundled along the street, and scenes from outside flashed by the window: a horse pulling a cart with a piano on top; seagulls perched along the peaked roof of a row of tall redbrick houses; shops – butchers, chemists, milliners – with canopied windows; an old man wearing a cloth cap spitting in the gutter; and endless rows of narrow, cobbled streets. South Shields was big, much bigger than Esther had imagined. In awe, she cuddled into the security of Mam's chest.

'Are we nearly there, yet?' Dorothy's voice sounded strangled.

'Soon,' Mam replied.

Dorothy's chin quivered and she turned away.

Tears welled in Esther's eyes and the scene outside the tram's window blurred. The outing wasn't exciting any more. Her new coat felt tight around her chest and the velvet bits on her collar that touched her neck itched, and so did the black woollen stockings that reached to the top of her legs – but when Esther scratched, the itch just moved to another place.

'Be still, child,' Mam said, tetchily.

Esther didn't like her new clothes any more or the black shiny shoes that earlier she'd been so proud of.

After a time, Mam shuffled her off her knee. 'Our stop,' she announced.

She stretched out her hand to stroke Esther with the lightest of touches, on her hair, her cheek, like she did at night when a bad dream awakened the little girl.

Mam led the way along the aisle, and when the tramcar stopped, she alighted from the platform. Esther came next, followed by Dorothy, and then the conductor handed down the suitcase.

As the tram clanked away, Esther studied her surroundings. They stood at the bottom of a pleasant, tree-lined walkway that tunnelled into the distance. Esther, admiring the row of impressive houses set back from the road by a sloping grass verge and white fence, felt somewhat cheered. She considered this a beautiful place to live and said so to her mother.

'These houses are known as Georgian and Victorian,' Mam explained, liking to keep her children 'knowledgeable,' as she called it. 'This place is called Westoe Village.' Mam looked around. 'Like most of Shields, the surrounding area has been built up but this corner,' she nodded towards the walkway, 'still feels like the old village and has nothing like the smog in town.'

'Do rich people live here?' Dorothy asked.

'Indeed they do. Mostly owners from the ship-building and coal-mining industries.'

Esther had no idea what Mam meant but nodded all the same. Their mother frequently talked to them as though they were grown-ups and woe betide either sister if they spoke as the neighbours did, in 'common Geordie' dialect.

'It pays to speak properly.' Mam instructed them, 'You'll thank me when you're older.'

Esther wasn't so sure, because when Mam was out of earshot, the neighbours called her 'Mrs High and Mighty'.

Mam heaved up the suitcase and led them around a flat-roofed building.

'Keep up, girls,' she called as she headed up the walkway, 'it won't be long now.'

Tall trees blotted out the sky and Esther had to crane back her head to see the tops of them. Accustomed to narrow, smoke-filled streets crammed with houses, she gazed in wonder at the space all around.

Mam diverted through a gap in the wall and the path led them to a road with fields either side. In the distance was a row of imposing houses whose windows gazed out over parkland. They crossed the road and took a gravelled path set between two green fields.

It was raining now, the soft kind of rain that soaked you through, and Esther thought she saw sleet in it. She grew excited at the thought that snow might fall.

'Here we are,' Mam pointed to some chimney pots that rose above trees on the skyline ahead.

'Where… where are we?' Esther wanted to know. But nobody answered.

Through the trees, the threesome followed the gravelled path and when they came to a clearing, a house came into view. Peering in through a wrought-iron gate, Esther could see that inside the grounds were lawns, a vegetable plot and a wooden greenhouse painted white.

'The place is called Blakely Hall,' Mam said, a hint of reverence in her tone, 'and was once owned by Sir Stanley Blakely.'

'Who is he?' Dorothy asked.

'Part of the gentry.'

Esther had no idea who the gentry were and was about to ask but, staring up at the towering façade, the words dissolved in her mouth.

'Does this Sir… Stanley… still live here?' asked Dorothy.

'He died a long time ago.' Mam shook her head. 'Poor man… didn't have children of his own…' She faced Dorothy.

'A good Christian… he bequeathed his house as an asylum for orphaned children.'

'Who owns it now?'

'A religious charity.'

'Is this the special place?' Esther asked.

Their mother, moving on, didn't answer.

The gate creaked as Esther opened it. Walking beneath the stone arch on this drab November morning, the scene beyond looked bleak. A path leading up to the house separated lawns strewn with sodden leaves; bushes with dead flower heads sprouted from the grass, and the air was filled with the stench of rotting foliage.

Esther waited for Mam who, by now, trailed breathlessly behind. She caught up and together they climbed the sweeping stone steps that led up to the house.

The building, with rows of sash windows and ivy-clad walls, did indeed look grand but Esther, jittery now, was disinclined to set foot inside.

Mam banged the doorknocker, and they listened as the noise echoed inside. The door opened and a girl, older than Dorothy, stood inside. She wore a navy-blue frock covered with a white frilled smock. Her mousy-coloured hair was cropped and beneath arched eyebrows, opaque brown eyes scrutinised them.

'I'm Mrs Makepeace,' Mam told her.

The girl nodded. 'I'm Sandra. The Mistress said to show yous to the office when you arrive.'

She stepped aside.

Inside the dim hallway, a strong smell of beeswax polish hung in the air. Sandra led the family along a passageway and, turning right, continued along a corridor paved with black and white linoleum flooring that squeaked beneath Esther's feet. They came to a door that had black writing scribbled on it. Esther, who couldn't yet read, wished she knew what it said.

Sandra rapped lightly on the door.

'Enter,' boomed a voice.

Mam led them in.

The room appeared cramped and the heat from a coal fire was overpowering. A large desk, piled high with papers, dominated the room and tall fixtures with shelves crammed with metal containers lined the walls. The fire, glowing in the grate, spat coals, now and then, onto a tiled hearth. Esther's fingertips, beginning to thaw, tingled painfully.

A lady sitting behind the desk spoke. 'I'm the Mistress Knowles. Welcome to Blakely Hall.' The Mistress's smile was more of a grimace – it didn't look at all welcoming. Her eyes held no warmth in them, and dull and glazed, they reminded Esther of dead fish eyes. Unsure of the lady, Esther clung on to her mother's coat-tail before taking a step back and hiding behind her.

Mam placed the suitcase on the floor, rifled through her handbag and produced a slip of paper.

'The contract's signed as you advised.'

Mistress Knowles stood up behind the desk. Taking the paper, she read it through. Dressed in a navy frock, her large bosoms strained the buttons which looked as if they might pop any minute. Her grey hair, covered by a mop cap, straggled to beefy shoulders.

She looked up. 'Aye. All seems in order.'

She paused, her lifeless eyes boring into Esther's, making the little girl shiver.

'Divvent leave it too long,' she told Mam, 'it'll only make matters worse.'

Esther expected her mother to correct the Mistress's speech but Mam just stared as if bewildered.

'What happens next?' she asked.

'It's no concern of yours.'

'Can we go home, now?' Esther found her voice.

Mam didn't answer but started to cough – a spluttering noise she couldn't seem to stop and one that made her clutch her chest.

'I'll get Sandra to bring water.' The Mistress made towards the door, but Mam waved a hand to stop her.

'I'll be fine…' she gasped, 'in a minute.'

Esther knew otherwise. After such a prolonged spell of coughing, her mother needed to lie down.

Mam brought a lace-edged handkerchief from her pocket and, covering her mouth, spat discreetly into it. Then, deftly, she brought the hanky down and returned it to her pocket. The Mistress's eyes bulged in horror and she shielded her mouth with a hand.

'I'll thank yi' to leave,' her tone was brusque.

Alarmed by this change of events, Esther stared disbelievingly up at Mam. Why didn't she give this nasty lady a piece of her mind?

Mam bent down to Esther's height. 'Tell you what…' she spoke in the sugary voice she used when she wanted to convince her daughter of something. 'Why don't you both go and take a look around? I've heard there's a dolls' house in the baby's department.'

'Are you coming?' Esther asked.

'No. I'll rest here awhile. You go ahead.'

Neither girl budged.

'Do as yer mother says,' rapped the Mistress.

Esther looked uncertainly at Dorothy. But Dorothy's eyes grew wide, warning Esther not to say another word.

As she stood in front of the nasty lady, a spark of defiance jabbed Esther. 'I'm staying here with Mam.'

The Mistress bristled with outrage. She opened her mouth to speak but Mam stopped her.

'You'll do no such thing.' Esther's heart sank at the firmness in Mam's tone. 'Now go ahead without me.' She attempted a reassuring smile.

'Haway, girls,' The Mistress waddled to the door. 'Be quick about it.'

At a loss to know what else to do, they followed the Mistress out of the room. The events too puzzling to take in, Esther's eyes, swimming with tears, looked down at the linoleum squares at her feet, automatically avoiding stepping on the lines in case it brought bad luck.

Presently, the Mistress came to a halt outside a glass-panelled door. Peering in, she turned the doorknob. Esther, following behind, was overcome by the sickening smell of stale urine, camouflaged by disinfectant. She wrinkled her nose.

Cots stood at the far end of the room, where solemn faced babies stared through wooden bars, while older children sat at a low table. A stern-faced nursemaid wearing a blue and white-striped frock, apron and a starched cap perched on her head, read from a large storybook. Then, at the far end of the room, Esther spied the dolls' house. Though its front door was missing and no furniture adorned its rooms, her young heart lifted.

She smiled at the children who sat around the table but, with indifferent expressions, they stared glumly back.

Esther's hand crept into Dorothy's, who stood at her side.

The action caught the attention of the Mistress.

'You, girl,' she said, 'will stay put in this department till your next birthday.'

Dismayed, Esther cried, 'I won't be here on my next birthday.' She stared into Dorothy's apprehensive eyes. 'Will I?'

The Mistress strode over. 'You're in my charge now, girl. The sooner you get used to the idea the better for all our sakes.'

Esther refused to believe the ogre lady. She belonged to Mam. About to tell the Mistress so, she glanced at Dorothy. But some misgiving in her sister's eyes made her hesitate.

'Don't be frightened,' Dorothy's voice wobbled. 'I'll be here with you.'

The idea that she should be afraid alarmed Esther. 'Where's Mam? I want to go home.'

'We can't.' Dorothy's voice was flat, her eyes watery pink. 'I promised not to say anything but… I suppose it doesn't matter now… Mam's going away and we've to stay here for a while.'

Esther was stunned. She knew what her sister said must be true because Dorothy never told a lie, not even when it meant keeping out of trouble.

She disentangled her hand and made for the door. 'I don't like it here… I'm off to find Mam.'

'You'll do nee such thing.' The Mistress's large frame made to block her way but Esther, too quick, darted around her ample figure. Opening the door, she streaked along the corridor as if the bogeyman himself was chasing after her.

'Come back,' the Mistress shrieked. 'Else you'll be sorry.'

Only one thought occupied Esther's mind – to find her mother. She would plead with her; tell her how sorry she was and that she'd never be naughty again.

Breath hot in her chest as she ran, Esther rounded a corner, and then she saw her. She stood in the dimly lit hallway; arm outstretched as she opened the front door.

'Oh! Don't go.' The words wrenched from Esther. 'Not without me.'

Mam turned, her tear-stained face registering a blank look Esther neither recognised nor understood.

'Be brave, little one. I'll be back sometime soon.'

Then she was gone, the door clanking behind her.

CHAPTER TWO

Sandra came to fetch Esther, as she sat forsaken at the front door.

'The Mistress is livid with yi,' Sandra announced, folding her arms. 'I'd stay clear if I was you.'

'I want to find Mam.'

'You can't… she's gone. And if you want to be a cry-baby then, gan ahead… you'll get nee sympathy from me.'

Esther stood up and wiped her nose with the back of her hand. 'I'm no cry-baby,' she said.

'That's better. Haway. I've to take you to sickbay to see Nurse Bell.'

Too bewildered to argue, Esther followed the big girl through the house to a covered walkway leading to a redbrick building.

In the future, whenever Esther thought of that time in sick bay, she broke out in a sweat. She was ordered to sit on a high stool. A towel was placed roughly around her shoulders. Nurse Bell, a tall lady with sunken eyes with swathes of grey shaded beneath them, wielded a large pair of scissors and began to cut off Esther's ringlets. Once chopped, they lay like dead snakes on the floor. Horrified, for her auburn hair was her mother's pride and joy, she could hardly breathe for the tight band that seemed to squeeze her chest. Stripped of her clothes, which she never saw again, Esther was ushered into a large tub of steaming water. Nurse Bell commenced to scrub her skin until it was red raw, before washing Esther's shorn locks, and pouring a lotion that burned mercilessly over her scalp.

Pink and smarting, Esther emerged from the bath. Told to dress in 'Blakely uniform' – a navy-blue frock covered with a white frilled smock, she was then delivered back to Sandra who waited outside.

Throughout the ordeal, Esther refused to cry, partly because she didn't want to be a cry-baby, but mostly because her mother wasn't there to dry away the tears.

'You'll do, lass.' Sandra clapped her on the back.

The big girl led her back to the main building where Esther found herself in a long queue of children. All the girls wore the same uniform; all stood still and quiet as statues.

'Why are we queuing?' she asked Sandra.

'Shush… it's the dinner queue,' Sandra whispered. 'You'll be in for it, if you're copped talking.'

Then, gloriously, Dorothy appeared. She stood at the far end of the corridor with another girl at her side. Dorothy too was dressed in uniform and, with her fair hair standing up in wisps, and her skinny figure, she appeared more like a boy. Esther felt a pang of sadness seeing her sister in such a way. As she stood next to Sandra, the little girl's determination not to cry was tested.

The two sisters stared glumly at one another.

'You knew Mam was bringing us here,' Esther accused, forgetting Sandra's warning to keep quiet. She didn't know how Dorothy had kept such a big secret from her.

'Only since last night.'

'Where's she gone? Why didn't she take us with her?'

'She didn't say… honest.'

'Did she say when she was coming—'

'Be quiet!' a man's voice bellowed.

Startled, Esther leant sideways. Looking down the queue, she saw a man with a vexed expression on his face staring back at her.

'Come here,' he commanded.

She froze but Sandra pushed her forward. 'Do as Master Knowles says.'

Esther moved to the front of the queue, passing the watchful eyes of the other children.

She stood in front of the Master, her eyes level with his rotund tummy. Her gaze travelled up to his red waistcoat with a button missing, his crumpled jacket, and further still to his shiny, bald head.

'You've no number, girl,' he barked. 'What's the punishment for talking in line?'

Esther didn't answer.

'Sir,' a voice called out, 'she doesn't have a number, and neither do I.'

Dorothy.

The Master's eyebrows shot up, his forehead riddling with lines. 'Whoever said that come here at once.'

Dorothy appeared at Esther's side, the two sisters holding hands.

'Sir, we're both new here,' Dorothy said in her quiet way.

Then a peculiar thing happened. The vexed expression left the Master's features, his face relaxed and all of a sudden he looked less frightening.

Dorothy did that – she had a calming effect on people.

The Master craned his neck to look over the heads in the queue. 'Who is responsible for these two?'

'Me, sir, I am, Master Knowles,' Sandra called.

'Then you're not doing your job properly. Have they been shown the rules?'

'No, sir, there hasn't been time.'

'Do it now.'

'But, sir, what about my dinn—'

'Now!' he bellowed.

The girls shrank back in fright.

*

The three of them sat upstairs in the girls' dormitory on one of the wooden cot beds. Timber beams crossed the room, and attached to them were notices displaying bible passages. Dorothy explained that they read 'God is Good' and 'Blessed are the Poor'.

'How old are you?' Esther asked Sandra.

'Eleven,' Sandra replied.

'Have you any brothers or sisters?'

'A brother, Alf, in the boy's department.'

Sandra was hollow-cheeked and when she talked she ran her fingers through her shorn hair. She was so thin her legs were like the matchsticks Mam used at home to light the fire with.

Mindful of being polite, Esther didn't stare.

'Why are you in this special place?' she asked.

'Cos both me parents are dead and I'm an orphan.'

Esther stared, horrified.

Then she thought of her mother and her heart lifted. 'We have Mam.' She looked at Dorothy for reassurance.

'Makes no difference…' Sandra rolled her eyes. 'Blakely's governors changed the rules. If widows can't provide for their offspring they bring them here.'

'Who told you that?' Dorothy asked.

Sandra grinned. 'The Mistress. I listen through keyholes.'

Dorothy smiled appreciatively at Sandra. 'It's kind of you to show us around.'

The big girl shrugged. 'I've no choice. I'd rather be eating me dinner.'

They fell silent.

After a while Dorothy asked, 'What are the rules Mr Knowles mentioned?'

Sandra heaved a long-suffering sigh. 'They're on the walls and everywhere. The Mistress recites them the beginning of every month at breakfast for those that can't read. See… ' She pointed to a poster that was pinned behind the door.

Dorothy rose and, walking over, began to read.

'*That the house be swept and cleaned each morning and inspected by monitors. That no orphan is allowed absent from the house without permission...*' She took a deep breath before continuing, '*All in the infant department in the summer months are in bed by six—*'

'That's you,' Sandra cut in.

Esther protested, 'Dorothy too.'

'Nah! She goes to bed at eight up here in the junior department.'

The revelation that she'd be separated from Dorothy was one too many for Esther and she finally crumpled.

'I don't like it here,' she said, in a small voice.

Dorothy sniffed. 'Neither do I.'

*

As the weeks passed and Mam didn't appear, Esther grew downhearted. She cried at night in bed, not the sobbing kind that the other children in the dormitory might hear, but the silent kind when, hiding beneath the folds of the blanket, she stuffed a fist in her mouth.

She didn't belong here; she reminded herself, and it was only a matter of time till their mother returned. Esther trusted her and resolved to stay brave until then.

On Saturdays, Dorothy was allowed to visit the infants' department and she was permitted to come alone, without Sandra, her senior 'mother' who she was paired with the babies' department was self-sufficient with its dayroom, dormitory and kitchen, where a grumpy cook was employed. The sisters sat cross-legged in front of a meagre fire that had a tall mesh fireguard surrounding it.

'Do you think about Mam all the time?' Esther ventured to ask her sister.

'I try not to.'

Esther was surprised, for imagining their mother – the warm smell of her skin, how her eyes crinkled when she smiled – was what comforted her.

'Don't you want her to come and fetch us?' she asked.

'Don't be silly, of course I do. I don't want you to be disappointed, that's all.'

'Why would I be?'

'I don't know,' her sister said, evasively. 'You just might be.' Dorothy shifted as though she were uncomfortable. 'Have you made friends yet?'

'No, the Nurse is mean and all the children are frightened of her. They just sit on the mat. They don't talk, or play, or anything. Why are they like that, Dorothy?'

'I don't know but I promise I won't let that happen to you.'

'And you'll never leave me?'

'Never. You're my girl, remember?'

The saying was one Aunty Olga had often used. Of course, Aunt Olga wasn't a real aunt, but a family friend. Mam ran a corner shop from the two-roomed flat in Bream Street. The back room, with its smoky range, big double bed and feeble sash windows, was where the family lived. Aunt Olga helped her husband, Mr Gruber, run the butcher's shop further along the street.

As Esther thought of home, stirrings of excitement whirled inside her. Christmas would soon be here. Her mother would return for them by then, she was sure of it.

*

The days leading up to Christmas were dark and bitterly cold. Draughts howled through the bottom of doors, making the windows rattle, and in the babies' department, the wind blew down the chimney, causing billows of smoke to belch from the flue.

When Mam didn't return at Christmas, the sense of loss Esther felt was crushing.

When Dorothy visited her on Boxing Day, she suggested, 'Maybe Mam was too busy in the shop.'

'Mam closes the shop on Christmas Day,' Dorothy said, dully. She pursed her lips, as if she didn't want to talk any more and Esther felt compelled to defend their mother.

'Mam might have been too ill to visit. Remember the time she lay in bed, too sick to open the shop, and Aunt Olga served behind the counter?'

Dorothy averted her gaze. 'Esther, I don't want to talk about *her* any more.'

CHAPTER THREE
August 1934

At eight years old, Esther progressed to the junior department. Surprisingly, the past few years at Blakely had been tolerable. Friendships were made, lessons had been learned and Esther had mentally toughened up – the key to surviving at the orphanage. She had discovered she could endure anything, as long as Dorothy was by her side.

In the junior department, second-hand uniforms and shoes were left in a pile on the floor at the end of the dormitory on a first come, first served basis at the beginning of each school term. Junior girls were issued with a number to identify them and Esther was expected to stitch her number, twenty-six, on each item of her clothing.

'I can't sew,' she bewailed to Miss Balfour, the department's housemistress.

Miss Balfour, a robust lady with a kind smile, pink cheeks and an enthusiastic manner, was a committed Christian and had devoted her life to the Lord. And though intimidated by Mistress Knowles as everyone else was, Miss Balfour always put the girls first, no matter the cost to herself. The girls idolised her for it – Esther included.

Miss Balfour gave a reassuring smile. 'In a former life I was a seamstress.' But then her face clouded. 'The Mistress insists all her young charges learn how to knit and sew as it qualifies them to be a good servant.'

Esther frowned. She didn't intend to be a servant – good or otherwise.

Life at Blakely was tightly structured. Woken at six o' clock by a bell, Esther dressed and tended to duties distributed by the housemistress. At eight o'clock sharp, the orphans assembled in the dining hall, where hymns were sung and the Lord was praised for all his infinite goodness. Breakfast over, the orphans marched to chalk-smelling classrooms where the start of the academic day began.

Meals were unvaried in the oppressively quiet dining hall. Oatmeal gruel for breakfast topped with a dab of treacle, greasy broth for dinner – in which you would be lucky to find a shaving of meat – plus a slice of bread and a sliver of cheese, followed by stodgy rice pudding for supper. Forever starved, Esther ate everything placed before her, but still her chin became sharper, her features more defined, her frock size remaining the same for two years.

Then there were all the rules and the fear of punishment if they weren't obeyed. Anger festered in Esther, chiefly manifesting in defiance – and whenever she could, she broke the rules, much to the frustration of well-behaved Dorothy. She particularly enjoyed maintaining and cultivating her well-spoken accent which infuriated the uncouth Mistress Knowles. So, the once biddable Esther developed into a more insubordinate, cynical young girl.

But still, the ray of hope that one day Mam would return never left her.

Dorothy sat opposite Esther at the trestle table. She was taller and thinner, with an angular face and almond eyes. Today she seemed agitated.

Dorothy beckoned Sandra to sit alongside her. 'Sandra has got something to tell us,' she said without preamble.

Sandra drew in a breath. 'Mistress Knowles has arranged for me to go into service at a place called Lawe Top.'

'Is that in South Shields?'

'Yes. The Mistress says I'm lucky apparently,' she pulled a grim face, 'cos' the lady of the house doesn't want a premium to employ us. I'm to use the money to kit meself out with work clothes.'

Sandra would be fifteen in two weeks; it was time for her to leave the orphanage. She had no relatives, apart from her younger brother, Alf, segregated in the boys' department. It had never occurred to Esther to wonder where Sandra might live when she left Blakely.

'And you don't know who these people are you'll be working for?' Esther questioned.

Dorothy gave her sister an exasperated glare. 'What's your employer's name?' she asked their friend.

'Mrs Kirton.'

'That sounds a nice name to me.'

'You think so?' Sandra brightened.

'Will you come back to visit us?' Esther asked.

'If I can.' But Sandra didn't look hopeful.

A thought struck Esther. She turned to her sister. 'What if we're not here? Mam might have been for us by then.'

Sandra rolled her eyes. 'Has nobody told her yet?'

'Told me what?'

A guilty expression crossed her sister's face.

Before Esther could prompt Dorothy, a figure cast a shadow over them. 'Girls,' Miss Balfour said, sternly. 'Time to go.'

'Yes, Miss,' they chanted in unison.

The moment passed, and Esther forgot the question she'd feared to ask.

*

On the day of Sandra's departure, they were allowed to wait at the front door with Alf to say goodbye to their friend.

Sandra, swamped in a big black coat that reached down to her ankles, wore black stockings and lace-up shoes, and carried a small battered suitcase.

Esther noted the dread in her eyes.

'So long, Alf, be good,' Sandra gave her brother a half-hearted smile.

Ashen-faced, he mutinously kicked the linoleum floor with his foot.

Sandra regarded Dorothy. 'Promise you'll write.'

'I will.'

No one hugged, as expressions of endearment were frowned upon at Blakely. Mistress Knowles, arms folded over voluptuous breasts, watched from afar to ensure decorum was met.

When it was Esther's turn to say goodbye, Sandra gave a huge sniff. 'She isn't coming back… you know… your Mam. Better you find out now…' Her gaze met Dorothy's. 'And it's better it's me that tells you.'

'Time to move on,' Mistress Knowles cut in. Stepping towards the door and opening it, she handed Sandra a sheet of notepaper. 'The directions to your new address… here's the fare.' She shoved the coins into Sandra's hand.

Sandra stepped into the sunshine. 'Ta-ra,' she said, a quiver in her voice. The door closed and she was gone.

It was all too reminiscent of Mam's departure and the worry of it felt like butterflies fluttering inside Esther's stomach.

A shocked silence followed, and all that could be heard was a wail from the babies' department. Sandra's brother stormed off along the passage, not looking back.

Esther rounded on her sister. 'What did Sandra mean… Mam isn't coming back?'

'I won't have you raise your voice, girl,' the Mistress commanded.

Esther wouldn't be silenced. 'She is coming back. She promised me.'

For years, she'd held on to this hope. In her darkest days, it was the only thing that got her through.

'Divvent be so ridiculous, twenty-six. You're the property of Blakely. Your mother signed a contract to that effect years ago.'

Esther felt winded.

'Tell her, Dorothy, it isn't true.'

Dorothy's green eyes were swathed in torment. 'Oh, Esther... I should've told you long ago.'

As hope died, something shattered inside Esther and, inexplicably, she knew she wasn't innocent any more.

Mistress Knowles drew herself up. 'For your insolence, girl, you'll miss dinner. And be thankful I'm in a lenient mood.'

'I should've told you long ago, but, Esther, I couldn't bear to see you hurt.' Dorothy's eyes clouded with anguish.

Supper over, the two sisters were sitting across the table from each other. Esther wasn't listening – she was still puzzling over the question she'd been asking herself all day.

'What's a contract?'

'An agreement.'

'What did Mam agree to?'

Dorothy chewed a fingernail. 'She signed a piece of paper that said Blakely was responsible for us till we're fifteen. It's the rule.'

Esther's stomach lurched. 'How do you know this?'

'Sandra said Mam visited Blakely the week before she brought us here. The Mistress showed her around and then Mam signed the contract.'

'How does Sandra know this?'

Dorothy gave a weak smile. 'She listens through keyholes... remember?'

'And Mam never said a word?'

Dorothy hesitated. 'Actually, yes. She told me the night before, but she didn't explain things properly. She told me she was ill and couldn't manage and she was taking us to a special place and it was for the best. She said she'd been shown around and she was pleased we'd be fed and have a roof over our heads. She also told me to look out for you.'

Esther was stunned. 'Why didn't she let Aunt Olga look after us until she got better?'

'I was only young, Esther, but I seem to remember Mam didn't want us to go to Aunt Olga as she and her husband had the butcher's shop to run.'

'So, she dumped us here…'

As reality sank in, outrage sparked in Esther like a firecracker. Faced with the facts, she could deny the truth no longer. Mam wasn't the angelic saint she'd worshipped all these years but a stranger – a selfish stranger who had only thought about herself.

'I hate her,' she cried.

'Don't say that.'

'But I do.'

Dorothy stared at her sister with a look sad enough to break Esther's heart. 'She's still our Mam.'

'Why didn't she visit us, then?'

'Perhaps she was too ill.'

'Too ill to write to us or send someone else to check on us?'

'Oh, I don't know,' Dorothy admitted, crestfallen.

'I don't care if she never comes back for us.'

'Oh, Esther! You don't mean that.'

'Yes, I do.' Tired of waiting for her mother, Esther's heart hardened and she vowed never to trust anyone again. Except, of course, Dorothy.

'When you're fifteen,' she asked, 'will you be sent out to work like Sandra?'

Dorothy ran her fingers through her hair. 'Where else could I go?'

It had been a long and trying day, and Esther couldn't stay brave any longer. The thought of losing her sister was too much and unshed tears prickled her eyes.

'Don't get upset,' Dorothy's voice was unsteady. 'It could be the best thing to happen.' Her expression grew determined. 'I've thought about it, Esther. I'll find us a home so we'll never be parted again.'

Esther voiced her biggest fear. 'What if something happens and you're unable to return for me?

'I promise nothing will. You're my girl, remember.'

CHAPTER FOUR

November 1937

On the day Dorothy prepared to leave Blakely, sleet swirled down from a threatening grey sky.

Esther stood outside on the top step waiting for her sister.

Twelve now, Esther couldn't remember the last time she'd cried, but she felt like it now, swallowing a lump in her throat.

'Get back inside.' Dorothy appeared on the step dressed in a coat meant for someone bigger, wearing black lace-up shoes, a woollen hat and mittens whose wool had shrunk tight in the wash. 'You'll catch your death. Just look at you… you're soaked through.'

Esther's uniform was sodden. Droplets of rain streamed from her hair and down her face like huge tears.

Dorothy did what she did best and fussed over Esther, but both sisters knew this was only a ruse to hide their true feelings – the dread they both felt at being torn apart. These days, Mam was never mentioned and if Esther did think of her, it was with contempt. And when she found herself softening, feeling tempted to forgive her, she reminded herself of her mother's betrayal and hardened her heart.

Dorothy was the one Esther loved and couldn't bear to be separated from.

'Have you got the directions to the house?' she asked, anxiety bouncing around like a tennis ball in her stomach.

'In my pocket… but guess what, Esther?' Hope glimmered in Dorothy's eyes. 'The house is within walking distance from here. A place called Beach Road… behind the Town Hall. I'm to be a nursemaid, the Mistress says.'

Neither of the sisters knew the layout of their hometown, having spent most of their lives within the confines of Blakely, but the fact that Dorothy's place of work was in the vicinity made Esther sag with relief.

'Write as soon as you can,' she begged.

The Mistress maintained that if the orphans were taught to read and write in class, it would make it easier for her to place them in employment.

But the sisters stared knowingly at each other. Since leaving, Sandra had only corresponded once and they'd never heard from her again. She had written to say that she was employed as a general servant by a solicitor and his wife.

Her letter had ended:

> …If you think life gets any easier after Blakely then think again. From Cook to the Mistress and her three good-for-nothing daughters, I'm everyone's skivvy. I'm fed reasonably well but that's only so I keep up the strength to run after the lot of them.
> I miss you terribly but don't be surprised if I don't write, as I never have any spare time.

Dorothy wrote to the address but she never received a reply. Sandra's silence upset her and she wouldn't discuss the matter even when Esther pestered her. Esther's biggest fear was that the same thing might happen to Dorothy.

'I'll write the minute I can,' Dorothy promised, shivering. Whether it was from cold or fright, Esther had no way of telling. 'In three years it'll be your turn. And I promise, Esther, I will find us a home. Can you stay brave until then?'

A memory came flooding back of Mam requesting the same thing – but this was Dorothy, Esther reminded herself, and she trusted her implicitly.

As snowflakes began falling rapidly between them, Esther nodded.

A week passed and life at the orphanage without Dorothy was devastating. It was as though half of Esther – the part that stayed sane, the best part that only Dorothy brought out – was missing. With her sister gone, Esther, lonely and insecure, would erupt into fits of temper.

'My dear child, your recent behaviour won't do,' Miss Balfour reprimanded her one night as she readied to turn off the dormitory lights. 'You'll only suffer if Mistress Knowles finds out.'

Esther stood in her tent-like nightdress.

'I hate the Mistress,' she said.

'Hate is a strong word. You must pray for guidance.'

Esther knew Miss Balfour meant well but she'd had her fill of religion, forced upon her at the orphanage for years.

'When I leave Blakely I'm finished with prayers and church.'

'You're angry. You don't mean that.'

'Yes, I do. This doing-good business makes me laugh. My Grandfather was supposedly a vicar. Where was he when we needed help?'

Miss Balfour looked distressed. 'My dear, life won't always be a struggle. One day happiness will come your way.'

Esther refrained from saying that she didn't believe in fairy tales any more.

'Meanwhile…' a smile transformed Miss Balfour's face. She lifted a letter from her uniform pocket and handed it to Esther. 'This might make you feel better.'

Esther recognised Dorothy's loopy handwriting on the envelope. 'Oh! Thank you,' she said, grinning.

Miss Balfour went on. 'The Mistress said I was to give you the letter only if your behaviour improved.' A glint of amusement twinkled in her eye. 'I told the Mistress your conduct of late has been exemplary.' She moved to leave the room. 'Ten minutes more,' she smiled, 'before I switch off the lights.'

With something tangible in her hand to link her with her sister, the doubts in Esther's mind melted away. Legs crossed, head bent, she sat on the bed in the half-light, devouring Dorothy's words.

I'm writing this from my own room up in the attic. Imagine! I'm lonely though, and miss all the whisperings from the other girls. Across the landing is a girl called Alice, who is a year older than me and she's the house servant. But I'm getting ahead of myself.

When I left you, I followed the directions to Beach Road. The roads terrified me, as did all the people. I kept huddled to the wall like a frightened mouse.

Eventually, I found the house and it's grand, Esther. My employer is a doctor and his name is Brooke. His surgery is down some steps at the front of the house in a basement room. The Brookes have two toddlers, both girls, and cute kiddies – though Celia, the oldest, can be bossy at times.

Esther, I can't take everything in, there's so much. But the main thing is the family I work for are nice people and for that I'm grateful. I miss you dreadfully, though. I don't know when I'll get to see you. I understand I get a half-day off, but nobody has told me when.

I say a little prayer each night so that God will keep you safe.

Your devoted sister,
Dorothy

Esther carefully placed the letter under her pillow. Laying back on the hard mattress, a smile played on her lips. Dorothy was safe and well. Esther would have thanked God if she hadn't fallen out with him.

CHAPTER FIVE

October 1938

It was the orphan boys who heard the rumblings of war first. The Master allowed the older boys in the department to read his newspapers and so they had more of an idea what went on in the outside world beyond Blakely.

The rule forbade the boys and girls from communicating with each other but notes were passed in communal classrooms about all manner of things.

Dorothy didn't believe in the war rumours. She said Doctor Brooke trusted Mr Chamberlain – and therefore so did she. The prime minister had said in his speech after the Munich International Conference, 'peace for our time,' and that was enough to assure them.

Esther experienced a stab of jealousy that her sister was so close to the Brookes. She knew she shouldn't be so possessive but she couldn't help herself as Dorothy was all the family she had.

Dorothy's afternoon off was on a Wednesday, when she was allowed to visit Esther for an hour after dinner in the garden where her sister worked. For Mistress Knowles had refused to allow Esther, a senior girl now, to be a 'mother' to one of the little ones, like Sandra had looked after Dorothy.

'Esther Makepeace is a bad example,' she had announced one day at breakfast in the dining hall. 'She will help in the gardens where she can do nee harm.'

Esther enjoyed working in the open air and she was quick to learn from Benson, the gardener. She dug trenches, planted tiny seeds and watched as, miraculously, they grew into healthy vegetables; carrots, turnips, leeks and rows of green, leafy potatoes brightening her days. Flowers remained her greatest love, and she liked nothing better than to tend cuttings in the sunny and snug greenhouse. In summer, when the borders became an explosion of bright pinks, purples and oranges, she welled up at the beauty of it all.

It occurred to her that good things do happen sometimes. And Esther allowed her suspicious mind to relax for once.

The following May, on a blistering hot Wednesday afternoon, the sisters sat in the long grass beneath the shade of a sycamore tree. Dorothy, resting her head on the boundary wall, watched a bright blue butterfly flutter overhead. 'All the talk on the wireless and in the newspapers,' she said, 'speculates about war. It's quite alarming, Esther.'

Dorothy had been away from Blakely for about a year and a half now and considered herself to be Esther's eyes and ears to the outside world. She didn't tell Esther the more perturbing aspects of what was going on – the rumours rife in the town – that if war did break out there'd be thousands of casualties from aerial attacks and unruly mobs would descend on the country. In this disordered world, goodness knew what might happen but as the oldest, she'd keep her promise to Mam and protect Esther.

Thoughts of her father unexpectedly surfaced in Dorothy's mind. Just a young man when the Great War started, how had he coped? Had he been nervous he'd be called up or eager to do battle for his country? Whatever his thoughts, their father had travelled with countless of other brave boys to a foreign country to engage in a merciless war. The injuries he received there meant that he had been an invalid for the rest of his short life.

Sadness enveloping Dorothy, she wondered what their lives would have been like if their father had lived.

As the butterfly fluttered away, Dorothy realised she felt secure for the first time since Mam left them, and was loath to leave her safe haven with the Brookes. But there would not be a place for Esther there too when the time came for her to leave Blakely, as she had promised her sister they would live together. Dorothy would never go back on her word and she vowed to find the sisters a home. Yet how she was going to accomplish such a feat, Dorothy had no idea and the responsibility weighed heavily upon her.

Esther was sitting cross-legged in the grass making a daisy chain. She looked up. 'Miss Balfour says she's optimistic and refuses to consider the possibility of war. And I must say, I'm going to follow her example and stay positive.'

Dorothy smiled affectionately. Even though she was thin, there was robustness about Esther and her dogged spirit helped her survive the tribulations of Blakely. Dorothy was glad, hoping life would be good to her sister – and, perhaps, then the mistrust would vanish from her hazel eyes.

'I hope Miss Balfour's right,' she replied, 'but even Doctor Brooke has changed his mind. He now thinks war is unavoidable and it's only a matter of time.'

Despite the warmth of the day, Esther shivered. 'Let's not talk about war. It'll only spoil your visit.'

There were other subjects that Esther refused to discuss – Mam for instance. Although Dorothy hadn't wanted to talk about their mother when they were younger, she felt differently now. Because, as she'd grown older, Dorothy had come to understand that sometimes life intervened, meaning that people could not always do what was right but had to settle for what was best under the circumstances. She believed that of Mam, unable to bear the alternative.

As she lay back in the sweet-smelling grass, Dorothy's thoughts rambled down the years to life in Bream Street. She remembered the pungent smell of the store, with damp sawdust, exotic herbs and spices in the air; Mam serving in the shop wearing a long elegant skirt and a high-necked blouse, embellished with a cameo brooch. Tall and refined, she wasn't like the other women in the area and her aloof air caused a stir with the customers.

How Dorothy wished she could ask her mother all the questions that churned in her mind, to touch her face and feel if her skin was as soft as it was in her memory. The possibility of searching for Mam had crossed Dorothy's mind but she knew that her sister would view such an act as a betrayal of trust: Esther was unable to forgive their mother for leaving them – as far as she was concerned, she and Dorothy were on their own.

Esther broke the silence. 'Dorothy… I've started bleeding… down below.'

'Don't worry,' Dorothy smiled, 'you've started your monthly period, that's all. Have you seen Miss Balfour? She'll give you sanitary towels.'

Esther flushed. 'I'm not having a baby, am I?'

'Of course not, silly. And don't listen to what any of the other girls tell you.' Dorothy pulled a frustrated face. 'I wish I could tell you the facts of life but… I don't know them myself.' She sat up and hugged her knees. 'Mrs Brooke says my ignorance about such matters is Blakely's fault and they should prepare their girls for the outside world.'

Bitterness gleamed in Esther's eyes. 'The orphanage should take some of the blame, but Mam's equally responsible. She's the one who abandoned us here.'

'Oh Esther, I wish you could forgive her.'

'Never. I don't know how you can.'

'I can't hate her,' Dorothy cried. 'If you did something dreadful it wouldn't stop me loving you.'

'Hah! So, you agree that what Mam did was terrible.'

Dorothy shrugged, defeated. She watched as, in the distance, Benson came out of the greenhouse. A small man with bowlegs, he took off his cap, and wiped his brow on his shirtsleeve. Mind on his work, he didn't look up.

Dorothy sighed, hating unhappy silences. 'I decided to end my hermit existence,' she told Esther. She observed Benson as he took up the handles of the battered wheelbarrow and trundled along the cinder path. 'I've joined the local dramatic society.'

Esther gasped. 'Did you go by yourself?'

'No, with Alice.' Dorothy thought it wise not to mention that the outing had been Mrs Brooke's idea. She was the kindest person and seemed to care about her staff and their wellbeing. She reminded Dorothy of the caring Miss Balfour at the orphanage.

Esther stared at her curiously. 'You've changed since you left Blakely.'

It was true – but because of Esther's jealousy, Dorothy couldn't explain that her new confidence was all her employers' doing. Mrs Brooke encouraged her to try new things; a trip to the lending library, shopping on King Street's busy high street, walking with Alice along the Coast Road where Dorothy dreamed longingly as she looked out over the glittering sea. All frightening, yet exhilarating stuff.

'D'you go on stage?'

'Blimey, that's a bit much!'

'What d'you do then?'

'I paint scenery.' Dorothy's cheeks burned. She didn't add who she painted scenery with.

Best for now, she thought, to keep Lawrence Calvert a secret.

CHAPTER SIX

August 1939

Another Wednesday and the two sisters were enjoying the warm and bright sunny day in the orphanage garden.

It seemed outrageous to think war was looming. Seagulls soared high in the sky, and the grass was lush beneath Esther's supine body. She rested her head on an arm and listened to Dorothy as she read out loud from the newspaper. 'It says here we've to get on with the holidays… as long as Hitler, and the weather permit.' Dorothy looked up with a pensive gaze, 'Doctor Brooke thinks there's nothing for it but to defeat the aggressive spirit that threatens our nation.'

'He means go to war?'

Dorothy nodded.

Esther chewed thoughtfully on a blade of grass. 'Is everyone really carrying on as normal?'

'It would appear people are making a last ditch effort to enjoy themselves.'

Dorothy went on to describe how the beach was packed with families. How South Shield's sands were littered with tents and bathing boxes, where people changed into modest swimming costumes. How kiddies paddled at the water's edge, and weary-looking donkeys, with children on their backs, plodded along the seashore.

Esther gave a heartfelt sigh. She longed to be out of the orphanage and see it all for herself.

'How are things here?' Dorothy wanted to know.

'Us seniors are allowed to listen to the BBC news report before going to bed. Otherwise, life goes on as tediously as before.'

Esther couldn't imagine how anything, even a war in Europe, would disrupt the monotony of life at Blakely. About to point this fact out to Dorothy, she noticed her sister's faraway, dreamy expression. Studying her, Esther tried to work out what was different. Her bob had been replaced by a longer, sleeker hairstyle that reached her shoulders, topped by a fashionable sausage roll effect around her forehead.

'Since when have you worn make-up?' Esther asked, accusingly.

Dorothy laughed self-consciously. 'It's only a touch of lipstick and powder.' Her cheeks flushed pink and Esther knew there was more to come.

'All right, I'll blab... I'm seeing a fellow.'

Esther's jaw dropped.

'What d'you mean, a fellow?'

'His name is Lawrence Calvert but he prefers Laurie.'

That Dorothy might be seeing someone had never entered Esther's head. At Blakely they were taught it was improper to have anything to do with the other sex and the thought of Dorothy seeing a fellow made Esther squirm with embarrassment.

'I know it's difficult for you to imagine... me meeting a man...' There was a conciliatory note in Dorothy's voice, 'But honestly, Esther... Laurie is so comfortable to be with. I feel as if I've known him forever.'

'Man?! How old is he?'

'Twenty-two.'

He was old, then.

'Where did you meet him?'

'At the drama group. Alice only came for two meetings and I went on my own after that.'

Esther knew how much courage such an act would take and felt proud of her sister. But she was also peeved that Dorothy had been seeing someone without telling her – it only proved how much her sister had changed.

'I stood at the back of the hall like a wallflower,' Dorothy went on. 'Laurie approached me and asked if I wanted to help paint scenery. I painted the sky, but I was all thumbs and got blue paint everywhere.'

Dorothy sighed, as if recalling the most heavenly memory.

'Laurie led me into the cloakroom and dabbed my cheek with a wet handkerchief.'

'You were alone with him?'

'I swear the poor man was more nervous than me.' Dorothy sighed again, blissfully.

'And you've seen him since?'

'We went on a date. To the cinema and then danced at the beach.'

'The beach!'

'South Beach to be correct. Where a gramophone plays records and couples dance to popular tunes. It's quite informal… people dance barefoot or in plimsolls. It's super fun.'

Flabbergasted that Dorothy had kept her secret for so long, Esther gave an offhand shrug.

'Don't be cross,' Dorothy implored. 'I wanted to tell you but I was worried you'd be upset.'

'I couldn't care less.'

'Well, he wants to meet you.'

Dumbfounded, Esther didn't reply.

September was the month to prepare the garden for winter. The sky, grey and threatening, looked as though a storm was brewing.

Esther, carrying a long-handled spade, made her way to the far side of the house to the vegetable patch. There was no sign of Benson but evidence of his digging was beneath a high redbrick wall.

As she stood between rows of carrots, their feathery greenery grazing her fingertips, Esther was struck by the eerie silence, instinctively sensing that something momentous was about to happen.

Benson appeared around the corner of the house, a familiar figure in brown, coarse-material trousers, a collarless shirt and sleeves rolled roughly up to the elbows.

His ruddy face appeared perplexed. 'It's here then, the war.'

'The war?'

'Heard it from the man himself on the wireless.'

'Mr Chamberlain?'

'Aye. That's him all reet.'

He lapsed into one of his long silences and stared blankly ahead of him. He had been in the Great War and was apt to indulge in gruesome tales of life in the trenches. On these occasions, Esther was inclined to la-la-la in her mind, else she wouldn't sleep at night, haunted by the gory images.

In the uncanny silence, she shivered. *War.* She couldn't conceive what that would mean.

At suppertime, when the Mistress announced that war had been declared, no one in the dining hall reacted. The eagle-eyed orphans watched as bowls were handed along the table and the biggest question on their minds was if there was enough food for a decent helping. There might be a war on the horizon but that was in the faraway outside world – a place no orphan knew anything about.

During prayers – endless now there was a war to be delivered from – everyone stood to attention.

The Mistress looked expectantly at the Master by her side.

'His Majesty the King,' his voice rang out, 'has given a stirring broadcast on the wireless. He has called upon us… his subjects… to stand firm and be united.' Eyes burning with fervour, he continued to address the hall. 'His Majesty can depend upon us at Blakely. We will all do our best to promote frugality and peace in this house. We shall remember those who go to war in our daily prayers.'

As his voice droned on, Esther groaned.

How unfair, she found herself thinking, for those who had no one to pray for them. What happened to those people?

But uppermost in her mind was the imminent visit from Lawrence Calvert. Esther squirmed thinking about it. What if she didn't like him or what if he couldn't abide her? But Dorothy seemed gone on him and for her sake Esther must try to be civil to him. Even if she didn't want to…

On the Wednesday of Lawrence's arrival, Esther stood in Blakely's vast dining hall, the smell of greasy broth permeating the air, so nervous she could barely stand still. She worried that if Dorothy became entangled with this man, she might forget her promise to find the sisters a home.

Esther grimaced, dolefully. First the Brooke family and now him… more competition for her sister's affection.

As the hands on the clock moved to the designated hour, Esther pulled back her shoulders and straightened her spine. She was determined to rise above jealousy. The door hinges squeaked as it opened and Esther fixed a smile on her face. It was then that she saw him.

Lawrence Calvert.

He walked into the room, a bear of a man, dwarfing Dorothy. His face was friendly and his eyes crinkled at the corners when he smiled.

The pair of them came to stand before her.

'Esther, this is Laurie,' Dorothy said, looking nervous.

Taking his extended hand, Esther found her small one was lost in his and, for no apparent reason, she suddenly felt shy.

As the three of them sat down on the wooden benches, Laurie found it difficult to fit his longs legs beneath the table, giving up and turning the other way.

Dorothy's expression grew serious. 'You've heard the news?'

'Benson told me.'

'War. It's unthinkable. I don't know what to expect.'

They were both conscious of Laurie listening in, not used to having a man in their company.

Dorothy turned towards him. 'This is the dining hall,' she stated, unnecessarily. Laurie eyed the cracked walls, the damp patch on the ceiling. 'It's a bit grim, like,' he said.

'Laurie's in the building trade… he's a bricklayer,' Dorothy explained.

He gave a bellowing laugh. 'More like a man of all trades.'

He wore a dark suit and a matching waistcoat, a silver watch chain dangling from his top pocket. Reaching into his jacket, he brought out a bar of Fry's Chocolate Cream.

'For you,' he told Esther.

Esther's taste buds salivated. Never had she owned a whole bar of chocolate, just for herself. It would cause a riot back in the dormitory.

As the visit with Laurie continued, Esther found herself thawing in his company. He wanted to know all about life at the orphanage and, elbows resting on the table, he listened with genuine interest as she spoke. Esther surprised herself by telling him about the Mistress's meanness, the lack of food, how she missed Dorothy, and what a darling Miss Balfour was. Opening up came as a kind of release. Despite her earlier fears, Esther decided she liked Laurie Calvert.

'You're a brave lassie,' he commented when she finished. 'It puts the rest of us to shame... so it does... with all of our moans. I can't do much... but what I certainly will do is bring you treats of food.'

'The Mistress wouldn't allow it,' Esther said, aghast.

His good-natured face clouded. 'I'd like to see her try and stop us.' After a while, his face lit up and he grinned. 'Me Ma makes the best sponge cake with homemade plum jam in the middle. I'll bring you some next time I visit.'

'Will you thank her for me?' Esther replied, overwhelmed.

'Nee need for thanks. With us lot at home to feed and money short, it's second nature for Ma to bake.'

'Laurie's mam's a widow,' Dorothy explained.

Laurie's eyes lit up as he met Dorothy's gaze.

It was obvious – even to Esther who knew nothing about matters of the heart – that the pair were falling in love. And the amazing thing was, she didn't experience a scrap of jealousy.

The war, at first, was inconvenient more than anything else. It was worse in the evening, when the blackout curtains were drawn so that German raiders wouldn't know if they flew over built-up areas. Esther was one of the senior girls elected to walk around the orphanage, checking that not a chink of light shone out of the windows.

Shelters were built under the fields beyond Blakely and in the event of an air raid, the orphans were meant to sleep on straw-filled pallets placed on the concrete floor.

One day, at breakfast, while the orphans stood sleepily to attention at the tables, Master Knowles made an announcement from the balcony.

'It's feared enemy planes are going to use poisonous gas on the British people. When you leave the hall, I will distribute to each of you a box containing a gas mask. You must carry them with you at all times.'

The masks, when they were handed out, were heavy frightful-looking objects that reeked of rubber.

'Laurie says they remind him of beetle faces,' Dorothy said, when next she came to visit. Smiling, she shook her head. 'I ask you, who spends their time looking that closely at insects?'

But Esther was only half listening; she was worried about the latest war rumour.

'Is it true children are being sent away into the countryside?'

'It's called evacuation.' Dorothy's expression became serious, as she nodded. 'And yes, for safety's sake there's mass exodus from the cities into the rural areas.'

'What about the Brookes' children?'

'Doctor Brooke insists his children are sent to his in-laws who live in Lancashire and that his wife go with them.'

'Gracious… that's quick.'

'These days, Esther, people don't wait to act.'

All this talk alarmed Esther. The sisters might lose contact with each other – it had happened with Sandra, after all.

'What about you? Will you go?' Esther held her breath.

'There's no need. Mrs Brooke's mother is going to help look after her grandchildren. I'd only be in the way. Besides, I want to stay here with you… and Laurie…' Dorothy bashfully bowed her head and peered out from beneath her curled blonde eyelashes. 'I've fallen in love with him.'

It was no big surprise to Esther. 'Will… you marry him?'

Dorothy heaved a troubled sigh. 'We're both impossible when it comes to matters of the heart.' She ran slim fingers through her hair. 'Blakely has left its mark on me and I find it difficult to tell Laurie how I feel.'

'What about Laurie? He's such a direct person.'

'Don't let him fool you.' Dorothy's smile was tender. 'Beneath that tough exterior, he's one of the shyest people I've ever met.'

Esther hoped all went well because Laurie, the big softie, had found a way into her heart.

Time rumbled on and in December, Laurie and Dorothy came to visit. Esther sat nervously between them and the couple kept looking at each other as if they had something to tell her. The excitement in the air was tangible.

'Guess what?' Dorothy grinned.

'I can't. Tell me this instant.'

'Laurie popped the question.'

'He never did. How did he propose?'

'Don't mind me. I'm just an onlooker,' Laurie joked.

'He didn't ask me to marry him, exactly.' Playfully, Dorothy punched him on the shoulder. 'Supposedly, we were Christmas shopping but his lordship here had other ideas.' She beamed devotedly at her fiancé. 'Laurie stopped and looked in a jeweller's window and told me to choose the engagement ring I wanted.'

'That wasn't very romantic,' Esther said.

Laurie looked crestfallen, 'Aye, I suppose you're right. But the words just blurted out.'

'Clot,' his fiancée intervened. 'I wouldn't want it any other way.'

Laurie's expansive chest swelled. 'Haway then, show Esther the ring.'

The ring, a gorgeous diamond solitaire, gleamed on Dorothy's third finger.

'Oh! Congratulations. It's beautiful. So, when's the wedding?'

'Esther!' Dorothy appeared mortified.

'She's right,' Laurie said, 'why wait when there's a war on? Me call-up papers could come at any time.'

*

Two weeks later Laurie's prophesy came true.

As soon as Dorothy entered the dining hall, Esther knew by her stunned expression that something was wrong.

'What is it?' She ran to her sister, feet clattering on the wooden floorboards.

Dorothy closed the door and took a deep breath. 'Laurie's call-up papers came. Oh, Esther, he's gone.'

There was a moment's shocked silence as the news sank in.

'Do we know where?'

'To Skegness.'

'Where's that?'

'Further down the country on the coast.'

'When did he find out?'

'Two days ago. There was a warrant ticket for the train included with his papers. He was to report to HMS Royal Arthur, a naval training barracks.'

'The navy... that's the appointment he hoped for, isn't it?'

'He's thrilled.' Dorothy shook her head in despair. 'What is it about war that excites even peace-abiding men?'

Esther didn't know. She only knew that Laurie was the kindest man and he wouldn't hurt a fly. Would he?

During December it snowed. When the annihilation from the air didn't happen, folk were on edge and, according to Dorothy, were reduced to petty worries, such as burst pipes and slippery pavements. The first few months of war were labelled the 'phoney war' after so much anticipation.

Then came reports about evacuees. According to the media, some were filthy, unsocial and 'downright foul-mouthed'. Esther wondered about these badly behaved children who were unafraid of reprisal. They seemed worlds away from Blakely.

One dark and freezing cold January morning, when the orphans were glad to be up and busy making their beds, Miss Balfour spoke, her face grave. 'Girls, Mistress Knowles is to announce at breakfast that arrangements have been made to evacuate Blakely orphans.'

In the stunned silence, Esther looked around the room to the other equally shaken girls.

'When, Miss?' she asked.

'Soon. The mistress hopes you will make model evacuees. And it will be up to her who goes first. Probably the youngest children, attended by some of you senior girls.'

Esther wouldn't go – they couldn't make her. Fifteen on her next birthday, she could finally leave the orphanage. She wouldn't let the war rob her of the freedom she so desperately longed for.

Esther suffered for two days before her sister's next visit but when it came, Dorothy's news took precedence.

Breathless, she hurried into the dining hall. 'I've had a telegram from Laurie.'

She handed the envelope over to Esther. The message was printed on strips of white paper on the buff-coloured telegram.

Six days leave Friday. Arrange wedding by special licence.
Love, Laurie.

'Crikey.' Esther didn't know what else to say. Then, her face split into a smile. 'I'm so happy for you.'

And for myself, she might have added. Laurie was like a brother, and the fact that it would become official thrilled her.

Dorothy grinned idiotically, 'It doesn't feel real.'

She went on to explain that Laurie feared he might be sent to war and so wanted them to be married before his training finished. His barracks in Skegness was a former holiday camp and he lived in a chalet and wrote that he was perished for most of the time, but he was proud too, as he'd been considered signalman material.

'What's that?'

'A signalman sends Morse code which is dot to dash messages by radio from ship to ship and ship to shore, sometimes encrypted for security.' She clasped her hands against her cheeks. 'Gosh… it's both alarming and exciting to be getting married in such a short space of time… and so much to organise.'

'Such as?'

'Book the registrar, the chapel, flowers—'

'What do you plan to wear?'

'Mrs Brooke has been wonderful. She thinks I'm terribly young but with this war on, she doesn't blame me for reaching out for a bit of happiness. She insists I raid her wardrobe and find something suitable.' A shadow of regret crossed Dorothy's expression. 'She won't see me on my wedding day as she'll have left for the country by then.'

'Will the doctor go with her?'

'Initially, to settle the family in, but then he'll come back to his practice.'

'Will Laurie's family be at the wedding?'

'I doubt it.'

'Why can't they come?'

'Basically, it's finances. Laurie thinks his mam can't afford to rig the family out.'

'Surely, his mam could come?'

'Laurie thinks not. And he doesn't want to press the matter.'

'What about me?' Esther asked in a small voice.

'You, my girl, are chief bridesmaid.'

Esther, thrilled, was rendered speechless.

Then a dark cloud of dismay descended. 'What if the Mistress won't allow me to attend?'

'Esther, it's inconceivable you won't be at my wedding. You will be there – I promise.'

But Esther wasn't so confident. With a jolt, she remembered her news and told Dorothy about the evacuation.

Thoughtfully, Dorothy bit the side of her lip. 'I know it's distressing, Esther, but try to be brave. You're fifteen soon and hopefully the evacuations won't happen before then.'

'Miss Balfour reckons it'll be soon. Should we make a plan?'

Dorothy's expression became resolute. 'Leave it with me. I'll have a think… I promise I won't let us be parted.'

CHAPTER SEVEN
February 1940

'I did everything,' Miss Balfour assured Esther in the dormitory the next day, 'but the Mistress wouldn't budge on the subject. She insists she needs to know where her charges are at all times, especially now there's a war on.'

Esther could tell by the housemistress's embarrassed expression that she too knew this was only a ruse. The Mistress's real intention was to exercise tyranny over Esther – yet again.

Though disappointment hit her like a sledgehammer that she wouldn't be at her sister's wedding, Esther decided for Dorothy's sake to put on a brave face. She insisted she would be there in spirit. Meanwhile, she wanted to be included in every aspect of the arrangements so she could imagine the happy occasion.

Dorothy, in turn, played along and was equally adamant that the wedding was to be low key, just a formality, and they'd celebrate properly when Esther was free of the orphanage.

The day of the wedding arrived and, at the designated hour of eleven o'clock, Esther sat in the classroom, gazing out of the window imagining the scene at the little chapel over the road from the Brookes' house. Laurie, handsome in naval uniform, would recite his vows, his baritone voice reverberating around an empty church. Only two people were to witness the wedding;

Laurie's mate from the barracks, who acted as best man, and his sweetheart. Esther's mind, like a book, slammed shut. It was the most important day of her sister's life and she was missing the occasion – every fibre of her being wanted to be in that little chapel.

Her heart leaden, she followed the rest of the orphan girls as they marched from the classroom and formed a dinner queue. She jumped as a hand lightly tapped her shoulder. Miss Balfour, a hint of mischief in her gaze, beckoned Esther to follow.

She led the way to the so-called library.

'Only a half an hour,' Miss Balfour whispered as she opened the door, 'before Mistress Knowles is expected back from the evacuation process meeting.' She tittered. 'With God's help… the Mistress will never know.'

As Esther entered the musty-smelling room, a cry of joy escaped her lips. Dorothy and Laurie stood beside a tall fixture of aged books. Dressed in wedding attire, wearing a becoming grape-coloured suit, a navy halo style hat and black high-heeled peep-toe shoes, Dorothy looked as stunning as Esther had imagined.

'We came straight from the ceremony,' she grinned.

'How…?' Esther began.

'With help from Miss Balfour.'

'But it was all your idea,' Laurie gazed adoringly at his wife.

Overcome with joy, Esther couldn't think of anything adequate to say and grinned foolishly.

The pair of them went on to tell her about the ceremony, laughing and interrupting one another as they regaled her.

Then Laurie turned to Esther. 'But the day… petal… wouldn't be complete without your blessing.'

He did that, did Laurie – made you feel special.

Dorothy looked at him, overjoyed. And why wouldn't she be? Esther thought. Secure in the knowledge that she had married the love of her life, a man that cherished her, Dorothy's future shone like a brilliant star ahead of her. Esther vowed she wouldn't settle for anything less when she married.

The allotted time nearly over, Esther noticed Dorothy's pensive expression.

'Something wrong?'

Dorothy grimaced uncertainly. 'I promised I wouldn't mention it, especially today… but… I'll burst if I don't.' Her green eyes sought Esther's. 'Can you remember Mam's cousin Aunt Lillian? She used to visit us all those years ago at the shop.'

Esther recoiled. She couldn't believe that Dorothy would spoil the day by mentioning their mother.

She shook her head emphatically. 'No.'

'Aunt Lillian was plump with freckles and dressed expensively. She had a daughter… I think called Margaret… we wore her cast-off clothes—'

'I've told you. I don't remember.'

It was a fib, because of course Esther did.

Dorothy persisted. 'I'm sure I saw Aunt Lillian yesterday. I spotted this woman walking further up on this side of the street and there was something familiar about her. She turned to look both ways in the road before crossing and I saw her face. I swear it was Aunt Lillian… If not, it's her double. She walked further up and then guess what, Esther?'

Esther didn't want to know.

'She moved towards one of the doors and bringing out a key from her coat pocket, she opened the door and went inside. She must live there… or else she knows someone who does.'

'So?'

'She's a link to Mam. Esther, she might know something.'

'I don't want to know about Mam.'

'But I do.'

'Then you go and ask her.'

'I would never… not if you didn't agree.'

Esther knew she was being unfair but she couldn't change her mind… not even for Dorothy. Not when it came to their mother. 'Mam is past history.'

'I missed not having her at my wedding.' Dorothy's voice was barely audible.

'She didn't deserve to be there. She gave up that right when she deserted you.'

'She's our mother, Esther. I'll always love her, no matter what.'

Esther considered her sister's forgiving heart. If more people in the world were like Dorothy, she thought, there would be no wars.

Yet still she said, 'More fool you.'

'Haway, you two.' Laurie's good-natured face looked distressed. 'Let's not spoil the day.' He looked from one to the other. 'You realise, this is the best day of me life.'

There was something solid and dependable about Laurie that made Esther well up. She now had two people in her life to rely on. She wanted to convey some of this sentiment to him but, tongue-tied, the words died on her lips.

Laurie, the big galoot, smiled comically – as if he guessed what she was thinking.

'I'm the lucky one, petal,' he said. 'Not only have I married the best girl in the world but I've got the prettiest sister-in-law into the bargain.'

Three days later, his leave was up and Laurie was gone.

Time wore on. News from the war was that ordinary men in little boats had sailed across the Channel and rescued soldiers, stranded on the beach, at a place called Dunkirk. The feat, a comparative success, made Esther proud to be British.

'The new Prime Minister, Mr Churchill, told Parliament the affair was "a miracle in deliverance".' Dorothy told Esther in the dining hall when she visited. 'Mr Brooke thinks so too. He admires Mr Churchill and thinks he's doing a first-rate job.'

Esther refrained from saying that it wasn't so long ago since Mr Brooke had championed the previous Prime Minister. But really who knew what to think – war events were happening so fast these days, it was hard to keep track.

In June, Esther experienced the war at first hand.

Woken up by a siren wailing its shrill public alert, the host of orphan girls joined in screaming.

Miss Balfour's composed voice cut through the chaos in the dormitory. 'Girls, stay calm. Remember the drill.'

Gas mask, torch and blanket forgotten, Esther shot from her bed and ran with the rest down the stairs, out of the door and across the fields to the dark and damp underground shelter.

Cold and terrified they sat on straw pallets, surrounded by the sound of bombs shrieking and explosions as they hit the earth.

'How was it?' Dorothy asked, when she next visited.

'Terrifying,' Esther admitted. 'I didn't know what to expect. There was no light and we half froze to death. Even after the raiders passed we were too scared to sleep.'

'Same here,' Dorothy said. 'Doctor Brooke was home. We heard the siren and raced for the shelter down the yard. The bombs were a few peculiar crumps in the distance then all went quiet after a time. Doctor Brooke thought they came from the Harton area.' She shook her head as she continued. 'I guess it's the end of the phoney war… We're really in it now and its frightening.'

Esther didn't want to think of the realities of war. 'Any news from Laurie?'

Dorothy's features softened. 'He managed a night's leave on his way up to Scotland. He was full of himself, as he's passed his twenty words a minute test.'

'Is that like an exam?'

'Yes, now he's qualified to go to the next stage to become a signalman.'

'So when does that happen?'

'His class has been posted to HMS Scotia in Ayr to further their speed in Morse code and to familiarise themselves with naval routine.'

This was said with distinct pride, but then her expression became serious. 'Guess what? Doctor Brooke has joined up to the medical corps.'

'I thought only single men had to go.'

'He's volunteered.'

'Blimey.'

'Mrs Brooke will be heartbroken. Though I guess she wouldn't expect anything less of him.'

Esther knew by Dorothy's expression there was more to come, and she felt apprehensive.

'The Brookes leaving is easier for Cook as she doesn't live in. Besides, she's taking the opportunity to retire. Alice is going to join Mrs Brooke in the country to help out. Mr Brooke says I can stay on at the house… as caretaker.'

'Won't you be afraid all alone in the house?'

'I've refused the offer.'

Esther gawped. 'But where will you go? What about money?'

'I get an allowance from Laurie's pay but it won't be enough to rent a flat and live on. I'll have to get a job. Laurie and I talked it over. He wants me to find a home of our own. I explained to Mr Brooke and he understands. He says I can move out in my own time. He knows someone willing to rent the house.'

'A job? What kind of job?'

'I'll do anything. They're crying out for women to go out to work and help with the war effort.' Dorothy's face grew into a fond smile. 'Another reason to find a job is to make sure you have a home when you leave Blakely. Laurie can't wait to get you out of this place. It isn't long now till you leave.'

As though she'd swallowed a golf ball, Esther didn't trust herself to speak. It sounded too good to be true.

'Preparation has begun to evacuate Blakely orphans to Yorkshire,' the Mistress announced at assembly one morning. 'It's taken longer than I first thought.' She glowered at her husband as though this was due to his incompetence.

It was only a week before her fifteenth birthday. Esther couldn't believe it was happening. The Mistress liked nothing better than to break an orphan's spirit – though she hadn't succeeded with Esther. But if she was forced to be evacuated and lost contact with Dorothy, Esther feared she might finally crack. After years of staying so strong, she couldn't bear it.

On Dorothy's last visit, the sisters sat on the wooden bench in front of the ivy creeper on the mansion wall.

'I have news,' Dorothy told her. 'I've found a flat.' Esther's heart raced and Dorothy smiled, showing a row of perfect white teeth. 'I didn't tell you before in case negotiations fell through. It's not far from here. A place called Whale Street.'

'How did you find it?'

'A coincidence really. I got talking with one of the girls from the factory… a nice girl called May Robinson… she travels on my bus to work. She told me her uncle rents out property. She said she'd ask if he had a vacant flat. He offered me a two-bedroomed downstairs flat with vacant possession. I've been to view the property and though it needs some elbow grease, it'll do us just fine.'

Dorothy grinned and Esther saw the tiredness etched in her face. Young men were being called up and there was a shortage of manpower on the buses. When Dorothy had applied at the labour exchange for a job, she was offered work as a bus conductress.

The hours were long and involved shift work, ferrying miners and factory workers back and forth. It was an exhausting business.

'Dorothy! A place of your own, how exciting. When can you move in?'

'That's what this is leading up to,' Dorothy said with a smile, 'I already have… and there's a room ready for you.'

Esther's mind reeled. She couldn't take it in. To have space of her own and live with Dorothy… It was everything she dreamed of.

But then she fell back to reality. 'What about Mistress Knowles?'

'What about her?'

'She mightn't let me leave.'

'Leave it with me, Esther. She can't stop you. You're practically fifteen.'

Esther wasn't convinced.

But as it transpired, the Mistress was only too pleased to have one less orphan to worry about, and a troublesome one at that.

'Your sister has applied for you to go and live with her, twenty-six,' Mistress Knowles told her one morning, after Esther had been summoned to the office. 'It solves my problem. You're a bad influence, girl, and I'll be glad to see the back of yi. I've notified your sister to collect you the day after tomorra at noon.'

All this was said as the Mistress sifted through some papers on her desk.

'Haddaway and good riddance,' she sneered, looking up, and Esther stared into those cold eyes one last time. 'Mark my words, girl… you'll never come to any good.'

Hatred for Mistress Knowles simmered in Esther. Under her breath, she said, 'I'll show you – you old cow.'

On the day of Esther's departure, saying goodbye to everyone was difficult. For despite how Esther felt, Blakely had been her home and her fellow orphans the only family she'd known. Valiantly, she tried to stay brave and not let her distress show.

'We'll all be gone soon.' Miss Balfour's eyes shone, over-bright.

With everyone in the classroom, only the two of them stood in the dormitory.

'Will everyone be kept together?' Esther wanted to know.

'No. We'll be met by a billeting officer who will distribute orphans to the families they'll be living with.'

'What about Blakely?' Esther asked.

'There is a wind of change,' Miss Balfour said, 'and in the new world, hopefully Blakely will be no more.' She inhaled a deep breath. 'Esther... my child... I shall be both sad and glad to see you go. Glad you're beginning a new stage in your life... but sad we're losing you. Goodbye, dear, think of us with fondness. And may God go with you.'

Tearfully, she made a dash for the door.

Left alone in the dormitory, Esther felt light-headed. She couldn't believe she was free to leave Blakely. Shakily, she picked up the small suitcase from her bed and made for the door.

In the corridor, as she walked along the black and white linoleum floor, she was reminded of the day of her arrival. She was certain that the little Esther that was dumped at Blakely had been surer of herself. Her hair, then flaming red, had now toned to reddish-brown and though still short, it curled messily above high cheekbones. Strikingly tall, she hoped she was done with growth spurts. With a rumpled coat that fell inches short of her wrists, and woollen stockings that kept riding down her legs, Esther imagined she looked like exactly what she was – a dispossessed orphan.

Opening the front door, she emerged into the sun and as if on cue, a blackbird trilled from a tree branch. The moment felt surreal. She looked into the clear blue sky and shivered. Only days before, the country had been on yellow alert as a hundred enemy aircraft droned across the North East coast. Listening to the roar of planes and heavy gunfire with bated breath had become a familiar occurrence but the sound never lost its terror.

Outside, Dorothy waited at the foot of the steps.

'Oh, Esther, what a wonderful sight,' she cried.

It felt odd to wander down the path, and odder still to close Blakely's gates behind her. For years, Esther had waited for this moment and yet all she could think now was that inside the orphanage the dinner bell had gone, and everyone would be forming an orderly queue. She quashed the sense of dread she felt inside and, putting one foot in front of the other, tentatively followed Dorothy.

'Whatever you do don't look back,' Dorothy advised, linking arms with her sister. 'Laurie says in his letter he's waiting for a draft to a ship…'

As her sister chattered, Esther, studying her surroundings, was only half listening. They walked down a tree-lined walkway, past a row of pretty houses and, as they reached a main road, a cyclist went riding past.

It happened then, while Esther waited at the kerb to cross the road – the dizzying sensation that came with the knowledge that this great big world had gone on without her. She tried to assimilate what was going on around her; noisy traffic, busy pavements, posters on walls blaring wartime messages, fumes, vibrant colours. Feeling bewildered, Esther fought the impulse to flee back to the orphanage.

'It takes time to adjust.' Dorothy's voice washed over her like a balm. 'It was the same for me when I left Blakely. Mrs Brooke took me under her wing and if it wasn't for her, goodness knows what state I'd be in. Esther, I'm here to look out for you.'

Dorothy smiled in understanding.

Esther remembered the rivalry she'd felt towards Mrs Brooke and felt ashamed. How plucky her sister must have been, and Esther was determined to buck up and be the same.

Bracing herself, she stepped forward and crossed the road. They walked for a while, passing the tall and impressive Regent Cinema.

As she gazed around, a small cry escaped Esther's lips. 'Why… I remember this scene from all those years ago when—'

The sisters looked at each other, recalling that long-ago day. But this was the future, and a place Mam would have no part in. She pushed all thoughts of their mother aside.

'Gosh, look at all the rows of houses,' she said.

Dorothy stopped at the top of one of the terraced streets where redbrick houses ran down a hill as far as the eye could see. With a cobbled road and clouds of grimy smoke billowing from chimney pots, the scene looked austere and grim.

'Whale Street,' Dorothy announced. 'Our flat is on the second block.'

As she led the way down the road, two women, idly gossiping at their front step, wearing crossover pinafores and fur-edged slippers, eyed them critically. As she walked past, Esther could feel their eyes upon her back.

When they crossed the road by the off-licence shop on the corner, Dorothy rummaged in her shoulder bag and brought out a key.

She stopped at a brown door with a brass knocker. 'Here we are… home.'

Esther followed her sister along a narrow passageway into a homely kitchen-come-living room that had a high ceiling, floral wallpaper and a range fireplace where a large black kettle stood on the hearth. The saggy-cushioned chair and sturdy-legged couch were second-hand, as was the scratched table with a wireless on top, and mismatched set of wooden chairs. On the floorboards – scrubbed clean – sat a colourful hearthside mat, made out of pieces of spare material.

Dorothy noticed her gaze. 'I made it myself.' Her expression was proud.

'How?'

'By stretching a piece of hessian on a frame and poking material through with half a wooden clothes peg.'

Trust Dorothy to be industrious, Esther thought as she smiled.

'Honestly, Esther, it's so difficult to buy things these days because of rationing.'

'I've heard of that. What does it mean?'

Dorothy drew a laboured breath. 'It was brought in because of the shortages.'

'Why are there shortages?'

'Because enemy submarines are attacking the ships that bring food and other goods to us in Britain.'

'Oh dear. So how does rationing work?'

'Have you been issued with a book?'

'Miss Balfour gave me an identity card and ration book.'

'Yours will be blue, is it?' Dorothy asked. When Esther nodded, she continued. 'Because of your age you'll get full provisions of fruit, meat, and a half a pint of milk a day.'

Outraged, Esther exploded. 'I wonder who got my share, then, at the orphanage? Because it certainly was not me.'

Dorothy nodded, sympathetically. 'You'll have to register at the local shop and then each time you buy something on ration the shopkeeper takes the coupons out of the book – which means you can only buy the amount of food you're allowed.'

'You still pay, then?'

'Of course, along with the coupons.'

'It sounds complicated.'

'You'll soon get the hang of it.'

Esther looked around the room.

'Goodness all this space for two people,' she said, in awe. 'And you've managed to buy so much in such a short space of time.'

'Laurie left his savings to furnish our home,' Dorothy replied as she threw her coat over a chair. 'Not much, mind… but I had a marvellous time scouring the second-hand shops.'

Impressed by her sister's self-assurance, Esther was determined to one day be the same.

Later, as they sat side-by-side on the couch, they sipped a cup of warm Horlicks.

'This is delicious. What is it?'

'I knew you'd love it… it's a hot malted milk drink. I do know what you're going through, you know,' Dorothy commented with a grimace. 'The first time I saw fruit displayed outside the greengrocer's shop, I could only stare in astonishment. I mean, Esther… the only fruit we ever saw was an orange at Christmas. Even now, I can't tolerate wastage. Laurie, poor man, goes mad when I scrape mould off cheese… not that we get much now, with rationing.' A frown creased her brow. 'But believe me, decision-making is the worst bit of it all.'

'How d'you mean?'

'Think about it, Esther. From the minute we entered Blakely when did we ever have to make a decision? When did we have any control over our lives?'

Esther knew what she meant. She felt perplexed at what might be expected of her next.

'Come on,' Dorothy said, 'I'll show you the rest of the flat.'

She led Esther along the passageway to her own bedroom over-looking the front street and then to the diminutive back bedroom.

'This is yours,' she beamed.

Esther drew a sharp intake of breath. *Hers*. The walls were white and a picture of a vase containing sunflowers hung over a small Victorian fireplace, while a slim bed with a floral counterpane covering it stood against the far wall.

'It's lovely, thank you,' she exclaimed, eyeing the tall chest of drawers beneath the window. 'But I've got nothing to put in it.'

'Not yet,' Dorothy said, with a glint in her eyes.

She led them back through the kitchen into the scullery – a gloomy place that had room only for a gas cooker beneath the sloping stairs from the upstairs flat and a porcelain sink with wooden drainer.

It was too much to take in all at once. Esther made a beeline for the kitchen, where she sank into the saggy couch and finished the dregs of the milky drink.

Dorothy followed her in. 'I speak for Laurie as well as myself when I say… welcome to your new home, Esther.'

Such was her pent-up emotion that Esther's chin wobbled. Her eyes misting, she had a desire to hug Dorothy. But she refrained – the damage done at the orphanage meant she sat silent and wooden, afraid to reach out.

'You'll never forget Blakely but… you will get over it in time.' Dorothy commented perceptively. 'First, a bath to rid you of the orphanage smell and then a change of clothes.'

'What clothes?'

'All taken care of,' Dorothy replied, smiling.

Esther couldn't believe it. 'Where do I bathe?'

'In here in front of the fire.'

'Really?'

'Yes. I'm heating the water in the boiler in the yard's washhouse.'

'I think I'm going to like living here,' Esther said, feeling lucky.

'And I think I'm going to like having you here.'

'What about my keep?' At Blakely, orphans were never allowed to forget they were charity cases. 'Can you afford me living with you?'

'If you eat tiny meals, we can,' Dorothy laughed. 'In all seriousness, though, this isn't about money… this is your home.'

Esther's chin jutted. 'I'm going to pay my way.'

It was then that Esther made her first decision. Though the thought terrified her, as soon as she was able to, she'd find a job.

CHAPTER EIGHT

August 1940

There was news from the war that the German Luftwaffe had increased their efforts to destroy airfields. A fierce battle raging in the skies over Britain overshadowed life and folk felt besieged.

But for Esther, with her newfound freedom, none of the imposed restrictions registered, as she didn't know any different. Life at Blakely had prepared her for the austerity of war. People grumbled about bumping into things during the blackout, the strict rations, how the newspapers were exceptionally thin and how council workmen had carried off their gates and iron railings for munitions – but this new way of living, which brought independence to Esther, delighted her.

Though panicked when she had first left Blakely, overwhelmed by life on the outside, with Dorothy's help she soon got into the swing of things. As she adapted and saw how much she'd been missing out on, Esther vowed to live life to the full.

'People say you mustn't complain but everyone does,' Dorothy told her. 'This war is changing our way of life. But it's so refreshing, Esther, to have someone like you, who doesn't mind waiting in long, dreary queues to see what's on offer at the other end.'

There was truth in what Dorothy said. A night at the cinema watching Ray Milland, a dreamy actor with a fetching smile, or laughing at the antics of Old Mother Riley – a funny Irish washerwoman character who originally was a music hall act – all gave

Esther a thrill. Even the clothes that everyone declared drab were exciting to Esther, who had only known Blakely's tedious uniform.

Her favourite item of clothing was a two-piece suit – a square-shouldered jacket and knee-length skirt to which, in an inspired moment suggested by a women's magazine, she had added a colourful chiffon scarf that transformed the outfit. Her hair, still relatively short, was brushed into soft waves and when she looked in the mirror Esther felt grown up and thoroughly modern.

Of course, there was the appalling side of life that the war brought; the horror of bombings, the loss of homes, the greater loss of life, and the failures of Allied troops. But the outlook of the people – the patriotic attitude that the war summoned, the feeling that everyone was in it together – gave Esther courage. Hitler could do his worst but the British would not be beaten.

Determined to find work as soon as possible, Esther visited the labour exchange two streets away. As she stood in the queue of the large, echoing room, she reminded herself she didn't want to go into service and become a housemaid – Esther wanted a job that counted in this war.

There were six men sat behind the counter and Esther noticed she'd drawn the short straw. The officious looking man at the front of her queue had a purple nose and red veined cheeks, appearing very short tempered. Thoughts of the orphanage and of the Mistress came to mind and Esther fled the building. She'd had enough of people governing her. From now on, she would control her own future. Every night, she determined, she'd scour the situations vacant in the *Gazette* and find herself a job.

Two days later, at a loss how to occupy herself as Dorothy was working the day shift, Esther decided to borrow her sister's bicycle and venture to the seashore. She rode over the busy main road, past St Michael's Church, up Mowbray Road and when she came to the top of the hill she saw it – the sea. A vast, sparkling expanse of blue. She couldn't decide where the sea finished and the horizon began. Standing astride the bicycle, in rapture at the beauty of it all, Esther wished she could wrap the moment up forever to treasure.

Freewheeling down the hill, she reached the sandy promenade but was denied access to the beach, where rolls of spiky barbed wire – placed there for fear of enemy invasion – barred the way.

Looking into the distance, she froze in terror. Black blobs appeared over the sea as planes headed directly towards her. Terrified for her life, she didn't know what to do or where to hide. Fear gripped Esther – she'd heard how enemy gunners shot figures on the ground. Closing her eyes, she tensed as she waited for the rat-a-tat of machine guns.

Then her heart lifted as a squadron of Hurricanes came speeding across the North Sea, chasing the enemy. A dogfight ensued. Hurricanes swooped down, causing Jerry planes to take evasive action, diving to low level and scattering in all directions. As they thundered over the land Esther saw swastikas and German crosses emblazoned on them. Dropping bombs that exploded, alarmingly, on the town's harbour and clifftops, the raiders, with the Hurricanes still hounding them, turned east and made for home.

Her eyes raised to the heavens, Esther watched as an enemy aircraft, smoke pluming from its fuselage, nosedived and shrieked into the depths of the sea.

'Hurrah,' she screamed, a cruel gratification gripping her. Then she recoiled, sickened at her reaction. What was she becoming? Taking pleasure in the crews' death?

Like Laurie, the young men might not have known what to expect when they joined up. Maybe they too didn't have a mean bone in their bodies.

She'd seen enough.

She gazed at the tranquil scene, the acres of golden sand and swelling waves that looked reassuringly the same, and held promise that life would go on as before.

Mounting her bike, she pedalled up the hill and left the scene of carnage behind. Deep inside she couldn't shake the feeling of being grateful that 'our brave boys' would return to their wives and families.

The one thing she'd learned, she thought, as she rode towards the relative peace in the town, was that she was determined to count in this war.

One evening later that week after a scrap of cheese on toast for tea, Esther read the account of Winston Churchill's speech in the newspaper as he addressed the House of Commons on the state of the war. He paid tribute to the aircrews fighting the Battle of Britain by saying that, 'never in the field of human conflict was so much owed by so many to so few.'

As his stirring words sank in, Esther's thoughts turned to those brave boys who fought in the sky.

On the next page was a public notice that read: 'the war industry is clamouring for more women workers.'

Beside the notice was a blue and white picture of a serious faced pilot who wore a leather aviator cap with ear flaps and a chin strap. His gloved forefinger pointed out and the caption in red bold capitals beneath read, 'YOU can help make me a plane.'

'How do I apply?' she asked Dorothy.

'Go and see the supply officer at the labour exchange,' her sister advised.

'But I'm not skilled at anything.'

'You get trained, silly goose.'

Deeply suspicious of authority, Esther was doubtful. What if she was made to enlist in one of the services and was sent miles away from Dorothy?

She shook her head. 'I'm not going back to the labour exchange. I'd prefer to apply direct at one of the factories.'

'Remember my friend May Robinson… who helped me get this flat? She works in the canteen at a factory. I'll ask her.'

It transpired that May's place of work was indeed crying out for women to join the factory.

'She says to tootle along and see the labour manager.'

With nothing to lose, Esther made for the factory the very next day. As the bus left the town and made towards Tyne Dock, Esther's heart pounded. She was nervous – she didn't know the first thing about job interviews and she was terrified she'd make a fool of herself. A picture of Mistress Knowles' mocking face came into her mind's eye, making Esther sit bolt upright in her seat. She would make something of her life and prove that cow at the orphanage wrong.

When finally the bus stopped at the factory gates, Esther alighted and, squaring her shoulders, set off up the path.

The high, imposing wrought-iron factory gate was locked but at the side was a smaller one where a queue had formed. Esther joined the queue and when she reached the front, a man wearing a Local Defence Volunteer armband asked her to produce her pass.

'I haven't got one, I came looking for work.'

The man, middle-aged, with a brush of hair on his upper lip, looked nonplussed.

'I can't let you pass without proper identification,' he blustered.

'Haway,' came a nasal voice behind Esther, 'I'm late for work. Let the lass in… anybody can see she's nee spy.'

Esther turned to see a wizened man with yellow teeth, who winked at her.

The LDV man looked flustered, but then making up his mind, waved her past.

'Second building on your right, hinny,' the old man called after her.

She hurried past the bicycle sheds and low buildings camouflaged with green paint. The labour manager's office was a confined space in a cabin-like building with paper-thin walls. The labour manager was a portly man with a balding head, with a manner that suggested he was continuously irritated. Sat behind a desk, he drummed his fingers on the wooden worktop.

'Name,' he clipped, 'and address.' Esther provided her answers and he wrote them down on a form. 'Next of kin,' he went on.

All throughout the interview, the man kept glancing at his wristwatch. Esther might have been frightened, but his rudeness angered her and she fixed him an infuriated glare. After the Mistress at Blakely, she was afraid of no man.

Coolly and deliberately, she answered his questions.

'You'll do fine,' he surprised her by saying. 'Training starts next Monday. Seven thirty sharp.'

'Thank you,' she replied, her voice aloof.

Esther trained in a class of fourteen women of all ages, ignorant of what the factory produced. The foreman shed some light on the matter. He talked about the precision instruments the plant made.

'Speed is what's important,' he told the class. 'It takes fifteen people working flat out to keep a pilot flying.'

As reality dawned, Esther was elated. She was to play a real part in providing aeroplanes in the sky – and maybe make a difference to the war.

An instructor gave the class a lecture about safety aspects of working with machines. He then led them into the basement and the machine rooms. Here, as in the rest of the factory, the windows were boarded up and the room's artificial light was harsh on Esther's eyes. Women stood at machines, concentrating on their work. They wore navy overalls and peaked hats with fish nets covering their hair. The noise deafening and the atmosphere stifling, Esther felt an ache behind her eyes. How these women spent an eight-hour shift in such conditions she couldn't imagine. She hoped she wasn't assigned to this department.

It turned out that she was.

*

'Laurie wants to know if you've settled in at work,' Dorothy asked one grey and rainy morning that felt nothing like summer.

Dorothy had recently returned home from working the night shift. Tired and wan, she'd made straight for the bedroom and changed from her uniform into her husband's blue bulky dressing gown. She lounged on the couch, legs curled beneath her and read Laurie's letter.

'He sends his love and asks that you make sure I eat. Cheeky blighter says I'm too thin.'

Dorothy smiled and brushed the letter under her nose as if hoping to get a whiff of her husband.

'He has a point,' Esther rebuked. 'You eat like a sparrow.'

Busy getting ready for work, she opened a compact – a belated birthday present from Dorothy.

After being a nonentity at Blakely, Esther tried to feel special on occasion by wearing a touch of make-up and sometimes going to the hairdressers. Though recovering from the harsh treatment and deprivation of Blakely was a constant inward battle and Esther believed she didn't deserve such treats.

'I'll tell Laurie myself about my job.' Esther placed the compact in her shoulder bag.

Dorothy gave a tired smile. 'He'll be touched you made the effort.'

'Shall I make you a cuppa?'

'No thank you. I'm off to bed.'

Dorothy slipped Laurie's letter into her dressing gown pocket and Esther knew it would be read many times.

'Has Laurie any news of a ship?'

'He can't say because of censorship. But reading between the lines he seems to think he'll be going to sea any time soon.'

Which meant that Dorothy wouldn't hear from him for a while.

'Chin up, you never know your luck,' Esther said. 'He might be due some leave before he goes.'

Dorothy visibly cheered. 'D'you know, I never thought of that.'

As time went on, Esther not only took pride in her work, but also enjoyed the company of other women – not that she made any friends. The machine room had twelve benches and small drilling machines where Esther operated a drill press, forming holes in aluminium discs. Though monotonous, the work didn't drive her mad and, surprisingly, proved therapeutic.

The position of the holes was fixed by a jig and all she had to do was insert the disc and then raise and lower a lever. Not able to think while she worked, she became inwardly calm. In a world of her own, surrounded by noisy machines, Esther sang, as did the rest of the women, at the top of her voice – and the beauty of it was, she got paid two pounds, two shillings a week for the privilege.

Tea break came at ten. Most of the workers brought in flasks and preferred to sit at their benches on the shop floor and gossip. Esther favoured the canteen where she could purchase a hot cup of tea and a Spam sandwich. The rest of the morning passed quickly enough, though Esther kept an eye on the machine setter, who combed the room as he supervised work. At one o'clock sharp, the factory hooter blew and when the machines stopped, the silence was deafening.

Esther shot like a bullet out of the door, for queues in the factory canteen built up quickly. Sometimes it took the whole dinner break to get served. Some workers went to the nearby cafe for a meal while others made do with packed lunches from home. For Esther, a hot two-course meal was too big an enticement to miss.

At first, being in the canteen with masses of people and factory rules and regulations blaring from the walls reminded Esther of

Blakely, and she had to quash the urge to stand to attention at the table. But as time progressed, Esther forgot any comparisons with the orphanage. She found some comfort in the place; with its loudspeakers blaring BBC Home Service, the hubbub of noise, and the smell of delicious food in the air mingled with tobacco smoke.

The canteen was run on a self-service basis and Esther never knew whether to find a place at a table first, or join the queue. Today she opted for queuing up. Glancing around the room, she saw Bertha Cuthbertson wave over the heads and indicate a vacant seat next to her. Bertha – one of the machinists in the same shop as Esther – was somewhere in her late fifties, and a motherly type, who spoke her mind to a fault.

'Next – oh, it's you!'

May Robinson, wearing a white overall, stood behind the canteen counter, giving a diffident smile.

'I wouldn't have the vegetable pie, if I was you,' she said, oblivious to the sour look she received from the canteen supervisor who stood beside her. 'Have the corned beef hash… it's fresh on the day.'

Esther nodded.

Though May was years older than Esther, she radiated a child-like quality that made her seem far younger.

She piled a plate with food and handed it to Esther, watched by the disapproving supervisor.

'Any pudding?' May asked.

'Jam sponge and custard, please… and a cup of tea.'

May picked up a metal jug and poured steaming custard over a dishful of jam pudding, before handing it to Esther.

'I haven't seen your Dorothy for a bit.' She poured weak tea from an enormous teapot into a cup.

'No… she's on night shift,' she replied, shortly. Esther still felt quite protective over Dorothy, and jealous of other demands on her affections. She wasn't sure about May becoming too friendly with her sister.

'Ah! That'll be why. Mind you, I've been coming to work on me bike for the past two days, rather than the bus.'

She stood with the teapot in her hands as if she had all day. 'Tell your Dorothy me mam's given us a bag of wool. I'll try and get some to her.'

May and Dorothy had struck up a friendship when they realised that both their men folk were in the forces. They both liked knitting and spent many an hour together making socks for the 'boys on the front line'.

'Less talking, Robinson,' Miss Tait, the supervisor, a thin, impatient-looking woman, snapped. 'And get on with your job. We've a queue a mile long.'

May bristled. 'I was only telling her summik.' She handed the cup of tea over to Esther who placed it on her tray.

'Have you got your meal ticket?' May asked.

Esther handed the food ticket over the counter. She liked eating at the canteen because it meant she could save on her ration coupons.

Threading her way through the tables, she put the tray onto the bench and sat down next to Bertha.

Bertha remarked, 'My, you're slipping, Etty, lass.' For some reason Esther's name had been shortened at work, and she rather liked it. It made her sound more mature, not like someone who came from an orphanage – not that anyone knew about her past. She made sure of that.

'You're usually first to scarper when the hooter blows and make for the queue.' Bertha, a robust woman with a round friendly face, had two side teeth missing that were noticeable when she grinned.

She lowered her voice. 'My advice to you is to hang back and wait for the other lasses… else you'll be called stuck-up and get talked about.' She winked sagely, then slurped tea from a saucer.

The other machinists sat around the table, in full flow conversation, weren't in the least bit interested in what Bertha said. Esther was used to being ignored; when the lasses talked around her it was as though she was invisible. Bertha might have a point, she considered. She was so used to watching out for herself at Blakely, she didn't give others a thought.

'Give it time, lass.' Bertha's face expressed sympathy. 'They'll come round once they get to know you proper.'

'Thank you,' Esther said primly, and Bertha rolled her eyes.

'Hinny, it's the way you talk that puts folk off. Posh, like... and you act snooty.'

If only Bertha knew, Esther thought. Though she desperately longed to be accepted, the insecurity Esther had inherited at Blakely had left her lacking in confidence.

'See, you're doing it now... giving us a look as if I'm daft.'

Esther was appalled that Bertha – or anybody else – should think such a thing. And if any of the lasses did act friendly towards her, she found herself feeling uncertain and suspicious of their motives, ending up appearing aloof.

'Divvent take it so seriously, lass. We all have faults. I just wanted to help, like.'

Bertha gave a toothless cackle and Esther couldn't take offence at the woman.

'That's better. You're no raving beauty but when you smile, you're a bonny lass.'

Esther laughed outright at the woman's cheek. 'My dad was a Geordie,' she said as she picked up her knife and fork.

'Was?'

'He died when I was little, after the Great War.'

'Aw pet, that's too bad. What about yi' mam?'

'She's... she came from a well-to-do family – a vicar's daughter.'

Bertha nodded knowingly. 'Ahh. So, that's why you talk refined.'

Esther shrugged in embarrassment.

'Tell yer mam you do her proud.'

Esther didn't explain she could do no such thing.

Raids in the area continued during late August and early September, especially targeting aircraft factories. One dinner time, Esther was sitting outside for a breath of fresh air in the sunshine when she heard the drone of approaching planes in the distance. Fearing for her life, she threw down the women's magazine she carried and made a dash for one of the air raid shelters – a series of long and echoing tunnels underground. Dodging the other folk intent on the same thing, she ran to one of the entrances. Planes roared overhead and machine guns started to shoot at folk on the ground who scurried in all directions to avoid lethal bullets.

'Haway, hinny,' a male voice shouted as he took her by the arm. Together, they ran pell-mell for the entrance and, safely inside, Esther looked up into the face of a foreman who worked in the machine room.

'One of these days, lass,' he told her, 'management will think to arrange one of them barrage balloons to safeguard us. Sooner rather than later, I should hope.'

Esther imagined the balloon, which reminded her of a massive silver kite, sailing high in the air and tethered to the ground by cables. Its purpose, she knew, was to damage low flying aircraft and prevent attacks.

When a barrage balloon was delivered the very next morning the foreman responded, 'Only right an all.'

He asked if anyone was willing to do an extra shift on Sunday, traditionally a day of rest, and Esther volunteered. Dorothy, after nightshift, would be in bed and if Esther stayed at home, she'd be forced to creep around the flat, fearful of waking her sister up.

Her shift finished at two o'clock and by the time Esther made her way into the canteen, two of the staff were tidying the tables and putting dishes away. They gave Esther a disgruntled stare.

'I'll serve,' May Robinson said from behind the counter.

'We're finished. There's nowt to be had,' a blonde-haired woman snapped. 'And will you not stand on me wet floor,' she told Esther. 'I'll be here for the duration if *she* finds a footmark on it.'

'Miss Tait,' May said, by way of explanation, 'inspects the canteen afore any of us can go home. It makes her day if she finds fault.'

'And we are the ones to suffer,' Blondie commented.

'I haven't emptied the food trays yet,' May told Esther. 'I can give you a spot of cottage pie if you want.'

Famished, Esther nodded gratefully.

She sat as far from the counter as she could, not fancying the staff glowering at her.

As she ate the pie, Miss Tait marched in, and true enough, didn't miss a trick.

'Salt and peppers wiped... Trays cleaned...' the supervisor's sharp eyes travelled the room. She gave Esther a baleful stare. 'Right, ladies... when everyone's gone you can close up shop and go home.'

Esther, determined not to be hurried, finished the lukewarm pie, then rose and made for the door.

'See yi,' May Robinson called out.

Esther made her way to the cloakroom on the ground floor where stragglers from the machine room stood gossiping, cigarettes in their hands. The conversation stopped when she walked in. Esther collected her coat from the peg and, remembering the conversation with Bertha, turned and gave the lasses a friendly smile.

'See you tomorrow,' she said.

No one replied. Feeling downhearted, she made for the factory exit and, punching the time card, opened the door and emerged into the bright sunshine.

It was unusual to walk down the drive without hordes of workers pushing and shoving and bicycle wheels slamming into her legs.

'Hang on, Etty!' a voice called from behind.

She turned and saw May hurrying towards her, pushing a bicycle. The lass wore a grey two-piece suit with square shoulders and low-heeled slip-on shoes suitable for wear in the canteen.

'Eee, I'm sorry about the commotion in the canteen.' Flushed and apologetic, May came alongside. 'The staff get shirty when they want away on time.'

'I noticed.'

'They're a happy team, normally,' May said, loyally. 'Anyways, I wanted to catch up with you. I've a favour to ask but I didn't want to say in there,' she nodded towards the factory.

'What kind of favour?'

May's shining black hair hung naturally around her face and she wore no make-up. With thick, curly eyelashes and creamy skin, she didn't need any. But she was too thin and her bones stuck out prominently. There was no denying that May was pretty, and with her vulnerable look, she reminded Esther of the young actress Judy Garland.

'Tell your Dorothy I don't know when I'll next get to meet up with her.'

'Any specific reason why?'

'Billy's due some leave.'

Esther had noticed an engagement ring on the lass's left hand. 'Your fiancé?'

A look of adoration crossed May's face. 'Yes.'

'He's seen action, hasn't he?' Esther was sure Dorothy had told her something of that nature.

'Yes. In France at Dunkirk.' May's eyes grew enormous. 'Billy thought he was going to be taken prisoner but he managed to escape the beaches on one of those civilian boats. Poor lamb, with all the marching before, he was footsore and exhausted. His left foot went septic and he spent time in a military hospital in Leeds.'

'How is he now?'

'Champion… He's back with his battalion.'

'Where's he stationed?'

'He can't say. He's with the Northumberland Fusiliers. His battalion joined Home Forces and is somewhere down south.' Pride shone from May's eyes. 'He hitchhikes home whenever he gets a pass.'

As they neared the gate, the pair of them stopped and faced each other.

'Have you been engaged long?' Esther surprised herself by asking.

May shook her head in wonder. 'I still can't believe I am. Billy proposed the day war was declared…' She looked uncomfortable. 'There's not been an opportunity to arrange a time to get wed.'

'Have you known him long?'

May appeared at a loss to know how to continue. 'Billy and me, we… we went to school together. Oh, it's a long story…'

Straddling her bicycle, she rode off.

'Ta-ra,' she called.

As the bus passed the grain warehouse and turned the corner, Esther, gazing out of the window, watched the scenery go by.

The road ran parallel with the ribbon of the River Tyne and beyond a high brick wall were the timber yards, docks, and cranes that soared high on the skyline.

The air was humid and Esther fought to keep her eyes open. The long shifts at the factory were gruelling and left her drained, but the fact that she was helping the war effort made it all worthwhile.

Her only wish was that she had a mate. A high level of camaraderie existed amongst the factory women – which Esther was excluded from. Listening to the conversations and the scandalous chatter, usually about fellows, was an education, and enough to make her toes curl. She was positive the married women were making fun of the younger girls but how could she tell? Esther had no experience on such matters. What she did know – and was shocked to realise – was that she wanted to hear more of the banter.

Bertha usually obliged.

'Best you check out a lad's shoe size before courting him,' she told the machinists last Friday with a roguish gleam in her eye.

'Why?' came their cry.

'It's common knowledge,' Bertha pulled a knowing face, 'that big feet means big apparatus.' The sight of their incredulous faces sent her into hoots of laughter. 'And don't any of you think you can get away with a bit on the side without us older 'uns knowing. Isn't that right, ladies?' Her eyes swept the married women around the table.

'Aye,' they chorused in unison.

'How can you tell?' Maisie Beale wanted to know.

A brunette, Maisie was renowned for gormlessness.

'Suffice to say,' Bertha met Maisie's eye, 'don't go showing behind your ears.'

'Why?' Maisie's eyes grew big and frightened.

'Because, everyone knows, lass, it's the one place you can tell if you've had a bit of how's your father.' Bertha stretched forward. 'Shift your hair and let's have a gander. I'm sure you've nothing to fear.'

Maisie, scraping back her chair, fled from the table.

In the shocked silence, Bertha threw back her head and laughed till she cried.

Later, in the cloakroom, as Esther washed her hands, she looked in the mirror at the group of machinists standing behind her.

A pretty redhead, who drew nervously on her ciggie, said, 'I don't care what anybody says… why shouldn't me and Stuart go all the way? We're engaged.' She took another draw on her tab. 'What if a bomb's got our name on it, and we hadn't… y'know… tried it,' she pouted. 'Anyway, what Bertha says is a load of codswallop.'

'It worked on Maisie, though,' someone said and laughed.

'Who'd have thought it, though,' the redhead stubbed her cigarette out on the concrete floor. 'Maisie Beale of all people.'

Esther must have dozed because when the bus came to a halt, she jerked awake and the riverside scene had given way to the marketplace. She'd taken the long way around home and, changing transport, boarded one of the new trolley buses in King Street. Dorothy told her how only a couple of years before tramlines had been dug up in this street to make way for the modern trolleybuses. A lot of routes, apparently, had been taken over by the trolleys and they were a less jarring ride, and much quieter than trams.

As the trolley made its silent journey up Fowler Street, Esther saw the magnificent town hall, where the statue of Queen Victoria stared regally out from beneath a sweep of wide steps.

Staring out of the window, Esther saw a lad emerge from behind an anti-invasion blockade and sprint over the road to the bus stop, a lad she felt sure she'd seen before but couldn't remember where. He looked through the window and, as their eyes met, a spark of interest gleamed in his.

Climbing up onto the platform, he walked purposefully along the aisle and sat down next to her.

The trolley moved away from the kerb and the lad turned towards her. 'You live in Whale Street, don't you?'

Certain he was making advances, Esther was unsure how to behave.

'Second block,' she said. Their shoulders were touching and she felt self-conscious at such close proximity.

'I live at the top end, number twenty-eight.'

So that's why she recognised him.

'You been to work?' he asked.

'Yes.'

He had bright green eyes and his black hair, raked down, was parted at the side. Despite his somewhat aloof expression, she found him rather handsome.

'You headed for home?' he questioned, appraising her.

'Uh-huh.'

'So am I.' He wore a navy three-piece suit with high waisted trousers held up with buttoned suspenders. It was obvious from his black-rimmed eyes and grimy appearance that he worked at the coal pit. The lad had a quiet intensity about him and as he continued to stare, Esther felt herself flush.

'Have you got a boyfriend?'

Taken aback, she retorted, 'What's it got to do with you?'

'Absolutely nothing. But if you haven't, I was going to ask you out this afternoon.'

'To do what?'

'I don't know. A walk… a game of tennis in the park… anything you fancy.'

He was asking her on a date… Esther's first. 'What's your name?'

'Trevor Milne.'

'Yours?'

'Esther Makepeace, though I now prefer Etty.'

The idea of a game of tennis made her grin.

Trevor took her smile as confirmation. 'That's settled, then.'

The day, cloudy but warm, had a quiet, somnolent Sunday feel to it but, Etty, all of a sudden, felt carefree and daring.

'Why not? It's a beautiful day...' she replied, 'and it would be a shame to be indoors.'

'I'll have to tidy mesel' up a bit first.'

'Me too.'

As they approached their stop, Etty stood up, as did Trevor. She was pleased to discover that he was head and shoulders taller than her.

First to alight, he turned and helped her step from the platform. They crossed the busy main road and Etty, conscious of his long strides at her side, thought of the conversation in the cloakroom about a bomb having your name on it. Life was uncertain and she vowed, from now on, she would live a little. Not that she'd become a 'good time girl' with a rotten reputation. Heaven forbid. She fancied finding a fellow and enjoying a bit of gaiety. Some harmless, innocent fun – she certainly didn't want to settle down for a long while.

As they approached Trevor's front door, he said, 'I'll call for you when I'm ready.'

Opening the door, he disappeared into the dim passageway. As she ran down the street, it occurred to Etty that she hadn't looked at the size of Trevor's feet.

CHAPTER NINE

May bumped the Raleigh bicycle up the four concrete steps to the front door. Automatically, she cast an eye to the bay window where the net curtains tweaked. Ernie Robinson's gaunt and aggrieved face appeared, to be withdrawn when he saw that no one of great importance had called and that it was only his wayward daughter.

'Is that you, our May?' May's mother's voice called from somewhere in the bowels of the house.

May clattered the bicycle through the inner coloured-glass door and leant it against the passage wall.

She peered into the dim passageway. 'It is.'

'Thank Gawd for a bit of female company.' Her mother came to stand in the kitchen doorway. Wiping her brow with edge of her pinny, she gave her daughter an affable smile. 'The menfolk are driving me crackers with all their war talk. And not one of them thinks to give me a bloody hand.'

The 'menfolk' were May's father and Mr Grayson, one of the current lodgers. Mam ran a boarding house that took up most of her time and the work was never done.

Dad, in his younger day, was a celebrated lightweight boxer but his injuries in the Great War put an end to his career.

'Recuperating from his injuries has taken your dad a bloody lifetime,' Mam told May with jaundiced eye.

With no income, Mam – a shrewd woman – had used her husband's savings from his boxing days to secure a deposit on a house big enough to start a lodgings business.

She'd fumed, 'Your dad never lifted a finger to either help run the business or bring up his bairns. All that bugger does is sit in a chair with a jug of ale at his side. If you ask me,' which no one ever did because they'd heard it many times before, 'having his head bashed in when he was young addled his brain.'

Up until a few years ago, May, as the youngest and only girl, had been her father's favourite, but since her transgression he had virtually disowned her.

May came into the large kitchen where Mam stood at the sink that overlooked a red brick wall.

'Here, I'll give you a hand,' May took off her coat and hung it behind the door.

'You'll dee nowt of the sort. You've been slavin' all morning at work. Anyway, there's only the pans to drain dry.' Mam rolled the sleeves of her blouse down and fastened the buttons at the cuffs. 'Why are you so late?'

'Latecomers, dawdling over their dinner.'

'They should be telt to hop it. In fact, war or no war, working on a Sunday shouldn't be allowed. It's a downright disgrace.'

May was about to point out that Mam had slaved all morning making Sunday dinner but thought better of it. Her mother looked tired. Though still a bonny woman, she was round-shouldered with grey-tinged hair and a defeated look in her eyes, looking every one of her fifty-five years. May worried that she had been the cause of her mother's decline as she had loyally stuck by May in her darkest hour all those years ago. She would do anything to lighten her mother's load, not because she was indebted but simply because May loved her.

'Go and put your feet up and I'll bring you a cuppa,' May told her.

'You're a good lass, our May. Though, you'd better bring your dad and Mr Grayson a cup too, else there'll be ructions on.'

As Mam hung her pinny behind the door and left the room, a pang of sadness poked May.

Mam pretended to be tough and strong but May knew differently. She knew she missed her sons but they rarely visited or brought her grandchildren. And not a word of reproach did she make.

'They're good lads at heart,' she told May. 'And they've got busy lives of their own. I don't blame them. Yer dad's never made the time of day for his sons.'

May knew her two brothers despised their father because, in their eyes, he was a good for nothing layabout who'd allowed their canny mam to age beyond her years.

May dried the saucepans. Wiping her hands on the tea towel, she noticed the ovenproof dish on the table and recognised the contents as the remains of an apple suet pudding – Derek's favourite. May reflected, as she set the tray with everyday china, that it was good that her mother had Derek to lavish love upon. Once upon a time, May had considered her mother too old to bring up another bairn, but Mam had proved her wrong, and older and wiser this time round, she made sure she had time to enjoy her young son.

May padded along the passageway to the front room and, entering, placed the tray on an occasional table in front of the fire. The room was decorated with regal red and cream striped wallpaper, with a mismatch of faded high-backed chairs placed around the walls. Today it was bathed in yellow sunlight. Dad and Mr Grayson were sitting opposite each other in the bay window.

'I heard two unexploded sea mines were washed up on the shore yesterday,' Mr Grayson was saying. 'One of them only a hundred yards from Trow Rocks.'

As May walked into the musty-smelling room, her father gave her the usual disgruntled look.

'Were they British made?' he asked.

'Yes. The admiralty disposed of both.' Mr Grayson, a comparatively younger man, sat bolt upright. With his smart suit and round-rimmed metal spectacles halfway down his nose, Mr Grayson looked every inch the bank employee he was.

Mam looked up from where she sat in front of the hearth on the floor. With Derek at her side, she studied a jigsaw puzzle on the mat. 'Only the crown to finish.'

With a start, May noticed the bairn had had his haircut and lost all his lovely blonde curls.

'Whose crown?' she wanted to know.

'Why! King George's. It's a picture of his coronation.'

'That's too advanced for a lad of five,' Mr Grayson piped up.

'Rubbish,' Mam replied, looked annoyed. 'There's no flies on you, is there, son?' She ruffled Derek's hair.

With his plump cheeks and enormous blue eyes, Derek was as cute as any picture. May dropped on one knee. A clammy, boyish smell emanated from him and May gave him a hug, a rush of tenderness washing over her.

'Gerr-off,' he said, shrugging himself free and returning to the puzzle.

Mam gave her a sympathetic wag of the head.

'You'll have yon lad soft the way you gan on.' Her father's voice was nasal.

Mam stiffened. 'A hug never did anyone any harm.'

The two women's eyes locked.

May's father had no time for Derek, calling him a pest, but he could only go so far. Because of her father's drunken ways he was estranged from his sons and Mam was determined that history wouldn't be repeated with Derek.

He had complained only once about her devotion to their young son and like a tiger protecting its cub, Mam had turned on him.

'It would pay you, Ernie Robinson, to remember the hand that feeds yi,' Mam growled. 'Never let me hear another word against me son again, understand?'

Apart from harmless moaning, he never did cross his wife over Derek again.

May poured the tea and handed a cup to Mr Grayson. Noticing a bus pass by the bay window, she scoured the heads looking for Etty Makepeace – but on second thoughts, she realised the lass would have been home long ago. She was canny enough but her sister Dorothy was easier to get to know. Etty had a guarded look to her that always made May feel awkward, as if she'd done something wrong.

'Stop gawping lass,' her father broke into her thoughts, 'and give us me tea afore it gets cold.'

May never knew where she stood with her father, and wished for the idyllic relationship they had once shared. But since her disgrace, he'd never found it in his heart to forgive her.

'Our May,' Mam asked, 'when are you expecting that fiancé of yours home on leave? It's been some time.'

Now that Billy and May were engaged, Mam had agreed that he could stay in one of the attic bedrooms when he came home on leave. Billy's family lived in a two bedroomed house and now his younger sister had grown, Billy was required to sleep on the couch.

'Billy didn't say when in his letter. But he should be due some leave soon.'

The thought of Billy made May's heart swell with love and joy and she made a mental note not to be clingy – or to talk wedding plans – when he did arrive home, as she knew it would annoy him.

May had set her sights on Billy Buckley when they were both still at school. Though she'd idolised and fantasised about a future with him, she never believed such a miracle could happen.

Billy had had the pick of girls at school – and the talk was always about him behind the toilets in the schoolyard. He was the worst flirt and conceited with it, too.

'I'll see if I can fit you in,' he told a smitten lass.

He would consult a little black book he kept in his jacket pocket. With a lot of page-turning, and a look of concentration, he'd condescend to make a date with the besotted lass, much to the envy of her mates watching on.

'Mind, you're not the only one…' he'd impudently say. 'I've got other fish to fry. Just so's you know and I'm not accused of being a two-timing cad.'

This kind of behaviour was tolerated because where Billy was concerned, a girl lost her pride.

The reason May didn't go out with Billy wasn't because she had scruples, but because Billy never showed any interest in her. Shy and skinny with colt-like legs, she adored him from afar, and all through her schooldays, she'd have sworn Billy didn't know she existed.

When May left school and started work, Billy became a lingering memory. She had no qualifications, so when Aunt Ramona offered her a position as her parlour maid, May leapt at the chance.

Her mother was horrified. 'That sister of mine is just a jumped-up hussy, who thinks because she's married an undertaker she's a cut above everybody else.' She looked sorrowfully at her daughter. 'Our May, I want you to make something of your life and not end up a skivvy like me.'

May tried to explain that she didn't have the same confidence as Mam and a job with Aunt Ramona was better than nothing.

A month after her seventeenth birthday, on a wet and blustery December day, May hurried home from the marketplace. It was her afternoon off from work and she carried a brown paper bag filled with shopping from the market stalls; two second-hand romantic novels for her mother, whelks for her father and sherbet lemon sweets for Mr Grayson.

As she hurried along the road, hordes of workmen swarmed through Redhead's shipyard gates. Then she saw him – Billy Buckley. He walked along the pavement towards her, two other workmen at his side, wearing a worn navy suit and a cloth cap. May would have known him anywhere. He was stocky built, with the same swagger, and blonde hair, though darker now, with a forelock that swept his brow as if he'd fashioned it that way. She stopped in her tracks, unable to believe her eyes. Someone walking behind bumped into her and, overbalancing, she catapulted into the oncoming workmen.

'Watch out, pet.' Strong arms steadied her.

May's head jerked up and she looked straight into the ice-blue eyes of Billy.

'Why, it's May Robinson from school.' Brazenly, he looked her up and down. 'Man! Have you filled out... and in all the right places.'

All she could think was that he'd remembered her name.

He walked her home and all the while May couldn't believe it was happening.

She tried to think of something riveting to say, but blurted, 'My, aren't you the jammy one... having such a good job?'

What a clot, fancy her coming out with something as daft as that.

'Aye. If you can call working in a shipyard jammy.'

His answer annoyed her. 'You should be ashamed Billy Buckley. Most men... especially those that hang around the yard gates every morning, would be over the moon to have any kind of work.'

He grinned. 'Firstly, I'm not like most men and secondly, you look gorgeous when you're mad.'

Thrown, May gabbled. 'Did you get an apprenticeship?'

'Aye, as a fitter.'

'Your mam must be proud.'

'With me dad out of work we needed the money.' His face became serious and May reckoned she'd never seen this sober side of Billy before. He went up in her estimation. He wasn't just looking for 'a piece of skirt' after all. Billy had family he cared about.

Presently they came to the foot of the stone steps leading to May's doorway.

The rain started, the drizzly kind that felt like mist on your skin, but May didn't mind. She could have stood all day ogling at Billy's handsome face.

'D'you want to come out with us?' he asked.

She almost swooned. How many times had she dreamt that Billy Buckley would say those very words?

She nodded, too overwhelmed to speak.

He pulled up the collar of his shabby jacket. 'I'll call for yi' the morra night.'

'D'you not have to check in your little black book?'

'Are you poking fun at us?'

Conscience-stricken that she'd stepped over the mark, she replied, 'Eee I would never.'

'I'm only joking,' he laughed. 'I'll call for you at seven the morra'.'

As she watched him prepare to leave, she plucked up courage to say, 'You never bothered with me at school.'

He turned and walked away. His voice came over his shoulder with a laugh in it.

'I had bigger fish to fry, then.'

May giggled.

One thing Billy was not, was shy, and when he visited the house, he'd make straight for the kitchen and hail May's mother as if he'd known her for years. She, in turn would don a clean pinny, make fresh scones and check her appearance in the hall mirror. Her face lit up whenever he spoke and she hung on to his every word.

That was Billy for you, he had this magnetic charm that affected women – they visibly illuminated whenever he entered a room.

May walked out with Billy for four months. She was thrilled, feeling sure that one day soon he'd ask if they could become officially a courting couple.

Then one dark April evening, after the couple had kissed goodnight outside May's front door, she went indoors to find her mother waiting at the kitchen table.

'Sit down, our May.' Mam lifted the heavy china teapot and poured her daughter a cup of tea. 'We need to talk.'

'What's wrong?'

'I want you to be careful, lass… he's a right Jack the Lad, is that one.'

'Who, Billy?'

'I divvent trust the lad.'

'I thought you liked him.'

'I do, hinny, that's the point. I've met his type before.' Mam took a sip of tea, her troubled eyes never leaving May's face. 'I hope you're behaving. I don't want you doin' anythin'… silly.'

'Silly?'

Mam gave her a measured look.

'You know what I mean. That lad's a patter merchant and a bit of hanky-panky is all he's after.'

'Mam!'

'I'm warnin' you for your own good. Lads like him are only after one thing and they lose respect when a lass gives in.'

May put her cup on the table and stood up. Rarely did she disagree with her mother but on this occasion she was wrong. She wouldn't stand by and listen to Billy being criticised. 'How can you be so judgemental? You don't know Billy like I do.'

*

The next Sunday, Billy and May took a ride on their bicycles out of town to Cleadon Hills. It was a warm spring day and white marshmallow clouds hung in a paint-box blue sky. The air at the top of the hills was soft and energising, and May, overcome with a sense of freedom, had a rare moment of belief that, if she put her mind to it, anything could be achieved.

They found a spot at the foot of a knoll, hidden from view. May lay in the long grass and listened to birds twittering in the trees. Billy stretched beside her, his body warm against her skin.

Resting his head on her chest he told her, 'I'll go crackers if I don't talk to somebody,' he upturned his face to hers, 'and you're such a good listener.'

His voice was low as he spoke of his family; May had to bend her head to catch his words. He told her how his father had gone to pieces now he was out of work, how his mother was at her wits end trying to make ends meet and how his sister was broken-hearted because her once loving parents did nothing but squabble.

'That's terrible, Billy. How about you?'

'I hate me job but I have to graft at the shipyard as somebody's got to bring the money in.' His face looked bleak. 'If I had a choice I'd travel the world.'

'Wouldn't you miss home?' May asked.

'Not this dump.'

'Wouldn't you miss anyone?' she fished.

'Me family, of course… and you.'

Billy's indolent blue eyes probed hers and she knew why lasses found him irresistible – though, for the life of her, May couldn't put it into words. Peggy Daly, her old school mate, had tried.

'It's something to do with his chemistry,' she said. 'Some lads have it and some don't. Billy oozes it.'

Too deep for May, all she knew was that she ached for the love of him – and if she couldn't have him then she didn't want any other lad. Her mind was made up on the matter.

Billy looked at her and groaned. 'You know you drive me wild?'

May regarded his chiselled features, his piercing blue eyes, the dimple in his chin –and her heart twisted. She felt the urge to pinch herself to make sure she wasn't dreaming. She – May Robinson – was driving Billy Buckley wild.

He took her hand. 'Here, feel this.'

He unbuttoned his jacket and she saw he wore no waistcoat, just braces over his shirt. As he pressed her hand against his groin, her eyes grew huge. She'd never imagined it would be so big and hard. She knew she should snatch her hand away or, at the very least, show shame, but she was on fire and hungered for Billy's touch. Yet her upbringing proved too strong. For ingrained in May, like lettering in rock, was the fact that no decent lass would go the whole way before they were married.

She snatched her hand away.

'See what you've done?' Billy looked helplessly at the rise in his trousers. 'I'm in agony.'

Then he was astride her, sinewy legs pinning her down.

He bent over her, his eyes meeting hers and his husky voice whispered, 'I can't stand it any longer… I want you.' He sat up, his face tragic. 'You can't love me or you wouldn't put me through this… torture.'

Can't love him – dear Lord – if needs be she'd walk on hot coals for him.

'Are you frightened, is that it? I'll be gentle.'

If only there was some other way she could prove her love, but seeing the demand in his eyes, May knew there wasn't.

His hand moved under her skirt.

'Aw… come on, May,' he pleaded. 'You know I love you… it's only natural. I can't wait.'

May's heart soared. He'd said the words she longed to hear.

The next day May helped her mother change the lodgers' beds.

Mam, flapping the laundered sheet over the bed, told May, 'I know I go on but I can't help worrying about you and that lad.' When May didn't answer she went on, 'I suppose you think the right lass will change Billy.'

May shrugged. She caught the sheet and tucked it under her side of the mattress.

'And I suppose, our May, you think you're that lass?'

May did but couldn't think what to say.

Her mother gave her a troubled look. 'Such is the foolery of love… all I ask, pet, is you be careful what you get up to… save yourself a lot of heartache.'

May didn't say the warning had come too late.

May didn't hear from Billy. As the days passed, she began to worry. Agonised, she didn't know what to do. She couldn't believe Billy would simply walk out of her life. She tortured herself that her mother was right and that he'd lost all respect for her.

'Where's that lad of yours, these days?' Mam asked one day as May came home from work. 'I've not seen a sign of him in two weeks.' Suspicion was written on her face.

From her neck to her cheeks, May flushed red. What could she say?

'He's gone, hasn't he?' Mam folded her arms, 'I telt you the lad was flighty.'

May thought of going to see Billy in Laygate Lane where he lived, but what if his mother came to the door? May could hardly ask, 'Why's your Billy not seeing me any more?'

If Billy answered her knock, would May really beg him to start up with her again? No, she had too much pride, even if she did love Billy to distraction.

Weeks turned into months and as May's heart pined for Billy, she couldn't eat or sleep.

One June morning, feeling queasy, she raced to the lavatory down the yard, where she was violently sick. When this became a regular morning event, May was convinced that her yearning for Billy had caused the problem.

'When did you last have your do-dahs?' her mother asked after May had had another session in the lavatory.

'Do-dahs?' May asked, mystified.

'Your monthly… thingy.'

May cottoned on. She didn't have a clue when she'd last had a period. She didn't keep check but it must have been months ag—

She looked at Mam in horror.

'Yes, our May. I'd say by the evidence you're ganna have a bairn.'

When she missed her third menstruation, May realised it really was true. She was pregnant.

Her mother didn't flap or rant. She simply said, 'There'll be no seeing the doctor. Tis best, our May, that we keep this in the family and yi' have this bairn at home.' She sighed as if she carried the weight of the world on her shoulders. 'Folk around these parts are unforgiving about such matters – hypocrites that they are – and having a child out of wedlock could ruin your life.' Mam gasped a breath. 'Tis best, if we say this bairn your carryin' is mine.'

Such was her shame, May didn't argue. Besides, she reasoned, her mother always knew best.

Her father viewed things differently. 'A slut, me daughters become… I want her out of this house.'

Flint-eyed, his wife told him, 'She'll do no such thing. You've driven away your sons, I won't have you doing the same thing with our May.' Folding her arms, her eyes locked with his. 'I'm warning you, Ernie Robinson, you'd be wise not to cross me on this.'

He never mentioned May's pregnancy again but he never called her 'me little angel' again, either.

May's employer, Ramona Newman, was informed that May's help was needed at home.

'Won't Aunt Ramona be suspicious?' she asked.

'Miss high and mighty…' her mother said of her sister, 'is too wrapped up in her own affairs to be bothered with the likes of us.'

The subject was closed.

May's time arrived the next January, when her mother delivered the bairn in the attic bedroom and if any of the lodgers heard May's cries, they thought better than to mention it.

True to her word, her mother took Derek as her own. She understood, though, when May's arms ached to hold him.

'You can't, pet,' her voice was laden with regret. 'If this is to work, Derek must come to recognise me as his Mam.'

It was as if someone stabbed her in the heart. May doubted she could go through with the plan but what other option had she? For Derek's sake, she made up her mind that she'd conceal her feelings. If he cried during the night, or wanted a kiss better when he fell ill, she recognised that Mam was the one he needed and his big sister would never do. Derek's welfare was paramount and just to be near him would have to suffice. Cute little lad that he was, her heart soared with pride as she watched him thrive but that didn't stop the gut-wrenching turmoil May experienced inside.

Three years passed and in all that time May didn't hear a word from Billy but the gossip was he'd taken up with her old school mate, Peggy Daly. One crisp spring day, May stood on her top step polishing the brasses on the front door.

'Yoo hoo!' A voice called from below. 'Long time no see.'

May turned and was staggered to see Peggy Daly loitering at the foot of the steps. She wore a tailored suit with square shoulders and slim skirt that ended below the knee. The outfit was completed with a broad brimmed Easter bonnet.

Peggy had a lad in tow but he wasn't Billy.

May's hair was a mess, she wore a wraparound housedress, and her hands were blackened with metal polish. She was certain she had dirty smudges on her face.

Peggy linked arms possessively with the lad. 'You remember Melvyn? He was in the same year as us at school.'

'Hello Melvyn.' May remembered he used to be the school bully.

He grunted.

'Melvyn and me got engaged.' Proudly, Peggy held out her left hand.

May skipped down the steps to look at the proffered ring. 'Why, it's lovely,' she said of the tiny, solitaire diamond.

Peggy gazed adoringly up at her fiancé. 'Melvyn's in the Territorial army. He's off to summer camp in August. The week after he gets back we're due to get hitched.'

'Congratulations. It's not long to wait.'

Peggy laughed. 'Tell that to me Mam. She's making the wedding dress… and the two bridesmaids'.'

May marvelled at the dexterity of Peggy's mother.

As the couple made to move off, May plucked up the courage to ask, 'Have you heard anything lately of Billy Buckley?'

Peggy flushed to the roots of her hair. 'Not in an age.'

'Does he still work at Redhead's?'

'How would I know? Last I heard,' she gave Melvyn a nervous glance, 'which was long over a year ago, he was seeing a woman from Jarrow. An older woman by all accounts.' She sniffed. 'You know Billy. He's fickle. Goodness knows who he's got in tow now.'

Pulling an 'I'm fed up face' Melvyn tugged impatiently at her arm. 'Haway, we can't stand here gossipin' all day.'

'See you… bye,' May said as her fiancé hauled her away.

*

After her meeting with Peggy, the need to see Billy grew in May like a sickness. She made up her mind. She'd seek him out and perhaps then the madness that afflicted her would go away. She took to hanging around Redhead's shipyard, watching as hundreds of men swarmed out of the gates at closing time. She felt no guilt or shame and ignored the smutty remarks from the younger lads. Her behaviour was improper for a decent lass, May knew, but she stood her ground in the hope of glimpsing Billy.

Then, on the third day, as she leaned against the wall on the opposite side of the road, she saw him.

He swaggered out of the yard gates behind a group of older men dressed in trench coats and trilby hats. Pushing a bicycle with dropped handlebars, he wore a three-piece suit and red and black striped cap at a jaunty angle. One of the lads made a remark, nodding towards May, and the rest of them gave out hoots of derisive laughter. Eyes crinkling, mouth twisted in a laugh, Billy looked her way and, as recognition dawned, disbelief registered on his face.

He said something to his mates and, looking both ways, dashed with his bike across the road.

'What are you doing here?'

'Don't be mad. I had to see you.'

'I heard there was a lass hanging around the yard gates but I never dreamt it was you. Man, don't you know you'll get a reputation?'

'I didn't think.'

'That's patently obvious.' He stared over the road to where the other lads stood gawping. 'Haway walk away with me. We can't stay here.'

Hell's fire couldn't stop her.

While they walked, a cold northerly wind blew and she pulled up the collar of her coat. She looked sideways at him. He'd lost weight and his face looked pinched. As they headed towards the marketplace he stopped and watched a bloke pushing a handcart with a brass bedstead on it pass by. Billy turned towards her. Under the scrutiny of those gorgeous eyes, May felt herself wilt.

'Did you hear me dad died?'

'I didn't. Billy, I'm sorry.'

He gazed pensively over the road as if he expected to see his old man standing there.

'Heart attack.' He balled his fists. 'But if you ask me, it was bloody well being out of work that did it. He lost all pride.'

May touched his arm and felt the warmth of his skin beneath his clothes.

'That's awful. How's your mam bearing up?'

'Not so good. They had a row just before and she blames herself.'

May couldn't imagine having that burden of guilt but thought it best not to say.

His troubled eyes met hers. 'I thought about coming to talk to you.'

'Why didn't you?'

'After the way I treated you… I had no right.'

'What would you have said if you had?'

He proceeded to tell her what a scoundrel he was, how he'd made a hash of his life so far and how he was determined to make his father proud.

'I bet he was proud of you,' she said. 'Only men find it hard to show it.'

'You think so?'

'Me dad would rather do a hard day's labour than show emotion – and you know what he thinks of work.'

Billy laughed. 'You're priceless, lass. You always did me the power of good.'

He was touched, she could tell, and seeing his lovely smile made her ache for the love of him.

May needed to know where she stood. 'I've heard you took up with a woman from Jarrow.'

Billy became his cocky self again and grinned. 'I did. But you've nothing to worry about on that score.'

She watched the man with the handcart disappear around a corner.

'Am I forgiven?' he pouted.

She linked his arm. As if he needed to ask.

When May's mother heard that her daughter had taken up with Billy again, she was none too pleased.

Arms folded, she snapped, 'You want your head examinin', our May, getting involved with *him* again. He's a good for nothing waster and nowt will make me think otherwise.' Then her attitude changed and her brow creased into a worried frown. 'You wouldn't be fool enough to tell him about Derek, would you?'

Derek, three now, with his blonde hair and striking blue eyes, had a resemblance to his father. Best to leave Derek happy as he was and, besides, Mam doted on her son. Intuition told May that it would be wise not to tell Billy, especially as he had once joked that he liked kids – as long as they belonged to someone else.

'No, I'd never tell Billy.'

One morning at the beginning of September, May pattered along the passage to the kitchen to prepare breakfast. Mam, already there and fully dressed, sat at the table, a warm cup of tea in her hand.

Yawning, she told May, 'Mr Grayson says there's to be an announcement on the wireless and we've to stand by.'

'What for?'

Mam shrugged.

At the given hour, a huddle of them stood around the mahogany wireless in the front room. Her father, bending over, twiddled with the knobs and tuned in.

The Prime Minister himself confirmed what folk had suspected since the Polish invasion on Friday – that the country was at war with Germany. A shocked silence followed, broken by her father. 'That bugger, Hitler. Starting another war… he wants hammering.'

May's throat constricted with fear. All she could think of was Billy and his declaration that if war started he'd be one of the first to enlist.

May dashed from the room, fetched her outdoor jacket from under the stairs and, hands shaking, tried to do up the jacket buttons. She banged out of the front door, taking the front steps two at a time and tore along the pavement.

The day held a surreal quality and folk, congregated outside front doors and on street corners, stood with stunned expressions. May raced past, hell-bent on reaching Billy at his home.

'You've heard?' she asked, when he answered the door.

'Aye. That's me joining up.' His eyes held a serious glint.

Black fear crawled into May's throat. 'You don't need to. Not straight away.'

'I do. Besides, this might be me chance to see a bit of the world… me last chance at anything afore I'm dead.'

'Don't say that.'

'Now there's a war on nothing's certain.' Then he'd said the words that took May's breath away. 'Will you marry us? We'll get engaged afore I go.'

CHAPTER TEN

September 1940

'No time goes quicker than time spent on leave,' Laurie told Etty, as she sat beside him on a stool.

Laurie had been allocated a ship – a destroyer – which, by the luck of the gods, needed a boiler clean and was, at this precise moment, tied up alongside Commissioners Wharf on the River Tyne. Granted three days leave, he'd hopped it ashore and made it for home.

His huge bulk sprawled on the couch, Laurie dwarfed the aged piece of furniture.

Dorothy, wearing a frilly pinafore that tied at the waist, came in from the scullery and, shifting his leg, plonked down beside her husband.

Laurie stretched his arm around her shoulder. 'Champion dinner.'

With the realisation that war had arrived and might be a drawn-out affair, the couple didn't speak of the uncertain future, but the hollowness in their eyes gave their torment away.

Live for the day. This was the phrase on everyone's lips.

Etty's stomach felt uncomfortably full. She regarded Dorothy and her burly husband with fondness. She was glad the pair had found each other. It proved that in this mad, unpredictable world nice things could happen – and she held on to that hope.

She stretched luxuriously and said, 'Yes, scrumptious meal, thanks.'

'Was afters mentioned?' Laurie asked.

'Blimey, I forgot.' Dorothy leapt up and dashed into the scullery.

Merriment danced in Laurie's eye. 'I thowt I could smell something burning.'

Dorothy reappeared. Hands protected by a tea towel, she carried a round metal cake tin.

'It's ruined,' she wailed.

'Surely not.' Laurie regarded the contents of the tin. 'It looks fine to me,' he said, loyally. 'What is it?'

Dorothy, no expert cook, had surprisingly prepared a superb breast of lamb casserole. The meat was a rare treat and goodness knew how long she'd had to queue at the butchers for it. Rising early, she'd scraped, sliced and chopped all the vegetables, insisting she could manage herself.

But providing a pudding, in Etty's estimation, was a step too far.

'Incinerated treacle pudding,' Dorothy said.

Etty and Laurie stood side by side in the miniscule scullery doing the dishes, and though there wasn't much room, it was companionable, their elbows colliding occasionally. Remnants of the dinner – peas, carrots and potatoes – were put on a plate and placed in the cabinet for tomorrow's leftover meal.

'Aye, with these shortages of food, every little morsel counts,' Laurie said, picking up the tea towel. 'Being frugal gives families a sense of pride they're helping with the war effort.' His cheery face creased as he frowned. 'Blasted submarines… sinking our supply ships.'

'D'you really think by cutting our supply of food Jerry thought we'd starve and submit?'

'Aye, lass. I do. But the enemy didn't account for the British determination to survive.'

Etty sighed and blew out her cheeks. 'But nobody thought there'd be this extent of rationing, did they? In January it was two ounces of bacon and butter and eight ounces of sugar for everyone. Now it includes cheese, eggs, milk, canned foods...' she raised her eyebrows, 'and I suspect the list won't end there.'

'Aye... even sweeties for the kiddies.'

Laurie, as he dried dishes, lapsed into silence, then cocked an eyebrow at Etty. 'A little bird tells me you've been seeing a lad these past few weeks.'

Etty scrubbed an enamel dish. 'Trevor Milne. He lives up the street in the next block.'

'I hear he's in a reserved occupation.' Etty's lips twitched. Dorothy had kept him well informed. 'Which means,' he carried on, 'the lad's work is important to the country and he's exempt from going to war.'

'I knew that.' Her tone was indignant. 'Trevor works at the pit.'

There was a pause as Laurie put the cutlery away in the cabinet drawer. He straightened and, rubbing the back of his neck, seemed nervous.

'Aye, well... petal... there's plenty of fish in the sea,' he said awkwardly. 'Don't you go hooking the first one without trying the rest.'

Dorothy had clearly asked him to have a word, and the poor man was trying his best.

'Blimey, I'm not gone on Trevor,' Etty assured him, 'he's... just a friend.'

Was he? she thought. She was starting to rather like him and her stomach did a somersault whenever she saw him.

'That's that, then.' Duty over, Laurie appeared profoundly relieved.

'Only...' Etty gave a wistful sigh.

'Yes?'

'Sometimes, I don't know what to talk to Trevor about, you know... men's things.'

'Listen, pet, the lad's interested in you, not a lot of talk about football and suchlike.'

'He isn't interested in football.'

Laurie's bushy eyebrows shot up. 'A Geordie lad who isn't interested in football! Lord above, whatever next? What does he like, then?'

Etty explained how Trevor, in his spare time, enjoyed running and that he was a member of a Harriers club for cross-country runners. He'd also taken her out a few times to a supper dance and she'd found that, to her surprise, Trevor was a good dancer and she followed his lead as they twirled around the wooden dance floor doing the quick step, waltz and foxtrot to songs played on gramophone records. The couple enjoyed going to the cinema but Trevor's taste in films differed from hers, as he liked slapstick comedy, while she preferred romantic tales set in foreign places.

'Just like your sister.' Laurie's face split in a grin. 'She likes a soppy love story which she can have a good bawl at.'

Etty didn't mention that Trevor was prone to long silences when he grew serious, looking at her longingly as if he wanted to share something. But Etty, inexperienced with men, didn't pry in case she upset him.

She started to rinse the pudding tin under the tap, before remembering the government posters telling folk to conserve water. She complied by turning the tap off. Placing the tin on the wooden draining board, Etty thought about Trevor. He stood over six feet tall and with his swarthy good looks and rather fetching smile, he made her heart flutter. He displayed impeccable manners, pulling out seats for her, helping her on with her coat, and walking on the kerb side so that puddles wouldn't splash her as traffic went by.

There was an endearing side to him too, when he listened intently to whatever she had to say, appearing to genuinely care about her welfare – but, so far, he never spoke about himself or his home life and sometimes he'd clam up when Etty enquired.

But all men weren't as easy-going as Laurie and instinct told Etty that she must take things slowly with Trevor.

He had his uses too, Etty thought, appalled at her devious mind. With a boyfriend in tow, her status at work improved. Bertha had let it slip – intentionally, Etty felt sure – that she was seeing a lad and the lasses in the machine shop couldn't help themselves being nosy, wanting to know all about him. She was accepted now and skived off work in the cloakroom for the occasional gossip with the rest. It felt good to be part of something, even if it was only to impart the latest instalment of her love life – such as it was.

Dishes finished, Laurie draped the wet tea towel over the wooden draining board. 'Has Trevor got family?'

'Only his mam.'

Dorothy came and stood on the scullery step and by the intense look on her face, Etty guessed she'd been listening.

'From what I've heard,' she chipped in,' Mrs Milne... or Ma Milne, as she's better known... is a well-respected figure in the area. The type that folk in the neighbourhood send for when babies need delivering, or if there's a death in the family, she helps lay them out.'

'I know the sort,' Laurie replied. 'I had an Aunt Mabel who did the same thing. Lovely soul, she was... would do anything for anybody. There's not many of her sort about.'

Dorothy's gaze wandered around the tidy scullery. 'Thanks, you two,' she said appreciatively. 'Now come and put your feet up and we'll have a game of cards.'

'Is the inquisition over?' Etty asked.

Laurie winked. 'Aye, pet, it is. But remember, you're a precious commodity and you can tell that to any lad you meet. The present one included... else he'll have me to deal with.'

Etty thought of the years of being unloved and unwanted at Blakely and choked up.

The plan that Sunday afternoon was for Trevor to call for her as soon as he'd finished at the school hall. Trevor was a volunteer in the Auxiliary Fire Service and his duties were to patrol buildings, keeping an eye out for fires and watching for incendiary bombs during a raid. The school had been temporarily allocated as a base for the firewatchers. He managed this in his spare time, clocking up the required forty-eight hours a month. His stint this Sunday was supposed to finish at lunchtime, but at two o'clock there was still no sign of him. Etty, eager to be away, was sitting with her coat on. Laurie's leave was up the following day and she thought the married couple deserved time alone together.

'The ship's a beauty…' Laurie was telling his wife, who was sitting on the couch next to him, riveted by his every word. 'And there's some two hundred men—'

A knock on the front door interrupted him.

Etty, jumping up, flew to answer it. Laurie meant well, she knew, but if he answered the door she wouldn't put it past him to interrogate Trevor by asking what his intentions were, and she'd die of embarrassment.

'Toodle-pip,' she called as she hurtled along the passageway. Etty wore a green summer dress that had two little pleats at the front of the skirt. She'd found the dress in the second-hand shop and was delighted when it only needed the hem letting down. Stockings were a rarity these days but it was unthinkable to go out without them, so she'd pencilled lines up the backs of her legs to imitate seams.

Trevor stood at the front door, handsome in that unassuming way of his.

'Before we go anywhere,' he said, 'I'll have to go home and drop these off.'

He nodded at the steel helmet, trousers and waterproof leggings he carried.

Hello, she said in her head, *nice to see you too*.

'I thought you were never coming,' she responded, slamming the door behind her.

'I got delayed delivering stirrup pumps.'

The explanation would do, but an apology would have been better. He took off up the street and Etty hurried to keep up with his long strides.

'What d'you fancy doing this afternoon?' she asked.

'How about a breath of fresh air at the coast?' Trevor preferred to be outside but the beach was cordoned off by rolls of barbed wire. 'I can't be long, though, because me mother's not well.'

'Oh dear, what's wrong with her?'

'She's got a ropey chest.'

'D'you want us to stay at your house? Honest, I don't mind. It would be nice to meet your mam.'

'She doesn't know I've got a girlfriend.'

'Now would be a good time to tell her. Don't you think?'

'She frightens lasses off.'

This was a turn-up. Trevor didn't talk about his mother and from what Dorothy said earlier, Etty had imagined her a sweet old lady.

'In what way does she scare girls off?'

'Mainly with her sharp tongue.'

'She won't frighten me. I've come across the type before.' A brief glimpse of Mistress Knowles' cold eyes flooded Etty's mind's eye and she shuddered.

Trevor, she noticed, looked buoyant at her words.

'Anyway, what did your mam say to these girlfriends of yours?'

'There was only two.' He said, with astonishing frankness. 'She called the last one a brazen floozy.'

'Blimey… and was she?'

Trevor looked nonplussed.

'The girlfriend… a floozy?'

'Not that I noticed.'

'Is it true that your mam delivers babies?'

'Aye. Not so much now though.'

'How long have you lived in Whale Street?'

Trevor finally opened up, and told her about his parents. After they married, they had lived with his maternal grandfather – a retired sea-going engineer. His grandfather, a widower, resided in a rambling house with an orchard crammed with fruit trees. After his grandfather's demise the house was sold and the proceeds shared between Trevor's mam and a younger brother – a councillor apparently, and a prominent man in the town. With her inheritance, his mother had bought the pair of flats they lived in and rented the downstairs.

'Me ma was only interested in the top end of Whale Street,' Trevor said, 'where solicitors and the like reside.' All he said about his father when asked was, 'He was in the medical profession.'

His lips pressed together in a mulish way and Etty didn't pursue the matter. After all, she thought, she had secrets too. She felt honoured he'd confided in her and felt closer to him as a result of it.

'Mine died before I was born.' A sense of loss overcame Etty. She'd never known her father, didn't even have a picture of him and had never even known the timbre of his voice. Her own voice faltered. 'He… was called Harold and he died from war injuries.'

'What about your mam?'

'She came from a well-to-do family. But she… died when I was little.' She hadn't told a lie, Etty consoled herself, for, as far as she was concerned, Mam had died all those years ago.

'That was hard luck. Who brought you up?'

'An orphanage.'

Trevor's features softened in sympathy. About to reply, something caught his eye and he looked past her. Etty turned and followed his gaze. A funeral car drew up to the kerb, its bonnet gleaming in the sunlight. A man, short and dapper, wearing a black suit and carrying a top hat, climbed out of the motorcar and disappeared into a shop doorway.

'That's Mr Newman.' Trevor's voice held a note of reverence. 'A man I'm going to work for someday. He owns the funeral parlour.'

Etty shuddered. Death, especially these days, was something she'd rather not think about, let alone have to deal with in her line of work.

'Why would you want to do that?'

'Because it's a collar and tie job.'

It certainly took all sorts, she thought, but it wouldn't do if everyone was squeamish like her. Maybe though, like everything else, undertaking simply became a job. Somebody had to do this unsavoury yet essential work – and her respect for Trevor grew.

Her eyes travelled to the other side of the street, to the funeral parlour. Printed at the top of the window, in gold lettering, were the words, 'Newman's Funeral Directors'. A hand was painted on the door with its forefinger pointing to the bell and the inscription, 'we never sleep'.

As Etty pondered the ambiguous statement, the door was flung open and a rather stout woman emerged. Her feet were clad in brogue shoes and she carried the obligatory gas mask and wore the green uniform of the Women's Voluntary Service who, Etty knew, were valued for their service in the community. WVS women helped families find rest homes when they were bombed out, sought out second-hand clothes for children and ran mobile canteens for the rescue services. Etty held the women in high regard.

'I've no time to check the laundry, Roland,' the woman called over a shoulder. 'Do it yerself for once. I'm late for the staffing meeting as it is.'

She slammed the parlour door shut with such force that Etty marvelled the glass pane didn't shatter.

Trevor watched the woman bustle self-importantly up the street and grinned. 'You'd think the whole caboodle would collapse if she didn't attend.'

'Who is she?'

'Ramona Newman. She thinks she's somebody because she married a man of means.' He shook his head in amusement. 'But trying to be a lady is an upward struggle. She keeps lapsing into Geordie twang and by his expression you can tell it infuriates Mr Newman.'

Etty thought this all a bit harsh and was about to say so but Trevor started heading off up the street. As she caught up with him outside his front door she asked, 'Shall I wait here?'

Her expectation was to be invited in.

'Yes, I won't be long.'

His feet thudded up the stairs.

Left alone on the doorstep, Etty wondered about his mother, whom he was loath to let her meet.

CHAPTER ELEVEN

The rambling walk up the coast road took them to Blackberry Hills. They sat on a waterproof coat in a clearing, staring at the glittering sea far below.

'You can't escape it, can you… the war?' Etty stared at a concrete structure ahead of them. The pillbox – part of the war office defence system – was a stark reminder of a possible sea invasion. In her mind's eye, she saw the Jerry plane from the other day plunging into the sea, smoke billowing. The weather had grown cooler and, as she gazed to the expanse of sea far below she hugged the knitted cardigan she wore tightly around her chest. A life snuffed out, she thought. Gulls swooped to perch on a rock's jagged summit; their faint screeches floating across the sea to them.

Etty leaned back on her hands and inhaled the bracing sea air.

'Ow!' she cried, as a stab of pain jabbed her palm.

'What's up?'

Etty inspected the painful area. 'I've been stung by a nettle.'

'Don't scratch… it'll only make it worse. What we need is a dock leaf.' Trevor combed the grass. 'Here,' he tugged at a big leaf and, crushing it, rubbed its vein on Etty's palm.

His head was bent over her hand and she smelled the musky scent emanating from him. When he looked up, their faces inches apart, their eyes met and a sensuous ache came into Etty's abdomen. Her body longed for something, yet she knew not what, as she was inexperienced in such matters. Trevor leaned forward, his desire clear in his eyes. His soft lips touched hers, they kissed, and it felt natural as his tongue sought hers.

Their first goodnight kiss, standing outside the front door in the blackout, had been awkward. At a loss as to what to do, she'd puckered up and Trevor, missing her mouth, had kissed her nose.

'Oops,' she'd tried to make light of the uncomfortable moment.

This time when their lips met, the absurdity of kissing left her. Lost in passion, Etty forgot the throb in her palm, aware only of his warm, soft lips – that tasted curiously of peppermint – on hers. As arousal burned within her, her eyes blinked open and she pulled away, a little shocked.

He took her hand. 'Can we make it official; that we're a courting couple?'

'Blimey, we hardly know each other.'

His serious green eyes met hers. 'I know enough to want you to be my girl.'

Taken aback by his words, Etty wrenched her arm free.

'Trevor… I do like you but… I thought we were just having fun. Anything more serious takes time.'

His face darkened. 'You're the same as the rest… a tease… leading a bloke on.'

Her feelings injured, Etty stood up. She stomped down the hill. Trevor didn't call after her.

Retracing her steps along the coastal path and over the sand dunes, Etty made her way up the steps to the top of the railway bridge. She paused to look out over the sea, slate-grey now the sun had vanished.

She looked up the path but Trevor was nowhere in sight. Vexed at his insult, she told herself she didn't care. A tease, indeed!

Homeward bound, she walked through the allotments; long, thin strips of land running parallel to one another, where every type of vegetable grew and brick-built pigsties were fenced off from wooden chicken houses. With no gardeners in sight, presumably away home for their tea, Etty snapped pea pods from the vine and shelled them, popping them into her mouth. Firm and sweet, they reminded her of the orphanage vegetable patch. She pulled a wry face. Who'd have thought she'd miss anything from that dratted place? But she did. She missed the garden's variety of colour – the sweet-smelling green grass and the beautiful array of flowers: vibrant bell-shaped petunias; hydrangeas that retain their glorious blossom till winter; pretty marigolds and a profusion of busy lizzies dotted about in pots. And the trees, the tall and leggy silver birches, the towering oaks, the embodiment of endurance and strength – the trees she'd sit beneath in the shade and ponder life. But mostly, Etty missed the sense of space. She had never been happier than she was now but Whale Street, with its tall terraced houses where the sun couldn't filter through, left her feeling hemmed in.

A thought struck her, that made her infinitely sad. She couldn't live with her sister forever and, sometime soon, she'd have to move on. Although Dorothy and Laurie insisted they loved having her with them, the time would surely come when they would want the place to themselves. Unnerved, Etty wondered what she would do.

'Etty, wait!'

The shout broke into her thoughts. She threw the pea pods into the grass and turned to watch Trevor, his expression unreadable, striding towards her.

'You insulted me,' she said.

He stared into the distance as if trying to form the right words.

'I only spoke the truth…' he finally said, 'as I saw it. But I admit I might have made a mistake.' His expression was conciliatory. 'Do you then… do you still want to go out with me?'

She glimpsed a look of anxiety in his eyes and realised that this really mattered to him. Her heart melted because she knew past events shaped people's lives and she suspected Trevor could no more help his abrupt manner than she could overcome her mistrust of people. This knowledge made Trevor more human in her eyes. She gave him a tender smile.

'Will you give us another chance?' he asked.

Intuitively, she knew how much this cost him.

'I'm not doing anything on Tuesday. We could go to the flicks, if you like?'

He smiled. 'I'd like that.'

'But we're not going serious, mind.'

In September the blitz started in earnest. Cities were bombarded and civilians were given the worst taste of the war yet. London suffered the worst, with air raids every day, the cost in human life unthinkable.

Etty thought, as she read the latest reports, that if Hitler thought he could crush the British morale, he could think again. Citizens, outraged, were determined to withstand the onslaught and everywhere you looked, on boarded-up buildings and windows, was the slogan, 'Business as usual' chalked on walls.

Etty thought the shelter in the yard didn't provide much protection. Brick-built with a reinforced concrete roof, it had passed the council inspector's inspection. But so, probably, had the factory shelter she'd heard about that was blown to smithereens. No, Etty would rather take her chances under the stairs where it was warm and relatively comfortable. Up till now, she had got away with it – but not tonight when Dorothy was home from work.

As the siren wailed its chilling warning just before midnight, Etty was handed a blanket and pillow and ushered by Dorothy into the shelter that they shared with the Armstrongs, an elderly couple that lived upstairs.

'It'll be claustrophobic,' Etty told her sister, a wobble in her voice.

'Under the stairs isn't, I suppose.' Her sister raised an eyebrow. 'No, my girl, I want you safe with me in the shelter and no argument.'

Her girl. Etty was transported back to the orphanage… and the longing for her mother that was always under the surface came to the fore.

Then, the distant drone of an aeroplane brought her back to reality. As a cold hand of fear stroked the length of her spine, Etty tensed. Hearing bomber planes didn't get any easier. Dorothy grasped her arm and raced her to the relative safety of the shelter.

Cold and damp, the shelter had only two slim bunks. The sisters made do with basket chairs if they happened to sleep – almost an impossibility if a raid was on. Apart from a hurricane lamp, candles, a pile of books, flasks of hot water and makings for tea, there were no other comforts. Mr Armstrong, nudging seventy, didn't have teeth and his smiles were gummy. His wife, a wiry woman stricken with nerves, complained bitterly about the damp and draughty conditions, wringing her hands and talking non-stop.

'Lord help us… here they come,' she cried.

The throbbing of Jerry planes came terrifyingly closer. As planes roared overhead, a horrifying whistling noise pierced the air and time stood still. Then came a blast and a terrific explosion, the earth rocking, walls shaking, cups rattling. Mrs Armstrong was thrown from the lower bunk bed.

Etty, unable to move, sat frozen. Her fingernails, she realised, had dug into the palms of her hands. As clouds of dust filtered through the cracks of the ill-fitting wooden door, she began coughing.

As the plane roared into the distance towards Sunderland area, there came a lull.

'Are you all right, Mrs Armstrong?' Dorothy's voice was unsteady. She rushed with Etty and aided the old woman back onto the bed. Dazed and shaken, their neighbour didn't utter a word.

In the candlelight, Dorothy's scared eyes met her sister's. 'That was too close for comfort.'

Christmas 1940 came and went, not holding much hope for 'Peace on Earth' in the future. Images in the newspapers revealed the destruction in London after the latest enemy air attack. St Paul's Cathedral miraculously survived, majestic with its cross – a beacon of hope – towering high in the sky amidst the devastation of buildings burned to the ground.

'Apparently,' Dorothy told her sister, 'Winston Churchill ordered the cathedral to be saved at all costs to boost morale. I think they formed a special band of firewatchers to protect it.'

'Well, it worked,' Etty replied. 'And his rousing speeches helped too, I think the nation's courage and sense of unity has survived.'

It had been a while since Dorothy had heard from Laurie. She wasn't unduly perturbed as it was the way of the war, but she would have been greatly relieved if a letter had popped through the letterbox.

By the end of January, on a cold and snowy day, Etty lay on the couch, watching snowflakes as they fell, hypnotically, thick and fast outside the window. She had worked the night shift and considered her life turned upside-down. Finishing at six in the morning and home in bed by eight, she slept through until early afternoon – apart from, that is, when kiddies playing in the lane woke her up. She was lethargic, with scratchy eyes, and starving, but didn't know what kind of meal she wanted. She could never decide if her first meal of the day should be breakfast or tea.

As it was Dorothy's afternoon off work, she'd been grocery shopping, leaving Etty to rest. Pulling out items from the message bag, she ticked them off a list.

'Palmolive soap, flour, Drene shampoo, two rations of bacon, a smidgeon of butter and sugar.'

'Ooo! What's for tea?' Etty asked.

'Sardines.'

'Ugh! Not again.'

'I can't help it if the shelves are bare… blame Mr Hitler, it's because of him that foods are rationed.' Dorothy's face flushed in a rare fit of pique.

'I know we have to make do for the war effort.' Etty's tone was appeasing. 'And you do wonders, the way you manage.'

As she watched her sister carrying tins of food into the scullery, Etty considered that she would never be as skinny as Dorothy; she liked her grub too much. Yawning, she remembered the dubious compliment Trevor had paid her.

'I like a lass with a bit of flesh on her bones.'

Etty was reminded of meat hanging in a butcher's shop window. Trevor had redeemed himself by adding that she looked like the pin-up Betty Grable. Which was daft, because of course Etty didn't compare with the beautiful star – especially those famous legs – but it was lovely he thought so.

The couple saw each other regularly and, as he opened up, Etty enjoyed listening to him, especially his opinions which surprised her as he shared deep and meaningful thoughts on all kinds of subjects that set her mind thinking.

'I've never talked so openly like this to anyone before,' he admitted. 'I'm usually rather standoffish.'

That was another thing she liked about Trevor, his brutal honesty. She could easily be gone on him but memories of Blakely, and the bleak despair she had lived through at the hands of others, reinforced her guarded heart.

Now, Etty smoothed the dressing gown over her bust. She'd grown to a 36C cup and if she didn't watch out, she'd end up as top-heavy as her friend, Bertha Cuthbertson.

'You should think yourself lucky. Mine are like fried eggs.' Dorothy told her sister. She stood in the scullery doorway, staring down at the small twin peaks of her jumper. 'Small sized eggs.'

She cut a comical figure, standing there looking at her breasts and Etty started to giggle. Dorothy, seeing the funny side, joined in. It felt good to be untroubled and share a joke. It was rare these days, amongst the terrors of the war.

Later, after tea, when Etty should have been getting ready for work, she groaned, 'I do so hate the nightshift when time drags and everyone is in the doldrums. I want your job on the buses, with nothing to do but be sociable and take fares.'

'That's all you know...' Dorothy remarked. She sat in the armchair knitting what appeared to be a sock. 'What with grumpy drivers who take their grievances out on their fellow men by driving recklessly around corners... I've lost count of the times I've been tossed about in the aisles. And grouchy passengers who can be perfectly uncivil.' She turned her work and began another row. 'No, my girl, you're best off where you are.'

Etty felt comforted by Dorothy's words. The bad times at the orphanage, she realised, had been cushioned for her, because she'd had her sister to rely on – but what of Dorothy? Who had she to depend on? Wrapped up in her own misery back at Blakely, Etty had never given her sister a second thought. But she did now and said so.

'Ninny. You were little... there was nothing you could do.' Dorothy's needles stopped and she gazed into space. 'I can remember the day Mam left us as clearly as if it was yesterday.'

'And you've never despised her?'

'I was mad with her, yes... and I've had all kinds of emotions about her... but I've never hated her.'

'But what kind of mother leaves her kids with strangers?'

'The desperate kind.'

Mam had wronged Dorothy, yet she still had the capacity to forgive her. But Etty couldn't – she wouldn't – change her mind, not even to please her sister. She was in too much pain.

'Mam can go to the devil for all I care.'

The words rang in the air, and Etty regretted them as soon as they were spoken. She didn't want the subject of their mother to come between them.

Dorothy looked shaken. 'Etty, I'd be lying if I said I didn't want to find Mam and seek out the truth of what happened, but I promise I won't try. Not until you're ready. I'm sure you'll feel differently one day.'

Etty refrained from spitting out the word 'never'.

They sat in silence for a while other than the sound of Dorothy's needles clicking.

'By the way,' her voice conveyed the fact she wanted to be back on mutual territory again, 'I've been meaning to tell you something,' she looked up at Etty. 'It's strictly private, mind.'

Etty nodded. The sisters were used to sharing confidences.

'It's about May… She had a baby four years ago.'

'May Robinson? You're kidding me.'

'I'm not.'

'Did she tell you that?'

'The other night when she came around with a bag of wool. You were out with Trevor.'

'What did she say?'

'We chatted about starting a family and it just popped out. Poor girl. It's been hard for her.'

Etty knew why May had confided in Dorothy. She empathised with people and brought out their good side.

'Did she say who the father was?'

'No… but I have my suspicions.'

'And she abandoned the baby.' Etty heard the contempt in her tone.

'That's what she finds so difficult.'
'Why?'
'Because the child is Derek.'
'Her brother!' Etty sat open-mouthed.

CHAPTER TWELVE

January 1941

May gazed down at Billy as he lay sound asleep in the single bed, hand tucked beneath his cheek. She studied the contours of his face, his wide mouth, the deep creases like wings in his brow, the fluttering of his curled eyelashes as dreams played behind the lids.

It was Sunday, a day off work, and she'd crept up the stairs to see Billy before giving her mother a hand with the housework. Voices echoed from the lane and in the distance car tyres swished on a wet road. Then all was blotted out by the sound of a vacuum cleaner downstairs.

Billy had surprised her by arriving home late yesterday afternoon on a few days pass. May had heard his key in the lock and at the sight of him, smart and handsome in his khaki uniform, her stomach had curled in pleasure. His hair, cropped in regular army fashion, made his face appear boyishly round and the greatcoat he wore, almost sweeping the ground, gave him the appearance of a bairn dressed in adults' clothes. His lascivious smirk, however, was anything but juvenile.

'Hi, darling,' he flashed a heart-melting smile. 'I hitched a lift up the Great North Road to Newcastle. It was a Hillman. By gum, I froze!'

He squeezed past her in the narrow hall and dumped his haversack on the polished floor. Turning, he took May in his arms giving her a lingering kiss, the smell of damp wool, Brylcreem and cigarettes wafting up her nose.

His eyes darting along the passageway, he whispered in her ear, 'How about we vamoose upstairs and say happy new year properly.'

'Billy! Behave.'

Billy was always after 'a bit of the other', and May didn't see why not. As he said, they were engaged and she could never deny him anything, but timing was difficult. Mam was always about but there was the odd occasion when sneaking upstairs worked out. Yet a weight of guilt plagued May as, whatever Billy said, they still weren't legally married.

May hadn't seen or heard a word from him since November and, by rights, she should have been vexed but that wasn't May's style. Hers was a love that didn't ask questions or expect Billy to explain himself. The fact that he loved her at all was enough and she vowed that when they married she'd make him the best wife a man ever had.

*

Billy opened his eyes to find May staring at him with a faraway gaze.

'What?'

'Morning, Billy.' She bent and smacked him a kiss. 'I was thinking about after we get married.'

He sat up and stretched. He didn't want to go down that particular route; it would only lead them to the inevitable 'when will we get wed, Billy' scenario. And Billy was happy as they were for now. Maybe sometime in the future he'd want to settle down.

Somewhere downstairs the vacuum continued to whine.

'What d'you want for breakfast, Billy?'

'We could… '

'No… we couldn't… not with Mam about. Besides I said I'd help in the house.'

Billy stretched out an arm, slipped a hand beneath her frock and squeezed a firm buttock beneath her knickers.

'You're a scoundrel, Billy,' she arched away. 'What am I going to do with you?'

'I could think of a thing or two.'

He retrieved his hand.

'D'you want fried bread or toast?'

'Fried, please.' He stretched. 'By gum, it was worth the long journey home once in a while to get spoiled.'

Placing his hands behind his head, he laced his fingers and surveyed his surroundings. As soon as he was done with the army, he mused, he'd find them a home away from this mausoleum. Any man worth his salt wanted his own front door. Besides, he couldn't stand the way May fawned over that kid brother of hers. In Billy's opinion, the kid was spoilt rotten and needed a kick up the arse. To top the lot, her mother, once an admirer of his, looked at him with such disgust, Billy wondered what crime he'd committed to upset her so. Maybe she suspected what the couple were up to and wanted him to make an honest woman of her daughter.

'Don't be long.' May hovered by the bed. 'Breakfast will be ready in a jiffy.'

He pulled her down on the leaf-patterned eiderdown.

'Behave yourself,' she giggled, but he could tell she enjoyed his roving hands.

'We're engaged, May. We're allowed.' His voice sounded peeved.

'Clot. I know.'

'Not like them that do it in shop doorways, nowadays.'

'Billy!'

'Back at the barracks the talk is that since the war started some folk have lost all sense of moral decency. They get up to all kinds of *how's your father* in public places.'

'That's uncouth, Billy. I don't want to talk about it.' She jumped from the bed and smoothed her frock skirt. 'I must go.'

'I'll remember this, May Robinson, the next time you're gasping for it.'

Billy threw back the bedclothes and, reaching for his khaki trousers hung over the chair, pulled them on and did up the flies.

May passed over his shirt. 'Don't be mad, Billy.'

'Man! Can't you take a joke?'

'Sorry.'

'For gawd's sake stop being sorry all the time.'

'Sor—' May appeared stricken.

Billy strived for a lighter mood. 'What d'you fancy doing today?'

'We could help Mam. She needs to change the blackout curtains in the front room for thicker ones. And I don't want her climbing ladders on her own.'

Jesus. His wife was never happier than playing house and her idea of a grand night was sitting in front of the fire listening to the wireless.

'Then what?'

'We could take Derek to the park for a walk. He likes the swans on the lake.'

Hells teeth, things were going from bad to worse.

As he watched May leave the room, Billy wondered how he had got himself into this predicament.

It was after his father died, he recollected. Poor sod. After all those years trying to keep in work and out of debt, he couldn't take the strain.

At the time, Billy hadn't been able to get his bearings and the heart had gone out of him. Desperate for someone sympathetic to talk to, he had thought of his old girlfriend, May Robinson; the dumbest lass he'd ever known, but also the canniest. With her, there was no need for pretence. He could simply be himself.

His prayers were answered one day when who should be standing over the road from the yard gates, but May. Still mourning his father, sentimentality had got the better of him and he had started courting May, in the hope of making his dad proud. It had taken a war to spur Billy on and propose.

Picking up his cigarettes and matches from the chair, Billy acknowledged that he was a heel not to set a wedding date but now he knew why – he felt hemmed in and wasn't ready to settle down. He wondered if he'd ever meet his match in a girl?

Meanwhile, he couldn't bring himself to finish the affair with May because in spite of her neediness, he did love her in his own way.

'Billy, breakfast's ready!' May's shout came from downstairs.

Billy looked in the full-length mirror. Aye, for now his days of chasing women were over. Though, he told his reflection, that didn't apply to the nurse he'd met down south. In his book, nurses, especially nurses far away, didn't count.

He took the stairs two at a time, almost colliding with May at the bottom.

'I've got an idea what we can do this afternoon,' she said, caginess in her eyes. 'How about I take you to meet my good friend Dorothy Makepeace…You know, the one I've told you about. You'll like her, I promise.'

Billy had the distinct impression he was being shown off. But it was better by far than helping to hang curtains or babysitting a snotty-nosed kid.

Where was the harm?

*

Sunday was a lingering sort of day, spent drowsing in front of the fire. After a dinner of lentil soup made from chicken bones, followed by a baked suet jam pudding, Etty lounged on the couch, appetite satisfied.

Dorothy appeared behind her from the scullery, handing her a cup of chicory coffee. Coffee wasn't officially on ration but was scarce due to other imports being more essential, so folk had to make do with a chicory substitute.

'I heard an interesting fact while I waited in the queue at the corner shop,' Dorothy told her sister.

'What fact?' Etty took a sip of hot liquid.

'The woman in front of me said she'd heard that the royal family were issued with ration books too. Apparently, the Royals demanded they shared the same war experience as the British people.'

Etty's eyes twinkled. 'Can you imagine, though, His Majesty running out of milk and standing in the queue at the corner shop?'

Dorothy caught on, 'Wearing his crown.'

They looked at one another, dissolving into fits of laughter.

Etty took control and wiped her eyes, 'It just shows, though, how fair our system is. No matter how much money you've got, the food's shared out equally and at the same price. Good old Britain.' She gave a broad smile. 'That's why we'll win this war. We've got right on our side.'

Dorothy moved to the alcove cupboard door. 'Talking about sharing...' she said, bringing out a bar of milk chocolate. 'A present from Laurie on his last leave.' She snapped off a few squares and handed them to her sister.

'You don't get this at Blakely,' Etty grinned.

The saying had become a joke, uttered whenever the sisters were indulging in a treat.

A knock came at the front door and they looked at one another, puzzled.

'The only person I can think of is May,' Dorothy said.

Etty padded along the cold linoleum floor in the passageway.

There was no denying that May was a sweet-natured lass, but Etty found herself jealous of the friendship she had struck up with

Dorothy. She didn't like to share her sister with anyone except, of course, Laurie, who Etty now considered a brother.

And the way May went on about that fiancé of hers, as if he were God's gift, wore Etty's patience thin. Dorothy's too, she suspected, but her sister was far too considerate to let her irritation show.

Etty opened the front door, startled to see a soldier standing there. Stocky built and handsome, he had the bluest eyes she'd ever seen. As his compelling gaze roved over her body, they came to meet hers and gleamed in appreciation. There was a sense of familiarity about him, as though – in a different life, perhaps – she'd known him. Something stirred in Etty and she flushed.

'Blimey!' The soldier raised his eyebrows. He spoke to someone over his shoulder, saying, 'You never said your friend was a stunner.'

Unbelievably, May appeared from behind him.

So, this was the famous Billy Buckley. As the realisation hit Etty, the moment of intimacy between them passed, and she felt her hackles rise. The cheek of the man! Blatantly flirting with another woman in front of his fiancée and her, poor soul, didn't have a clue what he was up to.

'Clot. This is Etty, Dorothy's sister.' She turned towards Etty. 'I brought Billy to meet the both of you.'

'How d'you do, Etty.' He held out his hand, and it seemed churlish not to take it.

'Pleased to meet you, Mr Buckley.'

His hand was warm and calloused and he stroked her palm with his middle finger. Outraged, Etty withdrew her hand.

His eyes mocked her. 'It seems like I've got off on the wrong footing.'

Perplexed, she ignored him and addressed May. 'Dorothy thought it might be you. Go on in.'

May led the way and Etty, closing the door, followed Billy. She noticed his swagger when he walked and, to her shame, she observed how his buttocks were tight and firm beneath his khaki trousers.

*

Etty couldn't get Billy Buckley out of her mind. She reminded herself that he was May Robinson's fella and strictly out of bounds but still the Sunday when she had met him played repeatedly in her mind. The man was a charmer and arrogant with it but – blast him – whenever she thought of those gorgeous, transparent blue eyes, a delicious ache stirred in her groin.

Rather than be subjected to May singing her fiancé's praises, Etty took a lunch box to work, avoiding the canteen.

The whole thing was ludicrous, she rebuked herself, as she sat alone at her bench eating stodgy Spam sandwiches made with national bread. She'd only met the man once and here she was mooning in a lovesick fashion. She was in love with the idea of being in love. Really, all she wanted was what Dorothy had. A stable marriage with someone who cherished her. Thoughts of Trevor came to mind. Was he the one? Etty liked him and his handsome swarthy looks made her stomach melt like butter, but something was lacking. He didn't have charisma, the brazen, magnetic spark Billy Buckley had. Billy's appeal was more than just good looks, he set her pulse racing. But Billy was already spoken for, she reminded herself, and as such, he didn't come into the equation.

A couple of days later, having finished work for the day, Etty hurried out of the factory gates. As she tied the knot of her headscarf beneath her chin, she saw him. Billy. He leaned against a lamppost over the road and when he saw Etty, he threw his cigarette to the ground and ambled over.

'Hiya, bonny lass.'

'If you're looking for May, she'll be out shortly,' she replied, primly.

'She won't. She's working a late shift.' A warning bell rang in Etty's head. 'Anyways, it's you I want to see. Since I saw you I can't get you oot me head.'

His audacity astounded her. To come out with something like that, in earshot of others was downright… Etty couldn't think of a word that aptly described the bloke's nerve. Equally shocking was the way her heart pounded at his words.

'Go away,' she said, through gritted teeth.

The air was damp and she pulled up the collar of her navy waterproof coat and did up the belt. Wordlessly, Billy took her by the arm and, guiding her through the throng of crowds leaving the factory, led her to the far side of the gate where they could be alone. He loosened his vice-like grip and, leaning back, rested his foot against the gate's stone column. As he gazed at her, Etty experienced that déjà vu feeling again – as if she'd known him before.

She avoided looking at those spectacular eyes and his inviting, soft-looking, plum-coloured lips.

'Meeting a pretty lass like you makes me want to be fancy free again.'

She gave an impatient shake of the head and made to move.

'Haway, man, it's only wishful thinking. How old are you… seventeen-ish? Anyways I'm years older than you and I should have more sense.'

With his roguish good looks and rascally charm, Billy was a clever dick, but he'd met his match in Etty. She fancied him all right, but as far as she was concerned, that was where it ended.

'Leave me alone. I want nothing to do with you.'

He took a slim packet of cigarettes from his jacket pocket. Lighting one with a match, he took a deep drag and, exhaling a curl of smoke, he laughed.

'Your face darkens when you get mad.'

'It's not funny.'

'Neither it is, but I can't help what you do to me.'

'That's it. I'm going.'

'Can I see you again on me next leave?'

'Will you get it into your thick head? I'm not interested. You're engaged!'

'Ahh! You do fancy me, then. It's only the fact I'm "betrothed" to another that bothers you.'

'Only, indeed! Anyway, I've got a steady boyfriend.'

'I know… Trevor Milne.'

'How do you know that?'

'I asked May.'

The gall of the man. Etty shook her head in disbelief.

'You can dee better than that mammy's boy.'

'You don't know anything about Trevor.'

'He thinks he's a cut above the rest… so me mates at the yard tell us.'

So, Billy had been asking around.

She looked away, watching the stragglers appear from the gates. Along the street, factory workers had formed a queue at the bus stop. Normally, she would be one of them, with not a care other than getting home and the eternal question of what to have for tea. But now that chance had brought Billy Buckley into her life, she had a hunch that things had irrevocably changed. She wanted him, but she couldn't have him and Etty wondered if she'd ever feel the same about anyone else again.

Spiritedly, she told him, 'You know nothing about Trevor! He's responsible, dependable and—'

'Boring.'

'How dare you say such a thing?'

'I bet it's true.'

'Trevor wants us to become engaged.' There was a ring of defiance in her tone.

'And will you?'

She didn't answer him. She couldn't tell a lie. Her feelings about Trevor were muddled, and meeting Billy had made her more confused because she couldn't help but make comparisons between the pair of them.

As she stormed off, she called over her shoulder. 'I told you to leave me alone. My life is no affair of yours.'

After their run-in, Etty didn't see Billy again and she presumed he'd returned down South. As the weeks wore on, she swung from loathing him to daydreaming about him. She imagined tracing her forefinger over the dimple in his chin, up around his seductive lips, and wondered what it would be like to kiss them. She baulked, though, at the notion of squeezing that rear end of his and, scandalised, vowed to put all thoughts of Billy from her mind.

If only she could.

CHAPTER THIRTEEN

The raids were a regular occurrence now; the siren had gone off last night, and again this morning. Etty had spent the night in the shelter and sleeping had proved difficult, as enemy planes screamed overhead and the distant thuds of bombs penetrated the concrete walls. Then came the heartbreaking sound of ambulances and fire engines, and the toll on human life was unthinkable. To make matters worse, all water, gas mains, electric cables and sewers in the area were damaged.

Dorothy had talked to a neighbour at the door, whose husband worked as a shipwright carpenter at the docks. She reported back that raging fires had caused considerable damage down at the docks as well as to other parts of the town. The word was that the new aircraft carrier at Jarrow was thought to have been the raiders' objective but no hit had been scored.

Her eyes round with gossip, Dorothy added, 'Apparently it's business as usual in the town.'

As she readied herself for work, a surge of pride washed over Etty for the townsfolk. They could lose everything but never their fighting spirit. Incongruous though it may have seemed, with death and destruction all around, Etty had never been happier. Dorothy felt the same and the pair made a pact to feel no shame. Life was balanced on a knife's edge, and all it took – like the lass at the factory said – was a bomb with your name on it. In the face of such odds, the sisters agreed, life should be lived for every minute.

Accepted now by the lasses at the factory, Etty thrived at work
– and if she got bone-tired due to long shifts then so be it. Hers
was a pleasant routine and living with Dorothy after the terrors of
Blakely was like the rainbow after the storm. Of an evening they
sat enthralled, listening to light entertainment on the wireless.
There was comedy with Tommy Handley, and when Vera Lynn's
melodious voice rang out in the room singing her signature tune,
'We'll Meet Again', Dorothy's expression became full of longing.
With Laurie's destroyer somewhere out at sea, she hadn't heard
from him in a long while.

As the sisters listened to plays, swinging big bands and orches-
tral arrangements, they felt fulfilled, recovering from the years of
deprivation at Blakely. If Dorothy ever thought of Mam, she didn't
think to disclose the fact and for that, Etty was eternally grateful.

'Did I mention May's fiancé's home on leave?' Dorothy called
over her shoulder.

It was a surprisingly humid May day and Etty, stifled, had
opened the back door. She stood in the scullery rinsing a favourite
dirndl skirt through in the sink. Dorothy had the evening off and
sat on the scullery step, legs in the yard, darning a hole in the
elbow of a cardigan sleeve.

'Apparently, he's got a week's pass.'

The bar of soap Etty held plopped in the water.

Etty hadn't clapped eyes on Billy since he had waited for her
outside the factory. She supposed it had only been a flirtatious
episode and that she wouldn't see him again.

On both counts, she supposed wrong.

The next day, as she left work, the sunlight dazzled her eyes
after the dimness on the shop floor, and she shielded them with
her hand. She didn't see Billy at first, not until she was further
along the road and he fell in step alongside her.

In the baking heat, the sweaty scent emanating from him should have made her keel over but somehow, because it was Billy, she found the pungent odour curiously arousing.

'Hiya, bonny lass. Miss me?'

'I heard you were on leave.' She kept her gaze ahead.

'Did you expect us?'

'No.'

'But you hoped.'

Billy was incorrigible.

'Don't kid yourself.'

'D'you always play this hard to get?'

'I'm not playing anything. Remember, you're engaged to May.'

More is the pity, her mind said.

'You don't need to rub it in.'

'What's that supposed to mean?'

He shrugged.

'You'll be telling me next she doesn't understand you.' She'd read all about men's trickery in romantic stories in women's magazines.

He looked wounded. 'I would never.'

'Good.' She stopped and faced him. 'Because May's potty about you.'

'I know.'

'Her world revolves around you.'

'I know that too.' He gave a heartfelt sigh. 'I also know she's a lovely big-hearted lass and deserves better than me.'

They walked, side by side, locked in thought. Up above in a powder blue sky, painted as if by a child's hand, not a cloud or bird stirred – and it seemed unjust that evil, in the form of enemy planes, should taint such an idyllic landscape.

Etty stopped at the bus stop. 'This is as far as you go.'

'Aw! It's a lovely night I thought I could walk you home.'

'Goodbye, Billy.'

*

All next day at work, Etty couldn't concentrate. She hovered between hoping Billy was waiting at the factory gates and despising herself for the thought.

Her shift finished, she hurried with the rest of workers as they exited the factory gates.

Then she saw him standing at the bus stop, smoking a cigarette.

He caught up and walked beside her.

'I'd never willingly do anything to hurt May.' He spoke as if they'd never been apart.

Conscious of the throng around them, Etty hurried along the street.

She hissed. 'What d'you suppose she'd think if she saw us like this?'

'We're not doing anything wrong, just two friends meeting up...' His smouldering eyes told her something else. 'Besides, she hasn't got a jealous bone in her body.'

A thought gnawed at Etty and she couldn't help but ask. 'How long have you known each other?'

May once let slip that she and Billy went back a long way and Etty was curious.

'I've known her since schooldays. Why?'

'No reason.'

'I met up with her when she was seventeen and we went out for a while.'

Etty, too busy calculating, didn't comment. Derek could be Billy's son, she reasoned, before discounting the idea. Why would May's mam bring the kid up? And why hadn't Billy married her then?

She remembered Dorothy had told her in confidence and besides, she told herself, it was none of her business.

'Why did you wait such a long time to propose?'

A haunted look flitted across Billy's face. 'We met up again after me dad died. The war had just started and I suppose I got carried away. It seemed the thing to do.'

'Were you close to your dad?'

'I swore I'd never end up like him.'

'Why? What did he do?'

'Bloody fool, had no life. Working at the shipyard, that's all it amounted to.'

'He had his family.'

'Aye... and look where that got him. Because of us he couldn't walk away.'

An image of a broken man played in Etty's mind and she felt infinitely sad.

'Maybe,' she kept her voice controlled, 'he loved you too much to... abandon you all.'

She wanted to add, *he didn't dump you in an institution that scarred you for life.*

'More fool him.'

Enraged at his answer, Etty charged ahead.

He hurried to catch up with her. 'Now what have I said?'

'I wouldn't waste my breath telling you.' Etty let the matter drop, as she might start a full-scale row otherwise. She changed the subject. 'When d'you plan to marry?'

'Dunno. I don't know if I'm cut out for it. Not yet anyways.'

If he wanted sympathy then he'd come to the wrong place.

'Why are you here?' she asked him.

'I wish I knew.' He looked genuinely bemused. 'All I know is you're special. The way you walk, the posh way you talk... how your brown eyes sometimes change to green and have orange flecks in them. Most of all, it's easy to talk to you.' He gave a roguish grin. 'Believe me, conversation is a first with a lass.'

They came to the dank Tyne Dock arches. Halfway through and in the gloom, Billy rested his hand lightly on her arm. A bolt of electricity zipped through Etty. His blue eyes glittered in the dim light and she noted his adorable, jutting chin.

She couldn't deny Billy's magnetism and though she'd only known him for such a short while she was falling for him. But he could never be hers, she reminded herself.

'I wish you were the one I was engaged to.' His voice echoed around the dripping tunnel. 'I wouldn't feel so trapped.'

Etty shivered, not from cold air but from the intensity that shone in his gaze.

The words wrenched from her. 'Go home Billy, go home to your fiancée.'

Billy didn't stand at the gates after that – but Etty received a letter from him two weeks later. It was waiting for her behind the front door on the mat when she got home from work.

> *Hi, bonny lass*
>
> *I'm lying on my bunk at the barracks thinking about you. I know I'm being a nuisance but I meant it when I said you were special. The thought of you drives me crazy. Honest, I've never felt like this about any lass and it's hard to let you go.*
>
> *Think on, something like this only happens once in a lifetime. You can't blame me for trying.*
>
> *This is just to let you know I'm here if you ever get tired of Mammy's boy. We'd figure something about May.*
>
> *Wishing you were mine, Kiddo*

Etty didn't have to think as she knew she could never find happiness at another's expense.

Besides, she had Trevor.

*

By September, the nights were drawing in and the rain that threatened all day lashed against the windowpane. Etty checked her watch – quarter to eight. Trevor would be here any minute. He was her steady boyfriend now and though he hadn't asked again, it was accepted they were officially courting. They saw each other regularly and she felt comfortable enough with him now that she could just be herself. She didn't think of Billy these days yet her pulse raced whenever May mentioned him. But, she reminded herself, Billy Buckley was firmly in the past.

With Dorothy out visiting friends from the dramatic society, the young couple took the opportunity to spend a night in.

A knock came at the front door and with a final glance at her appearance in the oval-shaped mirror above the range, Etty hurried along the passage, switched off the light and opened the door.

Trevor bundled in. 'I'm soaked through,' he said, giving Etty a kiss as he squeezed past. She followed his lanky frame into the dimly lit kitchen.

He shrugged out of his jacket and shook it. 'Me ma had one of her coughing fits and so I waited till it was over.'

Etty still hadn't been introduced to the seemingly formidable Ma Milne and neither was she eager for this honour.

Trevor hung his jacket over the back of a chair and, collapsing on the couch, picked up the *Gazette* and proceeded to read the front page. Etty, sitting beside him, noticed his polished look. His hair was slicked back, his clean-shaven chin had a blob of dried blood on it and his nails were clean of coal dust, buffed until they shone. Affection for him washed over her – he'd made the effort especially for her. Resting her head against his chest, she heard his heartbeat through his grey woollen pullover.

A lad was supposed to take the initiative to start petting, Etty knew, but left to Trevor, their canoodling would never progress beyond a kiss. She didn't know why, and it was too uncomfortable a question to ask. Was he shy? Or perhaps he was afraid as, like her, he mightn't have gone beyond a kiss before? Etty was plagued by a mounting fear that because she was raised at Blakely, she might be damaged, unable to feel in that way. She needed to find out.

A coal spat in the fire and, by its warm glow, she undid Trevor's shirt button. Sliding her hand onto his bare chest, she ran her fingertips through a bush of fluffy black hair. He folded the newspaper and placed it on his knees.

'That's nice.' His voice was husky.

Following her lead, he placed a hand on her breast and teased a nipple beneath the material of her blouse.

Etty upturned her face, surprised by the raw need in his eyes. She strained her neck and his lips touching hers were warm and moist.

They pulled apart.

She asked. 'Do you want me to undo my blouse buttons?'

'If you want to. As long as you know I'd never ask you to go the whole way.'

'I wouldn't.'

'I've never… tried anything because… I'm worried I get carried away.'

So, that was the reason.

'I think if we went further than petting, we should have an understanding first.'

Etty stopped fumbling with her buttons. 'How do you mean?'

'We should talk about the future.'

'Is this your idea of a proposal?'

'It makes sense we team up.'

It was as if someone had thrown a bucket of cold water over her.

'Sense?' She leapt up from the couch.

Trevor looked like a man who didn't know what he'd said wrong.

'I mean… you can't live with your sister forever and it's time I found a place of me own.'

'And that's a reason for us to marry?'

He looked confused. 'No. It's just an expressio—'

'Tell me something, Trevor, d'you love me?'

He stood and towered over her. 'Course I do. I always have.' He hesitated while he found the right words. 'I'm not romantic like in the flicks, Etty... but I do know you're the one for me.'

He should have left it like that but the silly beggar, taking her silence as a sign he'd won her over, went on. 'But mind, if we do get engaged we can't broadcast it until me ma finds out. She won't be worth living with if we don't tell her first.'

Alarm bells rang in Etty's head. She was back at Blakely with the formidable Mistress Knowles.

Rebellion sparked within her. 'So your mam is going to rule our lives?'

'How d'you mean?'

'According to you, we have to ask your mam's permission for everything.'

'I didn't say that.'

'What did you say, then?'

'Look here... me mam's not a well woman and she can be difficult at times and it's best we handle her with ca—'

'Best! For who?'

If Trevor thought she was going to be bullied into submission by his mother, he could think again.

'There's no need to shout.'

Mistress Knowles' hostile eyes swam into Etty's vision and she was a defenceless child again. As she shivered, old resentments surfacing, she gave herself a mental shake. She reminded herself that life had moved on. No woman would rule her again – and that applied to Trevor's interfering mother.

'There's every need, Trevor.'

'What's got into you?'

'Common sense.'

'What's that supposed to mean?'

'If you can't stand up to your mother, then I'm not going to spend a lifetime doing it for you.'

Trevor pursed white lips together in anger.

'And don't sulk.'

Etty knew she had riled him but some devilish compulsion urged her on.

'You're as bad as me mother,' he snapped. 'And for your information, I please Ma to have a bit of peace but like you, she doesn't have the sense to know when to shut up.'

'Somebody I know once called you a mammy's boy... and they were right,' she retorted.

She watched the hurt cross his gorgeous face and instantly regretted her thoughtless words.

'What gives you the right to criticize others when it's blatantly obvious you don't know a thing about them? You think you're the only one who suffered a rough childhood? Just get on with it, Etty, like the rest of us.'

Shocked by his words, she reeled. Trevor appeared stunned, looking sheepish as though he wished he could retrieve his words. But it was too late, he'd stirred up a nest of bitterness.

'Trevor Milne, if that was your attempt at a proposal, forget it. Nothing would make me marry you. And, furthermore, when I do get engaged I'll tell who I damn well please.'

He tore his jacket from the back of the chair and shrugged into it. 'Do as you like. Only don't expect me to be hanging around.'

Without a backward glance, stiff-backed, he marched from the room. She heard his feet stomp along the passageway and then the front door clashed behind him.

*

As he walked up the street in the black night, Trevor didn't know what to think. He was shaky mad. The two of them had said terrible things in the heat of the moment – words they weren't likely to forget. Man, how Etty got under his skin but Trevor, seething at the words she'd flung at him, had his pride and would be damned if he'd back down.

He put his hand in his jacket pocket, feeling the little square velvet box that held the second-hand solitaire diamond ring he'd intended to give her. He'd bought the ring that very day and spent all his savings on it. He'd even rehearsed the words he would say.

Trevor sighed, disconsolately. Maybe some things just weren't meant to be.

*

One night in the first week of October, Etty braved the blackout to meet with Bertha Cuthbertson at the picture house in King Street. She waited in the pool of light in the foyer; the outer doors firmly shut, so that no chink of light could be seen from the outside. Tapping her foot impatiently, Etty glanced at her watch. If Bertha didn't show soon they'd miss the beginning of the B film.

Opposite Etty was a kiosk, where a blonde cashier was sitting behind a pane of glass.

'Fellas, eh!' The girl studied her fingernails and after blowing on them, polished them on her tunic top. 'Stood you up, has he?'

'I'm not waiting for a fella,' Etty protested.

Since the night that Trevor had bungled his proposal, Etty convinced herself she preferred her new-found freedom and that parting was for the best.

What if Trevor finds someone else? A little voice in her head tormented her. A stab of jealousy poked Etty that took her breath away. For all his faults she did miss Trevor, she'd grown fond of him and wanted him for herself. The night they'd argued put paid to that though. After what he said, no way would she make the first move to put things right. She stuck out a stubborn chin, telling herself she didn't need Trevor.

'I've known lasses,' the girl in the kiosk broke into her thoughts, 'wait for hours on exactly that same spot. It doesn't occur to them they've been stood up.'

'I haven't been stood up.'

The girl didn't look convinced.

Etty checked her watch. Bertha was half an hour late and Etty dithered over what she should do. That moment the outer door swung open and her friend came in and heaved up the marble steps.

'Sorry, lass,' her cheery face contorted with annoyance. 'That man o' mine hasn't shown up after work. He promised faithfully he'd be home to mind the bairns. I've asked the neighbour upstairs to look out for them.' She grimaced, 'If that bugger's gone to the pub he's in for a roasting. I swear,' Bertha was a little breathless with rushing, 'if it was up to that sod of a husband o'mine I'd never set foot outside the house.'

She rummaged in her purse and paid the cashier for a ticket. 'Haway,' she said, putting her change away. 'I divvent want to miss the film.'

Giving the cashier an 'I told you so' smirk, Etty led the way through swing doors into the picture hall, where an usherette showed them to their seats by the beam of the torch she carried. A newsreel on the big screen displayed images of bomb-damaged London and the male commentator's urgent monotone filled the hall. Pictures showed Home Guards removing mountains of rubble, risking their lives amongst teetering buildings.

In the kerfuffle, as the two women found their seats, took off their coats and placed handbags and gasmasks at their feet, the people behind them clicked their tongues in irritation.

'Aye, well,' Bertha raised her voice, 'if folk had more tolerance there mightn't be any war.'

Hardly had the pair settled in their seats when the newsreel finished and the house lights went up.

'We've missed the showing of the B film.' Etty folded her coat and placed it on her knee.

'Suits me. I'm happy to see the feature film, then haddaway home.'

'What's the picture called again?'

'*Goodbye Mr Chips*.'

'Who's in it, do we know them?'

'Robert Donat and a new lassie called…' Bertha's brow creased in concentration. 'Greer Garson… apparently it's her film debut.'

'How d'you know all this?'

'May Robinson. I mentioned this afternoon in the canteen we were coming and she told us she'd seen the film at the beginning of the week with that fella o' hers. She reckons we're in for a rare treat.'

So, Billy had been home on leave. Etty couldn't help the stab of disappointment but hot on its heels came relief. He'd heeded her words and left her alone. Etty should be thankful.

'I think I'll go to the lav before the main film starts,' Bertha whispered. She heaved herself out of the seat and glowered at the ruddy-faced man behind. As Etty stood up to let her friend pass, she did what everyone did during the interval – scanned the sea of heads to see if she knew anyone.

She froze.

He sat a dozen or so rows behind, on the other side of the aisle. Smoking a cigarette, his eyes narrow slits, he looked directly at her.

Billy Buckley.

CHAPTER FOURTEEN

Billy waved, before walking over and sitting down in the vacant seat next to Etty. It was ridiculous how guilty she felt, as though she'd engineered the whole thing.

'You never replied to me letter.'

'Go away,' she whispered.

Bertha returned and, squeezing past Etty, raised her eyebrows.

At a loss as to what to say, Etty shrugged.

'How did you know I'd be here? Did you quiz May?' she asked him.

'Yes.'

Etty couldn't believe his cheek or May's stupidity. 'Did May simply volunteer the information?'

'In a general conversation sort of way, yes.'

'And she wasn't suspicious?'

'May isn't the suspecting kind.'

'Where does she think you are?'

He took a drag of his cigarette and the smoke curled upwards towards the lights.

'At the barracks. Me leave's up tomorrow. I'm travelling back later tonight.'

Bertha, the other side of Etty, poked her in the ribs. 'That's May's fella isn't it? What's he doing here?'

'Believe me, I'm trying to find out.'

The house lights went down and the heavy curtains swished open. Music sounded in the vast hall. The film's title came up on the screen and Billy leant over and murmured in her ear.

'You smell lovely, clean and fresh. I'm pleased you don't wear perfume.'

The tension in Etty heightened. She couldn't believe he would show up like this in public.

The film started. Etty watched as boys arrived at a school, excited for the beginning of a new term. The scene was far removed from anything she'd experienced at Blakely. Mr Chipping, the main character, came bumbling into view in mortarboard and school garb, walking with the aid of a stick. A retired schoolmaster, Mr Chipping lived in the school grounds and Etty, warming to his character straight away, settled down to enjoy the film.

Billy nudged her elbow on the armrest and whispered, 'I came to tell you rumour has it me battalion's being sent abroad.'

Etty's heart rate increased. 'So? Why tell me?'

'I thought you should know. Will you miss me?'

'No.'

'Admit it. I'm irresistible.'

'Hop off. I want to watch the film.'

'Will you shurrup…' a male voice behind fumed. 'Some of us came to see the picture.'

Chastened, Etty slid down her seat. On the big screen the story flashed back to when Mr Chipping was a young man and met Katherine Ellis, the love of his life. The couple married and the strict master changed. He, and his wife, devoted to one another, led a charmed life and his pupils over the years all came to adore him.

Etty sighed. It was such a romantic story and it only confirmed her belief that there was someone special in the world for everyone.

Her thoughts turned to Trevor. As he'd told her, he wasn't romantic like in the flicks but he had other redeeming features. He was devilishly handsome and she could always depend on him for the truth. Plus, underneath his sometimes awkward exterior lay a giving heart, especially for Etty. But she'd finished with Trevor and there was no going back.

Aware of Billy at her side, she couldn't help compare the two. Billy, fun-loving, made life exciting and Etty flushed, wondering what it would be like to make love with him. She shivered deliciously in the darkness. But excitement was not what life was all about. Her mind switched to dear Laurie Calvert, his stability and integrity and how much he cherished her sister. She remembered the promise she'd made that she wouldn't settle for anything less than that kind of love.

'I came for a goodbye kiss,' Billy whispered.

Etty jerked away. 'Don't do this, Billy.' The word 'goodbye' registered. 'Have you got a posting?'

'No, but wherever it is I'll be thinking of you.'

He leant towards her as if to kiss her.

'You two,' the same voice of complaint behind spoke, 'will you sit still? I can't see anything with you writhing about.'

Mortified, Etty turned her attention to the film. Mr Chipping's wife was telling him that as long as he believed in himself he could go as far as he dreamed. Etty, entranced, guessed that something tragic was going to happen. When, heartbreakingly, it did, tears streamed down Etty's cheeks. To her surprise, the houselights went up and the projector, maddeningly, ceased to roll. Etty, wiping her eyes with her fingertips, looked around.

Mutterings of disgruntlement filled the hall.

The manager, a middle-aged man wearing a black suit and red dickey bow tie, walked onto the stage. Turning towards the footlights, he shielded his eyes with a hand.

'Ladies and Gentleman,' he said, his voice grave, 'I've an announcement to make. I've been informed of an enemy raid. Please leave your seats in an orderly fashion and make for the nearest air raid shelter.'

Before he'd finished speaking, seats tilted up and people made a dash for the exits.

'Haway, bonny lass, stick with me.' Taking Etty by the hand, Billy dragged her out of the seat. She bent to retrieve her coat, which had slid to the floor.

'No time.' Billy pulled her along the row of seats into the middle aisle.

Bertha dived under the upturned seat for her handbag. 'Wait for me!'

Etty tried to wrench free, calling out to Billy to make him stop but her voice was drowned in the hullabaloo. Folk swarmed up the aisle and she was carried along with them.

'What's Jerry got against this film?' someone at her side remarked. A bent old man with wispy grey hair shook his head. 'This is the second time I've brought the wife to see this picture and both times there's been a raid on.'

Then he was gone, his slight frame swept along in a tide of humanity, afraid for their lives. If it weren't for Billy clinging on to her hand, Etty would have lost him too.

As they made their way to the cinema's back door, Billy turned towards her. His expression grim, he yelled above the mayhem, 'We won't make it to the marketplace this way. Union Alley's blocked off from the last raid.'

He dragged her along a row of empty seats to the opposite side of the cinema, where the crowd surged to the front of the building. Then she saw Bertha, distress etched on her face as she was herded along the centre aisle towards the back door. Etty waved to attract her attention but Bertha simply didn't see her amongst the chaos.

In the foyer, Etty heard the warning wail of the siren from outside. She clung on to Billy's hand and was plummeted down the steps and through the open doors. A pedestrian running past on the pavement bumped into her and she lost her grip.

'Billy!' she cried.

Her eyes, unaccustomed to the dark, stared into a black abyss. People pushed and shoved, and an electric spark flared from overhead wires as a trolley bus passed by in the road.

'Where are you, Billy?'

But Billy didn't return her call.

A full moon riding high in the sky, veiled intermittently by cloud, cast a pale light that Etty could see by. Then the sound she most feared filled the night sky – the distant drone of aeroplanes as they flew in her direction.

Etty had never known real fear before, not even at the hands of Mistress Knowles, she decided – which was nothing compared to today's threat. She ran with the rest, looking over her shoulder once in a while, into the night sky. A mutter of guns came from the vicinity of the docks, followed by thuds and spirals of smoke, casting a sinister glow over the river. She stopped at the corner of King Street and stood transfixed, watching Jerry aeroplanes as they flew over in waves, tiny black dots at first, then big enough to induce bowel-slackening fear. It became sickeningly evident she was caught up in a large-scale attack.

'Bugger it. We're in for a reet time of it tonight,' a male voice yelled, making her jump. An Air Raid Protection warden, his face upturned towards the sky, stood at her side. 'Just look at them enemy planes,' he regarded her. Middle-aged with a good-natured face, his eyes were wide in alarm.

'Away with you, Miss, get yerself into the shelter… and lass, God bless.'

As though the warden broke a spell, Etty was galvanised into action. Her stomach lurched and she felt sick but she would never let fear show.

'You too,' she yelled over her shoulder as she fled.

She raced over the road into the marketplace, surrounded by familiar buildings – shops, a hotel, St Hilda's church, the old Town

Hall. As she ran, Jerry planes came over in waves, low overhead. Ear-splitting shrieks filled the night air and terrific explosions shook the earth beneath her feet. Figures ran full pelt in the direction that Etty was heading. Ahead, a man carrying a sack disappeared down the shelter steps, while another man, silhouetted in the moonlight, paused at the entrance. There were more whistling sounds and terrible crashes, and from over the road a cracking noise as a building collapsed. Etty fell down, got up again, and ran on. She toppled over a heap at the shelter entrance. A man lay dead on the ground. His war tragically finished, Etty could do nothing for him.

'The bastards,' a male voice yelled.

Strong arms swooped her up, and Etty was carried down the dark stairwell. The bombs mercifully ceased but in the distance came the sound of incessant crumps.

'Yi' all right, miss?' Her rescuer, a burly man with a blood-stained face, gave a stiff smile. 'Yi' had a close shave.'

'I'm grand, thanks,' she said, with as much bravado as she could muster.

The man put her down and, thanking him, Etty followed him around the blast wall. Her sausage roll hairstyle had become undone and wisps of hair fell about her face.

Covered in grime, she had a blood-soaked knee where she'd fallen down.

She stood in a crowded, dimly lit passageway, craning her neck to see if she could find Billy or Bertha but she couldn't spot either of them. People sat on seats that tilted from walls or on blankets in groups on the ground. The air, thick and foul, had a nauseating stench to it. The noise was incredible and further along the passageway an accordionist accompanied those folks who sang, half-heartedly, Gracie Fields's hit song, 'Wish me luck'.

It was cold and draughty in the shelter and Etty wished she'd had time to retrieve her outdoor coat before fleeing the cinema. Images of Bertha's terrified face as she was swept along by the throng at the cinema played in her mind's eye. Etty prayed her friend made it safely to the air raid shelter.

She picked her way around the bodies into the adjoining passageway, hoping it would provide space for her to sit down. Here, a similar scene met her eyes. People sat on the ground in groups while a baby in a siren suit slept in ignorant bliss in its mother's arms. Everyone appeared to know each other, which, because of the recent air raids, was hardly surprising. To keep her spirits up, Etty would have liked to sit and gossip but feeling very much an outsider, she moved along.

A sharp-featured old woman wearing metal-framed glasses sat on a blanket made out of colourful squares.

She looked up as Etty passed. 'Eee, hinny.' Her eyes were scandalised. 'I don't know what the world's coming to, just look…' she nodded to a few yards ahead, where two bodies writhed beneath a blanket on the ground. As she realised what the couple were up to, Etty's cheeks flushed and she averted her eyes.

Thuds came again from outside, faraway at first – then closer. As aeroplanes screamed overhead, Etty's mouth went dry and she clutched her chest. The ear-splitting explosion, when it hit outside, filled the passageway with dust and smoke.

'I want me man,' the old woman, dazed and dusty on the floor, cried.

Etty dropped to her knees. With a calm she didn't feel, she tried to pacify her. 'Don't be afraid. It'll be over soon.' Her words seemed to do the trick and the woman gave a weak smile.

At that moment, with all the dust in the air, Etty sneezed, a huge sneeze that threatened to burst her eardrums, and when she opened her eyes, a soldier towered over her.

Her eyes travelled up to his face.

'Billy.'

Relief shone from his eyes. 'Thank God you're safe, I've searched everywhere for you.'

His eyes over-bright, he bent, taking Etty by the elbow and helping her up. As she sagged against the coarse material of his uniform, the warmth exuding from him comforted her and it felt good to have someone who cared.

Here, in this overcrowded place, you could smell the fear, and though people put on a brave face, there was dread in their eyes – the terror that the end was nigh. Etty felt it too, but there was nothing she could do, no place to hide, no prayer to protect herself.

The guns were at it again, and the shrieks from planes overhead were deafening. Bombs dropped, intermittently, in the market-place, lights flickered, and the shelter walls shook, threatening to collapse. Jumpy and jittery, the urge to flee overwhelmed Etty.

A steadying hand came on her shoulder. Billy said in her ear, 'Bonny lass, I'll find us a seat.'

At the suggestion they should sit and wait it out to die, hysteria overwhelmed Etty and, inhaling deeply, she fought the urge to laugh. If she was about to be blown to kingdom come, she wanted these last moments on earth to count.

There was a lull overhead as aeroplanes receded into the distance. Etty knelt down beside the old woman, who stared blankly into space.

'Come with us,' she said, indicating Billy with a nod, 'we're moving further along the shelter.'

The woman gave a wizened smile. 'I can't, hinny. I have to stay here in me place.'

'How d'you mean?'

'This is where me and me husband sit.'

'Where is he, then?'

'I divvent knaa… they say they never found his body.'

Etty's spine went cold.

Apart from moving the woman forcibly there was nothing she could do. 'Don't you want company?' she asked.

The woman shrugged. 'Truth to tell, I'd welcome if I did cop it. It's lonely without me old man. We've no family, you see. Now, you toddle off with that nice young chap of yours and leave me in peace.'

This sort of thing happened when you lost someone you loved. It must be easier if they died, rather than just… disappearing without trace, never to be heard from again.

Billy placed his hands on her shoulders and guided her through the throng.

The raiders were back – only this time, it was as if Hitler himself had sent his entire air force to bomb South Shields' marketplace. As engines roared overhead, attempts at conversation proved impossible.

Billy steered her along the next passageway, then the next, where there were metal-framed bunk beds set against the walls. A young couple holding hands sat on the top of the first one while the bottom bunk, Etty noticed, was vacant.

A ghastly wailing noise came from outside and for a second the world stood heart-stoppingly still. The blast, when it came, shook the shelter, and the lights went out. An eerie silence followed, during which all Etty could think was that she was lucky to be alive.

She couldn't feel Billy's hands upon her and, groping her way forward, she made her way to one of the empty bunk beds, sitting down on the lower one. The metal springs sagged as Billy sat next to her. Relief flooded her that she wasn't alone.

Wave after wave of aeroplanes roared overhead. Etty couldn't see the walls but she imagined them, tons of concrete that, if hit, would come toppling down, crushing them all. She shuddered. She thought of the others, the young couple, the old lady. Billy and Bertha. Etty thought of her friend's kids at home worrying themselves sick about their mother.

Etty's prayer was simple. *Please God see us all safely through this night.*

When Billy's fingertips brushed her hair back from her brow with the lightest of touches, Etty realised with shock that his hand shook. This seemed so far from his usual bravado, Etty's heart melted. A finger tilted her chin upwards and his lips finding hers, Billy kissed her – a sweet kiss that she was helpless to do anything about and which tasted of dusty shelter.

As they broke loose, the raiders droned into the distance.

'For a split second I forgot where I was,' she whispered in his ear.

'Aye, it did me the power of good an' all. Can I do it again?'

'If you want.'

'I'm… engaged, remember.'

A jocular note was in his tone, but a hint of seriousness too.

'It's only a kiss, Billy.'

'But it depends.'

'On what?'

'On who you're kissing and what happens next.'

'It feels as if we're immune from life down here.'

He sighed. 'But we're not… life will go on after.'

'If we have an after.'

'True.'

Billy's groan was heartfelt. 'Part of me wishes I'd never met you.'

'That's not very nice.'

'You complicate life. I've always been able to love and leave a lass… but I know that's not going to be true of you.'

'Patter merchant.'

'I'd never kid about something as important as—'

'As what?'

'How I feel about you.'

An almighty crash came from overhead, as if a building had toppled down, and chunks of debris rained down upon them. Pushing her back on the bed, Billy covered her body with his. As she lay supine under his weight, the doubts came flooding back and, roughly, she pushed him off and sat up.

'You're not going to dupe me like that.'

'I was doing no such thing. I was trying to protect you.'

'Says you.'

'I don't know who it was hurt you so badly that you don't trust anybody but whoever he is... if I laid me hands on him I'd bash the living daylights out of him.'

He sounded like a bullyboy in the schoolyard and Etty laughed, a tinkling sound that surprised her. Here she was in the midst of destruction, with people cooped up like rats, a shelter that smelt bad enough to make you heave and kiddies who broke your heart crying out in the dark – and what was she doing? Laughing. She really had lost her grip on reality.

'It's good you can laugh...' Billy's voice was lighter. 'Many a lass would be sobbing her heart out.'

'I'm not any lass.'

'Don't I know it.'

He lit a match and, by its little flame, she saw his eyes smouldering in the darkness. The lasses at the factory, she decided, would call them 'come to bed' eyes.

As an exquisite pain rose in her groin, Etty weakened. Here, in this place where they might die, she wanted him to seduce her, but she was torn because in truth, he wasn't hers to have. But Billy hadn't taken an oath and this might be her last moment on earth, the voice of temptation told her, and against her better instincts Etty pushed all caution aside.

'I want us to make love,' she whispered, voice tremoring. She felt like a wanton hussy but she wasn't party to breaking marriage vows, she reminded herself. And this might be her last chance.

Silence.

Then Billy's husky voice. 'What about af—'

She placed a forefinger over his lips. 'Forget about after. There mightn't be an after.'

Billy drew on his cigarette and blew out the smoke. 'What about that boyfriend of yours?'

'We've finished,' she told him and was surprised at the twinge of regret she felt.

'So, it's just a case of trying it out in case you don't make it?'

'This isn't a time for jokes.'

'Who's joking? There's worse we could do.'

'Billy, I'm ignorant, I don't know—'

'So, you think I do?'

'I've got my suspicions, Billy Buckley.'

'Ah… so it's my experience you're after?'

The red glow from his cigarette fell to the ground, and Billy stubbed the end with his boot.

He took her gently by the shoulders, and in the darkness his lips found hers. Unsure what to do, she raked her fingers through his cropped hair, like she'd seen at the pictures. Yet this was no film; the passion that burned within her was real enough. Billy's kisses grew more demanding and hurt her lips but she didn't pull away. He laid her gently back on the bunk bed and, as the metal springs creaked beneath their weight, she stared into the darkness over his shoulder, every nerve in her being craving more. The thought that someone could see them plagued her mind but in the impenetrable darkness she knew they were hidden.

Then, in the passion of the moment all thought, save Billy's roving hands, was forgotten.

With patience she didn't know he possessed, Billy undid the little pearl buttons of her blouse and, slipping his roughened hand inside, found her breast. His tongue licked her ear and the side of her neck, each touch imparting a little electric shock.

'Are you sure?' he whispered in her ear.

'Yes.'

*

She drifted back to a dark and horrifying world, where the smell of burning prevailed. It took a moment to realise that the noise outside, growing louder by the second, was that of enemy aircraft as they crossed the marketplace.

'Billy!' she cried out.

In the pitch black she reached out for Billy's hand. He stood by the bunk bed doing up the buttons on his trousers and squeezed her hand.

As she lay, skirt up around her hips, reality hit Etty. Disgusted, she couldn't believe what she'd just done. Then, as a sweet ache of pleasure surged her groin, she dismissed her feelings and accepted that what had just taken place was the most wonderful thing.

That moment, bombs screamed overhead, and instinctively, Etty looked up to the ceiling and held her breath. An ear-splitting explosion followed. In the silence, an eternity passed, when Etty grieved for all that might have been – and strangely, felt too a calm acceptance of whatever would be.

'Mammy!' A toddler screamed from along the passageway.

Unexpectedly, Etty's bed collapsed and she sailed through the air to land with a painful thump. The last thing she remembered was her head cracking against a rock-hard surface.

She swam up from a pit of nothingness and opened her eyes to inky blackness. Her head ached, debris pinned her down and she could taste grittiness. It took time before she realised that all around her was deathly quiet.

She wondered how long she'd lain unconscious – minutes, hours – she had no idea. Tentatively, she moved her arms and legs. Miraculously, she appeared to have escaped unharmed. Shakily, she stood up, the debris falling from her.

'Blimey, that was a close call,' said a woman's wobbly voice.

There was the sound of someone moving through rubble. The same voice cried, 'My God, somebody help! Bill – me husband – he's not moving!'

'I'm sorry I can't see anything,' Etty told the woman in a shaky voice. 'I'll try and get help.'

She stood in the dark and brushed herself down. With the cloying heat and incinerating smell, this must be what hell was like. As she stood on legs that felt as if they'd had the bones removed, a headache pounded and her biggest fear took over – that the walls might cave in. She needed to get out.

Then she remembered Billy. She'd no way of knowing where he was or if he'd survived or not. She dithered, her muddled mind trying to decide what to do. It was best if she pushed on and found help for those that needed it.

Voices called out plaintively in the dark, but Etty could do nothing to help them. Stumbling over rubble, she made for what she hoped was the shelter's entrance. She bumped into others, intent on the same thing and, groping her way along the passageway, found the entrance, only to discover it had taken a direct hit and was impassable. Trapped in the hellhole, Etty, with the other survivors, dug out the earth with bare hands to be free.

When she touched an exposed shoulder, belonging to a lifeless form, Etty let out a scream. A hand came out of the darkness and slapped her hard across her face, the shock bringing her to her senses.

Then the 'all clear' wailed.

It took hours for the rescue team to reach them and Etty was one of the last. Her skin caked in dust, her hair soaked in sweat, she reached through the hole where strong arms pulled her out. Thankful for being saved, she breathed in the acrid air. But the world now seemed a more frightening place, and even the moon, soaring high in a clear sky, appeared to have a malevolent face. She then noticed fires raging around the marketplace, the area glowing a terrifying orange.

Disorientated, Etty gazed around. As far as the eye could see there was bomb damage. With a race of adrenalin, she thought of Dorothy. Was she safe?

A fireman wrapped a blanket around her.

'Is the bomb damage concentrated in this area? I've a sister, you see, who lives in the Westoe area.'

'Steady on, hinny.' He took by the arm. 'Chances are your sister's fine and dandy and worrying about you. Let's go and get you a cuppa, shall we?'

He escorted her to a mobile canteen, behind a cordoned off area, where Etty was given a tin mug of hot, sweet tea.

'You're a lucky lass,' the fireman took off his helmet and wiping his sweaty brow with the back of his arm, rolled his eyes. 'Some folk didn't make it.' He nodded to a few yards further away, where bodies lay on the ground covered with blankets. Etty shuddered. She thought of the lifeless form she'd touched in the shelter and wished she'd said a prayer. Then, thoughts all over the place, she hoped Dorothy wasn't frantic about her safety.

Her gaze turned to the marketplace and the scene of utter destruction. Shops were reduced to rubble, and not a pane of glass was left in St Hilda's church. The fire had spread to Crofton's draper store at the corner of King Street and the Grapes Hotel looked dangerously close to falling down. As fires raged and flames leapt against the backdrop of the night sky, firemen fought valiantly to bring them under control.

But it was the tram, lying buckled and destroyed on the pavement, that Etty found most poignant, and which brought tears to her eyes. She once again felt like the little girl being taken to a strange place by her mother, filled with panic and anxiety, all over again. And for an instant, Etty could swear she smelled Mam's fragrant perfume.

Then acrid smoke filled her nostrils. She was one of the lucky ones, she reminded herself, but the fact didn't help her. She felt only guilt that she'd survived when others hadn't.

The fireman, his face blackened, looked done in. He crinkled a smile. 'I'm glad you're all reet, Miss.'

Etty thanked him and, handing him the blanket, began searching the huddles of people for Billy. She prayed he wasn't back in the shelter buried in the rubble.

'Move along,' a policeman appeared and told the stricken folk. 'You can do no good here. Miss, away with you, home,' he said, as he spotted Etty.

He was a fresh-faced, decent-looking bloke. Etty wondered what he'd think if he knew what she'd done back in the shelter. Revulsion washed over her. A common slut – that's what he'd think, and he would be right. Her mind reeled. What about May? The lass didn't deserve this. Etty despised herself; she'd let everyone down. How could she face people again? Panicked, a new thought terrorised her. What if Billy crowed to his mates back at the barracks? She shivered at the thought.

Taking a steadying intake of breath, she reminded herself that she was in shock, out of control. Billy had good cause to keep quiet about this night. Besides, he had professed to love her. Why would he want to hurt her?

'What's the matter, Miss?' the policeman asked. 'You look shaken.'

'I'm fine, thank you,' Etty replied, rather than tell him the truth – that she wished she could start the day over again.

CHAPTER FIFTEEN

October 1941

Etty couldn't ask May if Billy had survived or not because she thought her fiancé was back at the barracks that night, where he belonged. She had no choice but to resist the urge to sound the alarm, for why stir up a hornet's nest if there was no need? Nervous and jittery, she did what she always did on fraught occasions – she ate everything in sight until she felt sick.

On the sixth day after the bombings, Dorothy, a perplexed frown furrowing her brow, said, 'I've seen it before, you're still in shock.'

She stood at the kitchen table making pastry for Woolton pie, a dish named after the Minister of Food that consisted of a mixture of potatoes, parsnips and herbs.

She brushed back her hair with a floury hand while tears welled in her eyes. 'I never want to go through a night like that again. I was sick with worry about you.'

Etty's memories, of running through rubble-filled streets, bombs crashing overhead, were like reliving snippets of a nightmare. She couldn't forget the acrid smell that hung over the town, the burnt-out buildings, the firemen, their hoses spewing water on raging fires.

A hulk of a man, silhouetted against the night sky, had waved a red lamp in the middle of the road, warning of danger ahead.

As she approached, he told Etty, 'Careful Hinny, this road's blocked. Queen Street took a hit and there's a crater filled with water from a fractured main. Fall down that and you'll never see the light of day again.'

An ambulance, its bell ringing, crawled out of the darkness. The man flagged it down and shouted to the driver, 'Got a lassie here needs assistance.'

'I'm fine,' Etty insisted.

The exhausted-looking ambulance man didn't argue the point. 'Where d'you live?'

She told him.

'Hop in,' he said. 'It's on me way to the infirmary.'

Etty couldn't recall the journey home, or thanking the driver; all she could remember was Dorothy's face crumpling when she opened the front door.

Now, as Dorothy rolled out pastry, her face creased in concern.

'It's natural you haven't recovered,' she said, 'not properly. Buried in that shelter not knowing if you were going to live or die. I do wish you would take some time off work, Etty.'

'I'm fine, honestly. The last thing I need is to be sitting at home, mulling things over.'

Etty resolved to buck up. The raid had left many dead and hundreds homeless – she was one of the lucky ones. If Billy were dead then he would have died a happy man. Her hands flew to her cheeks. She must be in shock, she thought, if she could be so composed about Billy's demise.

It turned out in fact that Billy had survived. Etty received a letter from him two days later. Picking up the post from the doormat, she recognised the sprawling handwriting on the envelope addressed to her. Hands trembling, she tore open the envelope as she made her way back along the passage and into the kitchen. Dorothy, on the late shift, was having a lie-in. Still in her dressing gown, Etty settled on the couch and began to read, her heart thumping.

Bonny lass,

Thank God you're all right! We had a close call, didn't we? May wrote and told me about the bombing and about your 'terrifying experience'. When she said you'd survived I've never felt so relieved.

What a brave lass. I never got to give you a cuddle or tell you how good I felt after… you know. Don't rebuke yourself – what we did wasn't wrong because we were both keen and it was meant to happen. I won't forget that night and all for the right reasons.

For the record, I was knocked out cold in the shelter. Apparently, the rescue team got me out and I was taken by ambulance to the infirmary where I regained consciousness sometime during the night. I asked about you but no one knew anything. I was at my wits' end but could do nothing without drawing attention to the fact we were together. And neither of us wants that. Man, did I have a stinker of a headache the next day.

I'm hunky-dory now and wish I had photo of you. Trouble is I don't know when I'll get to see you. Everything's hush hush here and I don't know when I'll get leave.

Minx, I can't get you out of my mind. Bloody war! I want to see you again. I'm thrilled I met you and go around with this idiotic smile.

What are we going to do, eh? It'll all have to wait. Can you wait? You must.

I promise I'll sort things out. I'm pining for you, kiddo.
Write to me,
Love,
Billy

Etty sat staring into space for a long while. Then, slowly, deliberately, her fingers betraying her pain, she ripped the letter into small pieces and threw them into the fire. Watching them burn, she gave a yearning sigh. If only, she thought, she could have a dalliance without care – but she knew she couldn't. Since the night of the bombing she'd thought about Billy every single day. Despite the fact that she ached for him, Etty couldn't cross the line of breaking up a relationship. Guilt tormented her, yet like a recurring dream, the scenes spent in the shelter with Billy wouldn't go away.

In disbelief at what she was doing, Etty wrote a brief letter. She told Billy it was over between them and he must never try to see her again.

*

Early one morning, nine days after the terrible bombing of Shields marketplace, Trevor nipped over to the corner shop for his ration of tea.

'Poor lass,' Mrs Moffatt, the owner of the shop, was saying to a customer at the front of a waiting queue. 'She was trapped in the marketplace shelter after them bombings.'

'Who d'you say it was?' the customer asked.

Mrs Moffatt measured a ration of sugar into a blue bag. 'Etty Makepeace… from across the road.'

'And was she saved?'

'Aye. She was one of the lucky ones.' Mrs Moffatt handed over the bag of sugar.

As though someone had thumped him in the gut, the wind went out of Trevor. Racing from the shop and over the road, he stood uncertainly outside Etty's front door. He ached to see her but feared her reaction.

God, how he'd missed her and how he'd berated himself for the mindless anger that had caused him to hurl such hurtful words. She, too, had said her share of unkind things but on reflection, it had been two wilfully stubborn people having a lovers' tiff. Now especially, having heard of her ordeal, it was the time to forget foolish pride and patch things up.

As he raised his hand to the knocker, Trevor was startled to see the door swing open and Etty's sister standing on the front step.

'Oh, hello, Trevor... how lovely to see you. You've come to see Etty, have you?'

'How is she?'

'To be honest, not as good as she thinks.' Dorothy's brow was furrowed. She stepped down onto the pavement. 'I'm so glad you called. I've to go to work and I loathe leaving Etty on her own. It's her day off and she's got too much time to think.' She touched his arm, looked knowingly at him. 'Go on in, she needs a friend right now.'

Etty sat on the couch staring into space as was her wont these days. Her emotions dulled, she felt neither pleasure nor pain and kept reliving those hours in the shelter when the drone of enemy planes thundered overhead. In those snatched moments, under the cloak of darkness, she had really thought she was going to die and selfishly hadn't thought of the consequences. Now, her conscience wouldn't let her forget.

Hearing footsteps along the passageway, and the kitchen door opening, she turned.

'Dorothy, what have—'

Trevor stood there, his sparkling green eyes observing her with a concerned expression.

'Dorothy said to come in.'

Etty smiled. He sounded like a school kid, unsure if he'd be scolded or not.

She regarded his familiar features, his broad shoulders, his air of solid dependability – so different from Billy – and she found she was glad he was here. A warm glow radiated within her, though the loathsome words she'd flung at him rang in her ears and she too felt unsure.

'It's good to see you.'

His face relaxed.

How could she be in love with two men? Etty thought, two men as different as chalk and cheese.

'Look here, I want to apologise for—'

Guilt pulsed through her. 'Don't, Trevor... we both said foul things that night we regret.'

He nodded and came to sit beside her on the couch. His familiar masculine odour masked the smoky smell from the fire. She inhaled deeply.

'How are you really?'

She wanted to confide in him, to tell him how terrified she'd been in the shelter but how could she with the secret she harboured?

'I'm doing fine... I'm back at work.' She kept her voice light.

'You don't fool me.' He placed his arm around her. 'Etty, you can't wish an experience like that away. It takes time.'

It felt good to be with him. She let herself sink into his embrace, resting her head on his shoulder.

'Can we start all over again?' he asked.

She sat bolt upright. 'Trevor, I'm not the person you think. I've done something...'

He tilted her chin and gave her a lingering kiss. So much for not being romantic, Etty inwardly thought.

When she surfaced, he pulled away, smiling tenderly. 'What's done is done,' he said, silencing her. 'It's what we do now that counts.'

A voice in Etty's head nagged that she was being unfair to Trevor, but she couldn't help wanting a second chance.

She nodded, forcing a smile.

Seven weeks passed. It was dinner time and, as Etty stood in the queue, the smell of food wafting from behind the counter nauseated her.

Choosing only mashed potato and peas with a bit of gravy, she found a seat at a long table with the rest of the company from the machine room. She tried to follow the conversation, but her grasshopper mind of late kept leaping from one disturbing thought to another. Scenes from her terrible ordeal flashed through her mind's eye – the screams of planes, the awful smells, the cries for help, the row of lifeless bodies beneath blankets. She felt so weary all the time, as though she suffered from some debilitating illness. She thought fondly of Trevor who was always there to help her through, caring for her like an invalid.

To add to her distress, she kept daydreaming about the experience she'd had with Billy. Something had awakened within her and she couldn't go back to being the innocent girl she once was. But she was normal, Etty realised with relief. She had amorous feelings and she wasn't a product of Blakely after all.

Then, there was the guilt that she was living a lie. Etty could hardly look at herself in the mirror. When she did stare at the haunted white face, overwhelmed with shame, Etty was stricken by how deceitful she was being.

Now, as she sat at the table, trying to eat a morsel of food, the band of her skirt digging into her waist, she was overcome by nerves. She sniffed and told herself to buck up. If what she suspected was true then she'd only got what she deserved.

The sight of May Robinson appearing, wearing an apron and a white cap covering her hair, only served to heighten Etty's guilt.

May began clearing the dirty dishes from the table.

'You haven't finished your dinner.' She stared with concern at Etty 'Are you all right?'

Etty coloured. 'I've got a stomach upset and I only fancy certain foods.'

'You should stay off work for a couple of days.' May scraped the remains off the plate with a look that suggested she would quite like to eat it herself.

Without thought, Etty blurted, 'Any word from Billy?'

A look of pleasure crossed May's face, and she balanced her tray on the back of Etty's chair.

'Not for a bit. Last time he wrote he said he was bored. He wishes his battalion would move on. What a fella… always on the lookout for excitement.' She shook her head in mock exasperation.

Regarding May, the innocent she was, Etty hated the deceiver she'd become.

Still, she couldn't resist asking the question, 'He's not been sent abroad, then?'

May blanched. 'No. Might he be?'

'I don't know… I mean, I just wondered.'

May brightened. 'What a fright you gave us. I thought you knew something I didn't. Tell you what, though, he's so canny. Since the bombings, he keeps asking after you.'

'That's… good of him.'

'I'll tell him we chatted.'

'I'd rather you didn't.'

'Oh!' May went pink as though she'd done something wrong.

The song, 'We'll Meet Again' blared from the canteen loud-speakers like an omen.

Bertha watched on from the other side of the table and gave Etty the blackest of looks. Etty squirmed uneasily. Bertha never mentioned the night of the bombing, but she'd been reserved with Etty, as if she was sizing her up ever since. Etty was upset because she valued the older woman's friendship but she never dared bring the subject up.

'There's no harm in my Billy, you know,' May's expression was anxious. 'He's a friendly lad… as friendly as they come.'

Didn't Etty know it.

*

Later, at home, Dorothy remarked, 'I still haven't heard from Laurie. I bet a bunch of letters arrives together next week. Honestly, talk about feast or famine.'

Her hair was pulled back with clips, black smudges from black-leading the fireplace marked her face like war paint, and she smelt of lavender polish. The furniture in the kitchen gleamed from all her hard work.

She didn't fool Etty, though, who knew her sister's need to keep busy when she hadn't heard from her husband in a long while.

Etty shrugged out of her outdoor coat and slung it over a chair. 'You should have left me something to do.'

'I did. I've changed the beds and there's a mountain of washing in the basket. I do mean to wash my undies out every day but I'm whacked after work.' Dorothy shook her head. 'How your friend Bertha manages to work and run a family, I'll never know.'

A picture of Bertha's disapproving face flashed in Etty's mind. 'Dorothy…'

'Uh huh.'

'I'm… pregnant.'

There was moment of silence during which Etty could swear she heard her heart beating.

Dorothy's eyes brimmed with compassion. 'You're sure?'

'I thought you'd be shocked.'

'Not shocked… more surprised. How long have you known?'

'I've sort of wondered for a while. It's been two months now since… you know. And I feel dreadfully queasy most mornings.'

'Ahh! That's why you skipped breakfast. Poor you… carrying the worry alone. Why didn't you tell me?'

'I was ashamed.'

'Nothing you ever do, Etty, would make me lose respect for you.'

Nothing? Etty winced.

In these parts, a child born out of wedlock was tantamount to mortal sin. Folk weren't apt to forgive or forget, and Dorothy would be tainted with the same brush as her sister.

Etty's eyes blurred. 'I knew I could count on you.'

'I should think so too. Have you seen Doctor Meredith?'

Etty shook her head.

'Then I insist that you do. Have you told Trevor yet?'

'He…' The urge to tell Dorothy the whole sordid mess overwhelmed Etty, but how could she confess to such an act with May's fiancé? 'No. Not yet.'

'If I may ask… are you two planning to marry?'

'Trevor has suggested we get engaged.' At least that wasn't a lie.

She hadn't yet had the courage to tell Trevor he wouldn't want her now she was used goods.

'Etty, I know Laurie will agree when I say this. I'll stand by you, whatever you decide.'

A rush of emotion engulfed Etty and she was so choked she couldn't speak. All she knew was that when God gave her Mam as a parent she was short-changed, but by giving her Dorothy as a sister, he'd more than made up for his mistake.

Thinking about what they'd been through together – Mam abandoning them, the ordeal of Blakely – how could she not tell Dorothy the truth? They were a team and had never kept anything from each other. Etty wouldn't start now or she'd never be able to look her sister in the eye again.

'Dorothy I…' A hard ball of anxiety in her stomach, she blurted, 'The baby isn't Trevor's.'

Dorothy stared open-mouthed. She recovered and asked, 'I don't understand… then whose baby is it?'

'Billy Buckley's.'

'May's fiancé?'

Etty would rather have crawled through a den of snakes than been responsible for the look of horror she saw register on her sister's face.

'Yes.'

'How…'

'The night of the October bombing.'

'Does anyone else know? Does Bill—'

'No one knows.'

Dorothy lapsed into a frowning, thoughtful silence.

Eventually, she spoke. 'I think we should keep it that way for the baby's sake – and all our sakes.'

Etty gave a weak smile. Trust Dorothy to consider this problem as hers too.

'But Etty, I must insist that if you accept Trevor's proposal you have a duty to tell him about the baby.'

Etty gulped.

The couple walked in inky blackness down Whale Street. Trevor, carrying a torch, pointed it down towards the pavement, its beam covered with tissue paper in accordance with regulations. Etty kept well away from the kerb because, although kerbstones were painted white, luckless pedestrians were known to trip and land in the main road. As she groped to link arms with him, she was reminded of the childhood game of blind man's bluff.

More confident now that she'd confided in Dorothy, Etty steeled herself to be truthful with Trevor. Yet she was nervous because he didn't deserve to be treated so shoddily. None of this was his fault and Etty was ashamed of the heartache she'd cause. And besides, over these last weeks their courtship had spiralled into something special. Trevor, on more than one occasion, had hinted at something long-lasting.

'Who's organising this dance we're going to?' he asked.

'The Home Guard. One of the lasses at work invited us. But Trevor, we need to talk first.'

'Yes, I agree. I've got something for you.'

'Why the secrecy?'

'I wanted to wait till you were fully recovered.'

He appeared jubilant and Etty was loath to spoil his mood. She wanted this meeting over and considered it best to tell him in the dark when she couldn't see his reaction. She'd be unable to bear it.

'I think we should break it off,' she gabbled, her heart pounding in the black of night.

Silence.

Then, 'Who is he?'

'Pardon me?'

'The bloke you're carrying on with.'

Her heart sank; there was no use in trying to pretend. 'It's not because of him. Anyway, it's over.'

'Pull the other one.'

'It's true.'

'If that's the truth, why do we have to finish?'

Why not tell him? He'd find out anyway.

Etty swallowed hard. 'I… I'm going to have a baby.'

'What? Is this some kind of joke?'

'It was one of those things… a one-night affair that happens in war.' Her voice tremored as she uttered the truth.

'Is that supposed to make me feel better?'

She'd done wrong and Trevor deserved an apology but what words would be enough? She didn't know how she would ever make it up to him.

'Trevor, I'm so sorry. I didn't intend to hurt—'

'Do I know him?' he interrupted.

'I'm being as honest as I can but please… don't ask me to tell you his name.'

He grabbed her by the arm.

'Trevor let go… you're hurting me.'

'I feel like strangling yi.'

'You can't make me feel worse than I already do.' She imagined his handsome face clouded with betrayal and it was difficult to go on, but she'd made up her mind to be forthright. 'You can walk away and there'll be no hard feelings.'

'You didn't imagine I'd stay, did you?'

With a flash of insight, Etty realised that deep down she'd clung to the hope that, against all odds, he'd look past her transgression and be her saviour.

'Trevor, I am very fond of you…' she heard herself say. 'I would very much like for us to marry and not just because of the baby.'

He let out a gasp.

'Please hear me out… I do want a home of my own. And by your own admission, you want to be independent of your mam. We could make a go of it. A contract, if you like. I'll cook and keep house and, for your part, all I ask is that you give the baby a name. And Trevor, there's no hard feelings if the answer is no.'

'Of course the answer is no.'

Footsteps stomped away. Etty didn't realise she'd been standing so rigid until a pain stabbed the side of her neck. Resigned now to the fact that the life inside her would be born a bastard, Etty straightened her spine and made to move down the street, tears pricking her eyes.

She heard footsteps approaching. Etty's heart hammered in her chest.

'You do know you've spoiled everything.'

'Yes. I'm sorry, really I am—'

'But I respect,' his voice changed, becoming conciliatory, 'that you could have married us without saying anything about the bairn.'

'I'd never stoop to such trickery.'

A pause.

'It's definitely over with… him?'

'Absolutely.' Shame and regret burned inside Etty.

There was ruffling noise, and then he took her hand and placed what felt like a little velvet box in it.

'I'll marry you,' he said, 'but I have a condition. On reflection, make that two. As far as anyone's concerned, the bairn you carry is mine. And we'll never speak of it again.'

'I wouldn't have it any other way. The other condition?'

A pause. 'You be the one to tell Ma we're going to wed.'

Etty despaired at Trevor's reluctance to cross his mother. He still hadn't introduced the pair of them and Etty wondered at his reticence.

'Agreed, but I also have a condition. Can we marry as quickly as possible?' She didn't want folk doing the sums.

A pause.

'Good idea. We don't want Ma suspicious about dates.'

Etty inwardly groaned. Mistress Knowles was turning out to be right, she was making a mess of her life.

*

'Man, is this shift never ganna end?'

The male voice came from Trevor's right. He swivelled his head and as he peered into the gloom, the lamp attached to his hard hat shed a pool of light in the dark tunnel.

Trevor worked as a filler at the coalface in a four-foot-high tunnel as black as night. Knees protected by leather pads, he shovelled lumps of coal onto a conveyor belt that ran behind him. The atmosphere was humid, sweat trickled from every pore and, in an attempt to keep the filthy air from reaching his lungs, he kept his mouth clamped firmly shut and breathed through his nose.

He didn't acknowledge the pitman who spoke, only grunting a reply.

'Right, lads,' the deputy hollered, 'everybody out.'

Trevor downed his shovel and, as he wiped his brow with a forearm, a rank smell of sweat wafted from his armpits. He wrinkled his nose in disgust.

Even if the work was classified as a reserved occupation, keeping him out of the war, Trevor hated the job. Not that he would have bleated if he had been called up. He would have gone all right, to do his bit, but killing his fellow man was something he would rather not do, given the chance.

Crawling on all fours, he followed the pitman in front, the beam from the lamp on Trevor's helmet showing the way through a forest of pit props that secured a rock-solid roof. He then walked along the mothergate where the coal, gleaming like black gems was spilled from a conveyer belt through a hopper and into four-wheeled tubs. He made his way into the main throughway and straddled the railway line, ever conscious that tubs ferrying coal might hurtle by.

The studs on his boots made a racket on the stone ground as he trailed behind the rest of the men, though he heard their voices echoing along the tunnel.

A boyish voice piped up, 'If I had me way, I'd be in Africa with the troops.'

'By, that would terrify Jerry,' a gruff voice said.

Great guffaws bounced off the walls.

'Me da says that's where the action is.' The young voice sounded peeved.

'Lad, had yer tongue. You're just oot o' nappies.'

As the men rounded a bend in the tunnel, the voices receded.

Noticing the steel rope beneath his boots vibrating, Trevor dived for cover in a refuge hole dug in the wall and waited. The air changed, becoming intensified, and then tubs of coal, hauled by steel rope, thundered past. In the eerie silence that followed, Trevor emerged from his cover and made for the mineshaft.

His thoughts returned to yesterday's conversation with Etty and how his guts had twisted when she'd told him she was expecting. What a shocker that was. What surprised him was the anger – no, the *jealousy* he'd felt when Etty confessed she'd been with another man. Trevor loved her and had scarcely been able to wait for the time they made love and… damn it… he wanted to be her one and only. He could never express how deeply he felt because words of love didn't come easily to him and besides, what man in his right mind confesses to such emotions?

Now, Etty had bloody well gone and spoiled it all.

Trevor would give his eyeteeth to know who this mysterious fella was. Where had they met? Was he a workmate? All Trevor knew was he'd knock the fella to kingdom come if he ever clapped eyes on him.

As anger had turned into disbelief, Trevor had calmed down. Etty was a lot of things but not a liar and in his heart he believed that it had been a one-night affair. He'd heard tales of folk driven over the rim, behaving out of sorts in this mad war. The realisation hit him, that if he and Etty were to have a future, he'd have to put this business behind him.

Trevor came to an air lock and, passing through, his lanky frame was able to walk upright. At the final bend, he swung round the beam, polished smooth by a generation of hands before him. At the mineshaft, he sat on a bench and waited for the cage. His mind foggy with lack of sleep, reality slipped away and he saw scenes in his mind's eye, like a play: Etty, head thrown back, laughing hysterically at something funny at the flicks; her voluptuous figure as they glided across the dance floor; how her chin jutted when she wanted her own way.

He rubbed his tired eyes and acknowledged that he saw through her game. She was in the family way and desperate for a husband and he – silly bugger – was happy to oblige. He cradled his chin in his hands. He found himself doubting her feelings for him but if this was the only way he could marry her, then so be it; he might never get a second chance. Despite everything, that was what he wanted. He would stand by her because one thing he knew was that Etty, proud and spirited, was the girl for him. If she carried another man's child then, so be it.

The cage came down the mineshaft, its metal doors rattling open, rousing him from his reverie. Trevor filed with the rest of the men into the cage and, squeezing between two mucky-faced workmates, he kept his counsel. A series of bells clanged and with a jolt, the cage made its rapid ascent.

Aye, Trevor thought as he hurtled upwards, the time was ripe for him to be free of his ma. She'd brought him up alone and Trevor was all she had. But she had a tongue on her, and Trevor knew he was weak where she was concerned. Etty, spunky lass that she was, was a good match for his mother. She was a good match for him too – where he was headed, he would need a classy wife like Etty, with her posh speech and ladylike ways. He wanted more than to be working down the pit for the rest of his life.

The cage reached the pithead and shuddered to a halt. Emerging into the bright November sunshine, Trevor vowed he'd be a good provider for Etty. No man worth his salt would want a working wife – he'd be a laughing stock of the community.

CHAPTER SIXTEEN

Etty stood at the foot of the sloping stairs and rapped on Mrs Milne's back door, as a gale-force wind howled down the lane.

Hair blowing wildly around her face, she smoothed it back with a hand. Nervous about meeting her future mother-in-law, Etty wanted to make a good first impression and had rehearsed what she was going to say.

As it was such a chilly day, she wore an Aran cardigan that Dorothy had knitted from yarn she'd unpicked from an old sweater of Laurie's. The board of trade had issued a leaflet telling everyone to 'make do and mend', and, ever resourceful, Dorothy had complied with the rules.

Her mouth dry, Etty rattled the latch and, finding the door unlocked, poked her head inside, peering up into the gloomy stairwell.

'Hello,' she called, 'anyone in?'

'Come up whoever you are… me legs are bad,' a wheezy voice called down the stairwell.

'It's me, Mrs Milne… Etty Makepeace.'

She climbed the creaking stairs towards the chink of light on the top landing. As she reached the top stair, an overpowering stench of fish turned her stomach.

A face peered around the door, a face furrowed with wrinkles.

'Are you the trollop that's been pestering my Trevor?'

The door opened wide to reveal Nellie Milne, who stood in a pool of light. An inconceivably small person, whose pigeon-like legs looked too spindly to support her stout body, what the woman lacked in stature, she more than made up for with her air of dominance.

But Etty would not be intimidated. She had faced bigger monsters at Blakely.

She held out her hand. 'Esther Makepeace… Trevor's fiancée. Pleased to meet you, Mrs Milne.'

The whites of Nellie's eyes bulged like ice cream in a cornet. 'Haddaway with you. Trevor wouldn't marry the likes of you.' Her chest heaving, she cackled, 'It's wishful thinking, hinny, on your part.'

'I know the engagement has come as a shock—'

'My son would've told us if he was betrothed. Wait till I tell him about your scheming lies.'

Etty didn't want to make an enemy of the woman but neither would she be spoken to in this manner.

'It's all arranged. Trevor and I can't wait to marry. It's arranged for Wednesday next week, at the registry office.'

'You… conniving hussy.' Purple in the face, Nellie launched into a paroxysm of coughing. She coughed and coughed, clasping her throat as if she were about to choke to death.

'See…' she spluttered, 'what you've brought on… and me with a bad heart. Wait till I tell my Trevor.'

She started coughing again, this time retching. Etty, looking around the makeshift scullery on the landing, noted it housed only a sink and gas cooker, where a fish head was poaching in milk in a pan.

Moving past Nellie, the smell of unwashed flesh making her want to gag, she filled a chipped cup with cold water from the tap. She handed it to her future mother-in-law, who had stopped coughing and wiped her eyes on a pinafore.

'Away with you,' she croaked. 'You'll marry me son over me dead body.'

'The wedding is at eleven, Mrs Milne. Trevor and I will be delighted if you would attend.'

The next day, Etty opened the front door and was surprised to see Trevor standing there.

'Ma's furious.'

'I'm none too pleased myself,' Etty replied.

'She's taken to her bed.' He ran his fingers through his hair. 'I telt you she needed careful handling. She's an ill woman.' He pushed past her and strode along the passageway.

Ill indeed! Etty thought. She banged the front door shut and followed him into the kitchen.

Dorothy, relaxing on a chair listening to the wireless, looked up. Etty widened her eyes at her sister, warning her not to say a word.

'Ma says you were full of cheek.' Struggling out of his coat, he nodded curtly to Dorothy. He faced Etty. 'Her heart's bad and she doesn't need aggravation.'

'I just told her the truth.'

He wouldn't meet Etty's eye.

'Ma says she'll come to the wedding on one condition.'

'And that is?'

'We live in the flat below her.'

Dorothy rose and discreetly vanished through into the scullery, closing the door firmly behind her.

'That's blackmail,' Etty cried.

Trevor shrugged. 'Think on it Etty, where else are we going to live? Ma owns the pair of flats... she says she won't charge a big rent.'

This was true. Decent property was hard to come by, especially these days when houses were being blown to smithereens. The only alternative would be to live in with Dorothy and that wouldn't be fair on her, or them, for that matter.

Trevor went on. 'Ma says she'll have Mrs McVay out of the downstairs flat by next weekend.'

Appalled, Etty replied, 'I'm not having it on my conscience that some poor woman got evicted because of us.'

'Ma says Mrs McVay's old and frail and her daughter should look out for her.'

If Trevor said 'Ma says' once more Etty thought she would slosh him one. She didn't know what was wrong with her these days. Tired and irritable, the least thing upset her. Dorothy thought she suffered from pre-wedding nerves, which could be the case because, in truth, Etty wasn't ready to get married – not yet. In her turmoil she had a fleeting thought about Billy. If she were to marry him, would she feel the same way? In her present state, with all the provocation, she would like to call the whole thing off – but that wasn't an option. As an unmarried mother, she'd be shunned and worse, her baby would be classed as a social outcast – a bastard. A chill ran down Etty's spine. The child she carried might learn to hate her as much as she did her own mother.

'Tell your mam,' she resigned herself to her fate, 'she can treat herself to a new hat.' Trevor visibly relaxed and she was quick to make it clear: 'But mind, living below your mam is only a temporary measure, until we find a place of our own.'

'Aye, Etty, we'll save as much as we can.'

A glint of triumph in his eye, Trevor didn't look like a man who wanted to be free of his mam.

Sometimes, life simply rolled on and, like a boulder gathering momentum down a mountainside, you felt you didn't have any choice but to roll along with it. That's how Etty felt on her wedding day. It was a surreal day, when all she wanted was to hide beneath the bed sheets and tell everyone she was too young to be a wife, let alone a mam – as she didn't have the faintest idea about either role.

Yet, there was a tinge of excitement too, she couldn't deny it.

'I've lit the boiler in the washhouse so you can have a bath whenever you wish,' Dorothy told her, when she delivered tea in bed that morning. Still dark outside, Etty felt cocooned in her bedroom, her sanctuary ever since she'd left Blakely.

An hour later she was sitting in the tin bath in front of a roaring fire, with steaming water a couple of inches above the wartime regulation line.

'If you can't bend the rules on your wedding day, when else can you?' Dorothy laughed.

'The water's lovely and soft,' Etty called through as she leaned back against the towel, strategically placed on the tin bath's cold rim.

'I dissolved a lavender bath cube in the water before you got in,' Dorothy said.

'It's heavenly. Are you wanting in after me?'

'Just try and stop me.'

Etty closed her eyes and relaxed and, as she drifted, a letter she'd read in a woman's magazine popped into her mind. It had been written by a girl who described herself as a 'distraught brunette'.

The girl explained she was going to have a baby. Two fellows could be responsible, which at the time, Etty had raised her eyebrows at. Both men wanted to marry her, but she couldn't decide between them. The so-called expert replied that, as the girl obviously didn't love either of them, she should make a fresh start and strive to be a morally stronger person in future.

The sanctimonious tone angered Etty. What right had this person to advise when she was obviously biased? But in truth, what rankled were the words 'morally stronger'. It had touched a raw nerve. She'd done the honourable thing, though, by telling Trevor about the baby. She might be young, but experience had taught her that it was wisest to be honest – for in the end, you still have to live with yourself.

Later, as Etty stood eyeing her outfit in the long mirror in the bedroom, it occurred to her that, at heart, people were kind. Clothes were on the ration, and when the women at the factory had heard she was getting married, they'd chipped in with their coupons so she could wear a new outfit. Her hair was coiffed into a style that befitted her halo-rimmed hat and she wore a mushroom coloured crepe-de-chine skirt, with matching jacket and shoulder pads, feeling rather special in it. The shoes were new, the net gloves borrowed from Bertha (who'd become her friendly self again once she'd heard Etty's wedding plans) and the blue lace-edged handkerchief tucked in her pocket was old.

Ready and, with a flutter in her stomach, she called to Dorothy.

'You look… stunning,' Dorothy gasped when she entered the room. 'Except for one detail.' She pinned the pink carnation she carried onto the lapel of Etty's jacket.

She stood back and admired her sister. 'Perfect.'

The weather that December day was wet and drab and Etty, afraid she might end up with dirty splash marks on her calves, took extra special care when she walked outside to the waiting limousine, kindly provided by Mr Newman.

It was the type of car in which, when seated, you faced each other. The Newmans sat erect as they watched her approach the car. While Mr Newman's smile was warm and genuine, his wife looked as if she had attended under sufferance.

Mr Newman opened the car door and alighted. 'You look as pretty as a picture, my dear.'

Ramona Newman looked scathingly at Etty.

'Eee, Roland,' she shrieked. 'I think I'm overdressed.'

She was wearing a two-piece suit trimmed with astrakhan, a skunk stole draped around her neck and a jaunty quill in her hat. Etty refrained from telling her that she certainly was overdressed.

Climbing into the limousine, the smell of leather and mothballs suffused Etty's nostrils. Dorothy came next, followed by Mr Newman. This is it, Etty thought, as she settled back into the sumptuous seat that scrunched whenever she moved – my wedding day.

For no apparent reason, she thought of her mother and, absurdly, a lump came into her throat. Quick to regain composure, she banished her mother from her mind and turned her attention to Mr Newman.

'Have Trevor and his ma left yet?' she asked.

'Over ten minutes ago in this very car,' Mr Newman closed the limousine's door.

Around these parts, a wedding car was a source of wonderment and folk emerged to gawp.

Trevor told her, 'Ma says it's Mr Newman's way of thanks for all the help she's given the business over the years. He was adamant, she says, and Mr Newman isn't a man you offend.'

Etty couldn't see why not. Trevor, obviously in awe of the man, didn't want him vexed, but she had personally felt it was a step too far when he insisted the Newmans should attend the wedding. After all, they had agreed that only immediate family members should be invited.

Mr Newman rapped on the dividing glass and, with a nod to the driver, they were off. As the limousine pulled away from the kerb, Mr Newman brought a handful of coins from his pocket and, winding the window down, threw them into the road. Kiddies appeared out of nowhere like hungry gulls, swooping on the coins and flapping each other out of the way.

Four guests waited outside the registry office: Mrs Milne, dressed head to toe in black (for heaven's sake, thought Etty, you'd think somebody had died); Bertha, wearing the same gaudy coat she'd worn to the cinema, along with her husband and lastly, May Robinson. Dorothy had requested that May be invited to the wedding as a substitute for Laurie.

Seeing May on her wedding day unnerved Etty. She'd cheated on the lass and it pained her to live with her shameful secret.

Laurie, somewhere in the Atlantic, had sent his love and blessing via a letter.

> *Pet, I would have liked nothing better than to give you away and it grieves me deeply that I can't. But thanks for asking, anyway.*
>
> *Remember that little bird I told you about way back when? Well, the same one informs me that you two lovebirds make a smashing couple and will prosper and have a long and happy life together. And I'm glad because that's what I hoped for you. Your wedding day will be a long and lonely one for me, but I'll be with you in spirit. I've warned people on the ship that at eleven o'clock sharp I'll let out a yell that'll make them jump.*
>
> *Tell that man of yours to look after you. You're a precious girl.*
>
> *Heaps of love,*
> *Laurie*

As Etty stepped from the car, the rain stopped and a weak yellow sun shone above the rooftops opposite.

Dorothy stood next to her. 'A good omen,' she beamed.

Her words calmed Etty, giving her the boost of courage she needed. Then, as she saw Trevor's lanky frame waiting in the doorway, she involuntarily shivered with excitement despite all her fears. This was for real, she thought. There was no turning back; she was getting married. Dorothy, misreading her sister's reaction as nerves, whispered in her ear, 'You can pull out if you want to. This is for life, remember?'

Etty's heart swelled with love for her sister. In Dorothy's eyes she could do no wrong and she was always there to protect Etty.

She would make good, she determined, and show Mistress Knowles. Marrying Trevor would be the start of a new life.

She gave Dorothy a trembling smile. Dorothy nodded and, taking charge, herded everyone into the registry office. Trevor held out his hand and as Etty took it, she noticed how steady it was.

The service, it seemed to Etty, was over before it had begun. One minute she was smiling at the tall, silver-haired man, who looked kindly at her from behind round-rimmed glasses, and the next she was listening to him tell Trevor that he may kiss his bride.

Trevor did exactly that – a smouldering kiss that took Etty by surprise. She felt self-conscious at first but, as she closed her eyes, a picture of Billy's face surfaced in her mind. Her eyes snapped open. She railed at herself guiltily. For heaven's sake, what kind of hussy was she that, while marrying one man, thought of another? But Billy's presence lingered nonetheless.

Trevor took her arm and guided her from the room, where they fought their way through the next wedding party that waited in the foyer. Outside, it rained again, and someone thrust a black umbrella into Etty's hands.

'You're all invited back to my place,' Dorothy told the gathering. 'Mrs Milne, you lead the way.'

Etty looked towards Nellie and was surprised when everyone laughed.

'Oh! Of course,' she said, feeling foolish. 'That's me!'

As she took off up the road, she noticed Nellie's face darken. Mrs Milne senior was not amused.

'Where on earth did all this food come from?' Etty asked Dorothy in surprise as they entered the kitchen. She eyed the joint of ham in the centre of the table. 'I thought the ration allowance for a wedding was only two pounds of cooked ham?'

Dorothy tapped the side of her nose knowingly. Tall-stemmed sherry glasses stood on the sideboard, and the table was filled with delicious-looking food: bacon and egg pie, corned beef hash, a tureen of mashed potatoes, preserves, bottled beetroot, vegetables and in pride of place—

'A wedding cake!' Etty exclaimed.

'Don't get too excited,' Dorothy quickly put in. 'It's a cardboard cut-out made to look real.'

Bertha gave Dorothy a knowing look. 'Who's been dealing on the black market?'

'Goodness, not me.' Dorothy flushed pink. 'The meal was made possible by some very kind neighbours who chipped in with ration books.'

Etty should have guessed. They'd come to Dorothy's rescue with precious provisions, because she was friends with everyone in the street. Folk were good at heart, she thought, especially when there was a war on.

By mid-afternoon, the wedding party was in full swing. Pink-cheeked and sparkly-eyed, people chatted animatedly with one another.

Mr Newman chinked the side of his stemmed glass with a fork.

'Everyone… could I have your attention, please? I'd like to take this opportunity to wish the happy couple the best of health and happiness.' His face sobered. 'And to remember those absent friends we would wish to be among us.'

No doubt Mr Newman was thinking of his son, Danny, away serving in the air force. As each of them thought of their own absent loved ones, the atmosphere turned sombre. Etty's thoughts turned to a mother she could barely remember. For a brief moment she understood why Dorothy had missed having her at her wedding. A picture of herself, the little forsaken girl leaning against Blakely's door ran through Etty's mind but she closed her mind, refusing to get sentimental.

Soppy fool, she thought, as she sniffed hard and brushed away a tear. Mam had discarded them like garbage and Etty would never forgive her.

The atmosphere needed jollying and Bertha raised her glass. 'To the happy couple,' she grinned, devilishly. 'And may their troubles be little ones.'

As everyone toasted the newlyweds, Etty was reminded of Dorothy's wedding day, and her own promise to herself to marry for true love. She gazed at Trevor – had she settled for less? How, she wondered, would she feel if Billy was the one she'd married?

Trevor, his eyes unfathomable green pools, met Etty's over the rim of his glass. She flushed, guilty at her disloyal thoughts. It was a lot to ask him to take on another man's child, and in this moment her regard for him went up a thousand fold.

'Speech… speech,' Bertha exclaimed. All eyes on Trevor, he held up his hand and declined.

At that moment, Mrs Milne rushed from the far side of the room, where she'd been in conversation with Bertha's husband.

An expression of abject dread on her walnut-wrinkled face, she cried. 'Me son… me only son… take care of him.'

She buried her head in Trevor's chest and, shoulders heaving, she sobbed.

In the embarrassed silence that followed, Dorothy's voice was heard to say, 'More sherry anyone?'

Etty gave a wry grin. She could rely on her sister – no matter what the situation.

'Come come, Mrs Milne,' Mr. Newman walked over to Nellie. What with the heat in the room and the amount of sherry he'd consumed, his face had turned a ruddy shade.

A look of irritation flitted across his face. 'Consider it like this. You're not losing a son but gaining a daughter.'

Short and bespectacled, with sparse, grey hair, what Mr Newman lacked in stance he more than made up for in influential clout. A man of means in these parts, he was highly regarded.

Trevor's ma, quick-witted enough to know not to annoy the great man, quickly regained her composure.

'Eee, I don't know what came over us, then,' she replied, sniffing at some vile smelling salts she'd taken from her coat pocket.

A conniving look in her eye, she told Mr Newman, 'Trevor won't forget his old Ma, will you son?'

Mr Newman filled with sherry and good cheer, clapped Trevor on the back.

'I admire a young man who looks after his elders.' His shrewd eyes shone. 'Lad, I've got a proposition to make. With all the young men being called up, I'm finding it difficult finding anyone to help with snatches. That being said, I'm offering you the job.'

Being a snatch – a coffin bearer – was a position much sought-after by Trevor, who longed to better himself in life.

'You seem a bright, upstanding lad. The sort folk would respect. The kind of man Newmans employ.'

Trevor positively glowed. 'Aye, Mr Newman, I'd like nothing better.'

'I've been looking for someone for a while. You could lend an occasional hand in the workshop when I'm rushed. Especially after there's been a raid on. What with a full-time job at the pit and all, I know you're a busy lad but… maybe when you do the night shift you can have a second job—'

'Aye, that would suit us champion. I'm up for it, all right.'

'One thing more, lad,' Mr Newman lowered his voice. 'If you work for me it would be wise if you dropped the Geordie twang.'

Trevor smothered a smile. That was rich coming from a man whose wife spoke in Geordie dialect.

*

Later, as the newlyweds made their way up the street in the dark, a crescent moon glided from behind a cloud. By its ethereal light, Etty made out the number twelve on one of the front doors.

'Home,' she said, with a hint of awe.

Trevor brought a key from his trouser pocket and opened the door. He stooped and, gathering her in his arms, carried Etty over the threshold. The romantic gesture touched her. They didn't kiss but the air around them felt charged.

The flat, with its small scullery, kitchen and two bedrooms, was a replica of Dorothy's. The similarity ended there, however. While her sister's home was cosy and crammed with personal knick-knacks, here the furnishings were sparse and of a practical nature – a table and two chairs bought from the previous owner (much to Trevor's disgust as he loathed anything second-hand), a cabinet for the kitchen scrounged from Dorothy, a rather lumpy horsehair couch, and a double bed on loan from Trevor's mam. The fire burned brightly on the blackened range, a kettle sang on the hob and from the oven came a meaty aroma. Only Dorothy could provide such a housewarming and, overcome by her sister's thoughtfulness, Etty's eyes misted.

'Can you believe all this is ours?' she said, overwhelmed.

Arms winding around Trevor's neck, she rested her head lightly against his shoulder, and a heightened sense of being surged through her. Here she was, she thought in wonder, with a husband, a home and sometime soon, a baby of her own. As reality sank in, a happy radiance spread over her. She dared to believe that life might be kind to her, after all. Then a thought struck her; what if the child she carried wanted to know about its heritage? What would she say? Her knowledge of family history was scant, and she certainly wouldn't frighten a child with stories about orphanages, or tales of a heartless grandmother that had abandoned her children. But perhaps none of these things mattered, only that her child was loved and felt secure. And she'd make sure of that.

Her child. Her own flesh and blood. Etty smiled.

Trevor put her down and she removed her jacket and kicked off her shoes.

'This place needs new furniture.' He looked glumly around.

Etty laughed, a tinkling sound that echoed in the high-ceilinged room. 'If you were brought up as I was at the orphanage,' she reproved him, 'you would consider this the height of luxury.'

She eyed her husband. She'd do the best to make Trevor happy and meanwhile, she must be patient. They had the rest of their lives to work out their differences.

Impulsively, she stood on tiptoe and kissed him.

He looked surprised. 'What's that for?'

Etty thought of the film she'd seen on the night of the bombing. It had left an indelible mark on her – the couple's endearing love for one another, and the way that Mr Chipping, the aloof and reserved schoolmaster, had mellowed with married life.

'Do I have to have a reason? Other than, you're my husband?'

'I suppose not.' He appeared rather pleased.

Later, as Trevor went to refill the coalscuttle, his mellow mood changed. Picking it up, he gave a disapproving, 'Huh!'

'What's the matter?'

'Is this your sister's doing?' He nodded to the fire, then the oven where a meat casserole simmered. 'Did you give her a spare key?'

'Yes.'

'Then ask for it back.'

'Why?'

'I don't want her barging in when I don't expect it.'

'She wouldn't.'

'She already has.' He gestured to the full coalscuttle.

'Dorothy did us a favour.' Confused, she nodded to the fire to make a point. 'I'll ask her for the key back when you ask your mam to return hers.'

In an instant, the atmosphere became strained, setting the mood for the rest of the evening. Though polite with one another, they avoided each other's eye. Etty dreaded what was expected of her in the bedroom and postponed it for as long as she could. Finally, when she could avoid it no longer, she yawned. 'That's me off to bed… it's been a long day.'

He grunted something about having to bank the fire first and it occurred to her that perhaps he too was nervous.

'Don't be long,' she said. 'Remember you've got work in the morning.'

As if he could forget. There was no honeymoon for the pair, as his shift was short of men and besides, they didn't have spare money for luxuries such as holidays.

Making her way into the bedroom, she changed into the parachute-silk nightdress Dorothy had made for her as a wedding present. Slipping between the cold sheets, Etty's feet were like blocks of ice. But you couldn't bring a stone hot water bottle to bed – not if you were expecting a bit of romance.

She stared up at the ceiling and waited.

When Trevor finally entered the bedroom, he flicked off the light switch and took forever to undress. Sliding between the sheets, he kept to his side of the bed.

'We don't have to… you know… do anything tonight, if you don't want to,' Etty told him.

'I'm tired,' his voice was gruff, 'and like you say, it's been a long day.'

He turned on his side, away from Etty and appeared to go to sleep. She didn't know what to think. If it were Billy, she knew things would have turned out differently. Then guilt at making comparisons with another man swiftly swamped Etty and she loathed herself for it.

The same thing happened the following night, and the next. Etty was at a loss to know what to do. None of the lasses at the factory had mentioned this kind of carry on. She couldn't ask anyone, not Bertha and certainly not Dorothy. Such a thing was too mortifying.

The next Saturday night, as Trevor undressed and pulled back the covers, sliding his lean body into bed, Etty attempted to broach the subject. But try as she might, she couldn't find the words because, what if Trevor was repulsed by her pregnancy? A sense of being ugly and undesirable overwhelmed Etty, and she knew her body was only going to grow bigger and feel worse as the pregnancy progressed.

Time wore on and the longer she remained silent the harder it was for Etty to approach the subject. She put the matter to the back of her mind – for sanity's sake she had to.

In other ways too, marriage wasn't what she had expected. When she lived with Dorothy, it didn't matter if beds weren't made or dust gathered on surfaces. The sisters, having had their fill of structured life at Blakely, where each day brought endless chores, were determined to live a more relaxed way of life.

'Once dust lands it never gets thicker,' was Etty's attitude.

Not so Trevor, who liked the place spotless. She fought to keep a sense of humour but it was tried one day when Trevor, as he came home from work, wrote 'clean me' on the top of the new sideboard in the dust.

The oak utility sideboard, their first new piece of furniture, had cost ten pounds seven shillings, and six points from the newly married furniture allowance. It was Trevor's pride and joy.

Tired and deflated, Etty stormed, 'If you're that pernickety, do the housework yourself.' She rifled through the ragbag and threw a duster at him. 'Laurie's a godsend when he's home… he does the washing up, most of the cooking and when Dorothy's at work he's—'

'Truly a saint,' Trevor finished for her, his lips twitching.

Etty wouldn't be humoured. 'Laurie's the kindest, gentlest soul, a man in a million.'

Trevor's convivial mood changed and tight-lipped, he replied, 'Unlike me.'

And so the row escalated. Etty said things she didn't mean and he retaliated by raking up all her faults.

'Call yourself a man,' she shrieked. 'You haven't the courage to consummate our marriage.'

There, she'd said it. She clapped a hand over her mouth.

Trevor looked startled. 'Is that what you think?'

'If you must know, what I think is that you find me… repulsive.'

Goodness, she'd gone all snivelling.

He came over and took her in his arms. 'Etty, the truth is I don't know about these things. I didn't want to damage the baby. I thought you understood.'

She sniffed. 'I'm not a mind reader, Trevor. You're going to have to learn to speak out.' Suddenly, she felt shy. 'There are ways for both parties to enjoy sexual intercourse,' she said, feeling brave.

He stiffened and let her go. 'Look here, I don't need instructions.'

Then the cosy atmosphere became one of suspicion and the knowledge of what she'd done with another man grew like an insurmountable wall between them.

They didn't mention the subject again but that night, as he climbed into bed, his face contrite, Trevor said, 'Etty, I want yi' to know that I think you're absolutely gorgeous… and if it's all right with you can we—'

She put her hand over his lips.

'Yes.'

As he pulled back the bedcovers and took her in his arms, she thought of Mr Chipping. There was hope for Trevor yet.

Trevor never did retrieve the key from his mam, nor did she stop calling in at their home at all hours.

Trouble started when Etty came home early one morning from the nightshift. She crept along the passage so she wouldn't waken Trevor and, opening the kitchen door, she saw Nellie stood at the range, a spitting frying pan in her hand.

'What are you doing home so early?' Nellie didn't so much as turn her head.

The smell of heated fat made Etty queasy. She drew a few deep breaths.

'More to the point, Mrs Milne, what are you doing at my range?'

'I'm cooking for me son. He hasn't had a proper breakfast since the day he wed.'

'Your son is capable of making his own breakfast.'

'Call yourself a wife, you're an apology.' The outburst took Etty unawares and she felt her hackles rise. It was shades of Mistress Knowles again and she wasn't going to let this tyrannical mother-in-law blight her life.

'Another thing; me son can't eat his bait because that national bread you give him tastes foul.'

The vindictive look on her face suggested Nellie was gunning for an argument.

'Your son is a grown man. If he has a complaint, he can speak for himself.'

It rankled that Trevor had discussed her with his mam. Then again, she shouldn't jump to conclusions. She didn't know in what context Trevor had spoken, and Nellie might be out to make trouble.

'Whatever happens in this household is no business of yours.'

'Cheeky hussy.' Nellie flipped a sizzling sausage with a fork onto its other side and as hot fat spilled onto the fire, angry flames whooshed up the chimney. 'Mark my words, Trevor will rue the day he married you, if he doesn't already, that is.'

'I think you've said enough, Mrs Milne,' Etty fought to stay calm. She refused to give Nellie the satisfaction of losing her temper. 'I'll take over now. I'll thank you to go and you can leave the back door key on the table.'

'I'll do nee such thing.'

'Trevor and I would like our privacy.'

'I'd like to hear what me son has to say about that.'

'In the future if you want to visit, rap at the back window and if we're not busy we'll let you in.'

'I damn well won't. Anyways, who takes notice of you? If it wasn't for me—'

'What's all the commotion about?'

Trevor stood in the doorway. He wore striped pyjamas, his hair mussed and his face puffy from sleep.

'It's her fault, son,' Nellie clutched her heart and appeared to shrink. 'I don't feel well,' she gasped a few breaths to prove a point. 'That wife o' yours says I'm not welcome in your home.'

'No I didn't,' Etty told Trevor. 'I said we wanted privacy and that I wanted the house key back.'

Trevor looked from one to the other. He ran his fingers through his hair. 'Seems a reasonable request to me, Ma.'

Nellie's face turned puce as an overripe plum. 'You're forgetting yourself, son, and whose flat you're living in.' There was a hint of menace in her tone. She stabbed a sausage with a fork and placed it on a plate heating in the oven. 'I wonder what Mr Newman would think if he heard you'd turned your old Ma out of your home. An upstanding man is Mr Newman. I can't see him employing you then, can you?'

She cracked their one and only egg into the frying pan. Then with a smirk of triumph, she left.

CHAPTER SEVENTEEN

December 1941

Like most Shields folk, Etty kept up with the local news in the *Gazette*, growing despondent when she read of all the deaths. How many more young men must lose their lives?

Two nights before, even though the weather was thick fog, the enemy had mounted an attack on Tyneside. The city of Newcastle suffered the worst and Etty's heart went out to all those who'd lost loved ones, especially now when New Year loomed. She felt humbled – her own problems seemingly so insignificant against the backdrop of the world stage. Yet how she longed for her marriage to work and how she vowed for the bairn she carried to be brought up in a loving home.

As her stomach swelled with her unborn child, Etty speculated about her own mother. Did she have maternal feelings? How could she have done such a thing, abandoning her daughters? She made a silent promise to the baby growing within her womb. Come what may, she would always be there for it. Never would she treat any child of hers as disgracefully as Mam had her and Dorothy.

Etty wanted New Year's Eve, her first as a wife, to be special – a foretaste of their future lives together.

Minutes before midnight, she hustled Trevor over the threshold, indulging in the northern tradition of 'first footing'.

'Exactly what is it we have to do?' she'd asked Trevor earlier on. Being brought up at Blakey, Etty had been deprived of the tradition.

'It's a ritual,' Trevor explained, 'where a man… preferably dark-haired as the saying goes… waits outside till midnight. When he steps inside he brings prosperity and good luck to the household for the New Year.'

As she hustled him out of the door, Etty pressed a lump of coal and a twist of salt and tea into his hand.

'What's all this in aid of, then?'

'I read in tonight's paper that it's customary to do this so we won't go without.'

'Daft carry on,' he said, but Etty detected a hint of satisfaction in his voice. 'By heck, I'll freeze standing out here.'

'It's not long till midnight,' she whispered, conscious of the other men who stood outside their front doors that might be listening in. She lowered her voice, 'Then we'll celebrate just the two of us.'

'You're on,' he laughed. 'Meanwhile, get yourself in the warm and wait for me knock by the fire.'

Etty felt a surge of love at him for being so considerate of her.

Since their row, things had dramatically improved. As the pleasure in their bedroom filtered into daily life, they enjoyed each other's company and became friends as well as lovers.

Pattering through to the kitchen, Etty anticipated the night ahead. She checked the clock on the mantelpiece. Seven minutes to go until midnight.

She glanced around the darkened room and smiled at the little imitation tree where candles burned brightly in holders. The glow of flames flickering on the far wall from the fire opposite gave the night an expectant, magical feel, where everything seemed possible.

*

It was a perishing cold night, when the moon shone and ice sparkled on the cobbled street. Trevor stamped his booted feet to inject life back into them. He was never one to be sentimental but there was something about New Year's Eve and its reflective atmosphere that got to him. Here he was, a married man with a bairn on the way and, the icing on the cake, he had a foot in Newman's door.

Aye, life was looking up.

'If you work for me, lad,' the boss told Trevor, 'it'll pay you to remember that undertakers are like the clergy themselves, and people look up to us.'

Aye, Trevor considered, as he waited outside his front door with a lump of coal in his hand, the boss was a pillar of righteousness in the community, all right, and if Trevor played his cards right, folk would think the same of him.

That moment, as the bright moon sailed behind a cloud, a dart of unease clouded Trevor's jubilant mood. At dinner time he'd promised his mother he'd call at her house at twelve and first foot.

She'd collared him at the front door as he was walking down the street from work.

'A word, son.'

Ma had turned indoors, hand on the banister rail, hauling herself up the stairs with an energy he didn't know she possessed. There was nothing else for it; Trevor had followed. His favourite fish pie waited for him on the kitchen table – he should have known there was a catch.

'I can't stay, Ma. Etty will have me dinner waiting downstairs at home.'

Ignoring him, she cut a wedge of pie.

'You'll be out first footing tonight, son, I presume?' It seemed a trick question.

'Dunno,' Trevor hedged. 'Why?'

She placed the piece of pie on a plate and handed it to him. One bit of pie won't hurt, he thought, hungrily taking a bite.

'I suppose now you've got a home of your own, first footing yer old Ma is a thing of the past.' She sighed like a martyr. 'Even though you've never missed a year since you were a laddie.'

Crikey Moses, Trevor wished he'd had the good sense to forgo the fish pie.

'I'll drop by tonight,' he said, 'but I can't stop, Etty is expecting me to first foot at ours.'

His mother's smirk rattled him.

Now, the commotion in the street, with doors banging, shouts of 'Happy New Year' and ship's hooters blasting on the River Tyne, alerted Trevor that the New Year had begun.

Strong northerly winds strengthened further, and a few flakes of swirling snow landed on Trevor's head. All he wanted was to kiss his wife and wish her all the best in the new year.

Guilt taking over, he moved a couple of paces along to Ma's adjoining door, with grave misgivings. Finding the door open, he stepped inside.

He'd only be a minute, Trevor promised himself.

*

Meanwhile, downstairs, Etty couldn't believe the time on the clock. Ten past twelve and Trevor still hadn't knocked. Her eyes travelled to the ceiling where she heard thuds from upstairs. Footsteps made their way across the floor and Etty heard muffled voices. Suspicion grew, but she quickly dismissed it. Trevor wouldn't!

She rose, treading in her slippers along the passageway to the front door. Opening it, she looked out. Her heart sank – not a sign of Trevor. She stepped outside into the perishing cold night and moved along to Nellie Milne's door. It stood ajar and Etty walked in.

Standing in the lobby at the foot of the stairs, the obligatory smell of fish hitting her nostrils, she strained to listen. Noise drifted down the stairwell; the sound of high-pitched, excitable voices. It sounded like a party – a party no one had thought to invite Etty to, and she had no doubt Trevor was there. How could he? On the first new year in their home. She heard Nellie's wheezy laugh, but Etty wouldn't rise to the bait by rushing upstairs and making a scene.

She felt deflated, and then so mad, that she wanted to wail and scream like a toddler. It was such a silly thought it made her smile, and her mood lifted. Etty was determined to rise above such a childish reaction. She wouldn't allow her vile mother-in-law to turn her into a screechy wife. Neither would she play Nellie's game of battling for domination.

Trevor had let her down but, like the heroine, Mrs Chipping, in the film, Etty would remain patient. After all, he knew no better than to please his wily mam.

Proud of her sensible self, she made her way back into the kitchen. Once again, she checked her watch. Twenty past twelve. She marvelled at how the atmosphere in the room had transformed in such a short space of time. The fire needed coal, the candles were burnt out, and the room, cold and dim, held a jaded feel. The spread on the table that she'd prepared earlier in case any revellers called by – sandwiches, jam tarts, homemade ginger wine – only intensified her loneliness.

She considered going to her sister's, then remembered that without Laurie to celebrate with her, Dorothy was retiring early to bed. The night spoilt, weariness overcame Etty but she decided to give Trevor a minute or two longer. She banked the fire and, pouring a glass of milk, settled on the couch.

She must have dozed off for the next thing she knew she started awake, empty glass in hand. Something had woken her. There it came again – a noise in the passageway.

'Trevor, is that you?'

No answer. Too late, she remembered she'd left the front door open. Anyone could walk in. A sliver of fear shot through her.

She rose and switched on the light. In its naked beam, she stood hypnotised as she watched the kitchen door slowly open.

A figure in uniform emerged.

'Billy!'

His face was flushed and, somewhat unsteady on his feet, he swayed into the room and leaned against the wall. Taking a slim packet of cigarettes from his trouser pocket, he lit one with a match and, inhaling deeply, scrutinised her through a haze of smoke.

She tried to remain composed but a fire ignited in her.

'You married him, then, mammy's boy?'

His gait unsteady, he lunged forward and Etty smelt alcohol on his breath.

'It's got nothing to do with you. Go away… you're drunk.'

Billy concentrated on standing upright and, tilting his head comically, said, 'I'm only a teensy bit drunk. It's New Year after all.'

The desire to laugh overwhelmed Etty, but she stopped herself. The matter in hand was too serious.

'How did you know where I live?'

'I ashed May.'

She should have guessed.

'Trevor's due home any minute.'

Billy gave a silly grin. 'Nah! He's not. Saw him teetering down the shtreet into somebody's house… there was a mob of them. A right seshion it looked.'

Etty glanced at the clock. 2.a.m. *Trevor should be home*, her mind blazed.

An exaggerated look of hurt crossed Billy's handsome face. 'Why didn't you write? I waited, then I heard you married him. Don't say you love him because I know different.'

This was getting out of hand. 'You've got May,' she reminded him, 'what about her? Don't you love her?'

'Course I do, in me own way.' As he tossed the half smoked cigarette in the fire, Etty longed to touch his face, to trace the dimple in his chin. 'Silly lass tries too hard, she suffocates us and I can't stand it any more.' He heaved a dramatic sigh. 'I have to, though, cos it's hard to be cruel to someone as nice as May. It's you I want, though.'

Those amazing eyes beseeched hers, yet there was obstinacy in them too. Where women were concerned, Billy was used to getting his own way. It occurred to Etty that she was just another challenge. The more she resisted him, the more he wanted her.

Tipsily he slurred, 'I had to see you.'

This was getting them nowhere. She tried to make light of the situation, and laughing hollowly, said, 'Billy Buckley, you're drunk. Away home with you… you'll rue making such a fool of yourself in the morning.'

'Be honest. You want me as much as I—'

'It stops here, Billy.'

'Why? Who's to know?'

Even though drunk, his nerve astounded her.

'I won't have an affair.'

Clarity sparked in his eye and he straightened up, 'So, you're going to walk away from what we have.'

'We've got nothing, Billy. A chance affair, that's all it was, in the shelter. Two people afraid they were going to die.' In her distress, Etty raised her voice. 'We've no future together. Go away. This time stay away for good. Is that clear?'

Lord help her, as the words hung in the air, madness seized Etty. She was tempted to tell him the whole sordid mess; that the bairn she carried was his, and ask him what he was going to do about it.

He opened his mouth to speak and then, as if he thought better of it, shut it again. His face became a mask and with a stiff little nod, unsteadily, he left the room.

As the front door slammed, Etty wondered if the pain in her heart would ever heal.

*

Some while later, Etty heard a key rattle in the front door, footsteps plodding along the passage.

Trevor.

He entered the kitchen and the cautious gleam in his eye said it all.

'I couldn't get away because me Ma had—'

Etty held up a hand. 'Please, no excuses, Trevor.'

'Etty, I tried but Ma had a houseful of neighbours and they—'

'I'm tired and I'm off to bed.'

An acute sense of her hypocrisy overcame Etty – how dare she condemn Trevor? She was twice as bad, pandering to Billy when she should have shown him the door from the first.

Trevor brought something from his trouser pocket. 'This is for you, love.'

Nellie's door key lay in his palm.

Weeks passed. On a Saturday evening in late February, Etty sat by the fire reading a national newspaper. With paper rationed and the publications restricted in size, she reflected that there was hardly any reading in them any more.

She yawned, folding the newspaper and placing it on the couch, where Trevor could read it later. He was working the late shift at the pit and would soon be home wanting his supper.

The fire, burning embers now, needed tending to. Etty picked two pieces of coal from the coalscuttle with tongs, placed them on the embers and watched them ignite. Trevor would appreciate a warm fire to come home to on this cold winter's night. Coal was a precious commodity and every bit had to be conserved. Setting a place at the table, Etty thought about how hard miners like her husband worked, supplying factories to make weapons to help win the war and—

As she heard the public alert from the air raid siren, Etty's train of thought was interrupted. The kitchen door burst open and Trevor hurtled in.

'Get yerself into the shelter,' he demanded, throwing his haversack on the table. 'I'll boil a kettle of water for the flask.'

'Trevor, I can—'

'Haddaway. Don't waste time arguing.'

Etty hurried over to the redbrick shelter, a replica of the one she and Dorothy had shared with the Armstrongs many moons ago. Though Etty missed her sister's company during raids, she knew Dorothy would be safe. Laurie had insisted his wife acquire a Morrison shelter so she could stay safely inside the house. A cage-like contraption that almost filled Dorothy's kitchen, the Morrison shelter had a steel roof and steel mesh sides.

Hearing the ominous drone of planes in the distance, Etty tried to escape the terror that jittered inside by lighting the paraffin lamp and focusing on how to improve the spartan shelter, devoid of comfort except for a couple of deckchairs placed against the walls. As raider planes drew closer Etty imagined the bunk beds that Trevor intended to build, the shelves fitted on the walls where she could store the makings for tea, candles and books. She imagined her baby in a cradle on one of the beds. It was cold in the shelter, and the flame of the lamp cast shadows on the walls.

Trevor clattered in from outside, carrying fresh blankets, a flask and torch.

'Jerry's over by the docks,' he told her.

In the distance, guns began to fire from the ground.

'Our Trevor,' Nellie's voice screeched from the upstairs window, 'come and fetch us.'

Trevor's green, questioning eyes met Etty's. 'She's terrified when there's a raid on.'

Etty knew because Nellie never let anyone forget.

'Best go and get her,' she replied.

Nellie brought the usual carpet bag of pastimes: knitting, a book, a pack of cards to play endless games of patience, and homemade lemonade which she never shared.

'By, the moon doesn't help tonight.' She plonked down in a deck chair and placed the carpet bag on the floor. 'Jerry can see everything. I wish I could turn the damn thing off.'

In the distance the thuds came terrifyingly nearer, planes thundering overhead. With wave after wave of aircraft above, Etty placed her hands over her ears.

Still, she heard Nellie's shriek. 'God love us… this could be the night I meet me maker.'

The bombers mercifully screamed past, hurtling into the distance.

'Some other poor blighter's catching it,' Trevor said as crumps were heard far off.

In the lull, Nellie started snivelling, looking for sympathy from her son.

Ignoring her, Trevor brought tin hats from beneath the deck chair. 'Here,' he handed one to each of the two women, 'put these on.'

'I don't know, our Trevor, now you've got a wife, I don't get any consideration.'

'I've got to take extra good care of Etty, Ma.'

'Why? Is she sickenin'? The lass isn't made of glass.'

In the darkened shelter, Trevor gave Etty an enquiring look.

Why not? Etty thought, Nellie had to know sometime. Surreptitiously, she nodded and he smiled.

'When you're old nobody wants—' Nellie began the same old story.

'Etty's not sick, Ma.' Trevor interrupted. 'She's in the family way… you're going to be a nana.'

Nellie looked from one to the other, a delighted smile stretching across her wrinkled face. 'At least the lass can do something right.'

Etty felt a jolt of guilt, thinking about what she did wrong to end up 'in the family way'.

As guns blazed again from the dock area and planes drew closer, Etty heard the distressing noise of bombs falling, followed by disturbing thuds. Though terrified, she tried not to let it show.

Her ears hurt though, from Nellie's piercing screams.

'You're safe in here, Ma.' Trevor picked up the bucket of sand that stood on the floor, used for incendiary bombs, and picking up a shovel, he made for the door, but not before kissing Etty.

'I've got to go, love.' Without further ado, he opened the door and was gone.

Minutes later, a plane, hit by a gun, came screaming down. As it smashed into the ground there was an almighty explosion. The shelter walls shook and the room filled with dust, the paraffin lamp blowing out.

In the darkness, Nellie's unruffled voice spoke out. 'I don't want to be known as Nana. I want me grandbairn to call me Granny Milne.'

The next day, after a sleepless and uncomfortable night spent in the shelter, Etty had to go to work. She could barely keep her eyes open and yawned all through her shift.

The foreman too yawned while he did his rounds of the machines.

'Aye, a bit of tiredness never killed anybody. If Jerry thinks we're beaten, he can think again. We're a stubborn lot, us British, when we're rattled.'

When she got home and read the news, it was reported that most of the North Eastern area had suffered. Civilians were killed and brave souls from the police force and auxiliary fire service were harmed – but, thank God, Trevor wasn't amongst them.

Etty's last thought as she went to sleep that night was, what kind of world was she bringing her child into?

Weeks turned into months and then it was June. Etty, lethargic, with her stomach inflated like a balloon, had to leave work and she sorely missed both the company and structure to her day. Although nervous about the forthcoming birth, she was excited too, but wished she knew what to expect. Without a mother to tell her, there was no one she felt comfortable enough to ask and it was unthinkable to approach Nellie, as the two women barely spoke.

Today was pleasantly warm, the sun shining from a cloudless sky, and a welcome surge of energy seized Etty, so she spent the morning preparing for the baby.

'It's the nesting instinct,' Dorothy beamed when she called in on her way to work. 'Mind, don't overdo it.'

Etty eyed her sister's work trousers. 'Have you seen the latest restrictions?'

'No. Any more food restrictions and we'll waste away.'

'This time it's clothes. No permanent turn-ups on trousers, double-breasted suits are out, as are pockets on pyjamas. No embroidery on underwear…' Etty giggled. 'Fat chance with the enormous knickers I have to wear. Thank goodness for maternity tops.'

Dorothy smiled and blew a kiss as she left.

Etty washed dear little baby clothes in the sink and, hanging them out to dry, thought how ridiculously small they looked. She scrubbed the crib – that Nellie had kept since Trevor was a baby – and pressed the cot sheets and blankets with a flat iron. When finally the work was done, her fingers puffed like sausages, shoes digging into her swollen ankles, she lumbered into the kitchen and made a pot of tea. As if on cue, Nellie appeared at the back door.

'Make mine black with one sugar,' she said, brazenly.

Without invitation, she barged into the kitchen and made herself at home on the couch.

'My, haven't we been busy?' she called through to Etty.

As Etty brought the tea in and handed her a cup, Nellie stared blatantly at her bump.

'I hope you haven't been overdoing it. Has that bairn moved today yet?'

Etty bit her tongue, stopping herself from telling the infernal woman it was no business of hers, even if she was a so-called expert.

She'd spoken before with Trevor about his mam's interference.

'Where's the harm?' he said. 'It's her first grandchild and she's anxious.'

'Trevor, she monitors everything I do. If I so much as fetch a shovel of coal, or go to the lav, there she is watching me from the upstairs window. She'll be writing me a list of do's and don'ts next.' Etty waited for a response, and when none was forthcoming, she went on. 'And then there's the ridiculous old wives' tales she's forever spouting.'

'Ma has brought dozens of bairns into the world,' Trevor's expression was one of patience. 'She does know what she's talking about.'

Subject closed.

She hadn't told Trevor his mam's latest corker. That she was afraid if Etty drank too much tea, the bairn might come out yellow – it was too laughable to be repeated. Besides, Trevor was being decent about the baby and referred to it as his own, even when the couple were alone. It was as though he wanted to convince himself he was the child's father in every sense of the word. Where was the harm – apart from having an interfering mother-in-law? If that was the price Etty had to pay, so be it, she'd put up with worse before.

'I've been thinking about the bairn,' Nellie said, which didn't surprise Etty as the woman scarcely thought about much else. 'I hope it turns out normal.'

'Pardon me?' Expecting to hear another outrageous old wives' tale, she smothered a grin.

'It's no laughing matter. What if this bairn has no proper feelings?'

'Whatever gives you that idea?'

'I've never mentioned the fact before but it's different now that you're carrying me grandchild.'

'Go on.' Etty mentally prepared herself.

'It's well known that folk brought up in asylums are immune to normal feelings.'

'Well known by whom?'

'Most sane folk around these parts.'

So there it was; she was referring to Etty's upbringing at Blakely. It had only been a matter of time.

'Mrs Milne, even for you that's rich,' Etty replied, icily. 'How dare you? My upbringing had nothing to do with sanity. Mam abandoned me in an orphanage.'

'That's what I don't understand, hinny,' Nellie's pugnacious face crinkled nastily. 'Why would a mother do that? Give up her bairn? Unless, of course, there was something radically wrong wi' it.'

She'd touched a nerve. Etty had asked herself the same question numerous times and never came up with a suitable answer, save the relentless feeling that her mother leaving them was, somehow, all her fault.

'Even for you, Mrs Milne, that is despicable. I want you to leave. And I don't want you back unless your son is in.'

She expected a lashing of the tongue or, at least, a reminder of whose roof she was living under, but Nellie did no such thing. Her head held high in defiance, she left without a word.

Etty went over and over the conversation all day, working herself up into a frenzy. Later, when she knew her sister would be home from work, she made her way down to Dorothy's flat.

Letting herself in with a key that Dorothy had given her, Etty found her sister knitting on the settee.

'Blimey, what a rotten thing to say,' Dorothy said, aghast, when Etty told her.

Etty sat on the arm of the couch, watching her sister knitting white baby boots.

'It's only words,' Dorothy continued. 'The woman's ignorant. Don't let her upset you.'

'But why would she say such a thing?'

'I suspect, because she feels threatened.'

'Threatened?'

'Because you've married her son.'

Etty had the sinking feeling what Dorothy said was true. She remembered the resentment she'd felt when Dorothy had befriended May, but she would never treat anyone with such contempt. At the thought of May, guilt slammed into her. For she had betrayed the girl, which was far worse.

'You're right,' she told Dorothy, 'Nellie will never forgive me for marrying her precious son.'

'Now listen to me. It's you Trevor married and it's you he loves. The pair of you make a perfect team. You must be firm with Mrs Milne and don't allow her to interfere in your marriage. Once you've had the baby, she'll come round. She'll have to… she's too much to lose otherwise.'

Dorothy never alluded to the fact that the bairn Etty carried was another man's child, she simply carried on as if Trevor truly was the dad.

But the sisters were a team and that had been the way of things ever since Mam left them. Thoughts of Blakely surfaced in Etty's mind like spiders crawling out of a dark hole. They taunted her, telling her how useless she was, how unwanted, that nothing she ever did would be right.

Trevor might one day change his mind and challenge her to tell him who the father was. When he found out, that would be the end of their marriage, and Etty would only have herself to blame.

She could have said no to Billy, that night in the air raid shelter.

Just like her mother, Etty was making a mess of her life.

Etty's baby came obligingly in late July. No eyebrows were raised because in the eyes of the world – and more importantly, Ma Milne – the child was born prematurely.

Nellie was determined to deliver the child; Etty was resolute she would not. Trevor took his usual stance of not getting involved.

'Doctor Meredith is going to deliver my baby,' she told him, refusing to speak further on the subject.

In the end, fate intervened and Etty didn't have any say in the matter.

Her waters broke in the middle of the night and, when she prodded Trevor, he wakened immediately.

'Eh! What! Is it the baby?' Panicked, he leapt from the bed and, switching on the light, pulled his trousers on. 'Try and stay calm. I'll fetch Ma.'

'You'll do no such thing. Phone for the doctor.'

But Trevor had shot out of the room and was gone.

As fluid trickled down her legs, Etty was startled. No one had said such a thing would happen, or that her contractions would be so painful. She lay on the bed, her mind in a whirl as another contraction started, a powerful tightening in her back that moved into a long drawn-out pain and exploded in her belly. When the pain receded, Etty flung back the covers and attempted to stand but then another contraction began. Falling back against the bed, she let out a low moan.

At that moment, the door flung open and Nellie walked into the room. Through a haze of pain, Etty saw she wore a long dressing gown, tied at the waist; her fine, grey hair cascading over her shoulders.

Nellie took in the scene. 'Haddaway, son,' she told Trevor who hovered at the door, 'this is nee place for a man.'

Etty had never known pain like it and, at this critical stage of labour, she didn't care if the devil himself delivered her, as long as the baby got born. She would have liked to yell and scream blue murder, but with Nellie presiding over the birth, she resorted to biting her lower lip until it bled.

As another compulsive urge to push overwhelmed her, Etty, exhausted, didn't know if she could muster the strength.

'Don't push,' Nellie shrieked.

Silence. It felt like an eternity passed.

Then, 'Eee I can see the bairn's head. And he's got a widow's peak just like my Trevor.'

Etty gave one final push, going cross-eyed with the effort.

'It's a girl,' Nellie said, disbelievingly.

A baby's cry filled the room.

Struggling up on her elbows, she pleaded. 'Show me my baby.'

There was no answer.

Etty raised her head, and all she could see between her legs was Nellie swaddling the baby in a white towel.

'My,' Nellie exclaimed, 'even if she is early… what a whopper.'

Until she held her infant safely in her arms, Etty wouldn't believe such a miracle had happened. A thought flashed through her mind. She wondered about her own birth. Had Mam felt the same? Was she just as disbelieving she'd brought precious new life into the world? With that thought, Etty experienced an intense ache to hold her daughter.

'I want my baby,' she cried. 'Now.'

Nellie took the child in her arms and made for the door, calling along the passageway. 'Son, look who I've brought to meet yi.'

Etty, distraught, swung her legs over the side of the bed and tried to stand but, weak and dizzy, fell backwards against the pillow. Tears of frustration brimmed in her eyes. Desperate to inspect every inch of her baby, a sense of loss overcame her. The first moments of her daughter's life were spent in another woman's arms. Anger transformed into fear as Etty realised she'd failed as a mother already.

Presently Etty heard noises in the passage – Dorothy's voice.

Walking into the room, Dorothy gushed, 'I'm so thrilled I called in before work.' She sat on the bed and hugged Etty. 'I've seen my niece and she's beautiful and—' the smile dissolved on her face.

'What's wrong?'

It was all too much. Etty tried to check the tears but they came unbidden.

'Etty, you're scaring me. Tell me.'

Etty brushed away the tears with her hand. She gulped. 'I... I haven't... seen her yet... my baby.'

'You're kidding me.'

'Nellie... took her away and... my legs are too wobbly to stand... and I hate myself for crying.'

'How dare the woman?' Dorothy exclaimed.

Dorothy might have been of a mild disposition but any injustice, especially where her little sister was concerned, brought the savage out in her.

'Leave this to me.' Her back ramrod straight, she strode to the door. A hand on the doorknob, she turned. 'I'll be back in but a few minutes.'

She was back in two. Trevor was with her, the baby in his arms – his face one of disbelief.

Etty struggled up the bed to receive her baby.

Trevor began. 'I didn't know you hadn't held her, I would never—'

'Never mind that now,' Dorothy took the baby from his arms and gave her to Etty. 'She's the image of you.' Trevor smiled and there was pride in his eyes.

Looking down at her sleeping daughter, Etty took in the large nose, crumpled face, downy, blonde hair. She felt… nothing. She gazed up at Dorothy's smiling face, trying to explain but, exhausted, her mind couldn't find the words.

'Have you chosen a name?' Dorothy's voice seemed far away.

'Elizabeth,' Etty replied, mechanically.

'The same as the young princess. I like it very much.'

As drowsiness washed over Etty in waves she drifted in and out of reality. A weight was lifted from her arms and through slits of eyes, she saw someone bending over her.

Etty's mind grappled with the idea that her mother stood at the bottom of the bed.

The figure spoke. 'Not now. We'll see to her later. Leave her to rest.'

The voice was Dorothy's. As she drifted off to sleep, Etty's disappointment knew no bounds.

CHAPTER EIGHTEEN

August 1942

'It's baby blues,' Dorothy told Etty. 'I've heard it's happened to many a woman.'

Five weeks had passed since the baby's birth. After a particularly hot spell, the weather was cooler today and all Etty wanted was to be out of the four walls of her flat and breathing fresh air.

'And worrying about the baby during Jerry raids won't help,' Dorothy continued.

Neither of them mentioned the raid the other night when planes attacked a number of places in County Durham. 'And what with feeding the baby during the night and no sleep when a raid is on… It's wearing on the nerves.'

It was Dorothy's day off work, and the sisters had strolled up to Redhead Park, and now walked down Whale Street, heading for home.

'Aunty Dorothy', as Etty's sister delighted in calling herself, pushed the pram, where the sleeping baby was covered by a light cotton sheet, shielded from the sun by a fringed canopy.

Etty dreaded going home and blamed her melancholic state on the fact that she was in the house so much alone. She couldn't remember the last time she had felt at peace, and hadn't been wholly truthful with Dorothy about how she suffered. It felt as if her brain was smothered by a blanket and dark thoughts teemed through her mind while, at other times, she couldn't think at all.

But mostly she felt withdrawn, with no interest in anything, or anybody at all – even, God help her, her daughter. If Dorothy knew the extent of her malady, she'd insist Etty see a doctor. But Etty's fear was that she'd be certified as insane and locked up in an institution. For what Nellie had said preyed on her mind – that folks raised in an asylum didn't have proper feelings.

'Come to my place for a spot of lunch.' Dorothy spoke in an over-bright tone, watching Etty closely. 'I'm itching to show you the christening robe. It's finished, by the way, except for the name.'

The robe, made from parachute silk, was a gift from Dorothy for her niece's christening.

'What name?' Etty asked.

'It's an idea I've had.' Dorothy's face became animated. 'The robe can develop into a family heirloom with our children's names embroidered on it. Let's hope Norma…' she pulled a quizzical face and Etty knew she longed to ask about the baby's name change, '… Elizabeth Milne will be the first of many.'

Etty liked the idea; it gave the future a sense of the stability she needed.

They continued to wander down the street, passing Mrs Henderson on hands and knees as she scrubbed at her front step. Looking up and, seeing who passed, she pursed her lips. She wore a pretty apron, and her fair hair, wound around steel curlers, was covered by a turban-style headscarf. Etty shook her head in disbelief. Folk were being blown to smithereens and here was this lass worrying about the cleanliness of her step – the world had, indeed, gone mad.

Mrs Henderson gave Etty a black look.

'It's because you're not churched,' Dorothy muttered under her breath so Mrs Henderson couldn't hear.

'I'm not what?'

'Churched. It's a blessing by the local vicar, to thank God for the baby's safe delivery.' She shrugged, noncommittally. 'Supposedly, the blessing washes the sin of childbirth away. Unchurched people aren't allowed to enter anyone's home as it's considered bad luck for the household.'

'Superstitious nonsense,' Etty retorted. 'Some folks still live in the dark ages.'

At one time, Etty wouldn't have been able to stop herself making some cutting remark to Mrs Henderson, and Dorothy would have hissed, 'for goodness' sake, behave yourself, Etty.'

But in her present state, Etty hurried by without making eye contact, much to Dorothy's apparent amazement.

Coming to a halt and producing a key from her shoulder bag, Dorothy opened her front door and, turning backwards, bumped the pram over the threshold.

Etty followed her in. Standing in the gloomy passageway, an ominous dread gripped her. Involuntarily, she shivered. What if Mrs Henderson was right and she did tempt fate by entering Dorothy's home? A chill ran up Etty's spine.

Unable to tolerate the silence a moment longer, she spoke in the hope of bringing some normality back into the situation.

'Buck up, Dorothy. Leave the canopy where it is for now.'

'Won't Norma be frightened if she wakes up in the dark?'

'She's used to it… what with the blackout curtains.'

'What a treasure she is.'

The phrase, her mother-in-law's favourite, made Etty cringe. Nellie ruined the bairn. If Norma couldn't sleep, she had only to whimper and her granny would make a beeline for her cot. Lifting her out she would croon, 'Come to Granny, me little treasure.'

Used to being picked up, Norma would now only go to sleep if she was rocked in someone's arms – and those arms were generally Granny Milne's. Etty knew she should confront Nellie but overwhelmed by lethargy, she couldn't summon the energy.

'I don't like to interfere…' Stood in the kitchen, Dorothy chewed her bottom lip. 'But we… that is, Laurie and I… wondered why you've changed Norma's name from Elizabeth.'

By happy chance a fortnight ago Laurie's destroyer had sailed into the River Tyne for repairs. Given two days leave, Laurie was delighted to spend time with his wife and to be acquainted with his new niece. His eyes lit up when he was introduced to Norma, but crinkled worriedly when he glimpsed his sister-in-law.

'She is Elizabeth. Norma Elizabeth,' Etty retorted.

'I thought Elizabeth was your first choice.' When Etty didn't answer, Dorothy continued. 'I'm concerned it's got something to do with Mrs Milne.'

'Trevor did mention his Mam favoured the name.'

Dorothy's eyebrows shot up. 'Really.'

Hearing the uncharacteristic disapproval in her sister's tone, Etty stiffened.

'Trevor too,' she said, defensively.

She didn't add that, under the circumstances, she was pleased he'd had any opinion at all and that the name change had nothing to do with his mother. As for Etty, she felt frozen and couldn't care less what the baby was called.

Dorothy, crimson-faced, exploded. 'Etty Milne, what's wrong with you? You've lost your spunk. Laurie thinks so too. He made me promise not to say anything but somebody has to.' She gasped an intake of air. 'And while I'm on the subject, Norma's spending far too much time with Mrs Milne and it's not good for her... or you, for that matter.'

The idea that the Calvert's had discussed her affairs shocked and humiliated Etty.

Rarely did the sisters argue. By the distressed look on Dorothy's face, it had cost her dearly to say what she had.

'I know it's easy for me to say—'

'Yes, it is easy for you to talk,' Etty jumped in and, like a dam ready to burst, words gushed from her mouth. It was easy for Dorothy, she ranted, who didn't have a baby to care for and, until she did, she shouldn't criticize. Dorothy should thank her lucky stars she didn't have a battle-axe mother-in-law to contend with. Then, there was Trevor who, unlike Laurie, was no help at all and who Etty never saw because he scarpered over the road to the Newmans whenever he got the chance. When he did come home, he expected tea on the table and the house spotlessly clean.

Etty drew a much-needed long breath before going on. 'Just look at the state of me... with all the weight I've put on I look positively matronly. And with night feeds and early rising, I'm tired to the bone. Worse – much worse than anything else,' she met Dorothy's gaze, 'is the fact that I have no maternal feelings about Norma and I need help.' After another quivering breath, Etty continued in a small voice, 'What if this is what being brought up at Blakey's done to me? What if I never get better?'

The tirade finished, Etty dreaded what Dorothy might think.

Amazingly, her sister's face only registered relief. 'Goodness,' she said, 'I'm glad that's off your chest. First of all, this has nothing to do with Blakely, please believe me. We have left that place behind us. And you will get better... you must give yourself time. You're right,' she looked shamefaced, 'I don't know any of these things and it's a wonder how you cope with it all.'

'I'm a useless mam,' Etty confessed.

'Never say that. You're a new mother, that's all.'

'What kind of mam am I when I let Nellie whisk the bairn upstairs at every opportunity?'

'The emotionally exhausted kind, that won't ask for anyone's help. You've always been the same,' Dorothy chided, as if Etty were a child again. 'There's nothing wrong in admitting defeat once in a while, it's a sign of maturity. Laurie taught me that.' At the thought of her husband, Dorothy smiled tenderly.

Now that her outburst was over, it was as though Etty was purged. She'd been bottling things up, she realised, and it was good to share her fears with Dorothy. She thought affectionately of Laurie, who, on his precious days off, had found time to be concerned about her. How fortunate she was to have relatives she could depend on. In a flash of insight, she realised she wasn't mad at Dorothy or, indeed Trevor – but herself. No matter what Dorothy said, the way she gave into Nellie over the bairn was feeble. Etty despised weakness and vowed she'd never let it happen again. From now on, she would make getting stronger her first priority.

She told some of this to Dorothy.

'You see…' her sister said, rolling her eyes and shaking her head. 'Already, you're making getting well a contest. You need to relax, let it happen.'

'I suppose so,' Etty said, gravely.

She was conscious of her face looking solemn and, for some reason she saw the funny side. She met Dorothy's eyes and saw a spark of humour in them and the atmosphere, all of a sudden, was charged with fun. For no apparent reason at all, the pair of them started to laugh. And how they laughed, the kind when you couldn't stop, and your sides ached and your cheeks hurt.

Dorothy sniffed hard and wiped away the tears. 'Might I add, matronly does become you… but Etty, I've been longing to tell you… your hair really does need a trim.'

The pair of them dissolved again into shrieks of laughter.

*

Trevor tossed and turned in bed. It was four o'clock in the morning and Norma yelled in the back bedroom as if someone was trying to murder her. In an attempt to get some sleep, he pulled the bedcovers over his head. Etty came through from the passage and climbed into bed.

'Are you just going to leave her to yell?' he asked.

'There's no pacifying her. She's fed and dry and apart from rocking her to sleep, there's nothing else I can do.'

'For how long?'

'Norma's got to learn, Trevor, she can't be picked up every time she cries.'

'Says who?'

'Dorothy and I agreed—'

'Since when did your sister become an authority on bairns?'

His wife sighed deeply.

The floorboards upstairs creaked. Ma Milne was awake – no doubt she'd heard the bairn. Norma's screams pierced the air and for an instant Trevor wished his mother still had the key to the flat.

'I won't have your mother interfering.' Etty's voice was adamant in the dark.

'You've not complained before.' He knew he was being unfair but he was tired and had only a couple of hours before work.

'That was then.' Etty's voice implied the subject was closed.

When the bairn had yelled in the past, Ma Milne would appear as if by magic, and he could get back to sleep. Worried sick by the way Etty had been mooning about the place, not interested in anyone or anything, Trevor hadn't known what was wrong with her or how to put it right. But these days, Etty was firm and wouldn't let the bairn out of her sight, and though Trevor was pleased, he needed a full night's kip if he was to do a day's graft.

'Where's the harm in me ma taking the bairn for one night?'

'If you don't know, Trevor, there's no point me trying to tell you.'

'You need the rest.'

'Norma is getting too attached to your mam,' she said, 'and I want it stopped.'

Trevor made up his mind that he wouldn't take sides between the two feisty women. They were both capable of fighting their own corner and what he wanted was a peaceful life and a full night's kip. It didn't pay to get involved. Then Trevor remembered when he had had no choice but to get involved over the naming of the baby. It hadn't been his finest moment. Personally, he didn't give a monkeys what name the bairn was given as long as it wasn't something outlandish that would make them a laughing stock in the community. His ma, however, approaching him with that 'careful how you tread, son' look in her eye, had demanded the bairn be called Norma, as that was the name she'd chosen for him, if he had been born a girl. Etty, equally, had her heart set on Elizabeth.

At a loss to know what to do, he tested the waters by telling his wife he thought Norma a grand name for their daughter. Turning towards him, Etty, with her gorgeous hazel eyes shining in appreciation, had replied, 'It's lovely that you've come up with a name. Norma, it is, then.'

Trevor had never felt such a cad.

*

As months passed, Norma mercifully slept through the night and Etty became her old self.

Etty's daughter, a source of wonder, could now sit upright supported by a pillow and, with chubby little legs protruding, would rotate her head, owl-like, and watch her mother as she moved around the kitchen. With a crop of blonde hair and spectacular blue eyes, she was indeed a bonny baby, but her temperament was not an easy-going one. For, even at this age, if she didn't get her own way, she was prone to throw a temper tantrum. If a favourite toy was out of reach, or fell from the pram, her little body would go stiff with rage and, blue in the face, she'd hold her breath and Etty would panic until the little tinker would take an energising breath and let out an ear-splitting scream.

One Sunday afternoon, they sat in Dorothy's kitchen listening to some light classical music on the wireless. Norma, looking angelic, was asleep on her mother's lap, while Dorothy sat on the couch, needles clicking. Etty looked at the contour of the bairn's face and found herself searching for any similarity to Billy. With her hair colouring and eyes, Norma did resemble him, Etty realised, and the child would be a reminder of that fateful night for the rest of her life.

'The news will be coming on soon,' she remarked, to stop her train of thought.

There was a fire in the grate and the room was cosy and warm, creating a somnolent atmosphere. Etty could barely keep her eyes open.

She sat up and stretched. 'I can't stay, Trevor said he'd be home from his run by dinner time. The meat's in the oven but I've still got the vegetables to do.' She shrugged. 'Whoever said Sundays were a day of rest should be shot.'

'Probably a man,' Dorothy replied, and they both laughed.

Etty smiled fondly at her sleeping daughter. 'This tinker keeps me on my toes any day of the week.'

Dorothy counted loops. 'Just think of the amount of work we did at Blakely… and we were just children.'

'I'd rather not think about that, thank you very much.'

'What about Sandra… Miss Balfour… and the rest of the orphans? D'you ever wonder what happened to them?'

This was getting too close for comfort to the topic of Mam, Etty thought.

'Sometimes,' she admitted. 'I only hope that when this war is over and done, the orphans will have found homes and be spared from going back to Blakely.'

'I would think not… after all the damage that was done.'

'What damage?' Etty asked, suddenly wide-awake.

'Blakely took a hit during the bombing last October.'

'But… why didn't I hear of it?'

'Because you were in shock after your terrible experience in the shelter. And afterwards I didn't want you upset.'

'How did you find out?'

Dorothy shrugged. 'News like that travels fast. Later on, I went up to the site, to see for myself.'

Etty was dumbfounded that her sister had never mentioned any of this before.

'You're braver than me,' she said. 'I couldn't return... not for any reason.'

'I wanted to put the ghosts to rest.'

Dorothy's gaze held a faraway look, tears brimming in her eyes. 'Mam still lives in my mind.'

'Can't you let the past rest?'

'If only I knew the true facts, perhaps then I could.'

'But we never will.'

Dorothy's chin trembling, she nodded.

Etty worried at her sister's emotional state. Unable to comfort Dorothy with platitudes, she changed the subject. 'What about the Knowles?'

Dorothy wiped her eye with the heel of her hand. She sniffed. 'A man from the demolition squad told me that Benson, the old gardener, had been killed, so had Mr Knowles, and that the Mistress of the establishment was taken to the infirmary in a bad way.'

Poor Benson, thought Etty. All he had wanted from life was decent weather to work in his garden and watch the plants grow. He had had a wife who he'd adored, but had confided in Etty that she'd died from tuberculosis. The only comfort Etty felt at his tragic passing was that he would now be reunited with her.

Etty's mind then turned to Mistress Knowles and those horrid dead fish eyes. Scenes from life at Blakely ran through her mind, disturbing her.

'Don't, Etty,' Dorothy spoke softly. 'Leave the memories in the past where they belong.'

Dorothy was right. Mistress Knowles had blighted her childhood, and Etty would be damned if she'd allow the woman to intrude on the future.

'I thought it time you knew.' Dorothy took up her knitting again.

'You did right. We can now close the door on that chapter of our lives.'

Norma started to stir.

'I must be off.' Etty scooped the bairn up in her arms and stood up, kicking the ball of white wool on the floor. 'Anyway, what are you making?'

'A bonnet and mittens.'

'But those won't fit her in the winter?'

'Who said they were for Norma?'

Dorothy gave a sly smile, and the full impact of what she meant hit Etty.

'You're kidding me.'

'Afraid not… it's your turn to be an aunty.'

*

It was a Monday afternoon. Trevor had just got home from work and read the note propped up on the mantelpiece.

> *Gone to get the rations in. Your dinner's keeping warm in the oven. Try and get some sleep. See you after.*
> *xx Etty*
> *PS I might call in at Dorothy's*

Might indeed! Etty was never away from that sister of hers and, as far as his kip was concerned, Trevor couldn't sleep because he was too wound up. Finishing the six till two shift, he'd come home to an empty house, the fire practically out, dirty pots piled high in the sink and the dust so thick he could write his name in it. To add insult to injury, the unappetising smell of overcooked food wafted from the oven.

On one occasion, he'd confronted Etty.

'You might as well pack your bags and live with your sister,' he'd said, his tone more antagonistic than he'd meant.

They'd quarrelled and he'd ended up sleeping on the couch. He shook his head; it wasn't a moment he was proud of.

He had a mind to nip upstairs to his mother's flat for a bite of dinner, but then he thought better of it – she'd only gloat, calling his wife a lazy good-for-nothing, and him a mug for marrying her.

To be honest, he thought, as he sagged into a chair, after months of thinking Etty had gone doolally, he was relieved the feisty girl he'd married was back.

It clicked, that as it was Monday, Mr Newman would be driving the van to the timber merchants. No doubt he'd need a hand carrying heavy timber into the backyard. Trevor wolfed down his dinner, a plate of pig's liver, taties and carrots, so dried-up it clagged to the roof of his mouth.

He changed into decent clothes and slammed out of the house.

As he crossed the cobbles, Mrs Raffle came out of one of the self-contained houses over the road. Her husband was a dentist and the woman – about the same age as him – had that refined look that spoke of money. Whenever he gave out his address, Trevor was always quick to point out that he lived at the top end of Whale Street, where professional folk like the Raffles resided.

The lady gave him a pleasant smile. 'Good day, Mr Milne.'

Mrs Raffle wore a classically smart grey frock, black high-heeled shoes, lisle stockings, and she was rake thin. Trevor sniffed; no self-respecting bloke would want his wife to look that skinny, it shrieked that he couldn't provide properly. Trevor had no worries on that score; his wife was suitably well endowed. There again, he thought, these genteel women folks were always painfully thin.

Surprised to see her carrying a pail filled with leftover food, Trevor put on his Sunday best smile. 'Good day to you. I'll take the scraps up the lane for you, if you want?'

Galvanised bins were placed at lane ends, so that folk could put scraps in them for the street pig.

'Would you? How kind. It's a task I hate. Though I'm in favour of the end result.'

He took the pail from her and, walking up the street, lifted the bin lid. Depositing the scraps, he pulled a disgusted face. The contents of the bin smelt to high heavens.

He returned to Mrs Raffles, who thanked him kindly.

She beamed a pleasant smile. 'How's that baby of yours, Mr Milne? A girl, isn't it?'

'Aye... she's champion, thanks. She's called Norma.'

'Delightful name. You must be a very proud dad.'

'I am that.'

Watching Mrs Raffle disappear into the house, Trevor realised in mild surprise, that he was. She was cute, was Norma. Her bonny blue eyes and gummy smile turned heads when he took her out for a stroll in the pram. As far as Trevor was concerned, the bairn was his, and let no man say otherwise. Yet the seed of doubt niggled in his mind. No matter how he tried to banish the fact Norma wasn't his, the truth kept surfacing. Trevor reasoned that if he knew who the bloke was, he might be able to come to put the past behind him. But like a dog gnawing at a bone, he kept wondering about it.

By heck, Norma could throw a paddy, and her screams went straight through him. Aye, he loved his little lass, but bairns were women's work.

Mind you, not that he saw much of her these days. Since Dorothy had announced she was expecting, Etty might as well have moved into her sister's flat. There was a health complication, apparently – that Trevor didn't want to know about – and whatever it was, the doctor had ordered complete bed rest. So, while Dorothy was waited on hand and foot, he went without.

His ma's voice rang in his ears. *Son, if you had any self-respect, you'd stop your wife's gallivanting. Call yourself a man... you're nowt but a mouse.*

Trevor's lips bunched. One of these days he would tell his mother exactly what she could do with her advice.

*

It was a blustery, though sunny, December day and Etty was giving Dorothy a hand hanging out the washing in the lane. As Dorothy stretched to peg out a sheet, her maternity smock rode up and Etty glimpsed the satisfying mound of her abdomen. But elsewhere her sister was still painfully thin. In the early weeks of her pregnancy, Dorothy had bled and it was feared she might miscarry. Four months on, all seemed well, but it was Etty's firm belief that her sister couldn't be too careful.

She eyed Norma, who sat propped up against a pillow, watching the kiddies up the cobbled lane take turns with a skipping rope. Earlier, the bairn had caused a rumpus because she hadn't wanted to go into her pram. Her screams could be heard up the lane and, embarrassingly, folk poked their heads out of yard doors to see what was going on. When, finally, after a walk, Norma was pacified, Etty had called in at Dorothy's, where she confessed she didn't know how to handle her daughter when she had a temper tantrum.

Etty took a pillowcase from the pail. It wasn't just her daughter who was being troublesome. She remembered the last time she and Trevor had rowed. He chided her in an uncivil tone about how often she visited Dorothy. They'd rowed and he'd stormed off and spent the night in the kitchen on the couch. Later, she'd tiptoed along the passageway to check on Norma and there was Trevor checking on the sleeping bairn. In that moment she'd forgiven the man. His heart was in the right place.

Dorothy faced Etty with a stricken expression. 'It's frightening isn't it, the thought of bringing up a child? I so want to do what's best for our baby.'

'You will… you'll make a wonderful mam.'

But Dorothy wasn't listening. 'I really do think,' she said, 'what happens to a child moulds the future person.' She had something on her mind, Etty could tell. 'Laurie and I… have made a decision. After the war's over we're going to live out in the country.'

Etty was stunned.

Dorothy's eyes shone with fervour. 'I know life's full of uncertainties, but I want to make sure I've given my baby the very best start.'

Etty felt the blood drain from her face. 'Where in the country?'

'Somewhere in Northumberland. Laurie believes he can set up a business on his own in the building trade and we could rent a cottage.'

Etty couldn't believe her sister hadn't breathed a word of this before, and said so.

Annoyingly, Dorothy only laughed. 'I'm telling you now.'

'What about me?'

'As if I'd leave you behind! Our plan is to include you and Trevor. We could all go; there's nothing to stop us. Trevor will find work too.'

As the idea grew in her mind, Etty saw the possibilities.

An easterly wind whipped up and, while Dorothy swilled the yard with the water out of the washtub, Etty went inside. She gathered Norma's spare nappies and her handbag in readiness for home as Trevor would be back any minute for his tea.

The more she considered Dorothy's proposal, the better she liked it. Trevor wanted out of the pit and there was bound to be work for him in Northumberland. The bonus would be no more interference from Mrs Milne, though Etty wouldn't deprive Nellie of seeing her grandchild and would welcome visits. But the real reason the idea appealed was the thought of endless green fields, big blue skies, and a life lived in a close-knit family – something Etty had always craved, and was denied as a child.

A knock came at the front door. Her mind leapfrogging with possibilities for the future, Etty made her way along the passage and opened the door.

A lad from the post office stood there.

He held out an orange envelope. 'Telegram for Mrs Calvert.'

For the second time that day, the blood drained from Etty's face and she resisted the urge to slam the door in the lad's impassive face.

'That'll be mine,' the voice came from behind.

Dorothy held out a trembling hand.

CHAPTER NINETEEN

Though of course the sisters knew about the heavy losses of ships at sea, they never spoke about it to one another. But the fact that German submarines did great damage to the British fleet was always on Etty's mind, plus the threat of magnetic mines – a device ships attracted at their peril. And she couldn't discount the enemy in the sky.

Destroyers such as Laurie's escorted the brave merchant ships that brought quantities of food and raw materials to British shores and munitions to Russia.

Laurie's destroyer, she learned later, was one of four that had escorted a convoy to the port of Murmansk in Russia. As it had plodded through the North Atlantic sea, the ship was torpedoed and went down with a great loss of life, Laurie's included.

Etty's reaction to the telegram was to go numb. She went through the motions, her only thoughts for Dorothy, and how to help her sister get through the initial unbearable shock. The only way she could think to help was by being practical. She brewed a cup of sweet tea, brought the washing in, helped Dorothy – who appeared to have frozen – into a comfy chair. Her sister white with shock, stared into space and seemed incapable of taking anything in.

Then panic seized Etty. Her hands shook, and her heart raced so fast she thought she was having a heart attack. She didn't know what to do for the best. Phone the doctor for a sedative for Dorothy? Encourage her sister to speak about what had happened? Worried that she might do or say the wrong thing, Etty ended up not doing anything. Feeling weepy, she slumped in a chair opposite Dorothy.

'There's nothing you can do here, Etty,' Dorothy spoke in monotone. 'It's best if you take Norma home out of the cold.'

Etty started, she'd forgotten all about her daughter. 'I'm not leaving you alone.'

Dorothy's lips quivered. 'Don't make it hard. I want… I need to be by myself just now.'

'As you wish.' Etty's mouth was dry. She swallowed. 'But once Norma's settled, I'm coming back and I'm staying the night. Norma can stay with Trevor's mam for once.'

They say that the good die young and in Laurie's case never was a truer word spoken. Etty couldn't cope with the loss of her brother-in-law. She loved the burly man with his big heart and gentle ways, and she knew there'd never be anyone finer in her life.

'It seems unreal,' she told Trevor one night as they sat by the fire. 'Any minute, I expect Laurie to walk into the room.' A pang of sorrow engulfed her.

'Now is not the time to think of your own grief,' Trevor replied, brutally honest. 'You have to concentrate on Dorothy.'

Etty didn't take offence because she knew her husband, in this case, was right – and with God's help, she'd find a way to get Dorothy through this.

Those first few days, Dorothy carried on as usual, not appearing to feel the impact of Laurie's death. Etty, deeply concerned, knew her sister was in shock. Her face tinged grey, eyes defeated, Dorothy appeared shrunken. She ate little, slept fitfully and chatted about daily affairs, but never once did she refer to her husband or his demise.

Desperate to know how to help, she approached Trevor for his advice at teatime. They were sitting at opposite ends of the table. Trevor's eyes strayed to the *Gazette* at his elbow.

'Are you listening, Trevor?'

'Eh!' He pierced a piece of fishcake with his fork.

'I'm at my wits' end what to do.'

He stared blankly at her. 'About what?'

'Dorothy.'

Fork mid-air, he averted his gaze and appeared uncomfortable. It occurred to Etty that his anxiety was due to the fact that they were on the verge of discussing emotion. She could identify with that particular problem. Years at Blakely had taught her to feel awkward whenever sentiment was shown and seeing this flaw in Trevor made her understand him a little more.

'I'd value any help you can give,' she told him.

A mixture of surprise and pleasure crossing his face, Trevor deliberated as he chewed his food.

She could talk over most things now with Trevor, she realised, his practical mind helping to find a solution.

Finally, he said, 'I'm no good at this kind of thing but if I were you I'd ask Mr Newman. If anybody can help, it's him.'

So Etty sought Mr Newman's advice the very next day. After all, she reasoned, his job was dealing with grieving relatives.

'I've seen this before, Mrs Milne,' he said. 'Your sister's in shock and shying away from reality.'

Mr Newman kindly invited Etty upstairs to his living room, a gloomy space overcrowded with dark, heavy furniture. Ramona Newman, overly gracious and dripping with sympathy, offered Etty a sherry.

'A treat for the nerves,' she said, with a wary glance at her husband. 'You should get your sister to try some.'

Etty declined but accepted tea that, surprisingly, was brought in on a tray by May Robinson. Etty briefly wondered why the lass worked for Mr Newman, before growing uncomfortable. She felt nervous around May and couldn't meet her eyes. She would be devastated if she knew the truth, Etty reflected guiltily.

Mr Newman paced the floor as he spoke. 'The trouble is,' he momentarily paused and pinned Etty with a brutal stare, 'there isn't a body for your sister to bury and with no arrangements to make, her husband's death doesn't seem real.'

Etty had experienced some of the same herself. At times, she expected Laurie to walk through the door and announce that his death had all been a ghastly mistake.

'I suppose you're—'

'There's no supposing about it. My advice to you is to let your sister come round in her own time.'

Mrs Newman took a cup of tea from the tray. 'You know fine well, Roland, when some folk lose a loved one, they niver get over the shock. Maybe that'll be the way of it for Mrs Calvert.'

Hysteria rose in Etty and she calmed herself by staring at the tapestry fire screen and, taking deep breaths, counted to ten. If the situation weren't so serious, Ramona's lack of subtlety would be laughable.

'My dear,' Mr Newman said with great restraint. 'This is not the time for comparisons.'

'I'm only trying to help,' his wife flounced.

'Would it be possible…' May butted in, 'if I came to see Dorothy to give condolences?' She looked uncertainly at Etty.

The lass stood next to an occasional table, a china teapot in her hand. Her face had a ghastly pallor as if she too had suffered some form of shock.

'I don't think Dorothy's ready to face anyone yet,' Etty told her.

'Have you asked her? If I was you I wouldn't treat her with kid gloves.' May's chin jutted and Etty felt a modicum of respect for her.

The lass had spunk, Etty thought.

'Though I wouldn't be as forthright as May, she has got a point. Tiptoeing around your sister isn't the way. Be natural around her and talk often about your brother-in-law with ease… even if she can't. That's the ticket.' The conversation undoubtedly over, he made for the door. 'And Mrs Milne,' he said, his hand on the doorknob, 'please give my sincere condolences to your sister for her loss.'

With no other authority to compare it with, Etty took Mr Newman's advice. She spoke about Laurie whenever she could and ignored her sister's uneasy silence.

Amongst other things, Etty wondered aloud about Laurie's family, reminisced about the past, and went on to deliberate what they should do with his clothes. She despaired when nothing seemed to get through to Dorothy. Throughout her life, Etty realised, she'd always relied on her sister. Now the roles were reversed, it was her turn to be strong and she vowed she wouldn't fail Dorothy. Then came the day when things changed – and it started with the most innocent of events.

It had snowed during the night, melting to slush by morning. Etty bundled Norma in warm outdoors clothes and, putting her in the pram and swaddling her with blankets, made her way down to Dorothy's. She banged on the doorknocker and her sister answered.

'I'm off to the shop. Do you need anything?'

Dorothy looked her up and down and scrutinised her feet. 'Your shoes are soaked through,' she said. 'Why aren't you wearing wellingtons?'

'They've got a hole in them and I need a new pair.'

'You're the same size as me. You can borrow mine.'

Putting on the pram brakes, Etty followed her along the passage. Dorothy opened the understairs cupboard door and disappeared. She seemed to take an age and when she reappeared, she held, to Etty's surprise, an aged tennis racket in her hand.

Tears rolled down her face.

'Laurie's?' Etty asked.

Dorothy nodded. 'He... reckoned he was a champ in his youth.' Her chin quivered. 'He's isn't coming back, is he?'

'No,' Etty said, gently. 'Laurie died, Dorothy. I'm so sorry.'

Dorothy appeared to buckle and Etty put an arm around her shoulders to steady her.

'I can't live without him,' her sister's voice was hoarse.

'You can. You will. You're carrying his baby, remember.'

Dorothy began to cry, great sobs that racked her body. She sobbed and sobbed and Etty held her close until she stopped.

She sniffed and gave a weak smile. 'I suppose I have to get on.'

'I suppose,' Etty said, tears brimming in her eyes, holding her sister tighter.

'I want there to be an afterlife, Etty, because Laurie might be with Mam.'

Etty thought it best not to say a thing.

One day, in mid January, Dorothy astounded Etty. They were in the kitchen, Etty changing Norma's sodden nappy on her knee while Dorothy squatted in front of the fire raking the ashes.

'I've been to see Mrs Calvert senior.' Her voice barely audible, she didn't turn, carrying on with her task.

'What did she have to say?' Etty held her breath.

'Nothing much, in fact, she was quite abrupt... but maybe she was upset. They're not a close-knit family. There's two boys, both old enough to be in the army. Mrs Calvert has trouble with her legs and gets around in a wheelchair.'

Etty digested this piece of news. There was to be no reminiscing about Laurie with the Calverts then.

Dorothy faced her. 'It's odd, isn't it? Laurie coming from a family like that when he was such a warm and loving person.' She heaved her shoulders. 'I left a photograph of him in his uniform.'

Etty's heart somersaulted – she'd spoken Laurie's name. She prayed that this was the final hurdle and that her sister was coming to terms with her loss. A picture came into her mind's eye of Laurie in his uniform, and the lump in her throat hurt.

In other ways too, Dorothy progressed. She began sorting through Laurie's pitifully few belongings. Most of his personal possessions had sunk with him on the ship. His civilian clothes were sent to a second-hand shop, his cricket bat, sheets of music and keepsakes he'd had since he was a lad were boxed up and placed on top of the wardrobe for his child.

When Dorothy eventually opened up about her loss, to Etty's mortification, it was to May.

Etty, leaving Norma asleep in her pram at the front door, called in to see her sister. May Robinson was sitting at the table – the Morrison shelter that Dorothy had thrown a yellow checked tablecloth over. With her feet up on a chair opposite, eating a jam sandwich, May appeared as if she were part of the furniture. The lass had got into the habit of calling at Dorothy's during her dinner break and Etty was thankful as it meant Dorothy had daily company – even if May's presence did make Etty feel uncomfortable.

As she entered the kitchen, an awkward silence followed. It occurred to her that she still hadn't found out why May had left the factory. With a remorseful start, Etty wondered if it had anything to do with Billy.

She left May and Dorothy alone while she went into the scullery to make a pot of tea.

The conversation in the kitchen resumed and Etty strained to hear.

'As I said…' May's voice sounded a tad nervous, 'I think you're brave.'

She heard Dorothy sigh. 'When I received the telegram… the shock was so great all I wanted was to die too.'

'Eee! Don't ever think that, not when you're having his bairn.'

'I don't now, but I did then. The worst part was getting angry with Laurie for leaving me.'

'The baby's part of him too. Just wait till the bairn's born... you'll feel differently then.'

The lass had a way of talking straight that Etty, given the circumstance, envied. She returned to the kitchen and taking the kettle from the hob, poured boiling water over the tea leaves.

Dorothy's smile was sad. 'Laurie reckoned his life only began when he met me.'

'You should be proud of the fact. I know I would be.'

'It's difficult to go on without him.'

'You're made of stern stuff... you'll think of a way.'

'He was so thrilled he was going to be a dad. His letters were full of plans.'

'Isn't it lovely, then, that he died a contented man.'

'I'd never thought of it quite like that before.'

A childish sense of being left out nettled Etty and, struggling with her composure, she tried desperately not to let it show. There was no real harm in May, she reasoned, and wondered why the lass vexed her so. Was it really to do with her relationship with Dorothy, or because she was Billy's fiancée? With a lurch of the stomach, she realised the latter was probably the reason.

Etty's mind didn't want to travel down that route; she'd end up feeling even more disgraced. 'Tea's brewed,' she called.

'Not for me, thanks.' May stood and gave Etty a sidelong glance. 'I'll have to get back to work. Besides, you and Dorothy will want to talk privately. You don't want me around. I'm not family.' This was said with a friendly smile.

When May had gone, Dorothy went to the alcove cupboard and brought out two cups.

'You're awkward around May. Is it because of...'

'Billy. I...'

'Etty! You either let it be known who the real father is or banish the fact from your mind and get on with life. It's up to you. Otherwise you'll torture yourself no end.' As she regarded her sister, Dorothy's expression softened to one of understanding. 'But it's not just about you, is it? Believe me, you're not a coward if you don't own up. You must think about other peoples' lives too. How it will affect them.'

'It's not just about the disgrace,' Etty admitted. 'I could never tell May because of the hurt it would cause. Poor lass… she's caught up in something she doesn't even suspect. And I've left telling Trevor too long. I wish I had told him from the beginning.'

Dorothy nodded. 'There's your answer, then. Don't prolong the guilt, as it will only ruin your life… Trevor's, too.' Dorothy looked upset and Etty hated that she was the cause. 'You must find the strength, Etty, to leave the past behind. For everyone's sake.'

'I know you're right but—'

'I'm not saying it will be easy but don't let it affect relationships… such as your friendship with May. She thinks highly of you.'

Etty, ashamed, had never felt so bad. She promised she would make a friend of May from now on.

And here Dorothy was in the midst of grief, trying to comfort her.

Etty gave her a hug. 'Thank you.'

Dorothy laughed, 'You don't get one of those at Blakely.'

Etty went on to lighten the mood by relating the tale of Mrs Milne believing that drinking too much tea could turn a baby yellow.

'There's not much hope for mine, then!' Dorothy placed the tea cups on the make-do shelter table. 'I've drunk gallons of the stuff since…' it hung in the air '…Laurie died.' A vein ticked in Dorothy's temple. 'The thing that hurts most is that our baby will never know its father.'

'We won't allow that to happen. We'll always keep Laurie's memory alive.'

Dorothy smiled gratefully.

They lapsed into silence, and when Etty thought about her brother-in-law, how he would never get the chance see his baby, she felt infinitely sad.

'I never knew our father.' She was surprised she'd spoken out loud.

'Neither did I, really,' Dorothy replied. 'I know he worked from home as a cobbler because he was ill. And that he died from his war injuries. I've only a shadowy picture of him in my mind.'

Dorothy had a faraway look in her eye and Etty wondered if she was recollecting about their father.

'Tell me.'

Dorothy started guiltily. 'I've never told you before because I thought it would make you sad as you've no memories of him.'

'It's sadder not knowing anything about him.'

Dorothy nodded. 'As I say, my memories are shadowy... me sitting on his knee getting cuddles and feeling sharp whiskers on my cheek. Him bending over and pulling the covers up around me when he kissed me night night in bed. I have an impression he was very tall – of course he would have been to me – and thin. Oh, and he pulled silly faces.'

'He sounds fun and kind.' Etty gave a wishful sigh.

'That's the sense I've always had of Father. Another thing I remember... our parents laughing.' Then a stricken look. 'After he died, I can't remember Mam's laughter again.'

Etty hastily changed the subject. 'Do you know what his injuries were?'

'I seem to remember he was gassed. Isn't that tragic? It's such a shame there's no one to ask.'

'There's the Grubers from the butcher's... if they haven't moved on. They might have known our dad.'

'So you do have memories of that time.' Dorothy looked piti-fully hopeful. 'Don't forget Aunt Lillian. Remember, I thought I saw her in Beach Road on my wedding day. She must know something about our father. Aunt Lillian was Mam's cousin, her surname was Stanton.'

They were entering dangerous territory, a region Etty wasn't prepared to go.

Dorothy had no such restraints. 'Etty, do you realise, I'm in the same boat as Mam? Our dad died just before you were born.'

The difference, Etty said in her head, *is that you'll never desert your baby.*

Dorothy went on. 'You did know her father was a vicar? And that she came from the Hexhamshire area.' Etty nodded. 'And that her mam died when she was little.'

'I never knew that. Who told you?'

'I've always known. I don't know how.' A wistful expression crossed Dorothy's face. 'Oh, Etty, I wonder what happened to her.'

She struck a forlorn figure, standing in the doorway, and Etty's heart wrenched. She would do anything to ease her sister's pain, to make up for her loss. An idea formed in her mind – an idea she instantly shied away from. She couldn't do that, not even for Dorothy.

Yet the thought niggled on.

She changed the subject. 'I've been meaning to ask. Why did May leave the factory to work for the Newmans?'

Dorothy hesitated. 'She's got troubles.' Dorothy moved to the hearth and poked the fire.

'Am I allowed to know?'

Poker in hand, Dorothy faced her. 'I wasn't sure whether or not to tell you, but we never keep secrets from each other.' She grimaced. 'Poor girl… Billy has broken it off. She couldn't handle factory gossip and she asked Ramona Newman, who is her aunt by the way, if she could have her old job back.'

Etty went cold. 'Did she explain why?'

'Etty, leave it.'

'Did she?'

Dorothy gave a troubled sigh. 'Can you remember when I told you ages ago that Derek was her son?'

Etty nodded.

'It's as I suspected; Billy is the father. They'd met before, when she was young, and she'd never told him about the baby. It's all rather complicated and I don't understand why the man didn't know about his son until then.'

'What was Billy's reaction?'

Dorothy's steady gaze met hers. 'He left her.'

As the full impact of what Dorothy had told her hit Etty, she went weak at the knees and had to sit down.

'You realise what this means,' she told Dorothy. 'If Billy has a son, and it's Derek, then he is Norma's half-brother.'

*

May was late for work. Usually, she rose in plenty of time but this morning she struggled to raise her head from the pillow. Her head ached, as did her bones but she refused to take time off, because she didn't want to stop and think.

She looked around the kitchen, with its swept stone floor, kettle whistling on the hob and oval table set for breakfast, concluding that everything was shipshape for her mother.

'Lass, there's no need for you to do all this,' Mam told her, time and time again. But May wanted to, as guilt still plagued her and it was the only way she could show her mother her appreciation.

Clever as she was, Mam knew something was up but May wasn't ready to tell her yet about Billy, and Mam didn't pry. May wished the folk at the factory were the same but everyone wanted to know everyone else's business. It was difficult keeping secrets and May would die if they gossiped about her.

Much to everyone's surprise, not least Mam's, May left the factory and went back to work for Aunt Ramona as a parlour maid. She didn't divulge that Billy had left her, making up a story that all leave had been cancelled at the barracks to explain his absence.

'Why?' Mam wanted to know.

Flummoxed as to what to say, May improvised. 'His regiment might be going abroad.'

Technically, this wasn't a lie because, at some point, Billy would be posted abroad.

The answer seemed to satisfy Mam because she didn't ask any more questions.

Billy had changed since New Year's Eve, May thought as she banged the front door closed and left the house for work. She didn't question why but she knew it had something to do with him going out first footing. She reminded herself to be patient and not to pester him. Her biggest fear was that one day he would tire of her – and it appeared that day had finally arrived.

It was on his last leave after the new year, she remembered, when he'd arrived unexpectedly and gone straight to the attic bedroom without a word. May made up a supper tray and, entering the bedroom, didn't question what was wrong as she knew her fussing would only infuriate him.

He paced the floor. 'It's not working, any more.' He stared at her with a wild look in his eye.

May would swear her heart stopped beating. She placed the supper tray on the locker beside the slim bed. *Please God, let this not be real.*

'What's not working?' She knew, of course, his meaning.

'Us'

'It's my fault, I shou—'

'It's nobody's fault.'

'I'll change.'

'Don't do this.'

'I will. Just give us a chance.'

'It wouldn't do any good. I thought I could settle down but I can't. And you… loyal and trusting… deserve somebody better than me. I should never have proposed.'

'Don't say that, Billy.'

'You don't realise it now, but I'm doing yi' a favour.'

She heard the firmness in his tone and desperation took hold. 'Leave it be for a while. You like getting me letters and when you're on leave you have somewhere to call home. I won't ask for anything, honest. Then when the war is done… see how you feel.'

May stood at the bus stop and a trolley bus arriving interrupted her reverie. She boarded and found a window seat, paying the cheery conductor. Then, gazing unseeing out of the window, she continued her musings.

'Don't sell yourself short,' Billy had told her. 'You deserve better than a waster like me. Think on it. What have I ever done to make you happy?'

She could think of hundreds of ways but the main one was Derek.

One of those déjà vu moments tiptoed over May and she was certain it was an omen.

'Billy,' her voice was tentative, but she was convinced it was the right thing to do. 'I… should've told you this a long time ago.'

'What?'

'You know that time on Cleadon Hills?'

Billy frowned in concentration.

'When we… made love for the first time.'

'Yes?'

'I got pregnant.'

Silence followed, his body stiffening.

Then, 'You're having us on.'

'Honestly. It's true.'

'Where's this bairn, then?'

Her heart thumped in her chest. 'It's Derek. Me mam brought him up.'

As he stared disbelievingly at her, Billy's eyes bulged.

'You conniving bitch. I never thought you had it in you. That you, of all people, would stoop so low to get me to stay.'

'Billy, I would never!'

May had often dreamed about the moment she told Billy about his son. Like a fairy tale, she imagined he'd be bowled over and the three of them would live happily ever after.

'To use the kid... your own brother...' Billy's voice was incredulous. 'To hook your claws in me... it beggars belief.'

'I'm telling you the—'

'Leave it, May. I'll pack me bag in the morning.'

He turned his back on her.

She couldn't believe this was the end. Helpless as to what to do, panic rose in her chest and she feared she couldn't breathe.

She gulped at the air. 'Don't hate us,' she exclaimed.

He didn't reply, simply glowered at her. In that moment, May summoned her dignity. She wouldn't beg. She wanted Billy's memory of her intact. She was capable of letting him go if that's what he wanted – but, she thought, tell that to the pain that ripped through her heart.

Even in her heartbreak, she couldn't help but worry about him. 'Where will you go?'

Still, he didn't answer.

'Let me know, Billy, I'd like to know how you're getting on.'

As the trolley stopped at Dean Road, May jumped off. Walking down Whale Street towards Newman's, she checked her watch. She wasn't late for work, after all.

She opened the funeral parlour door and, putting on a brave face, May hoped to fool her employers.

*

As time went on, May understood Dorothy Calvert's grief – how she didn't want to go on living without her husband.

The day Billy left, all evidence of him gone, the attic bedroom had felt lifeless without his presence. May had had an overwhelming feeling that she didn't want to go on.

She had always known it wouldn't last with Billy. He was a free spirit – no one could tame him and neither would she ever want to. May had believed that the fact he'd been a part of her life at all was enough, but how wrong she had been. Life without Billy, she realised, would only be existing.

In bed one night, as May tossed and turned, desperation took hold as she couldn't tolerate the heartache any longer. Like a wave swelling for the shore, all she wanted was to end her suffering.

Throwing back the covers, she padded down the stairs where she couldn't escape memories of Billy. Moving into the large familiar kitchen she made her way to the gas oven. By the light of a silver moon that shone through the window, she turned on the knob of the oven and opened the door. May sat on the cold linoleum floor, and taking out the shelves, she placed her head on the oven floor.

Hearing a hiss and smelling poisonous gas, her mind screamed *no*. Her last thoughts should be of Billy. His melting, dimpled smile; how handsome he looked in his khaki uniform, his ambition to travel the world and— as if a switch had been turned, May's thoughts paused. She choked, coughing and coughing until she retched. Sense taking over, she withdrew her head, sat up and decided she wanted to live. Not for her mother, the poor soul who would find her daughter dead in the morning, or her son, but for Billy. She couldn't bear the thought that he would blame himself for her demise. She couldn't spoil his life in such a way, when all she wanted was for him to be happy.

CHAPTER TWENTY

March 1943

'Coal, gas and electricity are all rationed, so what d'you think's next?' Etty asked Norma who sat in her sturdy high chair, made by Trevor in Newman's workshop.

Etty had read in a women's magazine that speaking conversationally to your child helped them with speech and vocabulary.

She continued, 'In February, rice and dried fruit were added to the list, not that you were affected as you're not keen on either, are you? In fact,' she scooped food from the plate onto a teaspoon, 'there's not much you do like eating these days and Mammy is fraught with worry.'

Hair smattered with vegetables, snot dangling from her nose, the bairn turned her head from the spoon of food proffered as if Etty was trying to poison her.

Etty knew so little about kiddies that she sometimes felt Norma was teaching *her*, rather than the other way around. Today, she tried to feed her solids but the bairn had a mind of her own, and refused to eat. The pair of them sat at the kitchen table, Etty pretending to eat mashed carrot from a spoon, making a suitably delighted face.

'Mmm! See… Mammy likes it.'

Norma, unimpressed, lashed out and swiped the spoon out of Etty's hand.

'Why, you naughty little thing,' she snapped.

This brought on a fresh onslaught of howling.

With all the broken nights, Etty was exhausted. She felt at the end of her tether, cooped up in the house for days thanks to the wintry weather.

The war news didn't help brighten her mood, either. Last month it was reported that after a week of battle, the Empire of Japan now occupied Singapore.

Etty shook her head. Eighty thousand Allied troops had been taken prisoner and Mr Churchill was reported to have said that it was the worst disaster in British military history. Fear crept over Etty – they were all mothers' sons and she wondered how folk coped with such heartache.

She looked fondly at her child, with her blonde curls and striking blue eyes. Even when she cried, Norma was a delight. It seemed incredible that in those first few weeks when Etty had suffered the blues, she had doubted her maternal love. Norma was precious and Etty loved her more than life itself. At the terrifying thought of losing her child, Etty realised that in this uncertain war-torn world, anything could happen – and a chill shivered down her spine.

The unlocked back door opened and Nellie appeared. Norma, still hollering, swivelled her head.

'What's wrong, pet? Granny's here to make it better.'

Norma stopped yelling and gave Nellie a two-tooth grin.

'What's the matter with her?' Nellie averted her eyes from Etty. 'She won't eat.'

Nellie chucked the bairn beneath her chin. 'If Norma doesn't eat…' she spoke in that irritating baby voice she used, 'she won't grow up big and strong.'

Norma clapped sticky hands together.

Nellie picked up a clean spoon from the table and proceeded to spoonfeed Norma who – wouldn't you know – ate without a whimper.

'By, she's all there, is that one. She knaas how to get her own way.'

Etty ignored the implication.

The two women had called a truce and only spoke when their paths crossed. This was the first time in a long while that Nellie had ventured downstairs and Etty had Trevor to thank for that.

He'd put his foot down, telling his mother to stop calling at bedtime because they were trying to get Norma into a routine. Her face puce, Nellie had sensed determination in her son, because, for once, she hadn't argued, turning on her heel and storming out of the flat.

Thrilled that he'd stood up to his mam, Etty noticed other changes in Trevor, too. He became interested in Dorothy's welfare and didn't object to the times Etty visited her. He even did odd jobs around Dorothy's flat and Etty was thrilled to see this caring side of him emerge.

The few times Nellie called, Etty tolerated her, as she saw no reason to cause trouble – as long as the she behaved, that was.

Etty liked the bairn to experiment with a variety of tastes and today's addition was mashed peas. Sampling a spoonful proffered to her, Norma made a disgusted face and spat the peas on the floor.

'What's this muck you're giving her?' Tasting the food, Nellie pulled a similarly revolted face that made Norma giggle.

'For goodness' sake, Mrs Milne, don't encourage her... she'll think eating's a game.'

'Don't talk tosh, woman... she's only a bairn. I bet she's got a sweet tooth like her da and wants a pudding.'

'After she eats her dinner.' Etty was firm.

Nellie muttered something under her breath.

'She said what?' Dorothy's face was a picture of disbelief.

'That I was an apology for a mother.'

Late afternoon in March, the sisters were taking Norma for a walk in the pram. They'd walked through Westoe Village and were treading the path that led through the allotments to the sands.

Dorothy stopped in her tracks. 'I hope you gave as good as you got.'

'I told Nellie, apology or not, I was Norma's mam and what I say goes. Then I told her, politely, to hop off.'

'Good for you.'

'The thing is, the little tinker howled when her grandma stormed out.'

They both laughed.

Though perishing cold, the day was bright and sunny, and the sisters, bundled up in woollen hats, mittens and scarves, took the sandy track past the bridge over the railway line, that led to the dunes. A bracing sea breeze brought colour to their cheeks and it felt good to be alive.

Etty took a sidelong glance at her sister. For weeks now, Dorothy hadn't been able to sit still, and perhaps that was why she stayed slim even though she was pregnant. If only she could lose the purple bruises from beneath her eyes and the haunted look that pulled at Etty's heartstrings.

To Etty's dismay, because of her sister's fragile health, Dorothy had worked up until she was six months pregnant at a local factory that had once produced civilian clothes but now made uniforms for both men and women. Until Laurie's financial affairs were settled, she had no other means but her wage.

'It's light employment,' she told Etty. 'Besides, it keeps my mind occupied.'

The sand on the path grew deeper, spilling over the top of Etty's shoes so she could feel it between her toes. In the distance, coils of barbed wire prevented them from reaching the beach.

Etty, pushing the pram, found it easier to haul it backwards through the sand. Shouts came from towards the beach and soldiers wearing khaki uniforms and carrying guns with bayonets crouched behind the dunes.

'They're carrying out exercises,' Etty whispered. 'I think we should go back.'

'Our brave boys…' Dorothy, mesmerized, commented, 'They are watching over us in case of a sea invasion.'

Without warning, her face crumpled and she sobbed. 'Bloody, bloody war.'

Etty left the pram and rushed over. Instinctively, she knew this was what Dorothy needed. She held her sister in her arms. Dorothy's sobs turned to great gasps that made her shoulders heave.

When finally, she stopped, Etty handed her a handkerchief.

Dorothy, pink-eyed, blew her nose. 'It still hurts like hell,' she said in a quivery voice.

Etty realised that the brave face her sister put on was all a front. 'I know,' she said, doubting if she really did.

'In my worst moments I still want to join him.'

'It'll get easier, I promise.'

Dorothy looked stricken. 'I don't want to be healed of missing Laurie.'

The wind whipping up, sand swirled in the air, and the surf could be heard pounding on the shore. From the beach came an occasional male shout.

Dorothy looked pale and drawn and Etty's impulse was to do anything she could to help. Her thoughts turned again to the idea she'd had the day they'd discussed their father.

Without thought of consequence, she blurted, 'I've made a decision… about Mam.' Dorothy's head jerked up. 'I'm willing to try and find out what happened to her.'

Dorothy's eyes widened. 'Because of me?'

'Partly… but I want to know the truth too.' Her confession surprised herself.

'How will we go about it?'

'You won't be doing anything.' Etty's tone was firm. 'I'll start by trying to find Aunt Lillian in Beach Road. If that fails, I'll look into seeing if I can find the Grubers.'

'Any other time,' Dorothy's voice held an edge of frustration, 'I would leap at the chance to help find Mam. But you're right, I haven't got the stamina just now. I'll stay home and look after Norma while you go. But Etty…' she clapped her hands on her cheeks in delighted disbelief, 'I really do appreciate what you're doing.'

Emotionally spent, her eyes welled up, and sniffing hard, she laughed through her tears. 'Poor child, look at Norma… she's wondering what's going on.'

Peeping over the top of the rain canopy, transparent blue eyes watching her aunty, Norma's face crumpled.

Dorothy forced a smile. 'Ah, pet, everything is all right. See.'

Etty prayed that her sister was right.

Trevor had worked the night shift and after a few hours' sleep he'd headed over the road to the Newmans'. The bairn, awake after her afternoon nap, played happily with a china-faced doll in her cot. Etty, busy ironing, was grateful for the peace. She'd made a pie out of the last of the bottled rhubarb and the pleasant aroma of cooking pastry wafted in the air. Content, a sense of wellbeing enveloped Etty.

As she paired Trevor's socks at the kitchen table, Etty heard the backyard door rattle. The door slammed. Footsteps clumped up the yard and the scullery door squeaked open.

'Anybody in?' a male voice boomed.

Billy!

Etty's heart started hammering. She smoothed down the folds of her skirt, checked her auburn hair in the mirror and ran her fingers through the waves.

'You've got a cheek, coming here.'

Beneath his army greatcoat, he looked thinner and his cheeks were hollow but – blast – he was still as handsome as ever.

'I'm like the proverbial bad penny.' His face wore a cheeky grin. 'Can I come in?'

'No, I'm expecting Trevor home any minute for his tea.'

'Go on. We're not up to anything… more's the pity.'

'I've told you. No. Trevor might catch you.'

'Crikey, Etty. Don't you ever have people call? One of the reasons I've popped in is to say I'm sorry to hear about your brother-in-law.'

Etty relented. 'Two minutes, then.'

She pulled back her shoulders, held her head high and marched into the kitchen. Billy followed.

She turned to face him. 'Why else are you here?'

Billy cocked his head, listening. 'Is that a bairn grizzling?' he asked.

'Yes.'

'Yours?'

Nervousness stabbed Etty and she didn't know what to say. 'I… asked you why you're here.'

'First off to say I was sorry about Dorothy's husband, he was a good bloke by all accounts.'

'The best.'

He didn't explain how he'd heard about Laurie and she didn't ask. She had more worries pressing on her mind.

He stalled.

'It's… over between me and May.'

'I heard.'

'It's for the best.'

'The best for who? She's broken-hearted.'

'She'll get over it. She still writes and tells me what going on.'

'You're heartless, Billy Buckley. You'll never find anyone as selfless as May. She worships you.'

'That's the hard bit. But she's handling the break-up better than I thought.'

'Hah! Your male pride is wounded! Serves you right.'

He grinned lasciviously. 'Seriously… it's you I want.'

She had to ask him. 'You didn't finish with May because of me?'

'She told lies to try and keep me.' His face clouded with disgust. 'I don't want to talk about it.'

Etty was flabbergasted that he should think May a liar.

It occurred to her that Billy was incapable of staying faithful to anyone, and she doubted he'd ever change. 'You only want me because I'm forbidden fruit.'

'It's always been you since the first time we met.'

He leaned forward and made to kiss her but she stiffened and pulled away. Yet she still didn't trust herself.

'It's only a matter of time,' his voice sounded peeved, 'before I'm posted abroad. Will you wait for me? How about we do a moonlight flit and move to make a fresh start?'

'I'm married, Billy.'

Norma's plaintive cry came from the bedroom.

Etty mentally shook herself. She stared at Billy – really looked at him, noting his arrogant gaze.

She made a decision. 'The baby that's crying… it's yours.'

'Not another one. Ha ha, very funny.'

'This is no joke, Billy.'

Disbelief registered on his face and something akin to fear. 'But we only—'

'Did it once. I couldn't believe it either.'

'And I'm definitely the…' at the look on Etty's face, he improvised. 'I mean, it could be hi—'

'It's yours. Trevor knew I carried another man's child—'

'And he still married yi.' He pulled a bemused face.

When Etty didn't reply, he continued. 'Why didn't you tell us before?'

'It wasn't appropriate. You were engaged to May. I considered it my problem.'

'I had a right to know.'

This was true. Why was she telling him now? Etty honestly didn't know… save, maybe, to see his reaction.

'Would you have left May? Played happy families? You professed you didn't want kids.'

Norma wailed and Etty made a move to go to her, before turning to Billy. She had to clarify something first.

'This plan of yours,' she said. 'Does it include your daughter?'

He blanched.

'Give us time, Etty, I've just found out.'

'In other words, no.'

'Hell, Etty, don't put words in me mouth. It's not a definite no. Until this very minute I didn't even know she existed.'

'Her name is Norma.'

Billy stared blankly at her. Maybe, Etty thought, she'd told him because she wanted to put the record straight for her daughter.

'It wouldn't be fair traipsing a kiddie around…' His tone was half-hearted. 'We could settle first and then send for… Norma.'

As if their daughter was a parcel. Etty shook her head in disgust – Billy really didn't have a clue.

Yet, somewhere in her being, she hankered for what he said to be true; that she could shed her responsibilities and follow him wherever he might go.

Then she came to her senses. An image of Norma's cute face, jaw trembling as she watched her aunty cry, featured in Etty's mind's eye.

'To be parted from my daughter for one day would be too long.'

Like the rest, she'd chased a Billy Buckley dream, she now realised. Flattered by his attention, she'd let herself become besotted. She hadn't seen the real person, the selfish cad he truly was.

'We could sort details out later,' he said, lamely, and she knew the heart had gone out of his purpose.

'Your daughter is more than a detail, Billy.'

'I make no bones about it,' he said, brutally truthfully. 'I've never wanted to be saddled with kids. But when a mistake happens it's dif—'

'Never call Norma a mistake.'

They had reached an impasse. It was time for them to go their separate ways.

'Come on, Etty, it was a slip of—'

'Go, Billy. We don't need you. Norma has a splendid dad in Trevor. And I have the perfect husband.' She was being cruel, she knew, but she wanted to punish him for the hurt he'd caused.

He winced, then his expression changed to cold detachment.

'You'll find someone else, Billy. I realise now you were never the one for me. I need someone dependable like—'

'Like the dummy you've married.'

'Goodbye, Billy.' Her tone was stiff.

Without a backward glance, he made for the door.

He was gone, this time for good. She heard his footsteps receding along the passageway.

She didn't want him, Etty knew that now for certain, but neither did she want their relationship to end this way. They'd made something special together – their precious daughter.

She raced along the passageway and, peering out of the front door, saw him swaggering up the street. He was halfway up the block; it was too far to shout without attracting attention.

He reached the top of the street and, turning the corner, disappeared out of sight.

CHAPTER TWENTY-ONE

Trevor watched, fascinated, as Mr Newman took the nail he held between his lips and hammered it into a coffin. The boss never missed and would be mortified if he did, because a hammer mark on a coffin was a sign in the trade of shoddy craftsmanship.

'I've heard tell of some dodgy fellows,' he told Trevor, 'who knock up coffins in their spare time and haven't a clue how to seal the joints properly. They don't seem to realise that it takes more than a hope and prayer and lining the coffin with sawdust to stop leakage happening.'

Aye, Trevor thought, Newman's, with its solid reputation, was the place to be.

He stretched and yawned. The nightshift had taken its toll, but Mr Newman was not a sympathetic man.

'If you're tired, lad, go home. If not, I'd appreciate a helping hand.'

Trevor picked up pieces of oak from the floor and flung them on the fire. He fetched a brush and started sweeping wood shavings.

'Mrs Newman was in her element this morning,' the boss said conversationally, without taking his eyes off the hammer. 'There was a letter in the post from our Danny.'

Danny, their only son and heir, was a pilot in the air force.

'That's champion. You'll be glad when the war's over and you have him home again.'

'That I will. He'll be back in the business where he belongs.'

'Danny's joining the firm, then?'

Mr Newman gave him a critical look and Trevor wished he'd held his tongue. 'Danny has some daft idea that he wants to become a teacher. I've told his mam that after the war he'll come to his senses.'

'Newman and Son, has a nice ring to it.' He flattered Mr Newman because it would do him no harm. But what he really wanted to know was whether this plan for the business would include him. The boss, finished hammering, looked ready for a chat, and Trevor, leaning on the broom handle, was ready to accommodate him.

'It's like this, lad… the wife and me have ploughed all our money back into the business, like my father did before me… and I'm doing the same for Danny.'

Bully for Danny, Trevor thought, poker-faced.

A gleam shone in the boss's eyes.

'Between you and me, Trevor, I'm looking for bigger property, some premises with a fair bit of land. I intend to expand the business. An investment for Danny in the future.'

More like a carrot to dangle in front of his son, Trevor surmised, but it was good news for him. Bigger premises meant more staff.

Mr Newman's manner changed and his look became tentative. 'While we're on the subject of business, I'd like a word with you about your mam.' His brow furrowed in consternation. 'Don't get me wrong, I've nothing but respect for Mrs Milne… how she's seen to folk in need over the years but… her way of doing things is outmoded.'

Trevor knew the boss's hidden meaning. The business was now too grand for the likes of his ma, whose practise of giving a neighbourly hand to lay out the dead was outdated. The insinuation was that it was Trevor's responsibility to tell Ma to retire.

'I can't promise anything… but I'll try.'

Before he'd hitched up with Etty, Trevor would no more have confronted his ma than chewed tobacco but he didn't flinch at the thought now. He had Etty to thank for that. With a turn of phrase, or a supportive smile, she assured him that his opinion did matter. She had a knack of making him feel good about himself.

'I'd appreciate that, lad.' Mr Newman visibly relaxed. 'Your mam can be… tricky at times.'

Trevor was saved from replying when the workshop door opened and May Robinson appeared, carrying a tray with two cups of tea on it. Today, her complexion the same colour as the white pinafore she wore, she looked ghastly.

'Have you met May? She's back working for us.'

Taking the tray from her, the boss set it down on the workbench. Like a trapped bird, she looked wildly about as if desperate to flit away.

'We haven't met,' Trevor told her. 'But you know my wife, Etty. She worked at the same factory. She's told me about you… all good things.' He smiled.

'Yes…' she said, 'and I know her sister Dorothy. I often caught her bus when I worked at the factory.'

'Our May is kindness itself,' Mr Newman intervened, 'when it comes to that sister-in-law of yours.'

At the mention of Dorothy, May became animated. 'Me heart breaks for what Mrs Calvert is going through. Laurie was such a lovely man. I hope your sister-in-law has a boy and it's the image of him.'

'Eh-hem,' Mr Newman's deliberate cough implied there'd been enough gossiping. May didn't need a second telling and scarpered from the room.

Trevor's thoughts turned to Laurie Calvert's death and how he'd had nightmares about the bloke's watery grave. Truth to be told, he didn't know Laurie, but folk spoke highly of him and no way had he deserved to die like that.

Etty had taken it badly and Trevor had wanted to put things right. He came up with an idea about how to help her sister's plight. Better at solving practical problems, his plan was to fix jobs around Dorothy's house and not to complain about how much time Etty spent at her flat. The plan was a success – Etty was appreciative and their marriage had taken a turn for the better from that day on.

The boss drained his teacup and took up the hammer. 'Back to work, Trevor, lad. The coffin won't make itself.'

Later that afternoon, Trevor, ready for the off, made for the parlour door. Stomach rumbling, he fantasised about what Etty had made for his tea.

He called through to the boss. 'Remember, I can't make it in tomorra.'

'Tomorrow,' the boss corrected him.

Heartened that the days were lighter now towards teatime, Trevor opened the door and stepped into the street. A movement over the road caught his eye. A soldier appeared in a house doorway – his doorway, Trevor realised with a start. The bloke, young and stocky built, exuded arrogance and watching him swagger up the street, something wrenched in Trevor's gut. Instinctively, he withdrew into the cover of the parlour's entrance.

Etty appeared in the doorway and looked up the street, her lips parted as if she were about to call out to the soldier. Then, as if she thought better of it, she hesitated. She sagged against the doorjamb, watching him as he walked away. Turning the top of the street, the soldier disappeared out of sight. Etty turned to go inside, but not before Trevor saw the expression on her face; a look of profound disappointment.

Trevor wasn't daft. This was the bloke Etty had supposedly had a one-night affair with. Fuming, his heart thumped in his chest. By, what a mug he was. He'd been duped. Doubts crept into his mind, and all kinds of scenarios presented themselves. How many times had the bloke called at the house? And how convenient that Trevor worked the nightshift. What about all those times Etty said she'd visited her sister? No doubt, the bloke was married – why else the secrecy? – and strung her along and, fool that she was, Etty had swallowed his patter hook line and sinker. But what upset Trevor most was the deceit. He'd never thought his wife was a downright liar.

How long he stood there, Trevor didn't know and it wasn't till a rag and bone man's horse clopped up the street that he gathered his senses. He tried to analyse his feelings – anguish, betrayal, anger – but all he knew was that Etty had made a fool of him. Inhaling a lungful of air, he crossed the cobbles and, entering the flat, his mood darkened.

'I'm late with tea,' Etty told him as he entered the kitchen.

The bairn, in her high chair, played with a favourite dolly.

'I don't want nowt,' he said.

Etty's hands shook as she set the table.

In the silence, heavy with duplicity, she turned towards him. 'What?'

'There was a bloke,' he said, 'a soldier… it looked as if he came out of our front door.'

She hesitated, but was quick to recover, 'Oh, him. That was Billy, May Robinson's fiancé. Did you ever meet him?'

Holy Moses. It got worse.

'What did he want?'

She turned and looked directly at him. 'He came to give his condolences about Laurie.'

She was good, he would give her that.

'That was canny of him.'

She looked at him, warily. 'Wasn't it?'

'Anything else?'

'Just general talk.'

To think only this afternoon, he'd sung her praises. How wrong could a man be?

He thought of May's tormented face as she served him tea, wondering if her fiancé's affair was the cause of her distress.

'You look pale.' Etty didn't make eye contact. 'You might be sickening for something. I'll make you a cup of tea.'

'I don't want tea.'

The audacity of the woman – behaving like nothing was the matter! Trevor shrugged off his coat and slung it over the couch.

A worried frown creased her brow. 'How about a glass of milk while you wait—'

'Are you deaf, or daft, woman? I don't want anything.'

As a hurt look crossed her face, Trevor despised himself but he couldn't stop. He was so wound up with jealousy.

Etty banged the salt cellar down on the table. 'I don't know what's got into you, Trevor, but until you can speak civilly to me, don't speak at all.'

Cold anger rose in him and Trevor felt out of control. 'This is my home and I'll speak to you anyway I please.'

Etty had the nerve to look outraged, as if she was the injured party.

The full impact of her deceit hitting Trevor, he blasted, 'You'd like that, wouldn't you? For us to behave as if nothing happened?'

Hands on hips, she drew herself up. 'What are you implying?'

'You know damn fine. You and your fancy man carrying on under my roof.'

Fear struck Trevor. What if this bloke knew about Norma and he wanted to now be a proper father? At the thought that he might lose Norma, or at the very least have to share the bairn with another man, gut-wrenching insecurity washed over Trevor.

'What I think, Trevor, is that you shouldn't jump to conclusions.'

'It was written on your face when he left, what this Billy means to you.'

There was the rub. Trevor couldn't bear the pain inside, spreading like a bush fire in his chest. Not betrayal, but heartbreak.

Etty had the grace to flush.

He mimicked, '*It was one of those things… a one-night affair that happens in war.* Liar! It's still going on.'

About to retort, she opened her mouth but no words came out. She shook her head.

'Think what you like but the truth is I sent him packing… afterwards. He was engaged to May.' She folded her arms. 'And I did the same today.'

Trevor hesitated. Could he be wrong? He wanted to believe her. He didn't want to lose what they had. Then the memory of the solider came to the fore – and jealousy and outrage won.

'D'you take me for a fool, woman? I saw the evidence… I've a good mind to throw you out into the street.' His head fizzed with hopelessness. 'I've had enough, Just… go to hell.'

The words rang out. The bairn, watching, began to cry.

Etty glared at him for one long moment and, collecting Norma from the high chair, stormed from the room.

Trevor anxiously ran his fingers through his hair. He could never take the words back. If Etty left, he'd have lost everything.

Again, the scene of the soldier swaggering up the street and Etty pining after him played in Trevor's mind's eye. No man worth his salt would be second best to another bloke, his outraged mind concluded.

The wrath inside him exploded like a firecracker. He would keep his side of the bargain, provide Etty and his bairn a home, but for Trevor, the marriage was over.

*

Billy gazed out of the carriage window and watched the hordes of folk, milling about the platform. Ever since he was a lad, he had been both thrilled and fascinated by the railway station. The notion that, by simply boarding a train you were transported to another way of life, appealed to the wanderlust in him.

Soldiers in greatcoats boarded a train while womenfolk waved tearful goodbyes – some poor sods had lost limbs and walked with crutches. A group of sailors wearing duffle coats crossed the bridge, while beneath, a train roared into the station hissing steam. In the carriage next to his, a soldier hung out of an open window. His sweetheart, standing on the platform on tiptoe, gave him a kiss goodbye. The scene aroused Billy and his thoughts turned to Etty. She got under his skin. He wanted her that bad at times that it became a physical ache – and the fact shook him. He'd never felt like this about a lass before. He laughed, ruefully. Who would have thought it, Billy Buckley had met his match?

The kid was a shocker, and something he hadn't bargained for. A whistle shrilled and the train jerked to a start. His nose inches from the window, Billy watched as the station passed slowly out of sight. He settled back in his seat and massaged his temples.

He lay back and rested his head on the seat and, closing his eyes, a picture of May's face, wearing her brave expression as he told her it was over came to mind. The lass had more spirit than he gave her credit for. She had corresponded a few times but didn't refer to the break-up and Billy worried that in her head they were still a couple. He never replied, as he didn't want to encourage her, even though she kept things impersonal. The truth was, he now had no feelings whatsoever for May.

He should have written though, told her he didn't hold it against her that she'd lied about the kid. Billy felt a swine he hadn't done that. As, truth be known, she'd made it easier for him to finish the affair.

As the train hurtled along the tracks, he fell into a sound and peaceful sleep.

CHAPTER TWENTY-TWO
April 1943

Etty passed the impressive Town Hall, pausing in front of the statue of Queen Victoria, towering above on a granite plinth. She wished her own head were made of bronze so she wouldn't have to think.

Yesterday's row with Trevor had taken its toll and she tossed and turned all night in the spare bed. How Trevor could believe she'd be unfaithful and in broad daylight with Norma in the house?

Yet, Etty thought, every picture told a story and Trevor believed what he'd seen. Could she really blame him? She had to admit the picture painted in the street did her no favours. Etty despaired. They'd been man and wife for some time, and now they'd got to know each other – to talk and debate about everything under the sun, and cautiously divulge their innermost thoughts – Etty had begun to believe they had a future together.

As the scene of Trevor's accusations played back in her mind, she regretted that she hadn't been given the chance to tell her side of the story. Damn the man. She was innocent of his accusation. She'd seen through Billy for what he was and sent him packing for good. Heart sinking, she surmised that Trevor could think what he liked. Because if his trust in her was gone then what was the point? The bottom line was, Etty, as always, would depend on her own strength and resilience and work things out.

Etty rounded the corner into Beach Road, and saw, over the road, the house where Dorothy was once employed. Mrs Brooke still kept in touch and when Laurie died, she sent condolences, wondering if Dorothy might like to join her in Lancashire. But Etty's sister had declined.

She'd told Etty, in a voice tinged with sadness, 'It's extremely kind of Mrs Brooke but I could never think of such a move. I want to stay in the flat where memories of Laurie are all around. Besides,' she'd given a small smile, 'I've got you to look after.'

It had been Dorothy's first attempt at humour since her husband had died, and Etty was pleased.

It was peculiar walking past the Brookes' house, seeing it unchanged, when so much had altered in their lives. Inevitably, Etty's thoughts turned to Laurie, and memories came flooding back.

She walked on as the street, empty of pedestrians, rose up a steady incline. At the thought of what she hoped to achieve today – to meet up with Mam's cousin and finally find out the truth about their mother – anxiety made Etty want to run a mile, but she steeled herself and carried on.

Tall terraced houses with bay windows overshadowed small forecourt gardens, some displaying yellow daffodils that nodded their heads. A stiff sea breeze infused her nostrils. Seagulls screeched overhead and Etty saw a blue band of glittering sea on the horizon.

Etty didn't know which house to try first and was drawn to the one with a pillar-box red door.

She knocked but nobody was in. The next door she tried stood beneath a canopy supported by two stonework columns. Banging the doorknocker, she heard it echo hollowly in the lobby. She was just about to walk away when a gruff voice called from inside. 'All right... all right... I'm coming.'

The door opened to reveal an elderly gentleman with a shock of silvery hair. He wore an Aran sweater with a polo neck and, leaning on a stick, his suspicious eyes assessed her.

'I'm sorry to trouble you, but I'm hoping you can help me find an aunt who I think lives in the street.'

'The name is?' His tone was terse.

'Milne,' she said, absently, staring at his weather-beaten face.

'Don't know anyone around here with that name.' He made to shut the door.

'Wait,' she cried, blushing when she realised her mistake. 'That's my name.'

The man stared.

'It's rather silly,' she quickly put in, 'but I don't know her married surname.'

'Any clues?' he asked.

'Her first name is Lillian'

He scratched his head. 'It's the Mrs you want... we've lived here over thirty years and she knew most neighbours by name.' A dejected look flitted across his eyes. 'She recently passed on.'

'Oh! I am sorry.'

The man nodded, glumly. 'Miss, can you think of anything else you think might help?' His tone was now deferential.

'She had a daughter called Margaret, I believe. She'll be a grown woman now, though.'

'Ahh!' Comprehension dawned in his faded grey eyes. 'You could be talking about Lillian Davies. Husband was a decent sort – owned a barber's shop. Their daughter, cute little thing, she was called Margaret. We used to invite them in for a sherry at Christmas when our children were small.'

Etty nodded in encouragement.

'They live further along over the road.' He pointed with his stick. 'The brown door with the red step.'

Etty smiled appreciatively. 'Thank you for your help, Mr...'

'Pearson,' he said. 'Captain Pearson.'

As Etty rapped the doorknocker of the brown door, she noticed the net curtain in the bay window twitch. A moment passed, and then the door opened and a woman stood there. If this was Aunt Lillian, Etty had no recollection of her, but she looked the right age.

'Can I help?' the woman asked, a dazzling smile splitting her face. Mature, with rust-coloured hair, peppered with grey, she had a dishevelled appearance. The buttons on her floral overall were done up the wrong way and a white petticoat hung beneath the hem of the skirt.

Her grin wide and infectious, Etty smiled back, 'I'm here to see—'

'Lillian.' Her eyes twinkled. 'Everyone wants to see Lillian… and to attend her meetings. What she did with her time before the war and meetings, I'm sure I don't know.' In the silence, the woman gazed expectantly at Etty as if she knew the answer. When none was forthcoming, she went on. 'How do you do, by the way. I'm Rose, Lillian's sister-in-law. I expect you've come about the troops' comforts.'

'I'm afraid—'

'Do come in… you're the first to arrive.'

The woman disappeared along the hallway, and with nothing else for it, Etty closed the door behind her and followed inside. The house, dark and chilly, reeked repellently of dog and, after the brightness outside, it took Etty a moment to adjust her eyes. The narrow hallway was decorated with cornices and an archway, and led to a flight of steep stairs, covered with a red, threadbare carpet.

'In here,' the woman said, gesturing to a doorway on her right.

'I must tell you,' Etty felt compelled to say. 'I'm not here for the troops' meeting. I'm not even sure if I've got the right house.'

Rose looked amused. 'Which house do you hope we are?'

'I'm looking for my mother's cousin, Lillian Stanton. At least that was her name before she married.'

'Then you've come to the right place.'

Etty's heart skipped a beat.

Lillian Davies stood at the fireplace, an arm resting on the mantel-piece. She wore a box jacket with a matching tweed skirt, pleated at the centre front. Stout, with pale skin, her hair a subdued brown, she looked as if at one time she may have been a fiery redhead.

'Lillian…' Rose said, 'This is—'

'I heard… Eleanor's daughter.'

At the mention of her mother's name, Etty blanched. This was someone who knew Mam – and her life history.

'*The* Eleanor?' Rose pulled an intrigued face. 'The one that caused a rumpus at the time of your wedding, Lillian?'

'The same.' Aunt Lillian, removing her arm from the mantel-piece, locked both hands behind her lower back.

'Such a to-do,' Rose grinned, wickedly.

'Why? What did Mam do?'

'Skipped the wedding,' Rose said, gleefully, 'so she could meet with a forbidden beau, who became your father. Has she never told you? She must giggle about it nowadays. I know I would.'

'I wouldn't know.' Etty looked directly at Aunt Lillian. 'I've haven't seen her since I was little.'

Rose gave a sharp intake of breath but Aunt Lillian didn't bat an eyelid.

'You poor thing,' Rose looked uncertainly at her sister-in-law and then back at Etty. 'Why ever not?'

'I'm rather hoping Aunt Lillian will tell me.'

'You will, won't you, Lillian? Tell the child what she wants to know.'

Rose plumped up a cushion on a very sorry-looking couch. Removing the clutter – an open novel, sewing box and newspapers – she patted the seat next to her and Etty sat down.

'This was before my time.' She turned to Lillian. 'You never told me Eleanor left her children.'

Aunt Lillian pursed her lips and didn't reply.

As though she was used to rebuffs, Rose turned to Etty. 'I expect you're wondering,' she prattled, 'what I'm doing here. You see, when my husband Arthur died, Lillian and George – Arthur's brother – kindly invited me to live with them. The two men were in business together, a barber shop, then the business went broke… such a terrible affair that left us all without any—'

'I don't think, Rose,' Aunt Lillian interrupted, 'the girl has come to hear about our affairs.' She looked at the clock on the mantelpiece. 'Isn't it time you were off to work?'

'Gracious, is that the time?' Rose leapt from the couch. She shook her head ruefully, 'Such a pity,' she told Etty, 'I was enjoying myself getting to know you. We must do it again some time when I haven't to rush to work.'

'What do you do?' Etty enquired. She liked this rather potty woman and wished she could stay.

'I help run a nursery in the local church hall… It allows mothers to go out and do their bit for the war. And if I don't buck up they'll wonder where I am.' Rose stood and made for the door. 'I look forward to next time we meet… toodle-pip.'

After Rose left, a resounding silence followed. Aunt Lillian made a pretence of straightening a picture on the wall – a ruse, Etty presumed, to delay the moment of truth.

Her gaze wandered around the room. It had a jaded appearance; faded burgundy wallpaper covered the walls, while matching coloured drapes hung listlessly in the bay. The furniture – two fireside chairs and a heavy mahogany sideboard littered with bric-a-brac – had seen better days.

She became aware of Aunt Lillian watching her.

'You're Esther,' she said.

'How did you guess?'

'Your auburn hair. And you always resembled Eleanor.'

A thrill ran through Etty, which she quickly dispelled. She didn't want to look like Mam.

'Why exactly did you come?'

'To ask you if you knew…' Etty could barely breathe for tension. 'Mam's whereabouts after she left us at the orphanage?'

'How should I know?' Aunt Lillian looked taken aback. 'You all simply vanished. I didn't know Eleanor took you to an orphanage. Though nothing that woman did would surprise me.'

'You didn't know?'

'When she couldn't manage, I begged your mother to let George and me look after you. But would she listen? I can't believe she would rather put you into an orphanage.'

'Why couldn't she manage?'

'Huh! Made on she was frail. She was ruined at home. Didn't do a hard day's work before she met Harry… your father. After he died, the shop ran into debt. She was penniless but she still had airs and graces.'

'You wanted Dorothy and me to live with you?'

'No, just you. We wanted company for Margaret. George wouldn't allow me to go through childbirth again.' She shuddered. 'I told Eleanor she'd find it easier with only one mouth to feed.'

What a nerve the woman had. 'What did Mam say to that?'

'She wouldn't hear tell of it. We fell out. I never visited again after that.'

Hurrah for Mam, Etty wanted to shout. 'How did you find out we'd gone?'

'I didn't. That woman… the butcher's wife… Olga Gruber… she came to seek me out. How she found our address, I'll never know. She said your mother had shut up shop and vanished without trace. She wanted to know your whereabouts. I told the woman we were just as bewildered as her.' Aunt Lillian pulled an affronted expression. 'Fancy not telling us – her family – her intention… but George reminded me we weren't Eleanor's keepers, and I decided he was right. Shortly afterwards Margaret took ill with scarlet fever and everything else was driven from my mind.'

In simple terms, Aunt Lillian had washed her hands of the situation.

Etty's gaze fell on a framed photograph of an attractive young girl dressed in a uniform, on the sideboard.

'Is that Margaret?' she asked.

Scenes from childhood played in her mind's eye. A child who wore the prettiest frocks, and had flaxen pigtails bound at the end with colourful ribbons, and who, in Etty's childish mind, lived the life of a princess.

'It is…' Aunt Lillian's face radiated a rare smile. 'She's doing well for herself. She's in the air force and has recently been posted to RAF Gravesend as a radio operator.'

Bully for Margaret, Etty thought and then felt mean because she would be the same way about any achievement of Norma's.

Aunt Lillian didn't enquire about Dorothy, or how the sisters had fared in the orphanage or, indeed, what they were doing with their lives now. Wrapped up in her own life, she didn't give a damn about others. Etty didn't blame Mam for falling out with her cousin.

But she'd promised Dorothy and was obliged to ask. 'So nobody knows what happened to Mam?'

'Did I say that?' said Aunt Lillian, stony-faced. 'Some weeks later,' her manner was impatient, 'after the Gruber woman came to see us, I received a letter from Martha explaining that Eleanor had returned to Rookdale. Her hometown.'

Etty's mind reeled. None of this made sense.

'Who's Martha?'

Aunt Lillian gave an intolerant sigh. 'Don't tell me you didn't know Eleanor had a sister.'

'Why should I?' Etty's tone was equally sharp.

'I suppose I'm not surprised. The pair of them never got on. When Eleanor returned to Shields for the second time—'

'Second time?' Events were going too fast for Etty to follow.

'If you'd kindly let me finish.' Aunt Lillian clicked her tongue and when she spoke, she punctuated each word as if speaking to an idiot. 'Your mother came to South Shields to attend my wedding when she met up with Harry…' Her eyes unfocused, she appeared to look down the years. Something vexed her because her face contorted with bitterness. She shook her head before continuing with her narrative. 'Your mother spoiled my wedding when she didn't turn up at the ceremony – she was supposed to be my bridesmaid.'

'Where was she?'

'Your grandfather found her with Harry – a young man he'd never met. He was furious, especially as the man in question was not of our social class. Your grandfather made arrangements to travel home with Eleanor the same day.'

Crikey, Etty could imagine the uproar Mam had caused.

Aunt Lillian continued, 'The second time Eleanor came to South Shields, she'd run away from home to be with Harry – against your grandfather's wishes.' A look of annoyance crossed her face. 'It was to my father's house she returned, and he took her in even though…' whatever Aunt Lillian was about to say, she thought better of it. She rose to her full height. 'My father, you see, was a fair man and didn't agree with his brother, Elroy's, strict code of behaviour. He could never see through Eleanor that she brought things on herself.'

'What did Grandfather do?'

'It's ancient history. Suffice to say, Elroy didn't approve of your mother and father's union and so he, effectively, disowned her.'

Her lips compressed into a thin line. Apparently, that was all she was prepared to say on the subject.

Etty couldn't let the matter rest. 'Surely, after Dad died, Grandfather relented? After all, we were poverty stricken.' Although she rather hoped Mam had had too much pride, and had told her father what he could do with his money.

Aunt Lillian gave a mocking smile. 'I would assume he never knew about you two girls. Your grandfather, you see, though a man of the cloth, was the most insufferable tyrant and would never tolerate the thought of your mother having a child by Harry. Your mother knew this and, wisely, she wouldn't tell her father about you two girls.'

So, that's why Mam rid herself of her daughters, Etty thought. She couldn't manage without a man and wanted to go back to the luxury of her former life, dumping her kiddies at an orphanage. The sheer heartlessness of Mam's actions left Etty cold.

A knock came at the front door.

'That'll be my company.' Aunt Lillian, bristling with importance made for the door.

Then she paused. She hovered as if deciding upon something and then moved to the bookcase. Her eyes travelled the books and she took a slim, battered one from the middle shelf.

She thrust the small tome into Etty's hands. 'This belonged to your father. You may as well have the book as it will only get thrown out.'

Etty, flicking the pages, discovered a volume of poems. She spied a handwritten dedication on a page but she daren't read it in front of Lillian.

'Thank you,' she said, overwhelmed. 'One thing more before I go. Did Martha's letter say why, after Grandfather disowned Mam, he took her back in?'

Aunt Lillian's expression became livid. 'Your mother could wrap men around her little finger... my father included. Supposedly, she'd been ill and went home a semi-invalid. There was a tearful reunion and Elroy fell for it. Your mother, you see, was a spoiled, pampered brat, and one of those women men fall over themselves to protect.'

'Do you know what became of them all?'

'No.' Aunt Lillian stomped to the door. 'And I don't want to know. Martha never wrote back after that.'

As she stood outside the door, gathering her wits, Etty had one thought. What should she tell Dorothy?

Retracing her steps, Etty looked up at Queen Victoria's blurry face.

Somewhere out there, she inwardly told Her Majesty, Mam exists and lives a lie. With the knowledge came heartache almost too hard to bear. Etty shook her head in disbelief. What kind of person could live, carrying such a weighty burden? Perhaps she didn't. Maybe she was a heartless person, without feeling.

Part of her, Etty realised, had wanted to find some justification for Mam leaving them, but that hope crushed, she felt sick with rage. She hated her mother with a vengeance and wouldn't spend another precious moment thinking about her.

She worried about Dorothy, unable to bear the hope fading in her sister's eyes. What if the shock proved too much and affected the baby? Mam had ruined their childhood and Etty was damned if she'd let her ruin the future.

Her mind searched for a way to soften the blow.

As she traipsed up Westoe Road, weighed down by her discovery, a squad of Home Guard men marched by in the road, row upon row, looking proud and unified. Looking at them, an idea formed in Etty's mind. She knew exactly what she must do. She wavered – could she go through with it? Sometimes in life, she told herself, you didn't do what was right, but what was best for those concerned.

She gave a wry laugh and wondered if that's what Mam had told herself when she'd abandoned the sisters at Blakely.

CHAPTER TWENTY-THREE

'What kind of book?' Dorothy wanted to know.

It was dinner time by the time Etty arrived home, but the meaty smell of stew permeating in the kitchen did nothing to lift her spirit. Nor did seeing Norma, who looked adorable as she played with a little wooden boat that sailed in a basinful of water on the table.

After admitting she had indeed found Aunt Lillian, Etty procrastinated by telling her sister about the book.

'Poems from the Great War,' she said, handing the shabby black book over.

'Why would Dad give Aunt Lillian a volume of poems?' Dorothy's brow creased in puzzlement.

With less than two months to go, her bump, Etty noticed, strained the material of the maternity smock she wore.

'Look at the dedication,' Etty told her.

Dorothy flicked to the page.

'*To darling Lily. From Harry.*'

Dorothy's eyes widened. 'D'you think that's Aunt Lillian? And if so, why would our dad dedicate poems to her?'

'Look at the date.'

Dorothy's eyes travelled back to the book.

'Why, it's autumn 1918. The Great War.'

'If I've done my sums correctly,' Etty told her, 'this was before he met Mam. And that's probably why Aunt Lillian was so hostile towards her.'

'How d'you mean?'

'According to the dates, Mam must have met our father after the war.'

'Maybe it was love at first sight and Dad had to break it off with Aunt Lillian,' Dorothy's eyes held fervour as if she were writing a romance novel. 'And she's been a woman scorned, ever since.'

'Soppy romantic,' Etty laughed.

'Why d'you think Aunt Lillian gave us the book?'

'Who knows? Probably, she just wanted rid of it and forgot about the dedication, but guess what?' Etty had been longing to share this piece of information. 'There's some of Dad's poems scribbled in the back leaf of the book.'

Dorothy turned the pages till she found loose pages of poems written in pencil.

Her eyes shining, she looked up and beamed. 'Oh, Etty, it brings our parents to life, when they were younger, doesn't it? Poor Dad, though… just a young man, stuck in that rotten war and getting gassed. I feel as if I know him a little better now.' Her expression changed and became one of wonder. 'I've just realised… if Mam met him after the war, he would have been an invalid. She must have been very much in love.' She fanned her face with a hand. 'I'm so touched… it makes me want to cry.'

Etty didn't know what to say.

Dorothy's eyes gleamed with unshed tears. 'Like me, she lost the love of her life. I wonder how she coped with the grief.'

'Like so many things,' Etty kept her tone emotionless, 'that's something else we'll never know.'

Dorothy's face lit up. 'We've learned so much about our father thanks to this book. He was romantic and wrote poetry and he liked to be called Harry. He loved our mam so much he broke it off with his former girlfriend.' She clasped the book to her chest as if she'd never let it go. 'Tell me, what else did Aunt Lillian have to say? Did you recognise her?'

'I can't say I did. And you were right about where she lives. But by the look of things, she's down on her luck.' Etty stalled.

'And… come on, Etty, spill the beans. I can see by your expression there's something else. Is it about Mam? Did Aunt Lillian know something?'

'Yes.'

'Oh! I can't bear the suspense. Tell me.'

An air of expectation filled the room as Etty struggled with an answer.

She inhaled a lungful of air. 'Mrs Gruber sounded the alarm. She knew about Aunt Lillian and visited her to ask if she knew where Mam and her daughters were. It turns out that Aunt Lillian had no idea Mam took us to an orphanage. She tried to find us but with no one to ask it was impossible, and when her daughter took ill, she gave up the search.' So far so good, she thought, watching Norma's starfish fingers submerge the boat in the water.

She felt Dorothy's intense gaze upon her. 'And…'

'Aunt Lillian heard nothing more until a letter arrived from Rookdale… Mam's hometown.'

Dorothy gave a sharp intake of breath. 'Oh, Etty, I recognise that name.'

'The letter came from Mam's sister… Martha.'

'Mam had a sister?'

'Apparently so.' Etty wanted this next bit of the story over as quickly as possible. 'Martha corresponded with Aunt Lillian, informing her that the Infirmary in South Shields had been in touch. Mam, apparently, was a patient and very ill, and had given them her family's address in Rookdale. Martha requested of Aunt Lillian that she visit and report back.' Etty squirmed as she fabricated the lie but she reminded herself Dorothy's peace of mind was paramount.

'Why didn't she go herself?' Dorothy's tone was indignant. 'Wild horses wouldn't keep me away if you were ill.'

Etty explained about Mam running off to join their dad and how Elroy – their grandfather – had disowned his daughter. 'He probably forbade Martha to visit Mam and she was afraid to cross him.'

'What rotten luck for Mam… that she had such a weak-bellied sister. You hear of such things happening in families… authoritarian fathers and frightened females. But Grandfather was a clergyman. Where was his compassion?'

Etty shrugged.

'Did Aunt Lillian go to the hospital?'

'Yes… but Dorothy…' As she prepared to tell another lie, Etty's body went rigid and her mouth went dry, 'it… it was too late.'

A small cry escaped Dorothy and, her knees buckling, she sagged into a chair.

'It was as you said all along. Mam did die.'

'I don't feel like gloating.' Dorothy's voice wobbled. 'Did you ask Aunt Lillian what Mam died of?'

Etty improvised. 'I was in shock… and forgot to ask.'

Dorothy nodded, understandingly. Unshed tears glistened in her eyes. 'Oh, Etty, you know what this means? Mam knew she was desperately ill and that's why she took us to Blakely. Too ill to write, she must have got the hospital to contact her family, believing they'd visit and she could tell them where we were.'

'It would appear so.' Etty had never felt so rotten. This was the first and last time she would ever deceive her sister.

'Mam never got to make it up with her family.' Dorothy smiled through her tears. 'Oh, Etty, though I'm desperately sad, I'm glad too… not just for me, but you too. Mam did love us. She intended to return for us. You can stop hating her now.' She grasped Etty's hand. 'Thank you for finding out. I always knew in my heart Mam cared and there was a reason she didn't return for us.' Her face crumpled and tears rolled down her cheeks.

Etty knew something too. As long as she lived she would never forgive her mother.

*

A great source of worry for Etty was what to do about Dorothy when her baby was due. The practice these days, because of the threat of enemy invasion, was to encourage expectant mothers to evacuate to the country where they'd be safe and well looked after.

But nothing would budge Dorothy. 'I intend to have a home birth,' she told Etty, chin jutting as she eyed a photograph of Laurie in pride of place on the mantelpiece.

Doctor Meredith agreed, making an exception in Dorothy's case. Etty was convinced he didn't force the issue because the move, he believed, might be detrimental to her sister's health.

'What if your labour starts during the night?' Etty wanted to know.

'I've arranged with the Armstrongs upstairs that I'll knock on the ceiling. They can make it to the phone booth up the street to call the doctor.'

'You can't rely on the Armstrongs. They're ancient and he's deaf as a post.'

Etty's idea was to debunk from home and sleep in her old room but Dorothy wouldn't hear tell of it, especially if it meant disrupting Norma.

'Besides,' she said, 'what help would you be if Norma decided to wake up during the night?'

Etty conceded this to be true.

Though loath to think on it, there was only one other solution.

'The nights Trevor works, she can stay upstairs at her Grandma's and I'll sleep with you.'

'What if I'm a couple of weeks overdue? You know you hate Nellie monopolising Norma.'

This also was true.

Etty didn't know what to do. Normally, she would talk troubles over with Trevor, but since his accusation, things weren't the same between them. They barely spoke and, if looks could kill, Etty would be dead. These days she couldn't step a foot outside the house without an inquisition.

A voice nagged in her head. What would she be like if the situation was reversed? She knew she'd look at the evidence and, like Trevor, think the worst. She'd been so secretive, no wonder he mistrusted her.

Etty now rued not telling him the whole story from the first. The terror she'd felt when the shelter walls shook and she'd thought she was going to die, how Billy was the father and she'd had feelings for him. That she had come to her senses, seen him for what he truly was, and worked out that, after everything, she didn't love him.

Etty was frustrated as she knew even if she did tell Trevor the truth now, he wouldn't listen. He'd made up his mind and nothing would change his opinion of her. She realised she couldn't go on living a lie. Not just for her sake but for Trevor's too. Continuing as they were would make them miserable and they'd come to hate each other. There was Norma to consider too. The bairn loved her dad and he in turn idolised her. Etty would never come between the pair of them. There was only one thing she could think to do.

The war had opened opportunities for women in the workforce and even those with children helped out. They took pride in their work and gained a patriotic satisfaction in helping the war effort. When the time was right, Etty would ask her sister if she and Norma could move in down the street. Etty would apply for a job while Dorothy could stay at home and look after the children. And then Norma would stay close to her daddy.

Not yet, though, as Dorothy had problems of her own and Etty didn't want to add to them. She would wait until after the baby was safely here.

She told Dorothy now, 'If I have to leave Norma with her grandma then so be it. I won't have you sleeping alone when you're due… there's no more to be said.'

In the end, the decision was taken out of their hands.

During the final weeks of her pregnancy Dorothy's body swelled and, much to her dismay, her fingers puffed up sausage-like and she was forced to remove her wedding ring. A trip to the doctor confirmed that her blood pressure had shot up.

'He advises complete rest,' she said.

'At home?' Etty asked, already making plans.

'No. He wants me in the infirmary where he can keep an eye on me.'

When Dorothy was admitted to hospital, Etty went jittery inside. Her mind preoccupied, she dropped everything she touched and did the silliest things, like filling the sugar basin with flour, and misplacing objects, especially the tea caddy, only to find it in the strangest place.

She wished Dorothy's confinement was over and done and the baby safely arrived so she could breathe easily again.

On a sunny afternoon in May, Etty walked along the maternity ward corridor. Sun streamed through the windows, an antiseptic smell accosted her nostrils, and she heard the babies' thin cries from behind the nursery door. In the black message bag she carried was a newly washed nightdress, an egg with her sister's name printed on it and the most darling little white matinee coat and boots that Dorothy had knitted for the baby.

As she walked into the ward, Etty saw that Dorothy's bed had a screen around it. Peeping round and seeing it empty gave her a shock. She hurried out of the ward, finding Sister's office along the corridor she rapped on the door.

'Come in.'

Sister Hope stood calm and composed behind her desk.

'Could you please tell me where my sister, Mrs Calvert, is?'

Sister Hope gave a brief nod. 'Mrs Calvert delivered her baby a half hour ago. She's still in the delivery room. The baby's fine but your sister has lost a lot of blood and her temperature's raised.'

A rush of adrenalin raced through Etty. 'Is it serious?'

'We intend to keep a close eye on her.' Sister smiled encouragingly. Wearing a starched cap and navy uniform, a black belt encircling her ample waist, she exuded professionalism, and Etty was reassured.

'Can I see her?'

'For five minutes. She needs rest.'

As Etty entered the delivery room, it was smaller than she'd envisaged. A drip stand stood by the bed, and a chart hung over the bedrail which Etty was tempted to read. It occurred to her she hadn't asked the baby's sex.

'It's a girl,' Dorothy told her. Head resting against the pillow, she looked pale and wan, but a glimmer of triumph shone in her eyes. 'She's called Victoria.'

Etty placed the egg and the other paraphernalia she'd brought on the locker top and, kissing Dorothy on the cheek, stood awkwardly by the bed as no seat was available.

'Congratulations,' she beamed. 'I'm thrilled it's all over. What a lovely name.'

'It's what Laurie and I chose if the baby was a girl – for when we're victorious and win the war.'

Dorothy's chin wobbled, and neither sister spoke for a moment.

Dorothy recovered. 'The babies are in the nursery for a time in the afternoon. The nurse said it's so that we mothers can rest. And she said I'm supposed to lie on my tummy for a while.'

'What on earth for?'

'Apparently it's to get tummy muscles back into shape.'

'That's a new one on me,' Etty looked keenly at her sister. 'How are you feeling, really?'

'Light-headed, if I'm honest. I dread standing up.'

'Then don't. Promise me you'll stay in here as long as you can.'

'The way I feel I've no option. And they look after me so well.'

'How was the birth? Was it too bad?'

'At one stage I yelled so loud the midwife said I should be ashamed of my—'

'It's easy for her to talk,' Etty interrupted heatedly. 'What's the betting she's never given birth?'

'You couldn't explain it to anyone, could you?' Dorothy shrugged. 'It's something you have to go through and it's lonely when you're left to get on with it yourself.'

Etty nodded.

'I kept reminding myself that millions of women have gone through the same thing through the ages.'

'It doesn't help, though, does it?'

They both laughed.

'Go on…' Dorothy's eyes drooped. 'Have a look at Victoria. I know you're dying to. I'm afraid I'm off to sleep.'

When Etty walked into the nursery there was no mistaking her niece. Her cot was in a row with the others and, lying on her side fast asleep, she was swaddled in a white blanket. With her snub nose and blonde feathery hair, she looked familiar.

'Why,' Etty told her, 'you're the image of your cousin when she was born.'

When Dorothy was discharged from the hospital and settled at home, it soon became apparent that any similarity between Victoria and her cousin ended in looks.

'She's such a content little thing,' Etty peered at the sleeping child in her Moses basket. 'You hardly know you've got her.'

Dorothy wasn't convinced. 'Wait till you hear her howls when she's hungry.' She frowned in consternation. 'She's such a windy baby. D'you think it's because she's bottle-fed?'

It was a source of great frustration to Dorothy that Victoria wasn't gaining enough weight. 'The midwife thinks she's not getting enough food. She's advised that I supplement with baby milk from a bottle.'

'What I think,' Etty told her sister, 'is that you worry too much. Victoria is thriving and you can't call that feeble wail, a cry.' She shook her head in disgust. 'Can't you remember Norma's bellow? Now *that* was a cry.'

Dorothy laughed and admitted she did remember the ear-piercing noise.

'I breast-fed Norma and it didn't make a happeth of difference to her wind and she was never a picture of contentment.'

Overall, Dorothy was doing well and apart from her private grief, all her thinking time was taken up by Victoria. But there was no denying that recent events had taken their toll. Dorothy had lost the first flush of youth; her appearance now careworn. Etty, infinitely sad that life had been so tough on her sister, aging her beyond her years, was reconciled to the fact that the war had this effect on people who'd lost loved ones and it was no use getting maudlin, because life held its riches too.

They were both mothers, each to a beautiful daughter, and some weren't as lucky, as they hadn't made it this far.

Her thoughts strayed to Bertha Cuthbertson, who could cook up a wise saying on most occasions.

'Hinny,' she would say, 'don't go looking for trouble, it'll find you soon enough.'

Their paths hadn't crossed in a long while, and she missed Bertha's friendship and forthright opinions.

On impulse, she said to Dorothy, 'Why don't we invite folk for a knees-up? I vote Bertha Cuthbertson for one.'

Dorothy looked unsure. 'What about the babies?'

'Having babies doesn't mean we can't enjoy ourselves once in a while.'

Dorothy brightened. 'I'm game for some fun… I vote May Robinson. By the way.' She looked tentative. 'Did you hear Billy Buckley's been posted abroad?'

'No. Did May tell you?'

'She visited last night. She said she wrote to him but he never answered except this once to tell her to get on with her life and that he'd been posted abroad.'

Etty was staggered that she felt – nothing. No rush of adrenalin at the sound of his name or yearning of the heartstrings.

She was truly over Billy Buckley.

'Won't Trevor mind?' Dorothy asked. Etty looked blankly at her sister. 'About getting chucked out of his home for a party? We could have it here if you want.'

The whole point was to give Dorothy a night off.

'No, we'll have the party at my place,' Etty told her sister. No matter what Trevor thought, the flat was her home too.

And so, it was settled.

Trevor, when he heard, wasn't pleased.

'Who've you invited?' he asked, suspiciously.

'Mainly workmates from the factory. Bertha Cuthbertson and—'

'Her that came to our wedding?'

'Yes.'

'A right upstart, she seems.'

'She's my friend.'

It was the first time the couple had communicated since their big row – if you could call the heated conversation communication.

'I'm not asking, Trevor; I'm telling you. I don't need your permission to invite people to my home. Besides you won't be here.'

'This is not your home… and where else would I be?'

'Work, fire watching, over the road at Newman's. Take your pick.'

Silence.

Then, 'Who else would be coming?'

'Dorothy, and she's invited May Robinson.'

'Why her? I don't know how you can face her.'

'She's Dorothy's friend.'

'Does she know about—'

'If you must know, they've split up.'

'That's handy.'

Etty observed that her husband appeared a little lost and forlorn. And she couldn't help but feel a pang of sorrow. The trouble was they were both stubborn.

'Trevor… contrary to what you think, I am not a liar. Anyway, he's been posted abroad.'

Another silence.

Etty's patience wore thin. 'So, what you're saying is I'm forbidden to have people round?'

Trevor clenched his teeth. 'For God's sake, woman, do what you like, I'm past caring.'

CHAPTER TWENTY-FOUR
May 1943

As Trevor walked home from work, confusion rattled him. For deep down, he still had feelings for Etty, but his wounded pride wouldn't let him get over this Billy fella.

Etty's words played in his mind. *I sent him packing... afterwards... And I did the same today.*

He wanted to believe her.

Then he pictured again the soldier in the street. It was the swagger that did it, made Trevor unable to overcome his suspicions... For what man was that cocky when they'd just been shown the door?

Later, tea over, the bairn tucked up in her cot, Trevor sat on the couch reading the *Gazette*.

He felt Etty's eyes on him and looked up.

She towered over him, arms folded.

'Are you going over to Newman's?'

'I might.'

'When?'

'When it suits me.'

'You will be... sociable to May when she arrives?'

'Don't tell me how to act,' he snapped.

'It's just she's—'

'You're scared I'll say something.'

'You wouldn't.'

A knock came at the front door.

'That'll be Dorothy,' she said.

'Who's looking after her bairn?'

'She's bringing Victoria with her.'

Before he could retort, she was off along the passage, opening the door.

Trevor shot up from the couch and, shrugging into his coat, made for the scullery, slamming out of the backyard door.

'We've got a job on, lad,' the boss greeted him. 'We're needed down the block at number ninety-eight.'

'The Duttons' place?'

'Yes. Charlie died.'

Without further ado, the boss picked up the board, some clean sheets and pillowcases and made for the door.

Charlie – otherwise known as Slinky, for reasons unknown to Trevor – was a pitiful excuse of a man, who drowned his sorrows in drink. It was a mystery where he got the money.

Trevor, picking up the trestle, followed the boss down the street.

It was late May, and the evening hadn't yet surrendered to the dark, so neighbours were out on their doorsteps gossiping to one another. As the undertaker and his mate passed them by they fell into watchful silence as though death itself walked between them.

Outside the door of number ninety-eight, a handful of ruffian children congregated. One of them, a girl with matted hair and rough features, asked shrilly, 'Mister, is it true? Has Brenda's da died?'

'Away home the lot of you,' the boss barked, shushing them off with his free hand.

The kiddies scarpered.

Trevor, entering the hall, made his way along the rank-smelling passageway. He found himself in a sparsely furnished kitchen where four scruffy, grave-faced kiddies sat, unbelievably, on wooden crates. It had been a good few years since he'd seen Slinky's wife and he was appalled at the change in her. As she sat on a three-legged stool, staring at dead embers in the fire, her eyes held a profound look of hopelessness. Emaciated, and of indeterminate age, she had mousy, lacklustre hair that hung limply to her shoulders and, with a prominent nose and pointed chin, she reminded Trevor of a witch in a fairy tale.

The boss laid a gentle hand on her shoulder. 'We won't be long, then we'll leave you in peace.'

She rounded on him. 'Tek as long as you like… that lyin' sod's goin' nowhere.' Mr Newman retrieved his hand as if it were burned. 'Lying bugger, telt me he had a job and was gannin' to work. And there was him throwin' the drink down his neck. Where did he get the money from… that's what I'd like to knaa?'

Wouldn't we all? Trevor thought.

The last he'd heard of Slinky – which was over six months ago – was that he'd lost his job as a caulker at the docks. As far as Trevor knew, the bloke had never worked since.

'How did it happen?' He ventured to ask, then wished he hadn't when the boss gave him a vexed look.

'Bugger was drunk coming home from The Locomotive at the Mill Dam… toppled off his bike into the path of an oncoming trolley. Killed outright.' Tears sprouted from the woman's eyes. 'Serves the silly sod right.'

'Ah-hem! Shall we get on?' The boss rolled his eyes at Trevor. 'Mrs Milne… what are you doing here?' he asked, sharply.

Trevor's Ma stood in the bedroom. She was holding a flannel, which she wrung out over a dish that stood on a chair at her side, before washing blood from Slinky's face.

The boss raised his eyebrows questioningly at Trevor, as though this was his fault for not having a word with Ma as promised – but Trevor hadn't had a chance. Besides, what the boss didn't grasp was that folk around these parts didn't take kindly to change and they'd send for Ma no matter what.

'Trevor and I can manage here, thank you.' Mr Newman's tone was curt.

There was an awkward silence when it looked as if Ma might explode. Then, a look of purpose crossing her face, she bent over Slinky and continued with the job in hand.

'Take it up with Elsie Dutton,' she told the boss. 'It was her sent for me to lay her fella out.'

Looking infuriated, the boss quickly recovered and, after inhaling deep calming breaths, his professionalism took over.

'I assume, Mrs Milne, the doctor's been informed to issue a death certificate.'

'Aye.'

'And the priest, has he been notified to give the last rights?'

She shrugged. 'Nowt to do with me.'

Shoulders back, Mr Newman became his officious self. 'Trevor, lad, I'm away to arrange such things with the departed's wife.'

He marched from the room.

'Upstart.' Ma fumed. 'Poking his nose in where it's not wanted.'

Trevor thought it best to keep his counsel.

Charlie Dutton's skeletal body reposed on the bed. He didn't look dead. Trevor expected him to open his eyes at any minute, and wisecrack like he usually did.

Ma took one leg and Trevor the other and together they heaved Slinky's trousers off to reveal a pair of holed and stained long johns.

Trevor wrinkled his nose.

'This is no time for sensibilities,' Ma rebuked. She flapped a clean sheet from its folds.

Trevor's eyes wandered around the room. What a way to live, he thought. The only furniture was a wardrobe minus its doors – probably burned when the coal ran out – some rag-like clothes strewn over the bed rail, and a chamber pot under the bed, mercifully empty. That was it – apart from filth and no doubt, bed bugs. Trevor started to scratch.

'If you're that precious,' Ma said, tartly, 'you should have thought twice before taking this job.'

She gave him an infuriated stare.

'What?'

Ma rolled up her cardigan sleeves, then dunking the flannel in the water, she wrung it out again.

'You don't have a clue, d'you?' She faced him, her neck flushing a bilberry colour. 'All those folk arriving downstairs at yours and nobody thought to ask my permission.'

'For what?' Trevor asked, flummoxed.

'It's common courtesy to tell neighbours – especially when they're the landlady – there's ganna be a ruckus.'

The penny dropped. 'Ma, it's nothing of the sort, just Etty inviting a few mates round.'

'Let me be the judge of that. Anyway, where's Norma in all this?'

Trevor scratched his head in bemusement. 'In her cot, of course.'

'Don't "of course" me. She'll never sleep. Why didn't you think to bring her upstairs?'

So, this was the crux of the matter. Ma was vexed because she wasn't asked to look after the bairn.

'I've explained before, Ma, we're trying to keep Norma in a routine.'

'I don't want your explanations, what I want is for you to put your foot down.' She quivered with vexation. 'That madam downstairs thinks she can rule the roost. I've never heard the like… dictating to me when I can and when I can't see me own grandchild. You do know she's playing you for a fool. Call yourself a man, you're a mouse.'

That did it. Something inside Trevor snapped.

'For pity's sake, Ma,' he said, tightly, 'will you stop meddling in me affairs? I've had enough of you harping on all me life.'

'Well, I never...' Ma's mouth went slack and she looked as if she hadn't heard him right. 'This is the repayment I get for all me help.' She shook her head in disgust but he could have sworn there was a modicum of respect in her eyes.

Quick to recover, she continued. 'Son, I've always done me best. I'm on your side not like yon scheming wife of y—'

'Enough, Ma. From now on keep yer nose out of my affairs. Is that cl—'

The door flung open and Mr Newman marched in.

'What's all this rumpus?' he blazed. 'Have the two of you forgotten where you are?'

In answer, Nellie clutched her chest. 'Eeh! All these shenanigans doesn't do me heart any good.'

'Mrs Milne...' The boss's expression changed to one of qualified concern. 'Are you all right?'

She leaned against the bed. 'I'm fine... don't you go worrying about me...' She gave her son a meaningful look. 'Nobody else seems to.'

Her chin trembled and tears squeezed from her lids.

Holy Moses, Trevor thought sourly, Ma knows how to turn the waterworks on.

'I've just made Mrs Dutton a cup of tea,' the boss told her. 'Why don't you join her?'

As she left the room, Trevor would swear she smirked.

Once she had gone, the boss looked nervously at Trevor. 'What brought that on? You didn't tell her about—'

'No, it's nothing to do with that,' Trevor assured him. 'She's mad at the wife... something she's done.'

'Your wife?'

'Etty invited some folks around, and Ma isn't suited.'

'Oh, I see,' the boss replied, looking baffled.

'Matter of fact,' Trevor said, as an afterthought, 'one of them is your niece, May Robinson.'

The boss beamed. 'That is kind of your wife. The girl needs cheering up. She's split up from her fellow and he's been posted abroad.'

Trevor's rib cage relaxed. Etty had told the truth about that. Now, at least, he didn't have to watch his back every time he went out.

'Right lad, let's get on. Mrs Dutton says she wants her dearly departed buried in his suit.'

The news that Slinky was to be buried in a suit astonished Trevor. He would've sworn on his life the bloke didn't own one.

The pair of them worked in silence, dressing Slinky in a mothball-smelling suit they discovered at the back of the wardrobe. Mr Newman then took a little pot of rouge from his jacket pocket and, applying some to Slinky's cheeks and lips, finished off by combing the thinning brown hair. It occurred to Trevor that Charlie Dutton looked a sight better dead than he ever had alive.

'All that remains to be done is to put the finishing touches to the coffin. Let's see,' Mr Newman checked his watch, 'we could be finished and deliver the coffin by midnight. Does that suit you, lad?' It was common practice to move the coffin at night so that the neighbours wouldn't be disturbed.

'Aye... I mean, yes.' Trevor certainly didn't want to go home yet, not with Etty's mates in his house. 'That suits me fine. I can manage on a few hours kip.'

Trevor's eyes travelled to Slinky's feet and he noticed they'd left the bloke's socks on. They were the thick woollen type, held up by suspenders at the knee. Slinky's big toe poked out of a hole in one of them. As he removed the offending sock – so stiff with dried sweat it probably could stand up by itself – Trevor noticed something drop to the floor. He picked it up, astonished to find it was a wad of money. Crikey, he thought, as he leafed through the notes, it was a tidy sum.

The boss raised his eyebrows. 'Lad, it never ceases to amaze me what you come across in this line of work.'

He pulled back his shoulders, taking the notes from Trevor, and made for the door.

Mrs Dutton, still sitting by the fire, looked up at the boss in amazement when he pressed the roll of notes to her hand, a glimmer of hope shining in her eyes.

Aye, Trevor thought, another fool hoodwinked by the one they loved.

*

Dorothy was the first to arrive, carrying Victoria in a Moses basket.

'She's just settled after her last feed.' Her face wearing her perpetual worried expression of late, Dorothy hurried along the passage.

'Best you put her in the back bedroom with Norma, where they won't be disturbed,' Etty called.

Another knock at the door. Etty put out the light and opened it and made out the outline of May and Bertha.

'Leave the door ajar,' Bertha said, as she bundled in. 'Ada Barker, as per usual, is lagging behind.'

Etty took their coats, putting them on the bed in the front room and ushering her guests along the passage, into the kitchen.

Soon, the five of them were sitting companionably in front of the fire talking about mutual acquaintances at the factory but the mood became sombre when Bertha asked if anyone had heard about Joe Dent, a fellow factory worker.

'Poor chap… didn't make it…' she heaved a great sigh. 'His ship was torpedoed and he was one of the unlucky ones.'

Etty looked over to Dorothy, sitting on the couch, whose face had gone chalk white. The evening was supposed to cheer her up, but with this reminder of death, Etty feared the opposite might be true.

She pulled a warning face at Bertha.

The older woman mouthed surreptitiously, 'Sorry hinny, I never thowt.'

She leapt from her chair and, fiddling with the knobs on the wireless, found a programme broadcasting Glenn Miller's catchy music.

'Haway,' she chivvied the others. 'Take your partners.'

Etty pulled Ada from her chair. 'Come on, we'll show them how to do it.'

Etty leading, they danced the quick step around the room to the tune of 'In the Mood'. Bertha took to the floor with May and the four of them, bumping into each other like dodgem cars, ended up laughing hysterically. Dorothy, watching on, smiled at their silly escapades.

Bertha then produced from her handbag a bottle of spirit.

'Who's for a drop o'gin?'

Etty brought tumblers from the scullery cabinet and the five of them formed a circle and toasted one another.

'I'm just thankful, lass,' Bertha chinked her glass with Etty's, 'that you and me survived the bombing. That was a close shave if ever there was one.'

Etty cringed, worried that her friend might, inadvertently, let something damning slip about that fated night.

She changed the subject. 'If anybody wants, there's port left over from Christmas.'

The evening proceeded in full swing, with people dancing and May and Bertha polishing off what was left of the bottle of gin. May got maudlin at one point and looked as though she might burst into tears.

'Are you all right?' Ada asked.

'It'll be the gin,' Bertha assured. 'It does the same to me.'

May shrugged off the attention. 'The night's not about me.'

In the bedroom, Dorothy was feeding Victoria but she wouldn't settle.

'Bring her here,' Bertha called through. 'I'm a dab hand at getting bairns to sleep.' She opened her ample legs and made a hammock of her skirt. 'A bit of rocking in this will soon have her off.'

It did.

The evening ended with May and Dorothy asleep on the couch, while the other three nattered about women's place in the workforce, amongst other things, over a cup of tea.

Bertha, cheeks flushed with all the high jinks, said, 'Did you hear what Mr Attlee was reported as saying? That the work us women are doing in factories has to be seen to be believed… and he's right.' She pulled an indignant face. 'After this war is won, you won't catch me going back to being a dogsbody to my lot at home.' She turned to Etty. 'How about you, hinny? Will you make it back to work?'

Etty pulled a noncommittal face. If her plan to move in with Dorothy worked, it would be sooner than any of them might think.

'I've told my hubby,' Bertha continued, 'that if he thinks I'm going to slave—'

As if on cue, a knock came at the front door.

'That'll be him now, come to walk us home.' She rose to go to the door, and said, somewhat shamefaced, over her shoulder, 'Poor love, he'll be starved. I only left him a sandwich for his supper.'

Etty suppressed a grin. So much for her being a dogsbody. She woke May and Dorothy, and brought out the coats. 'I've had a lovely night, thanks,' May told her.

The company said their goodbyes while Dorothy stayed behind in the kitchen.

'Don't worry about these two…' Bertha nodded to Ada as they all stood inside the door, 'Bert and me will see they get safely home. It's on our way.' She turned to Etty. 'Thanks, hinny, I've had a grand night.'

'Yes, we'll do it again. It's done Dorothy the power of good.'

'Aye, but she looks done in.'

Bert, impatient to be off home, gave his wife a beady eye.

'Men,' she tutted.

'You looked pooped,' Etty told her sister, as she came into the kitchen. It was an understatement – Dorothy looked haggard.

'Victoria is so good,' she yawned, 'but the night feeds are taking their toll. I don't like to complain but it'll be wonderful when she sleeps through.'

Etty had a brainwave. 'Tell you what, why don't I have her for the night? It seems such a shame to disturb her now she's settled.'

'I couldn't, I—'

'Yes, you could… just this once. You've brought plenty of dried milk and bottles. And I've got lots of nappies.'

'Won't she disturb Norma?'

'I'll bring Victoria in the bedroom with us.' It was a measure of her sister's tiredness that she hesitated. 'Go on… you need a good night's rest and you'll be a better mother for it.'

That did it.

'If you're sure. I could do with the sleep.'

Etty bustled her sister to the door before she could change her mind.

'I'll be here first thing in the morning to collect her.'

Seeing the bruises beneath her sister's eyes, Etty doubted it.

*

As he walked Ma home, annoyance festered within Trevor and he couldn't bring himself to be civil enough to chat. Ma was just as bad, with aggrieved sighs and heavy silences.

When they came to her front door, she feigned weakness and leaned against the stanchion.

'Here, give us the key,' he said, shortly.

'I'm perfectly capable of opening me own front door.'

'Mother, I'll wait until you're safely inside.'

'Aye... you're full of concern now... when yon hussy's not here.'

She was itching for a row. 'Ma I've got to get back to work. It's been a long day, and I'm bone weary.'

'Heaven help that I should keep you.'

She fitted the key in the lock and hurried inside. 'Our Trevor, you'll be the death of me yet,' she said, head poking around the door.

'And good riddance,' he muttered as he stomped off down the street.

Later, around midnight, as he helped Mr Newman carry the coffin down the street, Trevor marvelled at the hours he could go without sleep. Despite his tiredness it was good to be out in the fresh air. The sky was clear and the smell of sea mingled with wood smoke drifted on a soft breeze.

Sealed and polished with wax, the coffin had a brass nameplate attached to its lid and, fortunately, it fitted through the front doorway. This came as a great relief because many a window had to be removed to allow a coffin to enter a deceased's house.

Slinky's wife waited for them in the kitchen.

Hands on hips, she demanded of Mr Newman, 'Where did you say you found this money?'

'Lodged down a sock.'

'The mean bugger. His bairns half starved, the rent man's breathin' doon me neck and all the time he's been hoardin' this.' She held out the roll of money in her hand. 'Mister,' she told the boss, 'I'll give that rotten sod o' mine a decent burial but I want everythin' done on the cheap... is that clear?'

'Perfectly,' the boss replied, poker-faced. 'Our aim is to please at Newman's.'

*

Trevor's thoughts, as he made his way home, turned to the wad of pound notes he'd found in Slinky's sock, money wasted on a man like Charlie who would only drink it away. In his mind, Trevor dreamed of the life he would live if he were a man of means. It wasn't so much the wealth, he concluded, but the doors it opened. He reflected on his present state, shoulders heaving as he sighed. What was the point of money if you had no one to share it with? He thought of a future without Etty – and it hurt like hell.

The flat was in darkness as he entered and he reasoned that Etty must be fast asleep in bed. An empty spirit bottle stood in the scullery sink and the last piece of pie beckoned from a plate on the cabinet bench.

Trevor scrubbed his hands under the tap and, drying them, picked up the piece of pie and ate it. Checking the back door was locked, he made his way along the passage, removing his collar and tie as he went. He opened the bedroom door and made his way over in the darkness to the mantelpiece. But something blocked his way.

'What the—'

'Shh! You'll wake her.' Etty hissed from the bed.

'Who?'

'The bairn.'

'Norma's in here?'

'No. Victoria. In her Moses basket.'

'Why's she here?'

'To give Dorothy a good night's sleep.'

'Hurrah, for Dorothy. What about me?'

'Shhh!'

'Don't shush me, woman.'

Silence.

'Why wasn't I consulted?'

Trevor felt undermined. He collected his pyjamas from the bottom of the bed.

Bedclothes rustled as Etty sat up. 'What are you doing?'

'I'm off to the couch to get a bit of peace.'

'Don't wake the bairn.'

Tiptoeing into the kitchen, Trevor made up his mind – life couldn't go on like this.

Trevor woke hot and sticky. Disorientated, he tried to think where he was. A baby was crying. He saw Norma's pram hurtling down a grassy slope towards a cliff edge. He tried to save her but as he ran, he ran on the spot. He broke out in a drenching sweat. Faster and faster went the pram down the slope. Norma's face – framed by a white frilled bonnet, as she looked out from the pram – was screwed up and angry-looking.

Trevor covered his ears, but he could still hear a baby crying.

His mind grappled with the idea that he was dreaming. Then the truth dawned on him.

In an instant, he was wide awake. God in heaven, it couldn't be – but the insistent wail of the air raid siren outside told Trevor that it was.

CHAPTER TWENTY-FIVE

Etty slept fitfully and at the first pitiable whimper from Victoria, she started awake.

She flung back the bedcovers, switching on the bedside lamp. Quarter past two.

Pattering along to the kitchen, she took the kettle off the hob. A short while after, back in the bedroom, she fed Victoria from the banana-shaped bottle, made up with national dried milk.

As she sat on the edge of the bed, Etty gazed down at the child nestled in her arm. A seductive smell of milk and warm skin wafted from Victoria and she watched her aunt with her navy-blue eyes. Etty felt a tug of longing. She'd like another bairn, she surprised herself by thinking, a sister for Norma. Then she shied away from the idea. The memory of those bleak months after Norma was born was still fresh in her mind. Besides, with the way things were between her and Trevor, conceiving a child was not an option.

She sat Victoria upright and, supporting her head, tapped her gently on the back. The little tinker let out a burp that would make any grown man proud. Etty started to laugh but before it reached her lips, the noise that bellowed outside made her stomach clench.

The wail of the air-raid siren.

'Move, woman.' Trevor burst into the room, raven black hair standing on end. 'I'll take Norma to the shelter. You bring her,' he nodded to Victoria in her arms.

He donned a jersey, pulled trousers over his pyjamas and dashed from the room.

Heart thumping in her chest, Etty placed Victoria back in her Moses basket and hurried to the cupboard under the stairs. She grabbed a suitcase, packed for such an occasion, and picked up nappies and the bag full of essentials that Dorothy had left for the baby. Etty hurried through to the shelter, only to bump into Trevor coming the other way.

'Take these,' she bundled the suitcase and nappies into his arms.

At that moment came the distant mutter of guns. By the light of a silver moon, she saw Trevor, a transfixed figure, looking up towards the sky.

'Move, Trevor,' she shouted.

Her mind surprisingly focused, she considered what else she'd need. She dashed back under the stairs and brought out the little paraffin stove. Hurrying into the bedroom she took hold of the Moses basket's handles and made a run for the outside.

Halting at the shelter door, she paused to glance over her shoulder, seeing circular beams criss-crossing in the darkened heavens.

She dived into the shelter and slammed the door.

The light was dim and the atmosphere reeked of damp and candle grease. Trevor, the pile of essentials dumped at his feet, searched the wooden shelf and brought out a torch. Built across the wall behind him were slender bunk beds. Norma, blissfully unaware, slept in the upper one, with a rail attached to stop her from falling out.

Etty placed the Moses basket on the lower bunk bed.

As she watched, Trevor pulled on his rubber boots, waterproof leggings and trousers. Etty asked, 'What about your mam?'

His green eyes, glistening in the candlelight, looked agonised and torn.

'I wouldn't normally ask but… Etty, can you go? You know how slow she can be.' He rubbed the back of his neck in an agitated fashion. 'Out of a team of five in this area there's only the three of us tonight.' He grabbed his stirrup pump, bucket and shovel. 'Two if I don't get a move on. And you know those incendiary bombs; if they're not spotted quickly they start a fire and lives are lost.' He hesitated, looking over to the sleeping bairns. 'The kids are tucked up and settled.'

Etty nodded consent.

'Thanks.'

Their eyes met and for an instant he looked as if he wanted to say something, then his face hardened and the moment passed. He put on his steel helmet and, opening the door, Trevor was gone.

Etty wondered what he wanted to say. Then she remembered his appalling behaviour of late. Likely, he wanted to pick another argument. Damn the man, he got under her skin. But she didn't need him… Etty could manage nicely on her own.

Their voices must have disturbed Norma because she started to whimper. Planes droned in the distance, crumps coming from the coastal area.

Etty, terrified the bairn would wake properly and would never go back to sleep, stroked her forehead with her fingertips and whispered a favourite lullaby.

> *Go to sleep,*
> *Go to sleep,*
> *Go to sleep little baby.*
> *Close your eyes—*

Hot and crotchety, Norma started to cry. Etty picked her up, rocking her until her arms ached, to no avail.

The raiders came nearer and then in waves, roaring alarmingly close overhead. Every nerve in Etty's body tensed and she prayed for their lives. The bombers thundered on and up the coast where sporadic thuds could be heard from the Newcastle area.

In the silence, Norma kicked and screamed. Feeling desperate, knowing she had to fetch Ma Milne, Etty didn't know what to do.

'Please baby…' Her jaw ached with clenching. 'Just this once… I haven't time… not tonight.'

She persevered rocking.

Finally, when Norma's eyelids drooped and she breathed evenly, Etty dared to put her on the top bunk.

She waited a few minutes before blowing the candles out and taking her overcoat from behind the door, slipping outside into the yard. By a luminous moon that hung in the sky, Etty gazed towards the dock area and saw in its spotlight, an enemy aircraft heading this way.

Fizzing with dread, she tore towards the sloping stairs. Pressing the door sneck, she stepped inside.

'Nellie!' she yelled.

Seconds passed and Etty hollered again. 'Are you there?'

The drone of aeroplanes came closer. High-pitched whistles pierced the night air followed by a tremendous explosion. Bits of plaster fell on Etty's head.

Legs trembling, she began climbing the stairs but stopped when a reedy voice called out, 'Who's there?'

'It's me. Etty.'

'I want me son. I'll not budge till Trevor comes.'

Etty's nerves jangled. The silly beggar would get them both killed. Frantic as to what to do she hit on an idea – if that didn't work she'd return to the children.

'Nellie. Norma's crying. She's frightened and wants Grandma,' she called into the darkness.

The door on the top landing slammed and movements could be heard on the stairs.

'I'm coming,' Nellie sounded stronger.

Relief surged through Etty. But, as the roar of aeroplanes returned, it was short-lived. The bombers came over in groups and, seemingly, skimmed the rooftops. Guns blazed from the ground and bombs made a screaming descent. There was a drawn out whistle and a blinding flash and the earth beneath Etty trembled. Another amazing flash and something caught her eye. Hair braided into a plait, and dressed in an ankle length dressing gown, Nellie's ghostlike figure glided down towards her.

'Hurry!' Etty screamed.

Her voice was drowned out as more bombs rained down, sounding as if they exploded before hitting the ground. Nails digging into her palms, Etty was scared and yet spellbound, as if she watched on in a dream. There was a sudden blue flash and she hit the ground, hands over her head. Buildings toppled down with an almighty crash and a long crescendo of noise from glass breaking. Etty couldn't breathe for dust and smoke in the staircase. Her eyes burned and she coughed until she retched.

Then there was a lull, when Etty realised the raiders had passed. Legs trembling, her only thought was for the shelter. Stricken by the thought of what she might find, she could barely breathe. She made to dash down the stairs – then froze and listened. Creaks emanated from all around her.

Before she could let out a scream, the staircase walls caved in.

*

Meanwhile, as Trevor made his way towards St Michael's Church, guilt gnawed at him and he regretted leaving his wife to manage on her own. He was the man of the house, it was up to him to protect his family. Torn on whether to go back, he reasoned that duty called.

'Is that you, Mr Milne?' a voice called out in the darkness.

Trevor crinkled his eyes and by the light of the moon, made out the uniform of the air raid warden – blue battledress and tin hat. Mr Thompson, a man in his mid-fifties had an air of authority and a world-weary countenance.

'Aye, it is. I'm making me way to the church tower, watching for incendiary bombs.'

'It's already covered.' The warden looked towards the sky. 'Man, it doesn't bode well, does it?'

A familiar noise throbbed in the distance.

They came like a swarm of angry wasps up the coast. His face upturned, Trevor watched as planes roared overhead.

A hand grabbed him by the shoulder. 'Haway, man,' the warden yelled. 'Take cover in the church till its ower with. We're no help if wi' dead.'

Crossing the main road, they ran up the winding driveway. Heaving the church door open, they sagged in the relative safety of the vestibule.

With its soaring roof and draughty crannies, the church was dimly lit. The only source of light was the moon shining through stained glass windows. A few folk sat in pews, heads bent, praying for dear life. As planes roared overhead, it felt as if the very foundations of the building shook. Then came a lull, when raiders droned in the distance towards the Newcastle area.

'That was a close shave,' the warden shook his head. 'It's not over yet… I feel it in me bones. We're headed for a full-scale raid.' He turned away. 'I'm off to central control. You, Mr Milne, check for incendiary bombs and fire incidents.'

The warden, boots clattering down the aisle, made for the door.

Trevor, following, eyed a stone pillar that towered up to the rafters. He shuddered; if one of those blighters toppled down they'd all be gonners.

Retracing his steps, he froze and listened to the throbbing in the distance.

Raiders.

He ran the rest of the way down the aisle, emerging into the cool night air, watching as enemy planes came straight at him. Wave after wave thundered overhead. Mesmerised, it didn't occur to him to run for cover. Black blobs fell from the planes, and when the bombs exploded, a crimson hue spread over the houses. His mouth went dry as he realised, with a jolt, that the bombs were falling on the Westoe area.

Galvanised into action, Trevor ran pell-mell through the streets into the thick of the destruction, with only one thought on his mind – Etty and his bairn.

His breaths came in hot gasps and he yelled to the gods, *I didn't mean it, that she could go to hell.*

Sweat dripping in his eyes, he stood at the top of the lane, out of breath and panting.

The raiders had gone, reduced to a distant drone out at sea.

A chill of fear ran down Trevor's spine; he was unable to take in what he saw. Fires raged all around and he could see wreckage piled high in the lane. Houses smouldered and an acrid smell of burning hung in the air; gaps loomed between buildings where dwellings had toppled down. Folk, buried in the rubble, were being brought out on backyard doors then ferried away by volunteers to the infirmary. By far the worst to bear were the cries for help from those still trapped beneath the wreckage.

Trevor braced himself and raced down the lane, not daring to look where his house should stand. But there it was, soaring into the sky. Trevor went weak with relief. *Hang on*, he thought as fear gripped him, *the back door's missing, so is the yard wall.*

He climbed over the rubble and, seeing the shelter walls intact, Trevor found he could breathe deeply again. His eyes travelled to his home, the shattered windows and then to the pile of rubble that once was his ma's stairs.

He made for the shelter. Opening the door, he shone his torch in the darkness. The beam picked out Norma sitting up in bed rubbing her eyes.

'Etty!' he called.

No answer.

He moved the beam around the walls.

'Ma!'

Still no answer. Realising what might have happened, Trevor's bowels slackened in fear.

Trevor needed help if he was to get Etty and Ma out from beneath the rubble. He ran, hell for leather, down the lane to a group of men on hands and knees, clawing through wreckage.

Putrid smells caught the back of Trevor's throat, causing a bout of coughing. He spotted the warden, noticing that his hands were cut and bleeding.

'Can you spare someone?' He struggled to stay calm. 'It's me wife and ma, I think the back stairs has collapsed on them.'

Mr Thompson looked up, his eyes red holes in a grimy face.

'I'm doing all I soddin' can, Mr Milne.' He removed his steel hat and wiped the sweat from his eyes with a forearm. 'You've a bairn, haven't you? What about her?'

'There's two of them, I've left them safe with the neighbour next door.'

'I'll be with you as quick as I can.' The warden resumed his work. 'Meanwhile, we could do with a hand here.'

No way would Trevor stay, his family needed him – he'd claw them out of the rubble himself if needs be. He made to dart away but boots clattering on the cobbles down the lane stopped him. A young lad addressed the warden.

'The incident officer's sent a runner off to control,' he reported.

'For reinforcements?'

'Aye. He says twenty or so buildings are wrecked in the area and a bomb's dropped outside the Regent Cinema. The A.R.P. stores and the entrance to the public shelter are wrecked... the garage is gone... tramlines are torn up and there's a problem with a burst water main. And…' he drew breath and looked hesitantly at the warden, 'the wardens' post in Dean Road is damaged.'

'Bugger! What about fires?'

'A house down the lane's still raging.'

The warden pierced him with a grim stare. 'I can see that for meself, sonny. What about the homeless?'

'Temporary Rest Centres are to be made in local schools.'

The warden looked at Trevor and appeared to make a decision.

'Son,' he told the messenger, 'I'm off to help this fella find his Mrs. You take my place till reinforcements arrive.'

Mission accomplished, Trevor raced up the lane, the warden following behind. As they approached the yard, Mr Thompson assessed the collapsed staircase.

'First thing we do… Trevor, isn't it?' Trevor nodded. 'Is to dig out the back door and work up from there. Steady as you go, though.'

They worked in silence, clearing bricks, mortar and slates.

As Trevor toiled, his back breaking, sweat dripping down his spine, the time spent digging seemed an eternity.

The warden froze. 'Shh! Did you hear that?' He cocked his head and listened.

'There it is again.' The warden pointed to a spot further up the wreckage. 'Sounds like someone calling… bugger me, it is.' As sweat tunnelled down his mucky face, he grinned. 'You know what that means… one of the women is alive.'

Trevor lunged forward, shovelling debris with his bare hands and soon they were as cut and bloodied as Mr Thompson's.

'Steady, lad,' the warden told him. 'Go slow, at this stage you might do more harm than good.'

Agitated, Trevor could've punched the fella. It was all right for him to talk, his wife wasn't buried beneath a mountain of rubble and possibly gasping her last breath.

Then he saw the warden's tired, defeated face, and all was forgiven.

'Look,' Mr Thompson's face broke into a smile, 'I can see a leg.'

Caked in grime, the leg was unidentifiable. With renewed strength, Trevor clawed through the pile of brick and mortar. Then an item of clothing appeared, a skirt the same fabric and colour brown that his wife wore. Trevor let out a gratified sob.

Gingerly, he crawled further up the heap of masonry. As he carefully sifted through rubble, a face surfaced, caked in white dust and streaked with tears.

Etty's eyes blinked open.

Trevor's heart soared with relief. His wife was alive.

They pulled her, head to foot in a film of dusty grime, out of the rubble. Together they carried her to a space in the yard and lay her down.

Etty stared wildly about. To Trevor's astonishment, she sat up and started pummelling the warden's chest with clenched fists.

'The girls… I need…' she implored in short gasps. 'I shouldn't have… Norma, you have to find—'

'Whoa, lass.' Mr Thompson took her hands in his. He nodded knowingly at Trevor, a sign he was used to this kind of behaviour. 'Your kiddies are safe… your old man, here, brought in a neighbour to look after them.'

Etty stared incredulously at Trevor.

'It's true,' he said. 'There isn't a scratch on either of the bairns.'

'Thank God.' Tears slid down her dusty cheeks. Then, she looked around. 'Where's Nellie?' Her voice was croaky.

'She was definitely with you when the stairs collapsed?' the warden asked.

'Yes. Further up, I think.'

The warden started back towards the collapsed staircase and Trevor, following, viewed the wreckage that was once his ma's stairs.

'Lad, it's been a while since the bombs…' Mr Thompson's look told Trevor he should be prepared for the worst.

As they climbed the rubble and started shovelling with their hands, Trevor noticed the door was missing from the top of the stairs. Stopping for a breather, he viewed the depth of the wreckage. If his mother was down there, he accepted, more than likely she was a goner. His heart ached at the thought. Though she drove him crazy and was a manipulative sort, Trevor loved his ma.

He started to dig again. His grimy and blood-soaked hands hurt like hell but still he carried on. Gritty dust swirled in the air, assaulting his nostrils and travelling to his chest.

He cleared the area of bricks and mortar and uncovered the staircase door. As he stood the door on end, he stared down into the face of his mother – an old woman entombed in a rubble filled grave.

'She's here.' Heart thudding, Trevor clawed the debris away with his bare hands.

'Bugger me,' Mr Thompson had taken off his helmet and bent over, checking Ma's pulse, 'she's alive and it's thanks to that bloody door.'

*

Etty watched as two strapping volunteers carted Nellie away to the infirmary.

Trevor continually asked Etty if she was all right, not leaving her side.

He took her arm to help her up but she shook him off. 'Go with your mam. She'll need you to be close when she comes round.'

His jaw set, Trevor replied, 'I'm staying here with you and the bairn.'

Etty nodded and smiled. She stood on rubbery legs and inspected herself. Apart from a few grazes and a painful wrist, there were no real injuries.

Her eyes travelled the yard where shards of glass and slates littered the ground. Apart from the collapsed stairs, there was no structural damage. With a heart full of gratitude, she thanked the Lord that her family had survived.

'I'll have to go. I'm needed elsewhere.' The warden gave a curt nod.

As he walked briskly away, Etty called an inadequate 'thank you' after him. Stepping over the rubble into the lane, a passing figure hurtling past almost bowled him over.

'Watch it, mate,' the warden complained. 'Oh, it's you, Frank—' he nodded to a burly fireman.

'Can't stop,' rumbled a deep male voice. 'It's all hands to a fire out of control down the lane.'

'Blimey…' said the warden, 'is that house fire still going?'

She felt a rush of adrenalin course through her. 'What house?' Etty demanded.

The warden, sprinting down the lane, didn't answer.

Moving into the lane, Etty looked to where clouds of smoke billowed from a building. Dread fixed her to the spot and she couldn't move. She clutched her heart. She didn't want to look but a voice of authority in her head said she must. She took off, oblivious to the fact that she wore only a nightdress under her coat or, indeed, that the babies might need her. Only one thought dominated her mind.

Dorothy.

The lane was piled high with rubble that she clambered over, skirting holes that slowed her down.

In the distance the 'all clear' siren sounded.

The burning house came into view, flames licking through the top floor windows. Two courageous firemen stood in the yard, hoses in their hand, spraying water.

'No!' Etty cried. Legs buckling, she almost fell to the ground.

The building was Dorothy's.

CHAPTER TWENTY-SIX

Etty ran as if the devil himself chased her. She raced to the end of the block, and rounding the corner, turned into the front street. A crowd watching the inferno from a safe distance saw who it was. Silently, they parted and let her pass.

Two firemen valiantly fought to bring the blaze under control. A third, hands on his hips, watched the proceedings. Tall and thickset, he had the bearing of a man in charge.

Etty stepped over the coils of hose snaking the ground and approached him.

Sensing her presence, he turned. 'Miss, stay back,' he ordered.

She held her ground. 'D'you know what's happened to the occupants?' she asked in a squeaky voice that sounded unlike her own.

'Are you kin?'

'Yes.'

The fireman blew out his cheeks. 'The old couple… Armstrongs, isn't it?… are in a bad way. The shelter collapsed on them.'

'What about the lady… Mrs Calvert… downstairs?'

'A neighbour said she met Mrs Calvert last night and she was excited because she was spending the night at her sister's place.'

Fear gripped Etty. She could barely breathe, let alone speak. 'That's me, I—'

'Frank,' Etty was surprised to see Trevor at her side. He addressed the fireman. 'Mrs Calvert went home last night.'

Frank rubbed the back of his neck. 'Trevor, mate. No one else was in the shelter.'

'My sister never used the outside shelter,' Etty found her somewhat quivery voice, 'she always used the Morrison shelter.'

The fireman looked perplexed. 'Bugger me…' he shook his head. 'Miss, even if I'd known I wouldn't have sent anyone in. The bomb hit the back of the house and the fire was out of control.' He looked intently at Trevor. 'The flames at the front of the property are now under control but the structure's unsafe.'

Terror seized Etty. 'You mean… Dorothy could still be in there?' Her eyes met Trevor's. 'Do something,' she pleaded.

He hesitated. Then she saw a flicker of decision gleam in his eyes. Removing his jacket, he protected his head and made a dash for the front door. Ramming the door with his shoulder, it gave way under the strain.

'Trevor, man. No!' Frank shouted.

Etty froze; she didn't mean for him to risk his life. *Yes, you did*, an inner voice said. She needed her sister to be saved.

Etty waited.

Flames licked through the front upstairs window, and then there was an almighty crash as the downstairs ceiling fell down.

Time stood still.

Smoke belched from windows and the doorway. Heart racing, Etty prayed that any minute Trevor would appear. Surely God couldn't be that cruel – to take both her husband and sister.

Immobilised by fear, she couldn't take her eyes off the burning house. Why had she let him go into the inferno? Because she needed Dorothy saved. The sisters had been through so much together, they could get through this too, couldn't they? As flames billowed from the door, panic seized Etty. She couldn't stand still a moment longer. She made to move but strong arms held her tight and wouldn't let her go.

'Look!' a male voice shouted.

A figure came running out of the door, head covered in a smoking jacket that burst into flames.

Trevor.

Frank rushed forward and grabbing Trevor, wrestled him to the ground, rolling him over to extinguish the flames.

Etty's eyes sought the door, but as flames leapt high into the acrid air, no one else came out of the raging inferno.

She raced over to Trevor, kneeling beside him. In her distress, she noted his singed hair, the whites of his eyes turned pink, his red and blistered face.

'Dorothy?' she whispered.

Shaking, he wheezed, 'Flames in the kitchen... but could see in the Morrison shelter.' He coughed and clutched his throat, 'No one there.'

The words filled her with hope. But Etty couldn't bear to look at his burned skin or to think of the torture he must be going through, all because of her. As he struggled to breathe, she feared for his life. Yet her heart soared for her husband. She knew Trevor had risked his life not just for Dorothy, but because he knew how much her sister meant to his wife.

Etty told him gently, 'Don't talk... just rest. I need you to get better.'

'This man needs medical attention. Now!' Frank yelled.

Two burly men from the crowd came forward. 'It'll be quicker if we take him to the hospital ourselves.'

They wrenched a door off its hinges from a damaged building and laid Trevor upon it.

He looked up at Etty.

'Stay...' he managed to croak. 'Go and find her.'

Etty watched as the men made off with him up the street.

'That's a brave man.' Frank stood at her side. 'And lucky to be alive.'

*

Hope surged through Etty but she didn't know where to look or what to do next. Then it hit her. Of course! She knew exactly what Dorothy would do when the siren wailed. She would seek out Victoria.

She took off up the street, choking from the smoke permeating the air and, passing a gap where Mrs Henderson's house should have stood, she stared in dismay. The building was blown to smithereens. In her shocked state, Etty could only think of that immaculately kept front step.

'Hinny, all I've left is what I stand up in,' a voice from behind said. 'But I owe me life to that sister of yours.'

Etty turned and saw the dishevelled figure of Mrs Henderson. She wore a pair of men's trousers and an army greatcoat was draped over her shoulders.

'Dorothy was with you?'

'Aye, she was that. You see, with me husband away, it's up to me to look after his dad.' Mrs Henderson's pupils were big dark pools. 'I took him on when I married my Jeff. He's an invalid from the Great War. He's a canny enough fella but the trouble is, he can't walk far and that makes for hard work.'

Etty's patience running thin, she pleaded, 'Where's Dorothy? How did she help?'

'When the siren went off, I couldn't get the old fella in the shelter meself. Frantic, I raced to the front to knock upstairs. Your sister went shooting past and I asked if she would help. What a lass,' she gave a fond smile. Warming to the woman, Etty remembered her earlier disapproval. It just went to show, she thought, you shouldn't be quick to judge folk.

'Jeff's dad isn't a big man, physically, and so we managed to carry him between us to the shelter. Dorothy wouldn't leave it at that and insisted she help fetch his paraphernalia… books, pipe, medication, and so on. I did ask her to stay but she said she was in a dash to seek her little girl. Just after that, Jerry came over. If it hadn't been for your lass, I would've still been in the house struggling with Jeff's father.' She grasped Etty's hand. 'I'm eternally grateful to your sister.'

Etty, in a hurry to be away, broke free of her hand. 'I'm sorry, Mrs Henderson, about your flat.'

The woman pulled a rueful face. 'I had it just the way I wanted. I'll have to start all over again.'

If she hadn't been so panicked, Etty would've quipped a clever remark.

The street – with some of the houses vanished, others damaged beyond repair – was in total chaos. One house had its side blown off, so that you could see the exposed upstairs where a clock, miraculously, stood intact on the range mantelshelf, a picture of a bullfighter hanging drunkenly on the wall above.

Hurrying on, Etty passed a team of rescue workers sifting through a pile of wreckage.

'Oi! Where d'you think you're going?' A male voice startled her.

A middle-aged bloke sporting a black moustache glared at her. 'Stay back. These buildings are unsafe.' To make a point he gestured to a house across the road where a chimney teetered precariously over the side of the roof.

An older gentleman with an unlit pipe dangling from his mouth gave Mr Moustache an affronted stare.

'Best to wait, hinny,' he said to Etty, 'till the demolition squad's been and made the area safe.' He pulled a long face. 'You don't want to be poking around here.'

His eyes strayed to where three bodies, covered by blankets, lay on the cobbles.

'And the injured,' Etty asked, eyes glued to the blankets. 'What happened to them?'

'Ferried away to the hospital,' the man said. 'If you're looking for somebody… I'd try there first.'

Etty's guts turned over and she felt sick. She had to know. She moved forward.

'Don't, pet,' the gentleman warned.

She bent over the first body and reached out a hand.

Please God, I promise I'll talk to you every day. I'll go to church on Sundays. Please, don't let this be Dorothy.

She drew back the blanket and, looking into the reposed face of an old woman, felt incredibly sad. It was difficult to believe that only hours before this woman had gone about her daily affairs. Etty shivered.

The second body was the woman's husband, a kindly man. It felt indecent, somehow, staring at him like this and she covered him up.

She bent and pulled back the blanket from the third body. She stared into the ashen face of Dorothy.

A cry wrenched from her. Bending over, she hugged her stomach.

Dorothy couldn't be dead. She couldn't be. Etty fell to her knees. She shook her sister to awaken her and then noticed her blood-soaked hair, the gash at her temple.

An unbearable pain squeezed her chest. Taking a handkerchief from her pocket, she began to wipe away the blood.

A hand touched her shoulder. Senses acute, she smelled stale tobacco.

'Come away,' a gentle voice said. 'You can't do anything here, lass. She's gone.'

Strong arms lifted her up. Etty fought them off. As she looked down at Dorothy's lifeless form, her world tilted. This couldn't be. A life without Dorothy was… inconceivable. A low guttural cry rose from deep within her.

The hand pressed her shoulder again.

Etty turned and looked into the weakened eyes of the elderly gentleman. 'It's my sister, Dorothy,' she told him. 'We're a team.

She can't stay here… not on the cold cobbles. Would you help me please, to take her home?'

*

Two days after the bombing, as Trevor stood at the front door, the overpowering reek of burnt-out houses still permeated Whale Street. He wondered if the stink would ever go away.

The burns to his face and hands were still painful, especially when they were cleaned and his dressings changed, but he was a lucky fella, according to the specialist at the hospital. Trevor's injuries were superficial and didn't go deep, the bloke said, and with proper care and a good standard of hygiene, they'd be healed in a matter of weeks. But Trevor wondered about himself. Whenever he thought of his lungs burned with smoke and how narrowly he had escaped the ceiling falling down, he still got the shakes.

Then there was the business with Etty. They were uneasy around each other, as if all that had gone on before was too big an obstacle to overcome. Etty was in mourning for her sister and for the time being, Trevor surmised, it was best he left things as they were. But despite all this he couldn't help feeling a little ray of hope for their future.

Officialdom had moved into Whale Street. A queue of folk waited in front of trestle tables for council officials to attend to them.

As Trevor watched, an official, a rotund man with balding head and red agitated face, told the woman in front of him, 'Mrs, it's too dangerous to stay in your flat. The building is in jeopardy of falling down. It's only a temporary measure. You'll be allocated at the school for now.'

The woman replied, 'Says you. That flat's been in me family for two generations. Once I go, I'll never get back. I've seen it before. I'm staying put.'

'Mrs. I'm only doing my job.'

So, the argument rattled on.

Meanwhile, gangs of workmen, some carrying hefty ladders and planks of wood, went about their business in the street. Folk, pushing homemade handcarts piled high with their belongings, went to goodness knows where, because no spare property was to be had – which was a pity, Trevor thought, because it would have saved his ma having to live in with them.

Ma was discharged from the hospital with a broken arm. She had had a lucky escape, especially as her concussion hadn't lasted long. She didn't see it that way, though, and her complaining was purgatory. With no home till the staircase was fixed, she'd established herself in the back bedroom – in a put-you-up bed the Women's Volunteer Service found for them – with the two bairns.

Trevor didn't fancy sleeping in the front bedroom, not with Dorothy lying in state and so he'd opted for the couch in the kitchen. Aye, he thought, it was one thing dealing with death at work but quite another when it affected his personal life.

Trevor shivered. The games your mind played. He'd never tell another living soul but he'd swear he could feel Dorothy's presence in the flat. It came over him at odd moments, mostly in the passageway when he was on his own, this sensation that Dorothy was behind him and looking over his shoulder. He couldn't explain it and would never try. Trevor wanted the funeral over and done with this afternoon.

His main concern was Etty, who was deeply affected by her sister's death. She had an unhinged air about her and was obsessively cleaning every nook and cranny in their home. Soot brought down by the bombs lay like thick black snow over every surface in the kitchen and Etty had apparently sorted it out by the first night. Rooms were dusted and mats removed and beaten over a line in the lane like they were the source of all that was evil. The irony was, while some poor buggers had lost their homes, Trevor's sparkled as though royalty was expected to call.

Trevor worried that, with the eyes of the street upon them, his wife's inappropriate behaviour at such a time would reflect on him. Appalled by this train of thought – Trevor realised he sounded like Ma talking. He'd finished for good with that outdated mode of thinking. He'd survived the fire and life was too short. If he hadn't spoiled his chance, Trevor wanted to start over again with Etty.

Coughing again, he held his throat. He loved her still, he realised, and always would. Jealous rage had eaten him up and he needed to apologise for some of the things he'd said.

From within the house, he heard a baby crying. He heaved his shoulders. Trevor thought about how unlucky Victoria was losing both parents. Laurie Calvert had no relatives to take her in, his brothers served in the army and his mother was now permanently confined to a wheelchair. Trevor was concerned that the responsibility of bringing up the bairn would fall on Etty as she had enough to contend with. But Etty was touchy about the subject of Victoria and he thought it wisest to leave the matter alone for now.

'I find it best to submerge myself in work,' Mr Newman told Trevor, who sat on an upturned tea chest in the workshop.

His head bent over a vice, the boss planed a slab of wood, ready for a coffin. 'I tell you, lad,' Mr Newman continued. 'The plight of some folk could break your heart. Not only have they lost a loved one, but their home and possessions into the bargain.' His features sagged and he looked every one of his fifty-eight years.

Mrs Newman bustled in, dressed in a W.V.S. uniform.

'Roland, dear,' she said in her affected tone. 'I can't be doing without water, it still isn't on.' She sniffed, 'I'm off servin' in the mobile canteen.'

'Serving anything tasty?' Both because of rationing and having such a long lean frame, Trevor's stomach was never full.

Mrs Newman, stuck up trout, didn't speak to lesser mortals such as him.

'Ahem,' Mr Newman gave her a questioning look.

'Oh yes… it's your sister-in-law's funeral. If there's anything we can do, let Mr Newman know.' She turned to her husband. 'I've left you a sandwich on the drainer, Roland.'

She made a quick exit.

The boss bent and examined the planed slab of wood, running his hand over it.

'I'm stowed out with work,' he told Trevor, 'it's a pity you can't lend a hand.' He looked down at Trevor's bandaged hand and coloured when he realised his gaff. But he went on, 'Two funerals in the morning.'

Weariness overcame Trevor and he realised that maybe coming over the road was a bit too much, especially with Dorothy's funeral this afternoon. No way could he miss that. He wouldn't let Etty down.

'Lad, I was just thinking.' Trevor knew that forthright tone – this conversation was going to be awkward.

'Will your wounds leave you scarred?'

'Pardon me?'

'On your… face.' Mr Newman had the grace to look sheepish.

'Why?' Dumbfounded, Trevor asked.

Then it dawned on him and he saw red. He was tired of folk messing him around. His interfering ma, the Newmans – who thought they were a cut above.

Mr Newman persisted. 'Maybe it's best you work in the workshop for a time, till we—'

'Where I won't be seen, you mean.'

'Now lad, don't take it personally. I only meant—'

'I know what you meant. Scars aren't acceptable. I might scare people off and the business would suffer.'

'Let's be reasonable, Trevor, talk this through.'

Weariness like he'd never known overcame Trevor. He stood up from the tea chest. 'I'll tell you what is reasonable: Mr Newman, you can stick your job.'

*

The hurt of Dorothy's death tainted Etty's every thought, every action. It was all consuming. Etty wondered sometimes how much pain the heart could take.

You must go on, the voice in her head said.

All Dorothy's personal possessions had perished in the fire. She didn't own much jewellery; a pair of drop amethyst earrings she wore on special occasions, a silver bangle, and a string of pearls – a gift from Laurie on their wedding day. It was a pity about the pearls, they'd have made an ideal keepsake for Victoria but at least she would have her mother's wedding ring. She made a mental note to tell Mr Newman to remove the ring from Dorothy's finger before the funeral.

Submerging baby clothes in a sink full of tepid water, she wondered if that was what her sister would want. Etty had no idea; they'd never discussed what to do in the event of either of their premature deaths.

Mostly, Etty felt numb and since the day of the bombing, she couldn't sit still. Even having Trevor's mam to stay, infuriating though the woman was, proved a welcome distraction as it helped keep her busy and sane. She didn't want to stop and think, feeling so bereft there were times she wanted to scream at the top of her voice. But what good would that do? Life without Dorothy was futile and she was powerless to stop the black despair that threatened to swamp her.

Trevor tried to help but said all the wrong things. She ought to be thankful towards him for risking his life to save Dorothy's, and she wanted to tell him so but feelings were a luxury she didn't possess any more. She felt frozen.

Shirley Dickson

'Try and get some rest,' he badgered. 'You'll wear yourself out, keeping a nightly vigil on Dorothy.'

Etty's mind kept flashing back to the moment when she had uncovered Dorothy's face: the shock; the denial she was dead. Then came the panic, when Etty worked in slow motion. Since then, the realisation had hit and nothing would take away the pain, the *injustice*, of losing a sister as precious as hers. Overwhelmed, Etty wanted to curl up and howl like a wounded animal.

'*Stop fighting, and let time pass.*' Dorothy's voice, like a salve, spoke in her mind.

When Laurie died, all Dorothy wanted was to be with him and, perhaps, in some universal order, her wish had been granted. But no, Etty decided, Dorothy would never leave her baby, not even for Laurie.

Thank God for May Robinson, who she could rely on. May promised to keep a vigil with Etty before the funeral.

May had a knack of saying the right thing when needed. Everyone acted embarrassed around Etty, worried they might say the wrong thing, and so they avoided speaking at all. Which was hurtful when a simple 'I'm sorry about your loss,' would do. Not May though, who treated Etty as normal and spoke naturally.

In this time of grief, Etty valued her friendship, grateful to her friend. She had tinkered with the idea of telling May about the affair with Billy. But that would be selfish, she realised, as she'd only be confessing for her own benefit – to be absolved of guilt. She had caused the lass enough suffering and heartache.

As she wrung out the baby clothes, Etty checked her watch that lay on the wooden draining board.

Two hours to go.

The pair of them sat on the end of the bed, staring at Dorothy's waxen face.

Curtains were drawn. Candles stood in saucers on the mantelpiece and lit the room.

'Will Dorothy be in a plot on her own at the cemetery?' May asked.

'Yes.'

'D'you know if your family's got a plot?'

'No.'

Silence.

'Have you decided on hymns? Did Dorothy have a favourite?'

'She liked "All things Bright and Beautiful".'

'Fancy… that's mine as well.' Pause. 'Apart from the wound, there's not another mark on Dorothy's face, is there?'

'I couldn't bear it if there was. Her body was crushed, and her injuries are from the chest down.'

They stared horrified at the white shroud that masked Dorothy's body.

May spoke again. 'Why d'you think she was out on the street after the siren had gone?'

'I reckon her one thought was to get up the street to be with Victoria. But she didn't make it.'

'I think that too.'

After a pondering silence, Etty said, 'I'm glad I told Mr Newman not to put lipstick on her.'

'Is that what undertakers do?'

'Yes. To make people look more… natural. Trevor says sometimes they apply rouge, too.'

'I agree, I wouldn't want that.' May shook her head. 'She just looks asleep, doesn't she?'

Etty didn't think so. Her sister's body now seemed a shell with nobody there.

'I still can't take it in,' May cried. 'What will we do without her?'

'I really don't know.' Etty's voice cracked.

'Dorothy dying has taught me one thing,' May's chin trembled. 'Life's short. I'm ganna get me job back at the factory where I was happiest… even though tongues might still wag about the split with Billy.'

Despite her grief, Etty felt a jolt of culpability. Perhaps if she'd never met Billy, the couple would still be engaged.

Concerned for her friend, she said, 'Don't do anything hasty.'

May's expression, as she eyed the coffin, became determined. 'Dorothy was a fighter and so am I going to be.'

'Good for you.'

They talked for a time about Dorothy, and it was good to speak of her in the present tense. Then, the floorboards outside the bedroom door creaked.

Someone was listening.

'It's unnatural, I tell you,' Nellie's wheezy voice whispered. 'Them two in there talking to the deceased.'

'There's no right and wrong, Ma… leave things be.'

'They're both doolally if you ask me.'

'Etty,' Trevor's authoritative voice boomed. 'It's time. Bertha Cuthbertson's here to look after the girls. Mr Newman will arrive soon.'

'My legs have turned to jelly,' Etty told May.

'Don't worry, Trevor will hold on to you.'

Maybe they both were doolally, Etty thought, but if that's what it took to keep strong enough to bury Dorothy in her final resting place – then so be it.

CHAPTER TWENTY-SEVEN

Whenever she thought of Dorothy's funeral afterwards, Etty could only remember it in befuddled snatches. How, as the coffin was carried out of the house, the sun disappeared behind a black cloud. Mr Newman dressed in a top hat and a black suit, walking in front of the funeral cortege; wielding a cane at the traffic, keeping it at a snail's pace. Men doffing their caps as the car carrying Dorothy passed by. The packed pews at the church and how, as the coffin was carried in, Etty's legs buckled beneath her and she clung on to Trevor's arm for support.

Etty's memory of the cemetery was equally selective. Cars slowly passing through tall wrought iron gates, a queue following behind. Umbrellas, like clusters of black mushrooms at the graveside, and the fragrant smell of floral bouquets.

Etty's everlasting memory of that time was when her beloved sister's coffin was lowered into the ground.

Back home, although it was a mild day, Etty's extremities were icy cold and she couldn't get warm. Bertha appeared with a steaming cup of tea, May at her side. 'How did it go?' Bertha's good-natured face was stricken with compassion.

'St Michael's was heaving.'

'I'm not surprised,' May said. 'Dorothy touched peoples' lives.'

The emotion of the day caught up with Etty, and she couldn't reply.

'What you need is a glass of sherry to fortify yerself.'

She bustled away, returning with a stemmed glass of brown liquid in her hand.

'This'll help take the raw edges away.'

Sipping the sweet liquid, Etty gazed around the room. She knew only a few of the people who had come back to the flat to pay their respects. Dressed head to toe in black, they stood in huddles reminiscing, no doubt, about Dorothy. And though distanced from the scene, she felt a sense of pride that her sister was so well thought of.

As she watched on, a thought disturbed her. What if it were true, that loved ones on the other side were there to greet you? Dorothy would expect to see Mam and she would then know that her sister had told a lie.

Silly girl, I was strong enough to hear the facts. Dorothy's voice again.

Guilt gnawed away at her. Etty now knew this to be true. She knew they could have faced the truth together.

Mam!

Her sister deserved better but if the afterlife were real then Dorothy would be there alongside Laurie. The thought was comforting, and Etty gave a teary smile.

Nellie, apparently, had taken it upon herself to be the family spokesperson. Her arm in a plaster cast, she was in her element as she mingled with the company.

How good of you to come. Yes, the family are bearing up… in these days of war you have to. A big sigh; *Dorothy will be a big miss to us all.*

Etty straightened her spine and held her head high. These people were kind enough to visit her home and give their condolences; the least she could do was pull herself together and mingle with them.

In turn, she spoke with Mrs Henderson, Dorothy's workmates and others, who Etty had never clapped eyes on before.

May hovered at her side, ready to interfere if things got too much for her.

Etty moved on to speak with the Newmans.

'Thank you,' she said, 'for such a dignified funeral.'

Mr Newman looked a little apprehensive. 'It's good of you to say so, my dear.' He nodded to his wife, who stood with a glass of sherry in one hand and a plateful of sandwiches in the other. Her eyes glazed, she appeared bored.

'If there's anything we can do then don't hesitate to ask.'

Etty, too choked to speak, couldn't handle kindness. Mr Newman appeared to understand and patted her hand.

'I can't believe all this grub.' Ramona Newman's shrill voice made Etty cringe. She wore a black pillbox hat with a white ostrich feather that wafted, ludicrously, above her nose.

Etty glanced at the table, laden with sandwiches, meat pies, and homemade cakes. The funeral and wake had been arranged as if by magic. She looked across the room to Bertha who winked conspiratorially. During this war, folk had their own troubles but they still found time to help each other and, on this occasion, Etty was the receiver of their generosity. Bad times brought the best out in people, she reflected. Especially for someone as loved as her dear older sister.

Mr Newman, giving his wife a warning eye, gulped the last of his sherry. 'Regrettably, we can't stay long.'

'It was good of you to come at all,' Etty said mechanically.

Nellie made her way over to join them. 'A word, Mr Newman.'

While Trevor talked to the woman who ran the corner shop over the road, he noticed Ma making for the Newmans. He recognised that conniving look in her eyes.

Tuckered out, all he wanted was an empty house, a comfortable chair to nod off in, and his injuries to stop hurting.

He made his excuses and shambled over to where his mother held court.

'What a week, eh, Mr Newman,' he heard her say. 'You must be exhausted with all those poor souls you've had to bury.'

Taken aback, Mr Newman ran a forefinger around his shirt collar. 'Ahem. It's my job, Mrs Milne... my vocation in life.'

'Here you are, son,' Ma exclaimed when she saw him. 'I was just about to tell Mr Newman here... when you're back to full strength you'll be an asset to the firm. Folk like a hero.'

The two men eyed each other.

Ma nudged the boss's arm. 'In my opinion, he's wasted working down the pit.'

There was an awkward silence. Etty pleaded with her eyes to Trevor to make his Ma stop.

The boss looked horrified. 'Come, come, Mrs Milne. It pays to remember that all our sons are called upon to make sacrifices... some with their lives. Trevor's job is vital. Coal is an essential part of winning the war.'

Trevor bristled. 'Ma, stop meddling. I can handle me own affairs.'

The boss gave him a look of respect. 'Spoken like a man, Trevor. Meanwhile...' he turned to Etty, 'it's time for Mrs Newman and I to take our leave of the proceedings. If we can be of service... be assured you only have to ask.'

About to move away, his wife planted a hand on his arm. 'Roland... you said you'd ask.' Mr Newman looked puzzled. 'About her sister's bairn.' She turned to Etty. 'Who will take it in?'

Mr Newman's brow corrugated. 'And I told you, dear, it isn't our affair.'

Trevor's guts clenched when he saw Etty's expression. He guessed what was coming.

'Victoria has no one but me.' Etty's voice was firm. 'I won't have her brought up in an orphanage.' She looked directly at Trevor. 'Dorothy would want me to bring her daughter up.'

'How can you think such a thing?' Ma intervened. 'It's not fair on Norma. She'll have to share everything.' She turned to Trevor. 'Tell her, son. It's pure selfish, if you ask me.'

All eyes on him, Trevor caught his wife's red-rimmed eyes imploring his.

'Nobody's asking you, Ma.' Trevor moved alongside Etty and put an arm around her. 'The decision is up to Etty and me. If that's what my wife wants then that's how it's going to be.'

Mr Newman, standing next to them, clapped Trevor on the back. 'That's the ticket, lad. It's admirable taking on another man's child. When this war is won, Newman's will be on the lookout for reliable men... I'll count on you.' He looked shamefaced. 'And that means fronting the parlour.'

Trevor nodded.

Life wore on. Etty slept, looked after the kiddies, existed.

Bertha tried her best and called regularly. 'How about we go to the flicks?' she suggested. But Etty didn't want make-believe, she needed reality, the incentive to get on with life.

May often called and took the children out for a walk. She'd return and have a cup of tea and, as if silence was the enemy, she talked non-stop. Billy was never mentioned and Etty was glad because she didn't need a reminder of her disloyalty to her friend. The shame never left her.

Sometimes Etty's mind strayed to what might have been; the life Dorothy had planned for them all in the country. The fresh air, green fields, with her family living just yards away, was the idyllic life she'd always wanted. But now with Dorothy gone, the dream was shattered, Etty was broken-hearted – and life just trundled on.

Today – washday – started out like any other ordinary Monday. Etty dragged the tub from the washhouse into the yard and filled it with buckets of heated water from the boiler.

A baby's reedy cry rippled in the air. Victoria had woken in the back bedroom and wanted a feed. Etty hung the nappies out on the line, white flags of achievement the neighbours judged you by. The nation was at war; an aerial attack might happen any minute, but if your nappies weren't blindingly white as they flapped on the line – then, according to housewife law, you'd failed as a mother.

It started to rain, light drizzle at first, before a cloud burst. Etty turned her face towards the heavens. She wanted the saying to be true – that all those brave boys at the front, the old man beneath the blanket, Dorothy, had left this earth and found a better place.

As Victoria's plaintive cries increased, Etty dragged her mind back to the present. She hauled the tub back into the washhouse and slamming the door, hurried indoors. She proceeded into the bedroom, taking Victoria from her cot and laying her on the couch in the kitchen.

Folk were sorry for her loss, Etty reflected, as she made up a bottle in the scullery, but they soon forgot. And rightly so; they had their own problems and sorrows to contend with.

As she cooled the bottle under the tap, Etty thought of the film, *Goodbye, Mr Chips*. How naïve she had been to believe such romantic fantasy – a made-up story contrived to have a satisfactory ending. Real life wasn't like that.

A door slammed and she heard Trevor's voice talking to Norma, in her playpen in the kitchen.

'Where's Mammy, then? I can't smell any dinner, can you?'

Something cracked inside Etty like ice on a frozen lake. She was only going through the motions, she thought. This was no ordinary day – there'd never be another ordinary day as she knew it. Dorothy was dead.

She went into the kitchen, cooled bottle in hand. Trevor started talking about collar studs.

'I can't find them anywhere,' he said, 'the boss was none too pleased when I arrived without a collar and tie.'

Pandemonium had broken loose in Etty's mind and all he could think about was collar studs.

'It pays to look smart and keep in the boss's good books,' Trevor continued. 'He's talking about expanding the business… and you know what that could mean?'

You made a mistake, Etty thought, and from that day forth your path was mapped out. Now she had the responsibility of two children, which she didn't feel ready for. She thought of her own mother. Was life so tough, bringing two children up on her own, that she discarded them like rag dolls? Etty could never do that to her beloved daughter and niece.

Dorothy had forgiven Mam but Etty knew her sister was wrong. Life was about options and what you chose made the person you became.

Mam, selfishly, chose wrong.

Trevor looked at her in a peculiar way and it occurred to Etty that he too might feel as trapped as she.

'What could expanding the business mean?' she asked, in a shaky voice that didn't sound like her own.

'That I could be a respected partner at Newman's… we could be somebody.'

Suddenly, the magnitude of what had happened hit Etty – and the floodgates opened. Tears spilled from her eyes, down her face, dripping off her chin.

'Dorothy's gone.' The words wrenched from her.

'I know.' Trevor hurried over and buried her in his arms.

'I… miss her… dreadfully.'

'I know that too.'

'There'll never be anyone like her. We were a team.' She sagged against him and he squeezed her tight. Upturning her face, he wiped away the tears with his thumbs.

'Etty… I've been waiting for a bit to say this… I've wanted to tell you but I didn't think you were well enough to ask… but I have to speak out now.' He hesitated, nervous to go on. 'We settled for a marriage of convenience but that's not for me any more—'

'Trevor, I know what you're going to say.' She sniffed back the tears. 'And it's all my fault… I should have told you from—'

'What I want to do is set the record straight… To take our wedding vows again… only this time just the two of us, with a man of the cloth present. Because despite how I've behaved, I do love you.' He lifted her chin so that she saw the tenderness brimming in his eyes. 'I didn't realise how much until I thought I'd lost you. You've set me free.' He grinned and his handsome face relaxed. 'Imagine me being this soppy a romantic before.' Then, his expression grew serious. 'Can we start over again? Can we be a team?'

Startled, she asked, 'Why the change of heart?'

'That's what I'm trying to tell you. There is no change… you've always been the one I wanted since I first clapped eyes on you the day we met on the trolley.' He cocked an eyebrow at her. 'Sometimes I didn't like you, but Etty… I've never stopped loving you.'

As Etty stood nestled in his arms, she recounted scenes from the past. How he had married her knowing she carried another man's child, forgiven her when she wouldn't tell him who the father was, how he sided with her against his mother, and how he had risked his life to save darling Dorothy.

What amazed her was how much Trevor had changed to outright declare his feelings for her. Her heart melted with love and joy.

'I've got ambitions for our lives,' he told her.

Etty struggled for a moment as the past caught up with her, taking her back to being the orphan girl from Blakely who froze and couldn't handle emotion. But then she'd always had Dorothy by her side. As if lightning struck in her mind, Etty's thoughts grew crystal clear and she realised the happiness she now shared with Trevor was because of Dorothy. They shared the same upbringing, the same betrayal by their mother, yet her sister was never rebellious or mistrustful. It was Dorothy's influence on her life, her honest and loving nature, that helped Etty become the optimistic person she'd become today.

But Dorothy was here no more and though her loss was hard to bear, Etty was thankful for the short life of her beloved sister. And from now on she would try to be the trusting and open person Dorothy always encouraged her to be.

She would start by telling Trevor what he really meant to her.

'Trevor…' her voice cracked and she cleared her throat. 'I don't blame you for not liking me as I've been trouble since we first met. I want to say how sorry I am but also how thankful I am that you've put up with me.'

The happy surprise in his loving gaze helped her go on. 'I thought you wanted us to separate and I knew that wasn't what I wanted. I realised, you see, just how much I love and depend on you.' She felt her lips tremble as she laughed. 'So, yes, I'd dearly love to marry you again… only don't tell anyone… I just want it to be us.'

As Trevor took her into his arms, everything clarified for Etty. The light became brighter, sounds sharper and her heart burst with love and pride. She stood on tiptoes and gave her husband a lingering kiss.

As the clock chimed the hour, she broke free. 'Blimey. I must feed Victoria,' she gasped.

'I'll get her bottle,' Trevor said.

Norma grizzled in her playpen and her daddy, swooping her up in his arms, tousled her blonde curls.

Love for them all burst like a colourful firecracker in Etty's chest.

'You'll do, Mr Chipping.' She smiled lovingly at her husband's puzzled expression.

EPILOGUE
May 1945

Etty closed the door on the display of red, white and blue bunting that hung merrily across the street, and showed the woman into the kitchen.

Mrs Gruber declined to sit on the couch and instead sat on a high-backed dining chair. Her hair was silvery and thin, and she wore round spectacles. Though frail, Etty would know her anywhere. To see Mrs Gruber after all this time was a wonderful surprise but the meeting caught Etty off guard and she welled up at the sight of the old woman. So much had happened since that far off day when she'd been but an innocent small child, giving Mrs Gruber an excited wave through the butcher's shop window.

'Mrs Gruber, I can't tell you how lovely it is to see you.'

'For me too… my dear child, I've been longing to find you. But please… call me Olga.'

Etty hauled Victoria, a shy two-year-old, onto her knee and Norma, now four, stood at her side staring in wide-eyed curiosity at the visitor.

'Two girls,' Olga said, her German accent apparent. She smiled. 'How fortunate you are.'

Etty nodded to Victoria. 'She's Dorothy's daughter.'

The old woman's eyes glistened with tears. 'I read about your sister's death in the newspaper. That's how I found you. As I read the article, it mentioned a Dorothy Calvert and her sister Etty

Milne, and that you both were brought up in an orphanage, so I thought you must be the family I was looking for. The article even said you both lived in Whale Street.'

'You recognised us from the article?' was all Etty's dumbfounded mind could think to say.

'I hoped it would be you. I think the article is a good way to commemorate the end of the war. Such an apt title, "The Folk Of Shields' War". Sad stories but uplifting too… though I was distressed to read Dorothy's.' Olga smiled sadly at Victoria. 'This is the dear child she risked her life for. Now, like you, she is an orphan too.'

Etty stiffened. 'I'm not an orphan, Olga. The truth is… Mam abandoned Dorothy and me when we were little. That's why I agreed to share Dorothy's information with the reporter. I hoped Mam would read the article and feel remorse.'

'My dearest, for years I hoped we would have this meeting, so I could put the record straight about your mother.'

'Pardon me if I'm rude, but I'm not interested to hear. I spent too many years broken-hearted. You do know she went back to live with her family?'

'That may be so… but please, hear me out.'

Other than being downright discourteous, Etty had no option.

Olga brought her hands together and laced her bony fingers. 'The day your mother took you away—'

'You waved through the window.'

Olga smiled and nodded. 'I told Kurt – my husband, you remember him –something was wrong. Why had your mother shut up shop when I could look after it? Kurt said it was none of our business and he was right.' Perplexity crossed her face. 'I never saw you girls or your mother again.'

Typical of Mam, Etty thought bitterly.

Norma, bored now with the visitor that didn't pay her any attention, fidgeted. 'I want to play outside,' she whinged.

Etty didn't see the harm, as long as the yard door was locked. Olga watched as she took the two kiddies and their toys – a wind-up monkey, colourful balls and a miniature tea set – into the backyard.

When she returned to the kitchen, Olga held a letter in her hand.

'From your mother,' she said. 'I received it three weeks after you left.'

The impact of Mrs Gruber's words left Etty feeling woozy and dizzy.

'Mam wrote to you… after she left us?'

'I've guarded the letter all these years… Eleanor would want me to keep it safe because she would want you, her little Esther, to read it.' She pushed the letter into Etty's hand.

As she saw the spindly writing on the aged brittle paper, Mam became real to her again. Not the person Etty had formed in her hardened mind over the years, but softly spoken and smiling, cocking her head at a sympathetic angle as she listened to little Esther's woes.

Carefully, in case the folds might tear, she unfolded the yellowed paper.

My dear Olga,

I know you will be concerned as to my whereabouts but I am in a safe place, though unwell. As we discussed of late, I'm not a businesswoman and my previous life as a vicar's daughter gave me no training or knowledge in this area. Since my darling Harry died, the responsibility of running the store has become too great. I have no energy to deal with the situation and the shop is going downhill. I have no money coming in, and life has been a struggle.

I now know why. I suffer from consumption. Yes, my dear, tuberculosis. However, I knew immediately when I found out about my illness what I should do. Quarantine myself from my little ones. I have returned to the shire to live with family and they propose to send me to a sanatorium, an institution quite close that has the best recommendation. There is talk of a procedure to collapse my infected lung to let it rest and start the healing process. I cannot go into the details as to why the girls are not permitted to be with me. Suffice to say I have had an altercation in the past with father over who I chose to marry.

Have no fear, the girls are well catered for. Though I'm heartbroken at leaving my dear Dorothy and little Esther, as they are too young to understand, the guilt is relieved in knowing I'm doing what's best at present for my dear children until I can return for them.

I shall inform you where they are later. I trust you aren't offended, as I know you would be an exemplary guardian, but it is for the best, as you and Mr Gruber have your own lives to contend with.

I miss my children already but I think of them every waking moment. I know that the thought of being reunited with them will get me through this.

I am well looked after, with good provisions and my location is in the country where I have plenty of rejuvenating fresh air.

My strength is failing and I must sleep. I shall write soon and give you more details.

Your good friend,
Eleanor

Etty stared at the letter, the words blurring. Reality dawned… *Mam didn't abandon Dorothy and me…* She had had no other choice but to leave them. She had intended to return for them.

Slowly but surely, Etty experienced a joyous surge of happiness that burst into the very core of her being. If only Dorothy were here to share this precious moment.

'I did try my best to find you and went to see your Aunt Lillian,' Olga told her. 'But she was no wiser than I.'

Etty didn't trust herself to speak but she knew she must hear the full story. 'Did our mam write again?'

Regretfully, Mrs Gruber shook her head. 'A few weeks later, Kurt saw an obituary in the *Gazette*. It stated Eleanor's name and that she had passed peacefully away in her sleep at Woolley Sanatorium.'

Mrs Gruber fished in her handbag and brought out a scrap of notepaper. 'I lost the original cutting when my possessions were taken from me but I made notes in case I needed to relate them to you.'

She screwed up her eyes and read from the paper. 'There was mention of an operation but, in the end, Eleanor was too weak to survive. She was described as a regular worshipper at the parish church in Rookdale who helped her father, the Reverend Elroy Stanton, when she was younger with his pastoral duties since her mother had died.' Mrs Gruber shifted uneasily in her chair. 'There was no mention of a husband and children. It ended by saying she was a devoted daughter and loving sister and would be sadly missed.'

So, Mam was afraid to tell her father about his grandchildren – it all made sense now. Her mind whirred. Her mother, after all, was dead.

Olga continued. 'When I read in the article that you and Dorothy were placed in an orphanage I knew it was my duty to Eleanor to find you and make the facts known. My dear girl, the anguish you must have suffered over the years… thinking your mother had deserted you.'

It was too much to grasp at once; Etty's mind was in turmoil. 'You said all your possessions were taken from you,' she blurted.

'Kurt and I were interred in 1940.' Mrs Gruber's eyes glazed, as she looked down memory lane. She recovered and drew a labouring breath. 'People changed during the war and who can blame them? Neighbours became suspicious. We were told that if we couldn't speak plain English we should be interred. My Kurt was spat on... called a "bloody German". The business suffered. Then the police came and took us away. We were sent to an internment camp on the Isle of Man.' Mrs Gruber looked sorrowfully at Etty. 'It wasn't so bad but Kurt and I were sent to separate camps. He couldn't take the strain and his heart gave out.' She shook her head. 'I do not blame anyone... it was the times we lived in.'

There was a silence, when the kiddies' shrill voices could be heard as they played in the yard.

'I'm sorry for your loss,' Etty told Olga, who nodded gratefully.

'But this isn't about me. I came to give you the comfort you—'

'Daddy's home!' Trevor's hearty voice called from the passageway.

Olga looked expectantly at Etty.

'My husband, Trevor. He had to work today.'

Olga raised her eyebrows questioningly.

Etty told her, 'His official job is working at the mine but he also helps out at the local funeral directors. He was called out as there's been a death in the street.'

Olga nodded soberly. 'So many deaths.'

Trevor came into the room and Etty introduced them.

'I must go,' Olga rose, 'and leave you two to get on with your day.' She regarded Etty. 'We must talk again.'

'Let's make it soon.' Etty's mind still reeling, she sought paper and pen. 'May I have your address for contact?' She was surprised to see that her hand shook.

Olga looked uncomfortable.

Etty took in the dishevelled appearance. Of course, like so many others, Olga didn't have a home to go back to.

'Please come back tomorrow when we can discuss... matters further.'

Olga held out her hand to Trevor and when he took it, she gazed at the scarring on his face, his hands.

'The war.' She raised her eyebrows.

'My husband risked his life trying to save... someone in a raging fire.' Etty's eyes, filling with pride, met her husband's. 'He was very brave.'

A cry came from the back bedroom.

'Our son, Alex,' Trevor told Olga as he headed for the door. 'He has a good pair of lungs.'

As Etty showed the old woman to the door, a thought struck her. She wondered whether she could convince Nellie to take Olga in as a companion. As well as being a solution for Olga, the company might help keep Etty's interfering mother-in-law out of their hair.

As she watched Olga lumber up the street, Etty felt indebted to her for mending her heart, which had lain broken for so many years. Though crushed to discover that her mother had indeed died, the truth had finally set her free.

Later, as the pair of them relaxed in comfortable chairs, Etty related to Trevor what Olga had said. Both girls were still outside in the yard, and Trevor listened intently as he dangled Alex on his knee.

'It's a lot for you to take in, sweetheart,' he told her, 'but you must find some relief, now you know the facts. And now you know your mam died, you didn't tell your sister a lie.'

Etty gave a huge sigh of relief. 'I still can't take in what Olga has told me. Even though it's a heartbreaking story... yes, I'm exonerated. Dorothy went to her grave knowing the truth, after all.'

She thought of Miss Balfour's words from all those years ago. *Life won't always be a struggle. One day happiness will come your way.*

And it had. Etty let out a luxurious sigh. With a family of her own – a beloved husband and three gorgeous children to take care of, the question about Mam didn't seem so important any more.

Excited squeals came from outside. Trevor, carrying Alex, followed her into the yard.

Etty smelled smoke.

'Look, Mammy!' Norma pointed to flames leaping above the yard door.

'It's a bonfire, darling,' Etty told her daughter, 'to celebrate the end of the war.'

Etty took each girl by the hand. 'Let's go and see.'

She turned towards her husband. 'I've been meaning to tell you, my love… we are somebody. We're the Milnes of Whale Street.'

A LETTER FROM SHIRLEY

Firstly, thank you so much for choosing to read *The Orphan Sisters*, my debut novel. Getting a book published is such an exciting experience and has been a dream of mine for a long time.

If you would like to keep up-to-date with my latest releases you can sign up at the link below. I will only contact you when my new book is released and will never share your email with anyone and you can unsubscribe at any time.

www.bookouture.com/shirley-dickson

I do hope you enjoyed reading about Etty and Dorothy, their special bond throughout their life's journey, and the setting in the North East seaside town of South Shields, where I was born amongst the warm-hearted Geordies. Though most of the locations are real, I have taken a few liberties. For example, some street names are changed and no such place as Blakely Orphanage or the factory exists except in my imagination and for the sake of the story.

If you did enjoy the story and have the time, it would be wonderful if you could give the book a review. As a new author it would be amazing to hear what you think. I would also be most appreciative if you could tell friends and family about this novel as it may help fellow readers find me for the first time, which is a big help to a writer.

I would love to hear from you. You can contact me on my author Facebook page, or on Twitter.

Your support is most appreciated.

Very best wishes
Shirley x

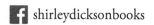 shirleydicksonbooks

ShirleyDWriter

ACKNOWLEDGEMENTS

It isn't just the author that makes books happen. There is a lot of hard work involved by many professionals behind the scenes. Therefore, I would like to thank every one of the wonderful Bookouture team for their help and support in getting *The Orphan Sisters* ready for publication. I'm so fortunate to be with Bookouture.

But firstly, for Wal, for his ceaseless support, it is you I rely on to read the first draft, who helps enormously with the research, and who makes meals and puts up with me. My love and thanks. My lovely family, three daughters, their husbands, four gorgeous grandchildren, my granddaughter's partner and the recent delightful addition, my great grandson. You all give meaning to my life and make it worthwhile.

Someone up there was watching over me when I met with Natasha Harding at the RNA conference. Thank you for your belief in me and being instrumental to me becoming part of the Bookouture family.

Special thanks to my amazing editor Christina Demosthenous, for all your hard work editing the book, your enthusiasm and faith in my writing. With your help and guidance, the book has turned out better than I ever dreamed. I'm truly grateful.

To the RNA New Writers' Scheme whose Readers comments helped enormously with the first draft I submitted. My friends in the RNA, especially Freda Lightfoot, who has been an inspiration and great source of help over the years.

Friends at the Border Reivers, who have been generous sharing writing knowledge over the years and who were there for the highs and lows, especially in times of rejection. To Chris Marples, for the hours it took one sweltering afternoon to help with 'computer tech'. For Hazel Osmond's informative writerly chat over coffee one pleasant morning.

For the rest of the family, friends and neighbours who followed my dream and are excited and delighted for me, thank you.

Made in the USA
Middletown, DE
12 May 2019